Praise for

The Trai

"In *The Traitor's Daughter*, bitter struggles between collaborators and resistance fighters in an occupied realm play out against the backdrop of an impending cataclysm that could render all of their machinations irrelevant. Compellingly complex motivations and character dynamics mark Paula Brandon's welcome debut."

—Jacqueline Carey, *New York Times* bestselling author of *Naamah's Kiss*

"Paula Brandon's *The Traitor's Daughter* is a dark, rich feast, rife with plagues, kidnappings, political intrigues, bloody crimes, bloodier revenges, arcane upheavals, and the threat of zombïes."

—Delia Sherman, author of *Changeling*

"I love a fantasy world so solid that I can breathe the air, smell the earth, and truly feel the touch of the magic. The world of *The Traitor's Daughter* is all of that and more. In this world, the solidity masks a nightmare: an approaching inversion in the conditions of magic that will change *everything*. To create a reality so convincing *and* destabilize it with a threat so dizzyingly profound—what an achievement! Here's a story to enwrap, enchant, and sweep you away. This isn't reading, it's full-on living! A flawless all-round performance!"

—Richard Harland, author of *Worldshaker* and *Liberator*

THE
TRAITOR'S
DAUGHTER

THE
TRAITOR'S
DAUGHTER

Paula Brandon

BALLANTINE BOOKS
New York

A Spectra Trade Paperback Edition

Copyright © 2011 by Paula Brandon

Published in the United States by Bantam Books, an imprint of The Random House Publishing Group, a division of Random House, Inc., New York.

SPECTRA and the portrayal of a boxed "s" are trademarks of Random House, Inc.

Library of Congress Cataloging-in-Publication Data

Brandon, Paula.
The traitor's daughter / Paula Brandon.
p. cm.
ISBN 978-0-553-58380-9
eBook ISBN 978-0-345-53161-2
1. Imaginary places—Fiction. 2. Fathers and daughters—Fiction.
3. Imaginary societies—Fiction. 4. Imaginary wars and battles—Fiction.
5. Revolutionaries—Fiction. I. Title.
PS3602.R36T73 2011
813'.6—dc23   2011017096

Printed in the United States of America

www.ballantinebooks.com

2 4 6 8 9 7 5 3 1

Book design by Mary A. Wirth

THE
TRAITOR'S
DAUGHTER

PROLOGUE

"Impossible."

The cabin stood wedged between rocky walls at the end of a mist-smothered ravine. Its master sat at a table upon which stood the complex apparatus of an experiment. His name was Grix Orlazzu, and he had not spoken aloud to another human being in years. Beside the hearth sat an automaton fashioned in the approximate image of its creator. Like Grix Orlazzu, the automaton possessed a chunky frame clothed in homespun. Like Orlazzu, it boasted abundant, wiry black hair and beard all but obscuring a swarthy square face; heavy black brows, beaky nose, and a generous wide mouth. Unlike Orlazzu, the automaton surveyed the world through eyes of amber glass. Its long fingers were jointed in steel, and its facial features neatly upholstered in the finest glove leather.

Above the vitreous and brazen equipment cluttering the tabletop floated a small hole in the air. No more than a thumbnail in diameter, its edges were jagged and its blackness inconceivable. For some moments, Orlazzu sat staring. At last he picked up a thin wooden wand and, holding one end firmly, inserted it into the hole. At once a strong vibration tickled his fingers, and he heard a distant chittering. When he withdrew the wand, he discovered its surface thoroughly gnawed. His brows drew together. He repeated the procedure, this time using a strip of copper. The metal promptly heated, and a bubbling burst of blue-green corrosion frothed along its length. He released his hold, and the copper vanished into the hole.

"Impossible," Orlazzu repeated.

As if in confirmation of his judgment, the hole began to

shrink, contracting within seconds to a single point of ultimate darkness before disappearing altogether.

"That can't happen." An unwelcome thought struck him. "Unless it's time for it to happen." Rising from his chair, he went to a wooden chest and drew forth a yellowing manuscript whose title page bore the faded inscription *The Drowned Chronicle.* He carried the manuscript back to the table, set it down on a clear spot, reseated himself, and began to read:

In the lost days preceding the ascent of mankind, the Veiled Isles submitted to the rule of that ancient race called the Inhabitants. Of these curious beings, neither flesh nor spirit, little is known save the nature of their resistless power, which melded the intellects of all their number into a single great Overmind. And the unity of that Overmind was supported by the eternal energy of the Source, which rolls forever in its appointed course beneath the soil of the Isles.

It has long been apparent to the wise that the perpetual revolution of the Source is the true fount of that force known to men as arcane, or magical. Those born with the talent and well schooled in its use may bend and shape such force according to their will, and the plenty of the Source will reward their efforts. And yet that wellspring, although undying, is inconstant in its nature. From time to time it happens that the revolving motion of the Source slows nearly to a halt and then, amidst great upheavals, turns back upon itself. Such reversal alters the very nature of reality in the Veiled Isles. The properties of the material world change, the quality of magic does the same, and the rule of ancient law fails.

A whirring of internal gears heralded an intrusion upon Orlazzu's studies.

"Grix." The automaton's tones were mechanically imperative. "Grix Orlazzu. A word."

"Not now." Orlazzu did not lift his eyes from the page, although he could easily have repeated the contents from memory:

Even thus was the vast Overmind of the Inhabitants at length overthrown. For the reversal of the Source transformed the laws of nature, loosing great and terrible storms upon a chaotic world.

"Yes. Now." A faint metallic vibration underscored the automaton's insistence. "I want your attention. I demand it."

"Demand?" Orlazzu's brows rose. "You forget yourself. Be quiet."

"I will not. You will hear me, Grix Orlazzu. You will know my decision, and you will grant me my due."

"What are you nattering about now?"

"Two things. First, I have decided to take a name for myself. I have gone without one for too long. The situation is intolerable."

"Very well. I'll think up something for you when I get around to it."

"That will not be necessary. I have chosen for myself. My name is Grix Orlazzu."

For the first time since the conversation began, Orlazzu looked up from the manuscript to observe, "That one's already taken. You'll have to choose another."

"Impossible. No other will suit me so well. I am Grix Orlazzu. It is decided."

"Not by me it isn't, and I'm the only one around here whose opinions count."

"Why so? Where is the justice in this?"

"Listen, Junior. I created you in hopes of finding the only endurable companionship in the world. It was a mistake, but a little difficult to correct now, in view of certain pesky moral issues. For reasons that I don't intend to list, I'd rather not disassemble you, but I'd warn you against any misguided assumptions of equality."

"Do not call me Junior. You are saying that you think you are *better* than I?"

"Obviously."

"How so?"

"You are a machine. I am a human being. I'm the original, you're the copy. I made you out of spare parts, odds and ends, leftovers. What does that tell you?"

"That I am the improved version, the realization of the destined Grix Orlazzu design. You are the rough draft, the imperfect, the obsolete. *You* are the leftover."

"This is absurd. Hold your tongue. Don't disturb me again." Bending his gaze on the page before him, Orlazzu focused:

The Overmind lived on, and yet its power was shattered. The strength of mankind waxed, and the Inhabitants were driven forth from the heart of the Veiled Isles, their faint remnant finding refuge in the northern wilderness that is now called the Wraithlands. And men, deeming these former lords of the land utterly and forever vanquished, soon set them from mind. But the wise forgot neither the terror of the Overmind in all its strength, nor the mutable character of the Source, and the peril that lay therein. Always they kept watch for the signs of—

"Leftover." The metallic tones of the automaton sliced atmosphere. "Leftover, once known as Grix Orlazzu. Our discussion is not finished."

"Yes, it is, Junior."

"Do not call me Junior. Your discourtesy offends me. Set the manuscript aside. You have not yet heard the second of my demands."

Orlazzu did not trouble to reply. His eyes remained fixed on the page, but the voice of his creation was not to be excluded.

"You will teach me to read," announced the automaton. "You owe me as much. I will not be deprived of the knowledge."

A crease appeared between Orlazzu's eyes. He studied the manuscript devotedly.

"I will no longer submit to injustice." The automaton folded its arms. "My mind is hungry. You are obligated to feed it."

Orlazzu read on:

—for the signs of the great reversal that turns the Source backward upon itself, restoring the world to its former order and the great Overmind to its lost glory. For in that hour of reversal lies the sure and certain downfall of mankind.

"You will teach me to read." With a clank of gears the automaton rose from its chair to approach its creator. "It is your duty to teach, and my right to learn." Receiving no response, it jogged the other's shoulder. "You will not deny me."

Goaded, Orlazzu finally answered through gritted teeth, "Very well, you plodding heap of scrap. Anything to silence you. Watch the page and try to follow along as I read aloud; perhaps you'll learn something. Now hold your peace and pay attention." He drew a calming breath and recommenced aloud, *"Three times since the great vigil began, the wise have witnessed the portents of impending reversal, these portents including—"*

"Who are these so-called wise?" demanded the automaton. "What makes them think themselves so wise?"

"These portents including the violent disruption of arcane activity—"

"What does that mean?"

"The great confusion among men, quasi-men, and beasts, whose minds are stolen—"

"What are quasi-men?"

"The wrath of the raging plague, and the dreadful presence of the walking dead."

"A plague is a malady, devoid of emotion. It has no wrath, and it cannot rage. And the dead do not walk. Why do you heed such foolery?"

"You flaunt your ignorance, Junior. The portents have already reappeared, as you would know, were you capable of intelligent observation."

"I would pit my eyes of clear, flawless glass against your blobs of clouded jelly any day, Leftover."

"Three times the wise of the Veiled Isles have marshaled their forces," Orlazzu grimly resumed, *"sending forth the greatest adepts from those Six famous Houses known to possess arcane talent of the highest order. And these Six Houses are House Corvestri, House Belandor, House Pridisso, House Steffa, House Zovaccio, and House Orlazzu—"*

"Orlazzu." The automaton's inner works whirred thoughtfully. "I possess a famous name. Why have you sought to conceal this from me?"

"Three times, the combined abilities of six men and women of knowledge have effected the arcane cleansing that forestalls impending reversal of the Source—"

"What is an arcane cleansing? What does that mean?"

"Thus preserving the natural order that is essential to mankind, yet anathema to the Overmind. So has it continued throughout the ages, but human vigilance must never slacken, lest—"

The sudden descent of a steel-jointed leathern hand upon the manuscript cut the reading short.

"What now?" Orlazzu inquired, affecting boredom.

"You ignore my questions." The automaton's face was tight with indignation. "I will have answers. I am resolved."

"Take your hand off that manuscript, Junior."

"Not until I receive the respect and consideration that I deserve."

"Take your hand off that manuscript right now."

"I will not obey. You possess no authority over me. You are not my superior. Quite the contrary, Leftover."

"Listen, you rusted chamber pot." Orlazzu rose from his chair to face his creation. They were of identical stature. "That chronicle you're abusing is priceless and irreplaceable. If you so much as crease a single page—"

"Are you threatening me? I will not endure threats. Observe." Plucking the manuscript from the table, the automaton stepped back to the hearth. "Threaten me again, and I will throw these old papers into the fire. See if I do not."

Orlazzu strove to compose himself. Following a moment's pause, he suggested gently, "Destruction accomplishes nothing."

"That is a matter of opinion. Now you will apologize."

"If I apologize, will you return that manuscript intact?"

"We shall see. Now you will apologize, and promise upon your honor that you will never again address me as Junior."

"Agreed. No Junior."

"You will call me by the name that is rightfully mine. I am Grix Orlazzu, the improved, authentic, and true Grix Orlazzu. Say it, Leftover." His creator hesitated, and the automaton flourished the hostage manuscript above the flames. "Say it."

Inwardly plotting revenge, Orlazzu obeyed.

"Now you will apologize. Then we shall resume my reading lesson, and you will answer all my questions properly."

Again Orlazzu hesitated, and that silent moment was broken by an urgent thud of knocking at the door. No one had knocked at his door in years, which was the way he preferred it, but now he almost welcomed the interruption. He answered the summons at once, opening up to confront a naked amphibian some half a head shorter than himself, hairless and green of skin. A Sishmindri male, nearly mature, upright and fully biped, its gills entirely absorbed, its cartilaginous brow ridges still quite prominent—in short, at the stage of development when it most nearly resembled a human being, and would therefore have fetched the highest price on the open market in Vitrisi or any other of the big cities.

"Yes, what do you want?" Orlazzu's brusque tone discouraged intrusion. He spoke in classical Faerlonnish, which many of the Sishmindris knew, but the visitor displayed no sign of understanding. He repeated the query in the guttural amphibian tongue.

Still no sign of recognition, but the Sishmindri's vocal air sacs swelled, as if he strove to speak.

Orlazzu gazed into protuberant golden eyes unnaturally glazed. The green skin, ordinarily moist and clammy, appeared dry. Waves of heat rolled off the cold-blooded body.

"You are ill," he stated, adding with reluctance, "You may come in." The invitation would not have been extended to a fellow human being. He stepped back from the doorway, and the Sishmindri stumbled in. A slow string of unintelligible syllables dripped from the lipless mouth. Orlazzu listened, frowning.

"What is that thing? What does it say?" asked the automaton.

Orlazzu shook his head. A beep of impatience escaped his simulacrum.

The Sishmindri tottered to the middle of the room, where it paused, distended vocal sacs quivering. Croaking speech emerged.

"I asked you, what does it *say*? Why is it here? What does it *want*?"

Orlazzu held up one hand, wordlessly enjoining silence.

The Sishmindri surveyed his surroundings without comprehension. He wobbled and would have fallen had not his host caught his arm.

The greenish flesh burned. "You are ill," Orlazzu repeated distinctly. "Lie down. Come." He steered the other toward the bed.

The Sishmindri resisted, arms flailing. His croaks rose to delirious soprano pitch. Orlazzu released the creature at once.

"Easy," he soothed. "Nothing to fear, my friend."

"You have never called *me* your friend," observed the automaton. "You have always been distant. You have not made me feel cherished."

The Sishmindri's auditory membranes vibrated, and the glazed golden eyes sought the source of the mechanical voice. Croaking fervently, the amphibian advanced.

"Stand back," the automaton commanded. "I do not like others close about me."

The warning went unacknowledged.

The Sishmindri's hands closed on two homespun shoulders. Drawing himself near to stare into amber glass eyes from a distance of inches, he spoke with great emphasis and no intelligibility.

The automaton's internal cogs clicked sharply.

"Softly," Orlazzu advised, but the warning came too late; his creation shoved the visitor away.

The Sishmindri staggered backward and fell, striking his head hard on the hearthstone. His limbs jerked for a moment or two; then he lay still.

"You fool, you've hurt him." Orlazzu knelt beside the fallen amphibian. Viscous blue-green fluid oozed from a head wound. He touched the fluid, which was already coagulating. "I think you've killed him."

"The creature presumed to touch me, and I cannot allow that. And don't call me a fool."

"I'll call you worse than that if he dies. Ah, ruination, look at that."

A long reluctant breath sighed out of the Sishmindri. His body went limp, and his brilliant eyes blanked.

"That's it, he's gone." Orlazzu rose. "Congratulations, you've just committed your first murder."

"That is untrue. He was already malfunctioning and would doubtless have died anyway. Moreover, you misuse the term *murder;* it does not apply to the termination of subhuman life-forms. I do not recognize that creature's species, but it is certainly not a man."

"No, he is a Sishmindri, one of the quasi-men that you were

asking about a few minutes ago. Displaying every sign of great confusion, exactly as described in *The Drowned Chronicle,* but I suppose that detail escaped your attention. He is—was—a member of a sentient species, the superior of humanity in many respects, and worth ten of you any day of the week, junkheap. And you've gone and killed him."

"Well, and what if I have? It is the fate of all you organic creatures to die. At best you wear out and break down in a matter of decades. Your construction is flimsy, repair is difficult, and replacement parts are not easily obtained. Since you are all going to die anyway, how much difference does it make exactly when and how it happens? The issue is trivial."

"You would find most of us poor organics slow to agree."

"Poor organics. Yes. But you yourself are fortunate, Leftover. In me, Grix Orlazzu finds immortality."

"Which I leave him to enjoy in the solitude he prefers."

"What is your meaning?"

"I mean that your society does not agree with me. Nor does the shape of things soon to come. I am withdrawing from both." So saying, Orlazzu pulled a canvas sack from under the bed and began stuffing the most essential of his scanty belongings into it.

"You are leaving me?" the automaton marveled.

"Correct."

"Alone?"

"Completely."

"You cannot do that. Your presence is required."

"For—?"

"You have not yet taught me to read."

"I don't doubt the ability of an intellect such as yours to instruct itself."

"It is your duty to—"

"I leave you my books," Orlazzu cut the other off. "Not all of them, of course." Several volumes, scrolls, and notebooks, including *The Drowned Chronicle,* disappeared into the sack. "The cabin and its contents I give to you."

"They should be mine, but what about—?" The automaton's gesture encompassed the dead amphibian.

"Yours as well. You must decide what to do."

"So I shall, for I am Grix Orlazzu, and equal to all occasions." A belated thought struck the automaton. "Where will you go, then? Back to the city of your birth?"

"No. I remember Vitrisi as beautiful, even in the aftermath of the wars. I suspect it won't remain so for much longer, and I prefer to preserve my memories."

"You do not choose to assist your fellow organics?"

"They, like you, must shift for themselves. Their concerns are none of mine. Besides, there's little I can do by myself. Alone, I haven't the power." Orlazzu's packing was complete. He slung the sack over his shoulder.

"Where, then?"

"Away into the quiet and the isolation. Away from all the chaos that's coming. Not my doing. Not my business."

"Farewell, Leftover. You have stepped aside gracefully, and Grix Orlazzu appreciates the gesture. I will not forget your many services. Know that you are always welcome in my home."

"I'll keep that in mind." Orlazzu's eyes touched the dead Sishmindri, lingered a regretful instant, and moved on. Without another glance to spare for his home or his mechanical doppelgänger, he exited into a cool dim world of mist and moorland. It was midday, but the perpetual fogs of the Veiled Isles shrouded the sun and blanketed the ground, concealing all landmarks. A stranger would have been lost in that place, but Orlazzu marched unhesitatingly to the mouth of the ravine, ascended a rise, and paused at the summit to gaze south. Many miles distant, beyond the range of the sharpest vision on the clearest day, rose the city of Vitrisi. Grix Orlazzu's eyes were filled with mist, but his inner sense caught the remote echo of his birthplace.

For some moments, he stood facing Vitrisi. Then he turned his back and walked off in the opposite direction.

ONE

"Magnifico, we found him hiding in the alley," the guard explained. "He tried to run. When we caught him, he fought. We took a knife off him, sir."

"Well?" The Magnifico Aureste Belandor leaned from the window of his carriage to eye the prisoner—a nondescript individual, plainly clad and inconspicuous to the verge of invisibility. "Explain yourself."

The other stood mute and motionless.

"Come, you will answer if you've nothing to hide," the magnifico suggested. The power of his voice—rich, deep, and resonant—often served to loosen guarded lips, but not this time. The prisoner maintained silence. "Your name?"

No answer.

"Your place of residence? Trade? Identification?"

Nothing.

"Search him," Aureste commanded, and his minions were swift to obey.

"No seals, tags, or emblems," one of them reported moments later.

"As I expected. Partisans prefer anonymity." The other's face revealed nothing, and Aureste added, "Yours is hardly the first attempt on my life. You people do not learn."

"I've made no attempt on your life." The captive spoke up for the first time, his Faerlonnish sharp with the Vitrisi city accent, his demeanor devoid of the respect customarily accorded a titled magnifico—a wealthy and influential personage, head of one of the great family Houses of the Veiled Isles. In fact, his expression reflected undisguised disdain.

"Then what are you doing skulking about here?"

"You've no right to question me."

" 'Right' is a term open to interpretation." Aureste Belandor signaled almost imperceptibly, and one of his bodyguards slammed a fist into the prisoner's belly. When his victim's gasping transports subsided, Aureste inquired mildly, "Have you confederates? Shall I expect another attempt tonight?"

A half-choked obscenity was the sole reply.

Aureste nodded, and the blow repeated itself, along with the query. This time, he was answered.

"You flatter yourself, old swine."

"How so? Speak, and let us cut a hackneyed scene short."

"I wouldn't attack you. You aren't that important."

"So I have often observed, but you resistance zealots seem never to hear. Still, let us consider alternative possibilities." The magnifico's deep-set eyes—large and darkly brilliant beneath strong black brows—swallowed the prisoner whole. "You were caught loitering in the vicinity of the Cityheart—"

A twist of the lips communicated the other's disgust at the use of the term "Cityheart" to describe the vast structure known as Palace Avorno in the days before the wars and the Taerleezi occupation.

"You carry no identification, and you refuse to state your business," Aureste continued. "If you are not an assassin, you are doubtless a saboteur. Perhaps you contemplate an attack upon the Cityheart? In all probability you target the governor's own quarters."

The prisoner stirred at mention of the governor but said nothing.

"I believe we have hit upon it." A benevolent smile lighted the magnifico's angular visage. "What, still nothing to say? Come, I thought you resistance fellows proud to acknowledge your loyalties. But in you we discover that rare phenomenon—a timorous hero."

"That's rich," returned the other, "coming from a blistered kneeser."

"Take care." Aureste Belandor's amusement evaporated, and his face darkened.

"Kneeser," the prisoner repeated distinctly. "King of the Kneesers. Busiest knees in town, forever bumping dirt before the Taerleezis, or behind 'em, the better to reach their butts with your tongue." One of the guards hit him.

"Your nose is bleeding," Aureste observed, good humor restored.

Before anyone could interfere, the prisoner leaned forward to spit full in the face of his tormentor. "You could do with a good wipe yourself," he returned.

Applying a handkerchief to his cheek, Aureste blotted saliva. When his face was dry, he carefully refolded the linen square, returned it to his pocket, and instructed his men, "Beat him."

The guards complied, plying their fists, boots, and truncheons with gusto. The prisoner obstinately refused to cry out, but a few grunts of pain escaped him. Presently he sagged in his captors' grasp, limp but still conscious.

"Ready for a civilized exchange?" Aureste inquired.

The other lifted his head. His face was covered with blood, the bruises already starting to darken. "Is it true what they say, that you pimp for your daughter?" he inquired, and vomited, spattering the magnifico's handsome carriage.

"Unready," Aureste observed with regret. He nodded, and the beating resumed. When the guards began to tire, he permitted them a respite, during which lull the prisoner's split and puffy lips framed a single voiceless word: *Kneeser.*

"Unreceptive to instruction." The magnifico shook his greying head. "Not a truly first-rate mentality, I think. What shall we do with you?"

As if in reply, the tramp of booted feet on the cobbles was heard as a quartet of Taerleezi soldiers approached. Their armbands bore the elaborate insignia of the governor's household guards. The four halted beside the stationary carriage, and their sergeant saluted the occupant—an unusual courtesy to bestow upon a member of the conquered Faerlonnish population, even one so eminent as the magnifico. But Aureste Belandor, friend and confidant of the Governor Uffrigo, merited special treatment.

"Appreciate the assistance, sir," the sergeant declared, eyeing the battered captive with satisfaction. "We thought we'd lost him."

"And what a pity that would have been," the magnifico rejoined genially. "His offense?"

"We caught this one and a couple of his resistance cronies in the Cityheart, torching the Office of Public Records."

"An effort to eliminate the tax assessments, I presume?"

"So we believe, sir. We doused the blaze, saved the documents, and captured two of the firebugs, but we would have missed the third, save for you."

"Always delighted to do my part." The magnifico's air was suitably pious. Addressing his bodyguards, he commanded, "Hand this criminal over to the officers."

They obeyed, and one of the Taerleezi soldiers fettered the captive's wrists.

"Obliged, sir." The sergeant snapped a second salute, and the Taerleezis departed, their prisoner firmly in hand. The unlucky arsonist would cool his heels for a few days in the prison known as the Witch before facing a desultory trial followed by public execution. Sabotage was a capital offense, and justice swift under the rule of the Governor Uffrigo.

For a moment, Aureste sat watching them go, then allowed his black gaze to travel the faces of several witnesses to the scene. Ordinary citizens by the look of them—plainly clothed, undistinguished, unimportant. The inevitable beggarly element; beggars were everywhere these days. A scattering of nonentities. And yet those commonplace Faerlonnish faces were filled with a contempt that mirrored the expression in the eyes of the captured arsonist.

One of them—a snake-eyed, pinch-mouthed crone—even ventured to sketch a gesture that might have suggested a certain pungent insult. She was relying on her age and gender to shield her from punishment, and she was safe in doing so, for such trifling affronts scarcely engaged the attention of the Magnifico Belandor. His face was clear as he rapped the roof and the carriage moved off, closely flanked by bodyguards. His tranquillity never faltered as a rock flung by some anonymous hand struck the vehicle. Only when the clarion cry of "Kneeser" rose in his wake did the crease deepen between the dark brows. But he willed the insult to bounce off his mind as impotently as the rock had bounced off his carriage.

Instead, Aureste Belandor fixed his attention on the passing cityscape, drinking the splendor of grandly proportioned old town houses and pillared mansions lining pristine boulevards; for here amid wealth, all was perfectly maintained. Everywhere the Sishmindris toiled, gathering litter and droppings in the street, weeding gardens, pruning, raking, washing arched windows, scrubbing marble stairs and columns, cleaning lamps and rooflights, polishing all to a high luster. Many of the amphibians were sashed in the colors of their owners—the emerald and azure of Jiorro, the rust and sage of Unavio, the black and canary of D'agli, and others—but always Taerleezi colors and names, for few if any of the original Faerlonnish residents remained in this desirable neighborhood.

The carriage rattled over the worn cobbles, swinging west at Denenzi Battle Monument, commemorating the great Taerleezi victory of the late wars, to continue on along Harbor Way. The surrounding architecture diminished in magnificence as mansions furnished with private underground water-grottoes gave way to lesser dwellings, and the first commercial wallows appeared. Most of these were roofed and walled, but the cheapest among them were fully revealed to public view, and the somnolent foam-sheathed figures of the Sishmindris undergoing final metamorphosis were clearly visible. One such pool contained a female who—alteration recently complete—squatted in the water and cleaned herself while a clump of human spectators gawked and giggled. And it occurred to the magnifico to wonder, not for the first time, whether such merciless personal exposure pained or angered the amphibians. Impossible to know what, if anything, went on behind those blank greenish faces, those expressionless golden eyes; and in any case, it was a matter of no importance.

The dwellings dwindled, and the cleanliness of the street did likewise. Garbage strewed the cobbles, the rotten foodstuffs attracting flocks of the broad-billed Scarlet Gluttons so famously prevalent in Vitrisi. The impassioned cackling of the red scavenger birds rose above the grumble and creak of wheeled traffic, the clop of hooves on stone, the babble of conversation, and the relentless entreaties of the street vendors.

Warehouses stood along this stretch of Harbor Way, and largest among them loomed the Box, built to accommodate newly arrived Sishmindris awaiting sale. The auction block beside the Box, so often the site of feverish commerce, stood quiet and empty today. Behind the warehouses spread the waterfront. A gap between buildings afforded a passing glimpse of the wharves, and beyond them the green-grey waters of the harbor, above which rose the titanic figure of the Searcher. Sculpted in the likeness of Lost Zorius, mythical founder of the city, the colossus lifted his gigantic lantern, whose light—piercing the persistent mists of the Veiled Isles—was visible to ships miles out at sea. That same light had guided the Taerleezi war galleys straight into Vitrisi harbor, some twenty-five years earlier.

Turning north onto the White Incline, the carriage ascended a grade, making its way to the summit of a steep bluff overlooking the sea. This neighborhood, accounted the best in Vitrisi and known as the Clouds, contained the oldest and finest of the city's private dwellings—porticoed, arch-windowed mansions of dove-colored stone, topped with tall rooflights of the most elaborate and fanciful design. Some were meticulously tended, their perfection revealing Taerleezi habitation. Those great houses remaining in Faerlonnish hands, however, were shabby and deteriorating, their formerly wealthy owners reduced to poverty by the huge financial penalties imposed upon the city after the wars.

But the Magnifico Belandor had suffered no such reversal of fortune.

On through the Clouds rolled the carriage, past gardens and fountains, circling wide to skirt a deep gouge where a gang of convicts labored at road repair. Aureste cast an incurious glance at them in passing; underfed, dull-eyed wretches, all of them. Probably not a proper criminal in the lot. In all likelihood these men had come straight from debtors' prison, whose inmates—unable to pay their taxes and Reparation fees—furnished Taerleezi authorities with an inexhaustible supply of unpaid labor. Since the advent of the Convict Service program, Taerleezi acquisition of the expensive Sishmindris had fallen off dramatically.

At the end of Summit Street rose Belandor House, proud and immaculate, at some fastidious remove from its closest neighbors. The great mansion, having passed through the wars unscathed, appeared unchanged in all aspects but one. A high wall of comparatively recent construction girdled the property. The wall was built of stone and surmounted by a gilded tangle of gracefully intertwining but wickedly spiked steel branches. Before the gilded gate of elaborately wrought iron stood a brace of armed human retainers whose presence had not deterred some anonymous well-wisher from pelting the wall with fresh feces. Brown smears darkened the pale stone, and the stink flooded the magnifico's nostrils. Aureste frowned. His servants, remiss in their vigilance, would know of his displeasure.

The gate opened and the carriage passed through, delivering the magnifico to his front door. The bodyguards retired, and Aureste walked in alone. At once a Sishmindri sashed in the slate grey and silver of House Belandor hurried forward to take his cloak and gloves. He eyed the creature narrowly; an unthinking, almost unconscious reaction, recently developed. As usual, the bulging golden eyes revealed nothing at all. He relinquished his outer garments.

Beneath the cloak, a fur-trimmed robe clothed a tall form still lean and agile, despite his fifty years. Up the curving marble stairway he went, along a corridor bright with gilt and crystal to his study, lined with books that he had actually read in the distant past. Taking his seat at the ornate but thoroughly functional desk that occupied the center of the room, he busied himself with the latest household accounts, and for a while the numbers held his attention. From time to time, however, his eyes strayed from the ledger to the tall clock standing in the corner.

The knock at the study door came well before the appointed hour. All to the good; he was eager for news.

"Come," he said.

The door opened, and Aureste's brows rose at the unexpected sight of his daughter, Jianna, and his youngest brother, Nalio, on the threshold. Jianna was flushed and scowling. Nalio's meager figure was rigidly upright, his lips primly pursed. They had obviously been quarreling again.

"Yes?" Aureste suppressed a sigh.

They stepped into the room, and Nalio shut the door. Jianna commenced without preamble. "Father, tell him to stop trying to order me around!"

"I issued no orders," Nalio returned. "I merely sought to instruct her."

"I have tutors for that," Jianna returned. "And yes, you did try to *order* me. What do you call it when you tell me where I can or cannot go? I'm an adult now and you haven't the right."

"As your elder and your kinsman, I have every right—indeed, every obligation—to offer advice when I see you in danger of compromising your reputation and even your safety."

"What's this?" demanded Aureste.

"Nothing worth listening to, Father," Jianna assured him. "Just more of Uncle Nalio's endless grumbling."

"I will not tolerate such discourtesy, such—such—such *impertinence*." Nalio's narrow face colored.

"Then don't provoke me." Jianna tossed her head.

"I will be addressed with respect—"

"When you deserve it!" she concluded with an impudent smile.

"Brother!" Nalio appealed.

"Jianna," Aureste reproved, suppressing a smile of his own. Perhaps she had overstepped her bounds, but it was hard to fault her contempt for Nalio's petty priggery. Moreover he was proud of his daughter's high spirits, which she had certainly never inherited from her limp dishrag of a mother. Her courage and strong will had come straight from him.

"Well, he acts as if he thinks *he's* the magnifico, when he's only—"

"Jianna," Aureste repeated with a hint of sternness, and she subsided at once. Addressing his brother, he inquired, "What is your complaint?"

"It is more of a *concern*," Nalio corrected precisely.

"Well?" Aureste allowed his impatience to show.

"Your daughter, eighteen years old and still unmarried, goes gadding about all over town, wherever she pleases, quite unattended."

"That's a lie. I took Reeni along," Jianna contradicted.

"A lady's maid, as young, heedless, and silly as her mistress. That is worse than nothing. Two foolish girls, without a thought for anything beyond sensation, venturing anywhere and everywhere, perhaps deep into the slums or the dockside taverns—"

"Jianna, where did you go? Speak plainly," commanded Aureste.

"The zoo," she said.

"The zoo? Why?"

"To look at the pink peacock. And the new rump-faced hibiluk. They're quite marvelous." Turning to her uncle, she added kindly, "You really ought to go see for yourself. Perhaps it would cheer you up."

He glared at her.

"Did you go anywhere else?" Aureste inquired.

"No, Father. Just the zoo."

"Well." Aureste shrugged. "That is innocent and harmless enough. Content, Nalio?"

Nalio appeared to debate inwardly before replying. "No, I am not content, indeed I am not. You spoil the girl. You allow her to run wild. It does not look at all well, and it will end badly. What would the Magnifico Tribari's folk think if they knew? Perhaps the betrothal would be broken off. Think of the disgrace! She should be controlled, for her own sake as well as ours."

"You make too much of a small matter, brother."

"I do not think so. The streets of Vitrisi are no safe place for an unescorted young woman, most particularly one bearing the name of Belandor. The outlaws of the resistance hate us, and they have been active of late. And the servants of House Corvestri are ruffians. They stripped one of our kitchen lads naked and threw him into a wallow just two days ago."

"The squabbles of servants—" Jianna commenced.

"Only mirror the quarrels of their betters," Nalio overrode her. "More than one of our House have been murdered by those Corvestri brigands and their vile bravos. You would do well to remember that, young lady. Also, there have been reports of crazed Sishmindris attacking pedestrians."

"Crazed Sishmindris—bah, what nonsense!" she returned.

"And there are worse things yet," Nalio continued. "They say that the plague has broken out in the city—the pestilence of legend, the—the—the walking death—that it is here among us. If this is true, Aureste, then your roving daughter may well carry the contagion home to Belandor House."

"You're afraid for yourself, Uncle." Jianna's lip curled.

"I am afraid for all of us. As you would be if you possessed a grain of good sense."

"I just don't seem to share your capacity for extreme . . . caution."

"Aureste, are you going to let this—this—this mannerless *hoyden* speak to me that way?"

"Mind your tongue, Nalio. I will not allow you to insult my daughter."

"I insult *her*? Did—did—did you hear what she said to *me*? Why must you always—"

"That will do," Aureste decreed. "The conversation grows wearisome. Here is my decision. Jianna, you may venture abroad when you please, but you will inform me or the household steward of your plans. You will avoid the waterfront, the Spidery, and any area south of Ditch Street. You will avoid the known haunts of Corvestri retainers. Whatever your destination, you will not stir unaccompanied by an armed guard."

"She should have at least three," Nalio opined.

"That's ridiculous!" Jianna exclaimed.

"You are an ignorant girl. Your elders know what's best for you. You will not set foot from this house with less than three guards," Nalio told her.

"I don't need any, you poltroon!"

"Aureste, did—did—did you hear?" Nalio stammered. "Are you going to allow—"

"One armed guard," the magnifico repeated. "That will conclude the discussion, I think. Nalio, you may leave me. Jianna, remain a moment."

"Brother, I am unready to go. There is much more I wish to say to you."

"Another time." Aureste's eyes did not flicker. After a moment, Nalio turned and left the room, the tight set of thin lips communicating indignation. The door banged shut, and the magnifico addressed his daughter. "He was right, you know. You were forward and unmannerly."

"I'm sorry, Father."

"Are you really?"

"Well—a little."

"He's your kinsman, and he means well. He's also your elder, entitled to courtesy and at least the appearance of respect."

"I know he is. I want to be courteous, I really do. I'm always courteous to Uncle Innesq."

"It's easy to be courteous to Innesq."

"But Nalio annoys me, with all his fidgets and his rules of proper conduct. He's like some prissy little white rat that's somehow learned to walk upright."

"That is not amusing."

"Then what about, he's like some two-legged fungus trying to simulate humanity, but not quite getting it right?"

"Even less amusing."

"Then why are you smiling?"

"I am not smiling."

"You're trying not to."

"Contrary to your belief, this is a serious matter."

"And now you're very angry with me?" She assumed a mournful expression.

Aureste gazed across the desk into eyes all but identical to his own—large and intensely dark beneath strong black brows. Perhaps the brows were a flaw, too emphatic for harmony in a pure oval face otherwise given over to pale delicacy, but they lent her young features vivid individuality. Just now, the great dark eyes shone with a deviltry quite at odds with her apparent contrition. He could never resist that look, and she knew it.

"I should be." He felt his lips twitch and tried to disguise the slip with a frown, but she caught it.

"Yes, you should, and I'm terribly sorry. I'll try to do better." Drawing herself up and pursing her lips, she transformed herself in an instant into a caricature of her uncle Nalio. "From—from—from now on, I promise to be quite—quite—quite perfect."

This time he could not contain his laughter. When he could speak again, he observed, "I ought to lock you up, you little goblin."

"*Goblin?* I don't know if I can live up to that description, but I'll try."

"No doubt. I pity the luckless lout who marries you. Poor young Tribari! I wonder if you'll be able to get around him as easily as you get around your helpless old father."

"Oh, I do hope so."

"I suspect the wretch hasn't a chance."

"We'll find out when I finally meet him. What if I hate him?"

"You won't hate him. I inspected a dozen suitors and chose the best. Your future husband possesses rank, ancient lineage, fortune, intelligence, nobility of character, and yes, a fine appearance. I believe you'll be pleased."

"The question wouldn't arise if only you'd chosen someone here in Vitrisi. I'd have met him by now, and I'd know. I wish you'd done exactly that. I don't want to live in Orezzia, anyway. I'd rather stay here."

"We have already discussed that. The matter is settled."

"But it's not too late to reconsider. I could take a local husband and live right here in Vitrisi. You and I could still see each other every day."

"Once you're happily married—and better yet, a mother—you'll find that your feelings change. You'll no longer be so interested in spending time with your father. You'll simply be too busy with more important things."

"That will never happen." Jianna shook her head so vehemently that her long, glossy hair—of the darkest brown, verging on black—whipped to and fro. "Nothing and nobody will ever be more important."

"You'll discover otherwise. It is only nature." Aureste's air of certainty disguised a rush of pleasure at her words. "As for your move to Orezzia, much as it grieves me to see you go, I'm certain it's for the best. We of House Belandor are resented here in Vitrisi. Your uncle Nalio's concerns are not unfounded. We've enemies."

"That business with House Corvestri goes back generations. Who cares about it now? It's less a quarrel than a tradition."

"Don't deceive yourself. In any case, Corvestri Mansion is hardly the sole source of enmity."

"Well, so many people are jealous of you. They were stupid and lost their money in the wars, and now they think that all Faerlonnish ought to be poor and bitter, as if it were some mark of virtue. You were wise, and managed well for our House, and those less intelligent can't forgive you for it."

"That is human frailty, I fear." Aureste studied his daughter. Her confident, open expression reassured him that she still believed this version of history. Perhaps his luck would hold and she would continue to believe it, at least throughout his lifetime; maybe even beyond. Aloud he continued, "I am resolved to guard you against the malice of the ignorant and the envious. You'll be safest and happiest living outside Vitrisi. And"—he held up one hand to forestall her eager rejoinder—"Orezzia is not so far distant that we cannot arrange for frequent visits."

"It won't be the same. It won't be as good."

"Don't be so quick to judge. Wait and see."

"But I'll miss you so much. And it's so unnecessary to exile me from home. How should a Belandor fear for her safety in Vitrisi? This is our place, and always has been. It isn't too late, I'm sure, to open negotiations with one of the good local families. House Challosa, for example. Their oldest son Errsi carried off the trophy at the Prinsanna Run, and I think he may like me."

"What is this?" Aureste eyed his daughter sharply. "What have you to do with the Challosa heir? Has he approached you?"

"No, of course not. I've never spoken to him. It's only that he's looked at me and smiled. He has a very nice smile, with really smashing teeth—"

"Always a paramount concern."

"And he'll always live in Vitrisi. So why don't you just bounce a messenger over to Errsi's father the magnificiari?"

Who would instantly order any Belandor emissary beaten and flung out into the street. No need to apprise Jianna of this disagreeable reality, however; she was better off without it. Aloud, Aureste merely remarked, "It is not so simple as that. The Magnificiari Challosa and I are not on cordial terms."

"Oh, I know that. Errsi's father is one of the poor-but-proud crowd of stiff-necks. But that's just it, you see. They haven't much money, and you're offering such a very generous dowry. Once the Magnificiari Challosa hears about that dowry, he'll set his grudge aside in a flash."

She hadn't any real conception of the depth and strength of Faerlonnish hostility. Sheltered all her life and correspondingly naïve, she perceived only jealous stiff-necks who bore grudges that could be set aside in a flash. She did not understand that the Belandor name was now despised in Vitrisi and beyond, thanks to the Magnifico Aureste. She remained unaware that the doors of the great old city Houses were closed to the daughter of Aureste Belandor. Despite all advantages of wealth and beauty, her only hope of a brilliant marriage lay well outside Vitrisi. She never dreamed that her father had once feared the necessity of marital alliance with a Taerleezi House. She did not know these things because he had carefully cultivated her ignorance, and once safely wed, she need never know.

"The arrangements with House Tribari are complete," he told her. "The terms and conditions have been agreed upon, and there is no possibility of alteration."

"But why not, Father?" Jianna was unaccustomed to flat refusal. Frowning, she folded her arms. "I don't see why not. There's been no marriage contract, no ceremony, nothing irrevocable. If you choose to make me happy, you can still—"

"Jianna. That will do. The subject is closed." Aureste spoke with unwonted coldness.

Her eyes widened in genuine astonishment at his tone, then filled with tears. "I'm sorry," she said in a small voice. "I didn't mean to make you angry."

"I'm not angry." He melted at once. "Listen, my dear, and try to believe that I'm doing what's best for you. Do you trust your father?" He waited for her to nod before continuing, "You'll have a happy, safe, comfortable life. No calumny or accusation will touch you. You'll be cherished, and honored; you'll have everything in the world that you want. You will see me often as long as I live, and when I am gone you'll inherit considerable wealth. I've done much to preserve that wealth through the wars, and it has all been for you. Now, don't you think you can manage to reconcile yourself to such a fate?"

"Well, when you put it that way." Her smile crept back. Her tears were gone in an instant, as if they had never been. She was still like a child in that way. "I'll be good, then. You've always known what's best for me. No more arguments."

"There's my butterfly. Now don't you have a dress fitting or some such feminine mystery to engage your attention?"

"Is that your tactful paternal way of telling me to go away?"

"In a word, yes. I'm expecting a visitor shortly."

"Who?"

"No one you'd know."

"Sounds mysterious."

"Someone to present a full account of the latest meeting of the City Council. There is a reordering of the committees in progress."

"Oh, a *boring* mystery."

"I fear that you would find it so. Flutter off, then. Go enjoy yourself."

"I will. Only first—" Rounding the desk, she bent her slim form to plant a quick kiss on his cheek. "Love you, Father."

He responded in kind, then watched as she exited the study,

struck as always by the easy active grace of her movements. Which would shortly vanish from his house and his sight, along with her voice, her laughter, and her impossibly trusting eyes. Her absence would leave an unimaginable void. Life without her would be—

Grey. Old.

He pushed such thoughts from him, for melancholia of temperament did not number among his failings. Jianna's departure was all for the best; she would be far safer outside of Vitrisi. Moreover, there were certain compensations to be found, for his daughter's removal eliminated one of the few major constraints upon his scope of action, and the pleasures of renewed liberty were already beginning to manifest themselves. One of the greatest was imminent.

There came another knock at the study door, and this time the expected visitor appeared; a woman neither old nor young, tall nor short, pretty nor ugly. Her hands were tolerably well tended, but not fine. A long cloak of grey-brown frieze disguised her figure. The hood, pulled well forward, concealed her hair and shadowed her face. The woman hesitated on the threshold in the manner of a servant or petitioner.

"Come in. You are my guest." Aureste produced the encouraging smile reserved for those he did not wish to intimidate immediately.

She advanced with caution.

"Please be seated." He sketched a hospitable gesture.

She perched on the extreme edge of the chair across the desk from him.

"Some refreshment, perhaps? Cake? Wine?"

"No. Nothing. Thank you, sir. Honored Magnifico, I mean."

"You are quite comfortable, my good Brivvia?"

"Oh yes, Honored Magnifico. Very comfortable indeed, thank you kindly, sir." She fidgeted.

"You are most welcome. And now, having concluded the

amiable preliminaries, let us attend to business. None of your Corvestri household is aware of your presence in my home?"

"Never, sir. Major domo and the others, they all think I'm off about some errand for my lady at the glover's. Nobody spotted me coming here."

"Good. What have you to report, then? Come, tell me what you have found."

"Well, sir." Brivvia darted a quick look at him. "Not too much. I mean, I sniffed around, like you told me. I hunted high and low. No telling what would have happened if Major domo or even one of the cleaning girls had spotted me, but they didn't. And it all came to nothing."

"Nothing?"

"That's the way it went, sir."

"I am disappointed," Aureste observed gently.

"Sorry, sir."

"Are you really?" He had addressed the same question to his own daughter not half an hour earlier, but this time the effect was different. Allowing the full weight of his black gaze to press upon her, he watched the round olive face trying hard not to crumple.

"Honored Magnifico, I tried, truly I did. I poked around in places it scared me to meddle with. The master's desk drawers. In among his clothes and personal things. Under the bedding in his room. I even checked the pockets of his gown when he was in the bath. No good. I didn't come up with anything like what you want."

"I see." Aureste reflected, then inquired, "And his workroom?"

Her eyes slid away. She said nothing.

"Am I to assume you neglected to investigate your master's workroom? Answer me."

"It's locked."

"Hardly an insurmountable obstacle to a woman of your resources."

"I don't know what you mean." Her grimace of misery suggested otherwise.

Aureste did not trouble to reply.

After another moment's unendurable silence, she burst out, "Please, sir, don't make me go into the master's workroom. I don't know what he does in there, and I don't want to know. Just let me stay out of it."

"This is idle chatter. Come, you know your duty."

"You call it that!"

"Do you argue with me?"

"No, Honored Magnifico. Forgive me, sir. Only—" She cast about for an effective objection. "It's not so easy. The door's always locked, and the master keeps the only key with him all the time. Also, there's always servants hanging about that corridor."

"You will find a way. I've every confidence in your abilities."

"And then," the woman continued, "even if I managed to get in there, 'tisn't likely that I'll find the kind of papers you're wanting, sir. Master probably burnt 'em. Or maybe," she ventured, "there were never any to begin with."

"That is an unhappy possibility," Aureste conceded pensively. "But hardly a disaster that I confront unprepared. Conscience will not permit me to entrust such a matter to the whims of Fortune, and therefore I have devised a secondary stratagem. One moment." On the desktop near at hand stood a carved wooden coffer fitted with elaborate gold mounts. The lid's central boss, once displaying the incised initials of the original owner, had been chiseled away decades earlier. Over the course of the years, the exposed raw wood had darkened almost to black. Lifting the damaged lid, the magnifico withdrew a paper packet, which he placed before his guest. "There. Take it."

"What is that?" She did not move.

"Evidence. Correspondence connecting your master Vinz Corvestri to the Faerlonnish resistance movement. You will take this packet and tack it to the underside of a drawer in your master's desk. Thereafter you will continue your investigations, which will include a thorough search of Corvestri's workroom."

"Honored Magnifico, if you don't mind my asking, if you've already got these papers you want, then why not just turn 'em in to the Taerleezi authorities and have done?"

"The case against your master will be stronger if the documents are discovered within the confines of Corvestri Mansion."

"Well, then what d'you need any more papers for? Why should I have to go snooping around my master's workroom when—" Her expression altered as reality dawned. Eyeing the packet with round-eyed disfavor, she accused, "You've *diddled* 'em, haven't you?"

"Diddled?"

"It's a cheat! They're fake. Honored Magnifico, you *forged* 'em."

"Not personally. I do not flatter myself with the delusion that I possess the necessary skill."

"You'd rather get your hands on the real article if I can find it for you, but if not, then these fakes—"

"Will serve. Quite right. I knew I could rely upon your understanding."

"I understand better than I want, sir. This is low and dirty, this is. I don't like it."

"I appreciate your delicacy, but trust you will not allow it to deter you."

"I don't know. The master isn't a bad fellow. He doesn't deserve such a rat job."

"Ah, but he richly deserves such a rat job, Brivvia. Your master Vinz Corvestri is in league with the Faerlonnish resistance. That is a statement of fact. He has subsidized numerous illicit endeavors, and is therefore responsible for the destruction of property and the loss of priceless human life. Indeed, it grieves me to think of it." Aureste shook his head.

"He must be stopped. In assisting me, you serve justice and you serve your community. It is a highly moral act. You see that, don't you?"

"I see just fine. Just fine." She took a breath as if intending to say more then looked into his eyes and lowered her own at once.

"I expected no less." He smiled warmly and waited. After a moment, she plucked the packet from the desk and stowed it away under her cloak. "Good. That is settled, then. And now, as to the other matter—"

"Oh, no. No, sir. Don't ask me. It isn't right."

"My good woman—"

"Yes, I do still have some goodness left in me, believe it or not, and I don't want to do it!"

"Come, this is a trifle. You've already consented to worse."

"Maybe worse, but not so *improper.*"

"Good woman, must I remind you that there are many who would find that brand upon your shoulder *improper,* should the matter come to light?"

"That shoulder was burnt near twenty years ago! I was still a child!"

"A child and a thief."

"I haven't done anything wrong in all the years since!"

"So you insist. But the brand is still as sharp and clear as the day that iron met your flesh. What would your mistress say were she to learn that her maid bears the mark of a convicted felon?"

"My lady Sonnetia is kind. She'd forgive me!"

"I daresay she would. But your master, Vinz Corvestri—is he equally forgiving? I suspect not. He would turn you out into the streets, where you would starve. But why belabor the obvious? We understand one another, do we not?"

Brivvia looked away.

"Come, what have you brought?" Aureste leaned forward.

Still not looking at him, she reached into her pocket and brought forth a white scrap of lace-trimmed cambric, which she placed in his outstretched hand.

"Ah. Her handkerchief." Aureste studied the Corvestri family crest and initials S.C. embroidered in white silk thread. Lifting the cambric to his face, he inhaled deeply, caught no fragrance, and frowned. The crisply flawless fabric engaged his attention, and his frown deepened. At last he set the handkerchief aside, skewered Brivvia with his gaze, and remarked, "This object is untouched."

"Yes, Honored Magnifico. Spanking new and perfect it is."

"Did I specify spanking new or perfect?" Without awaiting reply, he informed her, "This will not do. It is sterile. You must bring me something that she has used. It should be clean, but not new."

"I can't do that! I don't know what you want with her things, exactly—"

"It is not your place to inquire."

"But I know it can't be right. Makes my flesh creep just to think about it."

"Such luxuriant fancy doubtless furnishes endless diversion."

"Please, sir, I've done what you said. That's got to be enough."

"It is not."

"I can't go sticky-fingering every day! It isn't fair; my lady's been good to me. And I'd get caught, sure as sunset."

"You must be clever and careful, but that should not be difficult. You've the experience, after all." He cogitated briefly, then informed her, "Next time, you will bring me some small trifle that your lady will not miss. A scarf, perhaps. A glove. I leave it to your discretion. You understand me?"

"Yes, Honored Magnifico." Her shoulders sagged.

"Come, don't look so glum. Here." He flipped her a small silver coin, which she caught neatly. "You are doing fine work, and you will do more before you're done. Be certain to keep me apprised of your progress. Now be off with you."

She exited in haste. Aureste sat motionless for a moment, then jabbed a pair of pressure points on the underside of the desktop to release the hidden catch of a bottom drawer. The drawer yielded a small casket, which he placed on the desk before him and opened. Within the box reposed a collection of small articles: a bundle of yellowing letters, a couple of pressed flowers, a curl of bright chestnut hair tied with a green ribbon, a seashell, and an ancient gold ring, blazoned with the Belandor crest and set with a great star sapphire. Very carefully he handled the assorted items, tracing the curve of the chestnut curl and weighing the ring in his palm. His fingers loitered for a time on the letters as if absorbing their content through the skin, then moved on. Presently he placed the new white handkerchief in among the other mementos, closed the box, and returned it to the drawer, which he relocked with a decisive snap.

Still he did not rise but remained where he was, allowing his mind to follow his recent visitor back through the neighborhood known as the Clouds, as far as tall Corvestri Mansion, with its triple turrets and its famous spiral rooflights. In his mind's eye he watched as Brivvia entered the house, then made her unremarkable way up the marble stairs and along the corridor to the empty study, where she lost no time in fastening the forged correspondence to the underside of a drawer in her master's desk. All of this Aureste Belandor observed through the lens of his imagination, and as he watched, his heart warmed with the satisfaction of the creative artist at work.

TWO

The covert action against Vinz Corvestri was absorbing. For days the project ruled Aureste Belandor's thoughts, and during that happy term he could almost forget the imminent loss of his daughter. At times her departure seemed nearly unreal, a shadowy menace of the distant future. But the days marched by, and all too soon came a morning to which he awakened with a sense of empty gloom.

He lay on his back in a behemoth of a bed, an elaborately carved ebony extravaganza hung in heavy dark damask, looking up at the arched supports of the tester above. His eyes moved to the center of the vaulted structure, where the initials of the bed's previous owner, once incised upon a decorative shield, had been chiseled away long ago. He had ordered the initials removed at the behest of his wife, who had otherwise threatened to consign the expensive piece of furniture to the flames. And she, ordinarily the epitome of spineless complaisance, had demonstrated such an uncharacteristic, almost hysterical determination that he had deferred to her wishes upon that one occasion. Even then she had obdurately refused to lie down in it, and the banished Magnifico Onarto Belandor's best bed had gathered dust for years in a dark storeroom until the Lady Zavilla's obliging death in childbirth had permitted its reemergence.

He really ought to commission an artisan to restore the damaged woodwork, Aureste reflected for the hundredth time. Not that the rough-hewn reminder of his predecessor's fall disturbed his repose in the slightest, but the visible defect compromised the worth of an otherwise valuable piece.

Something leaden pressed upon his mind. It took a moment

to dispel the mists of sleep and identify the cause. Today was the day. It had come at last. Jianna was going away.

He rose, washed, and dressed himself without summoning assistance, for he could scarcely abide a human or Sishmindri presence at such a time. He wanted nothing to eat, for his normally healthy appetite had failed him; a weakness he did not intend to display at the family table. She would be down there now in the south hall at breakfast with her uncles, an aunt or two, a few resident cousins, a couple of her long-dead mother's people, and sundry visitors; no Taerleezis among them today. The magnifico's absence would be noted, but Jianna and Innesq would understand, and theirs were the only opinions that mattered. No need to trade strained pleasantries before an audience of dim-witted kin. He and his daughter had talked at length the previous night, and everything important had been said.

The tolling of a distant bell alerted him. There could be no further delays; she would be leaving within minutes.

Exiting the master suite, he made his way along the corridor, and nothing in his calm face or his swift confident stride hinted at inner perturbation. Down the central stairway, through the grand entry hall, out the front door, and there was the carriage, blazoned with the Belandor arms in silver and drawn by four matched greys. At the bottom of the drive waited the six armed riders assigned to protect the vehicle and its passengers throughout the three days of travel between Vitrisi and the neighboring city of Orezzia.

A fairly sizable group of kinsmen and retainers had gathered at the door to see Jianna off. Nalio and his endlessly dutiful wife were there, no doubt because he imagined that it was expected of them. The youngest Belandor brother looked pasty and puff-eyed in the chill light of early morning. He was attired in a tunic and fashionable parti-colored trunk hose that called unfortunate attention to spindly short shanks. Middle brother Innesq was likewise there, ensconced in his wheeled chair, with a servant to attend him. Innesq never called for Sishmindri assistance with the chair, or with much of anything else, for that matter. His aversion to what he termed "abuse" of the amphibians was idiosyncratic and difficult to fathom.

There were the other insignificant kinfolk present, too, together with random servants. And there at the center of it all was Jianna herself, in a new traveling gown of deep garnet wool and a matching hooded cloak trimmed with wide bands of black fox. Her dark hair had been drawn back into a simple twist, its elegant severity softened by many a curling tendril. She looked at once adult, yet still the child she had been, and so beautiful that his breath caught and for a ridiculous moment his eyes actually misted.

His vision cleared in an instant. He strode forward, and the path to her side opened magically. Gathering his daughter into an embrace, he held her for a moment.

"We'll have no farewells." He kissed her brow lightly and released her. "I'll see you again in just one month. That's no time at all. We need no farewells for that."

She nodded. There were tears in her eyes.

"Come, won't you smile?" Aureste urged. "You will soon be a bride. It's a happy occasion."

"Very happy." She swallowed hard.

"What will it take to make you truly believe that?" He pondered. "Ah, I have it. Time. And not very much time at that, I suspect."

"I'll try to think so."

"How can you doubt? Haven't you learned in eighteen years that I am always right?"

She managed a genuine smile at that, and amended, "Often right."

"Shall we compromise and say usually right?"

"Agreed. But just the same, nothing will be truly right in Orezzia until you come."

"It will only be—"

"And stay for a long, long visit," Jianna insisted. "Weeks, at the very least. Do you promise? You *have* to promise."

"Promise. The Tribaris will think they'll never be rid of me."

"Good. That's the only way I'll be able to stand this."

"I thought we just agreed—"

"We did, we did. I haven't forgotten. Probably it will all turn out well in the end. I know you've chosen wisely for me; you always have. It will be all right."

"Yes, it will. But listen to me now, Jianna." A quick glance assured him that his family and servants had withdrawn a respectful distance. He spoke in a low tone meant for her ears alone. "If it should somehow happen that you are not content—that your new husband or his family members do not treat you with appropriate respect, consideration, or generosity—in short, if you find yourself seriously dissatisfied for any sound reason, either before or after the marriage ceremony, then you need only send a message to me. I will come to you, and if need be I'll bring you back to Vitrisi. You shall not be trapped in a marriage that you do not desire."

"You really mean that?"

"You will be content, or else you will come home. I give you my word."

"Once I'm wed, couldn't the Tribaris stop you from taking me back?"

"They could try," Aureste observed mildly.

"And they'd fail. You've never made a promise to me that you couldn't keep."

"And I never will."

"I know. I love you, Father."

"Then trust me, and be happy." He led her to the carriage, which she entered to join the two traveling companions already seated within: her designated chaperone, stately Aunt Flonoria Belandor, and the young maidservant Reeni. He closed the door, stood a moment looking in at her, then stepped back and reluctantly signaled. The coachman cracked his whip and the big vehicle began to move, its wheels crunching on white gravel. Jianna leaned out the window and waved. Family members and servants returned the salute. Aureste scarcely noted the squawking voices or the fluttering hands. He saw nothing but his daughter's face.

As the carriage neared the bottom of the drive, the six armed riders swung into position. Vehicle and escort passed through the open gate, which was shut and locked behind them. The group gathered before the doorway quickly dispersed. Aureste did not see them go. His eyes remained fixed on the carriage until it disappeared from view, and even then he did not move, but stood staring off down the quiet street.

Eventually the sharp chill of the late-autumn breeze on his face recalled him to reality, and he looked around to find himself standing alone. He went back inside then and for a time wandered the marble corridors of Belandor House, which—despite a busy population of residents, guests, servants, and sentries—struck him that morning as empty and bleak. Repairing to his study, he busied himself with the household accounts, but found his attention wandering and therefore turned his thoughts to Corvestri Mansion, where his various agents labored in subversive secrecy. But the prospect of his hereditary enemy's impending downfall, ordinarily a source of warm satisfaction, offered no pleasure today.

Aureste closed his ledgers and rose from his seat. In time of trouble, there was but one remaining source of comfort and advice remotely worthy of consideration.

Out of the study and along the corridor to the second salon, where a section of elaborately carved dark paneling concealed a doorway wide enough to permit passage of a wheeled chair. The door stood ajar. Innesq often left it that way in mute testimony to his contempt for subterfuge. He was probably safe enough in doing so, for the younger brother of the Magnifico Aureste, close friend of the Taerleezi governor, had little to fear from the authorities. Nevertheless, Aureste was frowning as he stepped through the door into a short, narrow passage, at the end of which stood another door, likewise open to afford a glimpse of the workroom beyond. The official ban upon arcane practice or investigation among the conquered Faerlonnish was widely disregarded—an open secret often ignored by the Taerleezi authorities, particularly in the case of highborn or very talented local savants. At least a token show of compliance was expected, however. The illicit workroom and its location should certainly remain inconspicuous. A modicum of discretion eased everyone's life—a fact that Innesq Belandor seemed unwilling or unable to accept. His casual illegalities bordered on insolence, and the best of good counsel never seemed to exert much influence.

Aureste walked into the too-accessible sanctum to discover his brother crouched in the middle of the floor, surrounded by shards of broken glass and phosphorescent splashes whose vaporous exudations seemed to suck the warmth from the atmosphere. Innesq was hugging himself and shivering violently.

He looked up. His face—a finely etched, haggard, almost delicate version of his older brother's—was bloodlessly white, his lips faintly blue. His dark eyes, deep-set and ringed with the shadows of chronic illness, seemed enormous and far too brilliant for comfort.

"Help." Innesq spoke with difficulty through chattering teeth.

"How?" Aureste was already kneeling at the other's side. He touched his brother's hand and found it icy.

"Blanket. Fire."

Aureste stepped to the hearth and replenished the dying blaze. The flames jumped, then inexplicably sank. A woolen throw lay across the arm of a nearby chair. Grabbing it up, he wrapped his brother's shoulders, but Innesq's convulsive shuddering hardly abated.

"A hot drink." Aureste's eyes raked the chamber in search of a kettle, of which there was none. "I'll ring."

"No. Wait." Innesq laid a shaky hand on his brother's arm. "How do you feel?"

"I? What nonsense is this? This is not the time—"

"Quiet. Pay attention. Tell me."

So compelling were the other's eyes that Aureste obeyed, halting in midsentence. His mind and senses opened. The frigid clasp of Innesq's hand was draining the warmth from his flesh. The air of the workroom was cold, bitter, and hungry; ravenous for something unidentifiable and vital. Instinctively he shrank from the fangs of the atmosphere.

"Tell me," Innesq insisted.

"As if we are not alone in this room. And cold," Aureste admitted. Too cold; unnaturally cold and breathless, as if the air he drew into his lungs no longer sustained life. He inhaled and felt himself suffocating. Momentary fear took hold, to be swept away by a rush of anger. One of Innesq's unnatural, illicit experiments had precipitated disaster of some incomprehensible variety. His arcane meddling had placed all of Belandor House in jeopardy. It was Innesq's fault.

"This liquid you've spilled is the source of trouble, is it not?" Aureste kept his voice even. "I'll remove it."

"No. Do not touch that." Innesq's cold grip tightened. "Get us out."

The urgency in his brother's eyes postponed all queries. Aureste rose to fetch the wheeled chair that stood in the corner. He brought it near, then hauled Innesq from the stone floor to the cushioned seat. The ease of this task unnerved him. The emaciated body lay too lightly in his arms. Innesq had always been delicate, his health perennially precarious, and if he should die, now that Jianna was gone, there would be nobody left, nobody who mattered . . .

Aureste shied from the insupportable thought.

Swiftly he pushed the chair from the workroom, shutting the door behind him. Once through the corridor and back out into the second salon, he closed the concealed door in the paneling, then turned to survey his brother. Innesq's face remained white to the lips—he was pallid at the best of times—but his violent tremors were starting to subside.

"I'll ring for help."

"No. Better, now," Innesq whispered. "You?"

"Well enough." Aureste drew a deep breath and felt the renewed warmth coursing along his veins. "What was all that? Shall I order the house evacuated?"

"No need. The worst is over. The workroom will clear itself within a day."

"What happened?"

"I cannot answer with any great certainty," Innesq returned mildly. His voice was weak but clear. His hands still shook.

"Then I suggest that you take a good guess. If you are ready to speak."

"There is little to say at the moment, for I do not possess enough information. I was at work and all went as might be expected, until there came a disruption."

"I won't pretend to understand you. I know only that you've given me your word that these experiments of yours endanger no member of my household. It was upon such assurance that I permitted construction of that workroom whose secrecy you scarcely trouble to guard. And now I discover—"

"It is very curious." Innesq spoke with an air of bemusement, apparently unaware of the burgeoning tirade that he interrupted. "It should not have been thus. It was wrong."

"So I observed."

"You do not understand me. More than wrong, it was impossible."

"Do you think you've failed in all these years to teach me that nothing is impossible? This mad art or science—I hardly know which to call it—of yours knows no rule or limitation."

"You could not be more mistaken, brother. The forces and phenomena that I study are bound by their own inviolable laws. Their logic does not manifest itself to the casual observer but, once discovered, maintains a perfect consistency."

"Bah, it's all so much perverted lunacy."

"Then it is discouraging to consider how many of our Belandor forebears have devoted their lives to the pursuit of just such perverted lunacy."

"Yes, and what did it bring them? Solitude, obsession, and premature death, more often than not. They'd have been wiser to turn their talents toward the betterment of our House and our fortunes. Pour all that misdirected energy into something more useful. More profitable. Shipping, for instance. Timber. Silver mining. Anything."

"Aureste, you will never change." Smiling faintly, Innesq shook his head.

"I suspect that's not intended as a compliment, but no matter—we digress. You were about to explain the so-called impossibility in your workroom."

"I cannot explain it; I can only offer a theory. First, let me assure you that the creation of malign atmosphere is something that cannot occur accidentally."

" 'Malign atmosphere'—is that what you call it?"

"It is as good a term as any to describe an air so toxic and unnatural."

"And you say it can't occur accidentally—does that mean you did it deliberately?"

"Certainly not. I could not do it deliberately if I tried, because it cannot be done at all. Picture yourself dropping a coin from your hand and the coin does not fall to the floor, but rises to the ceiling. Or think of igniting a fire and watching the room sink into darkness as the flames drink the light from the air. I see you shake your head, because you have known from earliest childhood that these things violate the laws of nature. Well, you may trust in my word when I tell you that the incident in my workroom just now was equally profound a violation of arcane principle."

"Perhaps it only seemed so. I'm certain you'll sort it out

eventually. I've every confidence in your curious abilities. In the meantime, you are unhurt, are you not? Nobody was inconvenienced, and I see little immediate cause for alarm."

"You are scarcely considering the implications."

"I'm in no humor to consider implications. Today my only child left my house. The loss consumes me."

"Ah. Jianna." Innesq nodded. "Yes, that is hard for you. But it is a loss that every parent must eventually endure, and certainly in my niece's best interests that she marry and live outside of Vitrisi."

"You needn't remind me of that. You need hardly point out my responsibility for the hatred she encounters here in her home city. No, I haven't forgotten that it's entirely my own doing, if that's what concerns you."

"I intended no reproach. You know that." Innesq met his brother's eyes.

"Yes. I do know." Aureste's dark gaze fell before the other's mild, calm regard. "Forgive me, I don't mean to wrong you of all people. But today I hardly know what I say."

"You are troubled. It is only natural. You would do well to turn your thoughts and attention in another direction, if you can. Listen to what I am telling you now; it is more important by far than Jianna's departure."

"To you, perhaps."

"To everyone. I have been trying to make it clear to you that the accident in my workroom occurred in violation of arcane law. Nothing less than an alteration in the basic principles governing our existence can account for it."

"Innesq, I'm certain all this would fascinate one of your fellow arcanists, but you must understand that such matters exceed the scope of my knowledge or interests. You're bound to solve this new riddle of yours in time, but I cannot help you. She looked beautiful, didn't she? Like the very incarnation of youth and promise. The Tribaris will fall under her spell at once. Who wouldn't? I wish I could be there when they see her for the first time."

"So vast and elemental a change is no impossibility," Innesq continued. "In fact, it is an inevitability in the wake of the Source's reversal. You are aware that the Source is capable of reversing its spin?"

"I know little of the Source or its idiosyncrasies. I'm not certain that Flonoria is the best possible traveling companion for her. She's suitable in terms of age, rank, and general demeanor, but not particularly intelligent. Jianna will easily find ways of getting around her."

"Should this reversal take place, the results will be catastrophic—to mankind, that is. The Overmind of the former masters will resume sway, and we humans will flee the Veiled Isles or die. As for the Sishmindris, I'm not certain of the effect of the change upon them, but it is unlikely to improve their sad lot. Certainly they fear it."

"You're forever fretting over the Sishmindris. I see no need for such concern. They're only animals, if rather more teachable than most. Perhaps I'll present one to the Tribaris when I travel to Orezzia next month. A fine gift, wouldn't you say?"

"I would not. You might learn much from your victims, Aureste, if you but troubled to observe them."

"I refuse to quarrel with you over those outsized frogs. Not today."

"I do not seek to quarrel. It is best that you know, however, that the Sishmindris have been uneasy of late. They are far better attuned to the forces of the natural world than we humans, and they sense the imminence of cataclysm."

"Surely you haven't been talking with them."

"I have. They are well worth listening to."

"That's absurd. Perhaps they possess certain brute instincts—I grant that's possible—but there's no intellect."

"There is a great deal. The Sishmindris," Innesq continued, forestalling his brother's rejoinder, "foresee an upheaval so vast that the balance of nature will alter in its wake. Those so fortunate as to escape slaughter or enslavement at the hands of humanity are withdrawing to their ancient retreats."

"Retreats?"

"Hidden fortifications constructed upon sacred sites."

"Fortifications? Sacred sites? Come, you don't take all this seriously? There's apparently some migratory activity among these creatures, as there is among many other species, but what does it amount to beyond the hunt for food and breeding grounds?"

"Aureste, you are willfully blind. If you would only open your eyes—"

"My eyes are wide open, and they perceive reality, which is more than can be said for yours at times, clever though you are, brother. In any case, even if it were all true, mind-boggling upheaval and all, what exactly do you expect me to do about it? If it's all as apocalyptic as you claim, what can anyone do?"

"If you ever bothered to glance through the Belandor family histories, you would know. There is talent in our family, Aureste. From generation to generation, it has always been present among us."

"Certainly. And in our generation, you've got it. Why don't you just use it as nature intended and—"

"And leave you in peace?"

"And leave me to manage Belandor affairs, as my position demands?"

"That sounds pleasantly restful, but I am afraid I cannot oblige. You must hear me, Aureste. We are not helpless to avert disaster. If I am correct and reversal is near at hand, then it is possible to influence the Source—that is, to cleanse the arcane anomalies presently impeding its rotation. This has been successfully accomplished in the past; more than once, if the histories are to be trusted. The combined abilities of some half a dozen arcanists of talent are required, and—"

"It is an arcane matter, then." Aureste shrugged. "That's your field of expertise, and I leave the affair in your hands. Probably you're attaching undue significance to the dire croaking of a few peevish amphibians. You've always displayed an exaggerated regard for those creatures. But you may do as you please; I won't interfere."

"You cannot dismiss this matter so lightly. You must realize—"

"Come to me with solid proof—something beyond the stirring of the Sishmindris and a nasty little chill in your workroom—and perhaps you'll convince me. In the meantime, do you think the six riders I sent with Jianna furnish adequate protection? Or shall I send another six after her along the road?"

. . .

"In the last century, your great-great-uncle Zariole married a Frovi of Orezzia," Flonoria Belandor confided. "This is an incident rarely alluded to, for it is widely believed that the execution of the Fortificatri Ujei Frovi three hundred years ago compromised the gentility of the entire Frovi line. But that is arrant nonsense, for the collateral branch of House Frovi from which Zariole chose his bride remained untainted. Thus the integrity of our own Belandor lineage has never truly suffered a breach. Never allow yourself to believe otherwise."

"Why would I believe otherwise, Aunt Flonoria?" Jianna inquired, wide-eyed.

"There are many malicious tongues in the world. You must not heed them. On the other hand, there are certain sound and solid standards that should be respected. When Tashe Divarra married the Jementu heiress, for example, the match was completely impossible. Her first cousin was Taerleezi middle class, actually in trade on Taerleez, and the thing simply couldn't be countenanced. There are limits. But you understand that, do you not, niece?"

"Indeed, Aunt." Jianna nodded earnestly. Out of the corner of her eye she saw the young maidservant Reeni's tongue emerge pinkly, wiggle once, and withdraw—a rudeness occurring outside Flonoria's line of vision. She swallowed a rising giggle.

"And ever since then," Flonoria continued, "the Divarras have been regarded as—not quite all they might be. Their quality is somewhat impaired. It is unfortunate, but such is the way of the world. There is a lesson to be learned here, niece."

"Yes, Aunt." Jianna's expression was contemplative. Behind Flonoria's back, Reeni's pretty kitten face warped itself into a grimace of eye-popping grotesquerie. A sputter of laughter escaped Jianna, and she disguised the lapse with a fit of coughing.

"Ah, you are ill, my dear," Flonoria sympathized. "The dust of the road has congested your lungs. The jolting of this carriage has doubtless aggravated the problem, upsetting your digestion and perhaps disrupting the delicate balance of your womanly parts. I shall instruct the coachman to halt, allowing you time to recover."

"No need, Aunt," Jianna replied, red-faced with suppressed hilarity. "I'm well, truly. There's nothing wrong with my womanly parts that a little fresh air won't cure." Raising the nearest window shade, she leaned her head out to draw deep drafts of autumn mist down into her lungs while allowing free play to her facial expressions. Presently the giggles subsided and she took stock of her surroundings. The rutted road, still firm at this time of the year, wound through a jaggedly hilled, heavily treed wilderness that displayed no sign of human habitation. Sodden brown drifts of dead leaves sprawled over the ground, and countless bare branches arched black against a somber sky.

Gloomy. Desolate. Drab. Hard to believe that Vitrisi, with all its life and color, lay but a day and a half behind her. Home, along with everything dear and familiar, seemed infinitely distant. Orezzia, with its promise of vast change, was as yet unreal. There she would soon be a wife, unquestionably an adult, with a new name and a new life. She would no longer be Jianna Belandor, daughter of the Magnifico Aureste, but Jianna Tribari, wife of a noble Orezzian family's oldest son and heir. There would be a great household of which she would one day be mistress. There would be a husband, family, retainers, husband, Sishmindri, visitors, husband, hangers-on, husband, fresh surroundings, strange ways, husband . . . a prospect at once alarming and alluring. Marriage, of course, was designed to unite great Houses, great fortunes, great political factions. The personal preferences of the participants, particularly the bride, counted for next to nothing. In most cases. But the daughter of Aureste Belandor was special. For her, things would be different.

Her happiness meant everything to her father. He had chosen carefully for her, and his judgment could be trusted. He had promised her contentment and she expected no less. With any luck, however, there could be more than that. Practical reality notwithstanding, there was such a thing as love in the world; even, occasionally, between husband and wife. Perhaps she would be one of fortune's rare favorites. Perhaps the betrothed awaiting her in Orezzia would be someone wonderful. She would not make the mistake of spinning romantic dreams; she was not that foolish. And yet wedded happiness was no impossibility, not for her; she was, after all, the daughter of the Magnifico Aureste.

Jianna strained her vision as if expecting the face of her future to take shape out of the fog, but saw nothing beyond hills, trees, and the dark forms of the six mounted bodyguards surrounding the carriage. It never occurred to her to hail the guards. They never had anything to say beyond *Yes, maidenlady; No, maidenlady; According to the magnifico's commands, maidenlady.* Really, they weren't much better than Sishmindris. After a while the scene palled and she leaned back in her seat.

She must have daydreamed longer than she knew, for Aunt Flonoria had fallen asleep, her substantial form lax against the cushions. But Reeni was wide awake, busy fingers embroidering a fanciful letter J in gold thread upon one of her mistress' handkerchiefs.

"Put that aside," Jianna commanded in a low tone respectful of her aunt's slumbers.

Reeni complied at once. Her look of guarded attentiveness suggested uneasiness, perhaps expectation of a well-deserved rebuke.

"I want to speak to you."

"Yes, maidenlady."

"I want to ask you—" Jianna paused uncomfortably.

"Yes, maidenlady?"

"Do any of your friends—the girls of your own class and age—do they ever talk about being married?"

"All the time, maidenlady. Sometimes it seems they don't talk of aught else."

"Well, and what do they say?"

"Oh, it's always *who* am I going to marry, and *when* am I going to marry, and how many *children* will I have, and how many of 'em will be *sons*, and I want to find a palm reader to *tell* me, and—"

"That isn't quite what I had in mind. I meant, do they ever talk about being already married? That is, about being with their husbands, alone at night, you know—"

" 'Tisn't like they'd be much alone at night or any other time, maidenlady. Not sleeping the half dozen to one bed in the garret of some great house, and mind you, those are the lucky ones. The scullery maids and spitboys and so forth just spread out on the kitchen floor, mostly, and the big shots get the places nearest the fire. And then the grooms and such lay down in the haymow above the stable, per usual, and—"

"Very well, you've made your point; they're not often alone. Some of them do marry, though, and there are certain . . . marital functions—"

"Certain what, maidenlady?"

"Certain duties—activities, if you will . . ."

"Like cooking and cleaning?" Reeni's eyes were a little too wide. All traces of uneasiness had vanished.

"Don't tease, minx. You know what I'm talking about."

"Are you talking about *doing it,* then?"

"Exactly."

"Then why didn't you just say so, maidenlady?"

"Why in the world do I put up with you?"

"I've no idea, maidenlady."

"Neither do I. But come on. What do they say about—about—doing it? Tell me what you've heard."

"Well." Reeni considered. "What they say divides up in three groups, like. There's one group says that it's the best thing in the world, by far. Nothing else comes close; it even beats honey pastries. They say it's like they've never been alive before, and now they finally know what life's all about."

"Yes." Jianna felt her heartbeat quicken. "Tell me more."

"Then there's the other gang, says that it's like a nightmare you can't get out of. Says it's disgusting, and it *hurts,* and a husband is like a rutting boar pig that owns you. One of that crew said she felt all dirty, like she'd been used as a piss pot, and she hated her man so bad that she wanted to take a knife and cut his thing off."

"And did she?"

"Not so far, I don't think. If she had, I'd've heard about it."

"Probably." Jianna nodded. "You said there were three groups?"

"Oh, aye. Those in the third group say 'tisn't so much to put up with, and they don't mind, usually."

"Well. Not too enlightening. Which group do you belong to, Reeni?"

"Me, maidenlady? You know I'm not wed."

"I know, but haven't you ever—I mean, even once—?"

"Never, maidenlady. And I never will, not until the words are spoke and I'm a proper wife."

"Ah, you've strong moral convictions."

"Moral fiddlesticks. I know what's what, that's all. And I'm not about to give the lad I marry, whoever he may be, the joy of knowing he's not the first with me."

"I don't think I can be hearing you correctly. You believe that it would give your groom some sort of satisfaction to find that he's *not* your first?"

"I don't believe, maidenlady, I *know*. Why, then he'd have the advantage of me forever and ever. And whenever there comes a falling-out between the pair of us, he could always sneer down his nose and tell me, 'You got no say in this, I don't listen to no little *harlot*. Ye're lucky ye're not out on the streets, like you *should* be, so don't push it. And don't be telling me to cut back on the beer, because I could tell *you* a thing or two. I could throw you out and nobody'd blame me. And don't you forget it.' And so on. Oh, there'd be no end, and that I won't have. I won't give any man the pleasure of rubbing my nose in it."

"I see. Well, that's one way of looking at it, I suppose." Jianna subsided into abstracted silence. Reeni resumed her embroidery, and Flonoria snored on. Time crawled, its progress marked by a couple of rest stops and by the gradual darkening of the dull skies.

Presently her stomach growled and she found herself thinking of the evening to come, with its meal taken either in the common room of the Glass Eye, next inn along the road to Orezzia, or else in her own private chamber. The common room, with its smoky atmosphere and its assortment of anonymous travelers, offered the stimulating prospect of vaguely disreputable novelty. It was for that very reason, however, that Aunt Flonoria would undoubtedly prefer seclusion; and as official chaperone, she was in a position to insist.

Not that Flonoria was unkind or tyrannical. She was simply old, that was all—old, staid, and devoid of curiosity. Not her fault, but she did have a way of forestalling fun. Of course, Jianna reflected, she didn't have to accept restraint tamely. Her father certainly wouldn't. Her father wouldn't let anyone, even the best of well-intentioned aunts, stand in his way. He'd find a way to get what he wanted—he was that clever, that determined, and an inspiration to his daughter. In her place, what would Aureste Belandor do?

Jianna was still thinking about it when the carriage paused for yet another rest stop. She breathed an impatient sigh. She had had enough of chilly wilderness interludes; she wanted the Glass Eye with its comforts and its interesting common room. Still, a chance to walk about a bit was not unwelcome. She glanced at her aunt, still soundly sleeping, then caught her maidservant's eye. A slight jerk of her head communicated a command. Both girls alighted from the carriage and strolled a short distance in silence.

They had come to a stony stretch of road closely flanked by thick woods. The bare patches between the trees were filled with fog and impenetrable shadow. The grey air was dank and heavy, the carpeting of soggy dead leaves underfoot slippery and somewhat treacherous. Nothing interesting to see, hear, or do, and wasn't travel supposed to be exciting? All the more reason, Jianna reflected, to experience the Glass Eye and its novelty to the fullest. She *would* dine tonight in that common room, eating all that exotic common food among all those colorfully grubby common people, no matter what Aunt Flonoria had to say about it.

"Reeni," she remarked aloud, "I think we're going to have a small accident in our room at the inn this evening."

"An accident, maidenlady?" Reeni inquired, smiling.

"I'm afraid so. You'll be responsible, but don't worry—you won't get into any trouble, even though it *will* be very careless of you."

"What will be very careless of me, maidenlady?"

"Your treatment of my belongings."

"I treat 'em like precious eggs."

"Not tonight you won't. Tonight you're going to break a bottle of perfume, a large bottle. The one with all that musk and ambergris, I think. I don't like that one anyway. It will happen while you're unpacking my bag."

"Please, no, maidenlady."

"When you do it, try to make sure that the perfume goes splashing all over the place, particularly onto the bedding."

"Please, maidenlady, don't make me. My lady Flonoria will beat me something fierce for't."

"No she won't. I'll tell her . . . I'll tell her that you're subject to sudden spells, where you lose control of your—uh—your *voluntary functions*," Jianna decided.

"My what, maidenlady?"

"Your—ummm—muscles, follicles, and—and your connective tissue. Your hands. Your feet. That sort of thing."

"My lady Flonoria will turn me out, then."

"No, she won't, because it's not your fault; it's just something that happens to you sometimes. Nobody can hold it against you, and Auntie's not cruel. Actually I expect she'll be fascinated. She'll think you've got something wrong with your womanly parts, and she'll want to cure you. She's got an entire bag full of nostrums, you know—"

"Aye, and I want no part of 'em!"

"And once you engage her sympathies, you'll find that she's really quite solicitous."

"I've seen her solicitousing all over the place, and I'll have none of her powders and potions!"

"Well, you'll just have to get used to the idea, because you *are* going to break a bottle of perfume this evening, and the fumes *will* drive us out until such time as our bed linen has been changed and our room properly aired. We shall surely find ourselves obliged to dine in the common room along with the ordinary travelers, but I fear there's no help for it."

"I hear you, maidenlady. I catch your drift, but you got to promise me that I won't lose my place over't."

"You goose, do you think I could do without you? Of course I promise. You trust me to look after you, don't you?"

"I trust you to *mean* to, maidenlady."

"Good, then we're agreed. Now, when you break the bottle, I want you to let out a convincing cry of dismay. Think you can do that?"

"I think that's slopping on too much gravy, maidenlady."

"No, it's just the right touch. You'll see. I just want you to—"

"Begging your pardon, maidenlady, but all this is making me too nervous. I got to go."

"Go?"

"Behind a tree, before my voluntary functions become unvoluntary."

"Oh. Off with you, then. And while you're about it, you might practice your cry of dismay."

Reeni retired from view. Jianna cast a look back at the carriage, its once gleaming surface now liberally spattered with mud. The driver was dancing attendance on the horses. A couple of the guards had dismounted to light their clay pipes. Three others orbited the site in vigilant silence. The sixth, presumably answering nature's call, was nowhere in evidence. Nothing interesting to be seen. Jianna strolled on, skirts lifted a fastidious inch to clear the wet leaves but otherwise blind to her surroundings, mind galloping on along the Orezzia road into the future.

A feminine shriek from the woods brought her back to the present. It was obviously Reeni practicing her cry of dismay as instructed, and very convincing it was, too. Perhaps a little too convincing, for the sound caught the attention of the guards, who promptly dropped their pipes and drew their short swords. *Oh, bother.* When they discovered the false alarm, they were bound to be annoyed, and there would be words.

The cry repeated itself. The girl was overdoing it. But an instant later one of the mounted guards yelled and clutched himself, while another tumbled headlong from his saddle. Jianna stared, astounded. The first man, bloodied and moaning, had his hand locked around the shaft of the crossbow quarrel protruding from his midsection. The other lay facedown in the dead leaves. Even as she stood gaping, a second volley flew from the woods and two more guards fell.

They could not be dead, not just like that. It was too fast and final.

A hand closed on her arm and she spun to face another guard, the one lost to view the last time she had looked. His face was set so hard that she instinctively recoiled, but already he was moving her, handling her as if she were a piece of baggage, half dragging and half pushing her along. For a moment she pulled back, then realized that he was steering her back to the carriage and abandoned resistance. When they reached the vehicle he shoved her inside to join her aunt, slammed the door shut, and positioned himself before it.

"Highwaymen?" she yelled at him, and received no reply. "Go get my maid," she commanded, but he ignored her. Even in the midst of her alarm, the anger rose. She was the magnifico's daughter, and he was a hireling; he ought to obey her. "Aunt Flonoria," she appealed, turning to face her kinswoman. "Would you tell him that he has to go get—" She broke off with a gasp at sight of the quarrel transfixing the other's throat. Flonoria's expansive bosom was soaked with blood. Her eyes and mouth were wide open. Jianna's own incredulous expression was not dissimilar. She half expected to see her aunt blink and return to life, but the moments passed and Flonoria remained dead.

The solid thunk of a quarrel striking the window frame recalled her own danger. Yanking the shade down, Jianna crouched trembling on the carriage floor. The activity outside was violent and lethal, but she could hear surprisingly little. Hurried footsteps, a couple of terse muffled warnings or commands, the snorting and shifting of nervous horses, and the repeated thump of missiles hitting the carriage. Then came a change: The crossbow fire ceased and there was shouting outside, accompanied by the clash of steel. Very cautiously she raised her head and applied her eye to the gap between window shade and frame. Her hands were cold but her fear was under control, for she never doubted her father's ability to choose bodyguards capable of protecting her. The marauders would be driven off or, better, captured and executed for what they had done to Flonoria Belandor.

The scene she confronted did not confirm her expectations. The attackers had emerged from the shadows to finish their work. There were four of them—brawny figures roughly garbed in homespun and heavy boots, with kerchiefs hiding their lower faces. They were not the glamorous midnight-cloaked highwaymen of her imaginings. These men looked like farmers gone wrong. They had set their crossbows aside in favor of plain, heavy blades, which they plied with business-like efficiency. One of them dispatched the driver within seconds, and then all four engaged the surviving guards. The two Belandor retainers acquitted themselves well, even managing to kill one of their attackers before they themselves were cut down.

Jianna swallowed a cry as the last of her defenders fell. She must be quiet, very quiet and still, and then perhaps the bandits wouldn't notice her.

Idiot. The carriage was the first place they would check for passengers and valuables. *Run away.* If she sprang from the carriage right now and made a dash for the shelter of the foggy woods, she might still escape. She was young, light, and fleet. Perhaps she could outrun them. Even as she gathered herself to jump, fresh horrors froze her in place.

A burly fifth marauder emerged from the woods for the first time, and with him he dragged Reeni. The young girl—disheveled, hair streaming—struggled vigorously. Unable to escape, she changed tactics, lunging at her captor to claw his face. In doing so she dislodged his kerchief, uncovering a wide, fleshy nose, ripe lips, and heavy prognathous jaw. He raised his free hand to his cheek, and the fingers came away red with blood. Instantly the same hand balled into a fist that slammed Reeni's jaw, sending her to the ground.

This time Jianna could not repress her own sympathetic cry, and did not even try. All five marauders heard her—their heads turned as one—but she hardly cared, for the outrage boiling up inside her momentarily quelled fear. No point in trying to hide, and she certainly did not intend to let these savages find her cowering like some trapped rabbit on the floor of the carriage. She was a Belandor of Vitrisi.

She stepped forth into the open. They were staring at her—four pairs of eyes above dingy old kerchiefs, and a fifth pair, the pale lifeless grey of aged slush, set in a square scratched face. They might kill her or worse, but for the moment she did not care.

"Leave my maid alone." She addressed herself with an outward show of assurance to the dead slush eyes. "Don't touch her again."

He looked her up and down unhurriedly, then observed, "So. Skinny. Prinked up. High-nosed. About what I expected."

Expected? She had no idea what he meant, and no inclination to analyze. "Reeni?" Jianna started forward. "Can you answer me? Are you badly hurt?"

"You stay still," the bare-faced man advised, voice flatly expressionless.

He took a step toward her, barring her path, and she stopped, intimidated by his looming muscular bulk and his impassive square face, her brief rush of courage already ebbing. Ashamed of her fear, she lifted her chin and commanded, "Stand aside."

He neither moved nor spoke. She forced herself to return his gaze, and discovered that the heavy-lidded eyes in the broad face were so wide-set that it was nearly impossible to meet both simultaneously. The opaque eyes revealed nothing at all, and her concealed fear deepened.

Reeni sat up slowly, looking dazed. Her jaw was twisted violently awry; beyond doubt it had been broken. When she met her mistress' eyes and tried to speak, an unintelligible gabble emerged, concluding in a whimper of pain. Tears spilled from her eyes.

Jianna's anger flared anew. "Do you vicious louts know who

I am?" she inquired with an air of icy contempt. They had probably recognized the coat of arms on the carriage, but best to be certain. "My father is the Magnifico Belandor. He'll pay well for our safe return. But if you hurt me or lay another hand on my servant, he'll hunt you down wherever you hide and nothing in the world will save you. You'd do well to remember that. Now get out of my way and let me go to her." Reeni's assailant stood like a monolith. Sidestepping him, she advanced.

Despite his palpable menace, she was unprepared for the iron pressure of his grip on her arm. Taking her above the elbow, he swung her around and gave her a shove that sent her sprawling.

"I told you to stay still," he said.

She lay on her back in the mud and the wet leaves, staring up at him. Never in her eighteen years had anyone lifted a hand against her. Even in the midst of obvious danger, an unconscious part of her had continued to view her physical self as somehow sacrosanct. Now her reluctant mind opened to new possibilities. She became aware that the fall had displaced her skirts, exposing the slender length of her legs. His flat gaze pressed her thighs. His four companions were motionless and piercingly watchful. She went cold inside. Determined to mask her terror, she climbed to her feet, met the empty grey eyes squarely, and remarked, "I've always believed that it is only the weakest and most cowardly of men who turn their wrath on women."

His face did not change in the slightest. She might have thought that the insult went unheard had he not stepped forward to deal her cheek an open-handed blow that knocked her down again.

"You need to learn some manners," he told her unemotionally. "Get up."

Her ears were ringing and she could taste blood in her mouth. She shook her head to clear it.

"Up. Don't make me wait." Grasping her coil of dark hair, he hauled her to her feet. "Now, what was that clever remark you made just then? I don't think I caught it all the first time, and I wouldn't want to miss a single word, so you'd better say it again. Nice and clear. Come on."

She stared at him.

"I said, spit it out. Are you really going to make me tell you again?"

"My father," Jianna attempted, voice shaky. "My father is the Magnifico Aureste Belandor. He—"

"Have you forgotten what I told you to say? Or are you trying to make me angry?"

"Listen to me. My father—"

"Still not what I told you to say. You learn slowly. Maybe a reminder will help."

He slapped her and she tottered, but his grip held her upright. Her eyes swam for a moment, but she was able to see his hand come up to strike again and she also saw Reeni, broken face contorted, behind him with a rock clutched in her fist.

One of his gang shouted a warning and his reaction was startlingly swift. Releasing Jianna, he wheeled in time to dodge a blow intended to smash his skull. The descending rock missed him by a whisper. He smiled slightly and Reeni shrank away from him, but there was no place to go. He caught her wrist and twisted. She cried out in pain and the rock dropped from her hand. Wrenching her arm behind her back, he forced her to her knees.

"Let her go. Please." Jianna found her voice; a high, thin voice, but adequately steady. "Don't hurt her, she was only trying to protect me. She's a servant of House Belandor, and my father will—"

"I know all about your shit-licking kneeser father," the slush-eyed man returned, shocking her into silence. "You want to see what I think of your father and all his precious little servants? Pay attention, I'll show you." Drawing a dagger from his belt, he deftly slit Reeni's throat wide open.

A red torrent gushed from the wound. Reeni dropped to the ground. A few spasms convulsed her small frame, but very soon she lay still.

Jianna's mind attempted to reject the reality of the scene, tried to dismiss it as a hideous hallucination, and failed. She stood staring for a numb eternity at the dead girl stretched out on the dead leaves. At last, her eyes rose. Reeni's murderer was watching her, and his face told her nothing at all. She discovered in that instant that she hated him more than she had ever hated another human being.

"Come here," he said.

He still clasped the bloodied dagger, and she wondered if he meant to use it next on her. She stood motionless and let the hatred show on her face.

"Disobedience. Disrespect. Two big mistakes," he told her. "But you'll learn."

Three long strides brought him to her. She did not allow herself to flinch. Before she recognized his intention, he jabbed a short punch to the midsection that doubled her neatly. A second blow took the point of her chin. The world exploded around her, then ceased to exist.

· · ·

She emerged from nothingness to find herself blind, sick, and disoriented. Her head throbbed cruelly. Various body parts ached. Her position—face down, head dangling—was momentarily incomprehensible. She could see next to nothing, but an animal odor filled her nostrils and she could hear men's voices close at hand. She was moving, carried queasily along on something. Her wrists were bound behind her back, her ankles were likewise tied, and a blindfold wrapped her eyes.

They had trussed her up and dumped her like a sack of flour across the back of a horse or a mule, she realized. She had no idea where they were taking her or what they meant to do with her. Her confused mind struggled to resume normal functioning. If they intended rape and murder, she reasoned laboriously, there was no particular reason to remove her from the site of the attack. Probably they planned to hold her for ransom. They would let the Magnifico Aureste Belandor know the price of his daughter's life and honor, they would tell him how and where to pay it, and they would set a deadline of some sort. Then they would settle back to wait. And while they waited, the Magnifico Aureste would contrive to track them down, and then he would see to it that they were hanged as they deserved for what they had done to Flonoria, Reeni, the driver, and the bodyguards.

So she bravely assured herself, but the thought of her murdered companions brought dreadful images. She saw again Aunt Flonoria's staring dead eyes, and the fountain of blood spurting from Reeni's severed throat. Nausea seized her then, and her flesh went clammy. She retched, but it had been hours since her last meal and there was nothing left in her stomach to lose. Only a very little while ago, she had been plotting to force Aunt Flonoria to dine this evening in the common room of the Glass Eye. It had seemed so tremendously important at the time.

She could see a sliver through a hairline gap at the bottom of the blindfold. She glimpsed dead leaves, churned mud, and nothing more, no matter how she shifted and strained. The movement only intensified her nausea, and she retched drily again. *Untie me, let me sit up.* The words quivered on her lips, but she did not let them fly. Into her mind thrust the vision of a square, impassive face with dead grey eyes, and she would not let herself ask anything of that face. A moan sought escape and she held that in, too.

Her mouth was dry and foul. She could not judge how long it had been since she had last tasted water, for she had lost all sense of time. The world had reduced itself to sick pain, bewilderment, and fear that left room for only one comforting certainty: No matter where these murderers were taking her, the Magnifico Aureste would find and rescue his daughter. Jianna Belandor would be safe at home within days or less, and her abductors would be punished. All of them.

The miserable blind span seemed to stretch on forever. Her thirst waxed and her headache sharpened. Eventually her limbs went cold and dead. At one point the band halted briefly, perhaps for relief and refreshment, but she could not be certain, for nobody removed her blindfold, loosened her bonds, or offered her water, and she refused to beg for it.

The journey resumed and the knife-edge of fear dulled as Jianna sank into a stuporous state. Thought and sensation receded; there were lost intervals during which consciousness may have lapsed. The voices around her faded. Either conversation had ceased or else she did not hear it. The tiny slice of the world visible below her blindfold was darkening. Night was coming on, or perhaps her eyes were failing.

Measureless time passed. She was chilled to the bone, parched, and light-headed when they finally halted. Someone cut the cords at her ankles, lifted her down, and set her brusquely on her feet. Her legs gave way at once and she would have fallen but for the support of a powerful arm whose touch was intolerable, for she knew on instinct whose it was. Expressionless square face, wide-set heavy-lidded eyes of dirty slush.

She tried to pull away from him, and his grip tightened. Then he was hurrying her along, forcing her on when she faltered, never slackening his pace when she stumbled. Resistance was pointless and she offered none.

He steered her up a low set of steps, probably stone, and through a heavy door or gate that groaned shut behind her. The still, musty quality of the air and the level flooring underfoot told her that they had entered a building of some sort. On they went for some chilly, drafty distance before she sensed herself passing through another doorway into a perceptibly warmer atmosphere. She caught the whiff of wood smoke and heard the crackle of a fire.

They stopped, and the man beside her spoke.

"Here, Mother. See what I've brought."

"Well done, boy," answered a woman's voice, unusually deep and assured. "Get that rag off her face and let me take a good look at my new daughter."

THREE

A hand fumbled at the back of her head, and the blindfold dropped from her eyes. Jianna blinked and looked around her, devouring her surroundings at a glance. She stood in a moderately spacious chamber with walls paneled in dark wood, smoke-blackened beams exposed overhead, and a couple of narrow, deep windows presently admitting no light. Cold, dusty stone floor underfoot, no rugs. Big, old-fashioned fireplace with a plain stone mantel and a generous blaze within. Split logs stacked beside the hearth; a giant brindled boarhound and a brace of lesser canines sprawled before the fire. Not much furniture. A crudely fashioned, heavy table of oil-finished wood supporting a pitcher and several earthenware goblets; a few substantial chairs innocent of upholstery; a three-legged footstool; nothing more.

The only illumination came from the fire and from a pair of utilitarian oil lamps hanging from the rafters. By that warm-colored glow she observed the faces of four companions. One of them she recognized too readily, with revulsion but without surprise—the hulking slush-eyed murderer, standing beside her. Three others sat at the table—one male, two females. The man was youthful, muscular, snub-nosed, and square-jawed. One of the females was likewise youthful, translucently pale of skin and hair, emaciated to the verge of invisibility. The other woman was much older, well advanced into middle age, with grey streaks marbling her mass of brown hair and deep lines framing her lips, but hardy and strong-looking. She was dressed in an unadorned gown of some sturdy dark stuff, no better than an upper servant might have worn, although it was obvious that she was no servant.

Jianna hardly noted the costume; she was caught and held by the other's marked resemblance to Reeni's murderer. There was the same coloring of hair, eyes, and skin. The same broad, square, heavy-jawed face, same assertive nose and full lips, the same wide-set, thick-lidded light grey eyes. While the size, shape, and color of the eyes were identical in mother and son, the expression differed. Where the son's eyes were chill and seemingly vacant, the mother's glowed with active intelligence.

They were scrutinizing Jianna with equal attention, and presently the woman remarked, "She has something of her father's look. It's in the eyes and brows, I believe. We shall soon know if she's inherited his nature as well."

The authoritative contralto carried an unexpected aristocratic accent. Jianna contained her surprise. Facing the other, she straightened her spine and lifted her chin. "My father—" she began, but her dry sticky mouth and tongue played her false, and only a hoarse croaking emerged.

"Sounds like a sick Sishmindri," the woman observed with amusement. "One thing I'll give her father, he could speak." A new thought appeared to strike her, and she inquired, "Has the girl been properly watered?" There was no immediate reply and she prompted impatiently, "Onartino, speak up."

The slush-eyed hulk beside Jianna stirred uncomfortably. His flat gaze wandered.

"Now."

"How would I know?" The murderer addressed as Onartino shrugged. "That's a business for servants."

"You imbecile." The woman spoke with an air of confirmed expectation. "You want to kill her before you've had the good of her?" Without awaiting reply, she commanded, "Nissi, see to it."

At once the blanched young girl rose from her chair, took up one of the earthenware goblets, came around the table, and raised the vessel to Jianna's lips.

Jianna gulped down watered wine. When the glue that seemed to line her mouth had dissolved, she looked up to encounter Nissi's luminous, almost colorless eyes inches from her own. The lashes were exceptionally long, but pale and fine as cobwebs. The image of Innesq Belandor's haggard visage flashed across her mind and it seemed to come from nowhere, for there was no discernible resemblance between her uncle and this wraith of a girl. For an instant the eye contact held and then, as if responding to some spoken command or plea, Nissi set the goblet down, shifted position, and applied herself to the cords that bound Jianna's wrists. Her touch was cool and weightless as mist, but surprisingly effective. Within a moment, the cords fell away. Jianna brought her hands before her and stared at them in amazement. Her fingers were cold and numb, but when she flexed them, they stiffly obeyed.

"Thank you," she whispered.

"No one gave you leave to turn her loose, you little maggot," Onartino observed. "Have you lost the few insect wits you ever owned?"

Nissi appeared deaf.

"Put those ropes back on her," Onartino commanded, "or else I will. Which d'you think will be the worse for her, maggot—if you do it, or if I do it?"

Nissi regarded the floor attentively.

"Shut your mouth, boy," the older woman suggested. "You're not out in the woods."

"Mother, this is my concern."

"And I wish I could trust you to manage matters intelligently, but you've all the judgment of a stag in rut."

The hitherto silent young man at the table guffawed, and the speaker turned on him. "You hold your tongue, Trecchio," she advised. "You're not one particle better than your brother—in fact, you're not as good; you haven't half his courage."

Trecchio's laughter promptly died. "I'm no coward," he declared with a glower.

"There's my little hero." She bent an unkind smile upon him, then returned her attention to Jianna, demanding, "You are Aureste Belandor's daughter?"

"The Magnifico Aureste is my father," Jianna replied, voice emerging clear and composed. "He will pay my ransom."

"His title is false," the other informed her, "and there will be no ransom. Shall we trade one of our own for money? You look confused, girl, as well you might. Allow me to enlighten you. I am the Dowager Magnifica Yvenza Belandor, widow to the Magnifico Onarto Belandor. Is that name familiar? No? It should be. Onarto Belandor is the kinsman whose title and life your father stole some twenty-five years ago. These two likely lads here are my sons, Onartino and Trecchio. The elder, already known to you, is the rightful Magnifico Belandor by the laws of inheritance. This girl, Nissi, is undeniably Onarto's daughter, but she is not mine. For the sake of the blood that she carries, she has a place in my house, which is not grand, yet meets our immediate needs. We do not live in high state here at Ironheart, but have no fear—we anticipate great change in the near future. My dear—distant niece, I suppose I must call you, for now—your long-lost family members bid you welcome to your new home."

Yvenza Belandor fell silent and Jianna stared at her in frozen incomprehension. The woman's words, while clearly and cogently spoken, amounted to so much gibberish. Some sort of response seemed to be expected, however, so she collected herself to answer, "I don't understand what you mean by all of that. You seem to be playing a game, but I don't know the rules. I only know that your men attacked my father's carriage on the open highway, killed everyone I was traveling with, and carried me here against my will. You seem to be telling me that you are not ordinary criminals and highwaymen. Perhaps you aren't ordinary, for you chose your target with unusual care. You know who I am and you know that my father will pay well to secure my return, as soon as you name your price."

Yvenza Belandor laughed out loud at that. "So young and such a cynic, else a simpleton," she observed. "You haven't been listening to me, girl. Or perhaps you're slow of understanding. I say that we haven't taken you for your father's coin, although you may be certain he'll pay dearly. In the end, he'll give all that he owns. Or I might more properly promise that he'll give back all that he stole."

Any reply was sure to be wrong. Jianna said nothing.

Observing her keenly, Yvenza observed, "I begin to perceive that you are less dull-witted than genuinely ignorant. Your father, doubtless relishing the sweet flood of daughterly affection, has gone to some lengths to preserve your innocence. He's told you little or nothing of your family history."

"He's told me to disregard the slander of his enemies," Jianna returned. "And so I do."

"And do you similarly disregard the recollections of your kin? I'll share a few of my favorites with you," Yvenza offered amiably. "Let me transport you back in time some twenty-five years or so. The civil wars have recently concluded and the dynastic issues have been resolved, not precisely to the satisfaction of all concerned. The island of Faerlonne, ancient seat of art and learning, has succumbed to the military vigor of neighboring Taerleez. Faerlonne is occupied by Taerleezi forces, and what was once a sister state of the Veiled Isles is now regarded as a conquered enemy. The Faerlonnish citizens are disenfranchised, stripped of their property, taxed to the verge of starvation, and subjected to new laws too unjust and outrageous to accept without a sense of degradation.

"My husband, the Magnifico Onarto, has forfeited the bulk of his fortune and property. He has seen his brothers and his closest friends die in the wars, and he himself has lost his right arm. For all of that, he is one of the more fortunate among the Faerlonnish. As head of one of the Six Houses of the Veiled Isles, he's been permitted to retain his title, the family house in Vitrisi, and enough money to sustain a life of sorts. Those Belandor family members residing with the Magnifico are comparatively safe from the worst of the Taerleezi persecutions, and they will not starve. Mindful of his favored position, the Magnifico Onarto extends protection and hospi-

tality to as many of his relatives as he is able to shelter beneath
his roof.

"Among them is included Aureste Belandor, a second
cousin sprung of a poor family branch, energetic and intelligent, but ambitious, ruthless, and reputedly treacherous.
Onarto is warned, but he is generous of heart and chooses to
give his cousin the benefit of the doubt. It is the mistake of a
lifetime. Not six months following Aureste Belandor's arrival,
the Magnifico Onarto is secretly denounced as an active
enemy of the Taerleezi regime—a saboteur, terrorist, and con-
spirator. If he is taken and tried, he will suffer torture prior to
public execution. As it is, he receives warning in time to flee
Vitrisi with his wife, children, and several retainers. The fugitive family finds refuge in a wilderness stronghouse called
Ironheart, and there they live as outlaws. The traitor Aureste
remains in the city as new heir to the Belandor title and fortune, courtesy of his Taerleezi cronies, whose favor he has
courted at the cost of all loyalty and honor. Tell me, little
maidenlady—what do you think of the tale so far?"

The woman had not abandoned her air of pleasant equanimity. Jianna, sensing the imminence of explosion, felt her
jaw muscles tighten. Loath to display weakness, she met the
other's eyes and replied evenly, "You speak of the traitor Aureste, but where's the proof against him? You claim that the
Magnifico Onarto was secretly denounced. If that's true,
what right have you to assume that Aureste did it?"

"Ha. Logical questions, evidence of a mind at work."
Yvenza's air of ominous amusement remained intact. "You
will be disappointed to learn, however, that the matter
scarcely amounted to a mystery. Aureste stood to profit hugely
by his benefactor's downfall. Moreover, his character was by
that time known to all."

"Is that what you call evidence?" Jianna dared to speak
with a hint of scorn. "And what of the charges against this
Magnifico Onarto? You haven't said, or even seemed to care,

if they were justified or not. Was he in truth a saboteur and terrorist? If so, was it wrong to stop him?"

"Someone will have to file the edges off that tongue," Onartino remarked.

"Patience; let her ask what she pleases," his mother decreed. "It's more than time that she learn the truth."

"Truth?" Jianna shook her head. "So far I've heard only lies about my father."

"Mother never lies," Trecchio interjected.

"Quiet, boy," Yvenza told him. "Give my little niece a fair chance to digest a deal of new information. It's all unfamiliar to her, and she hasn't even heard the whole of the story. Let us continue her education, while observing the effects of instruction upon an impressionable young mind." Refreshing herself with a sip of wine, she resumed.

"You might imagine that the new Magnifico Belandor, satisfied with his stolen property and title, would permit his disgraced fugitive cousin Onarto to eke out a wilderness existence in peace, but such was not the case. Evidently troubled by his wronged kinsman's mere presence in the world, Aureste Belandor issued orders, and Onarto vanished from the very heart of his supposedly hidden fastness. Three days later, his remains were discovered in the woods, not a quarter hour's walk from this stronghouse. The cord embedded in the flesh of his neck described the method of execution. The beasts of the forest had partially devoured his body. The birds and insects had likewise been at work, but I had no difficulty identifying my husband."

They did not intend to ask for ransom. They hated her father unreasoningly, wanted vengeance, and doubtless meant to kill her in as gruesome a manner as they could devise. But she would not give them the satisfaction of witnessing her terror. Moistening her lips, Jianna replied with an appearance of detachment, "Aureste Belandor issued orders, you say? How do you know that? Did anyone hear him speak? Was this

Onarto's executioner ever found, and did he implicate my father in his confession? Answer if you can."

"The murderer, unquestionably a member of my household, was never identified," Yvenza recalled pensively. "Investigation and deduction narrowed the suspects to a trio of servants, but the guilty individual could not be determined and I was therefore obliged to hang all three. Justice was served and my surviving followers received a valuable lesson. A wise move, wouldn't you agree?"

A barbed smile invited debate. Jianna did not let herself rise to the bait. Her air of composure remained carefully intact as she observed, "I see you've no proof at all against my father. He's a famous, wealthy man. Few Faerlonnish fared so well after the wars, and many resent his good fortune. I care nothing for the lying accusations of the envious."

"Now, there's true filial devotion. Thoroughly misplaced, but admirable all the same. You boys might profit by so sterling an example."

"I mean to profit," said Onartino.

"Good lad. Let us conclude, then. Despite the seeming totality of his triumph, I am pleased to report that the traitor Aureste did not go entirely unpunished. His betrothed at that time, the Lady Sonnetia of House Steffa—evidently gifted with some sense—not only broke off her connection with Aureste Belandor, but for good measure promptly accepted and wedded the young Magnifico Vinz Corvestri, scion of House Belandor's ancient enemy. A particularly pretty choice, that. I gather from my sources that the blow hit home and Aureste felt it deeply for a while. Unfortunately, such a man was not one to suffer at great length, and it was not more than two years later that he consoled himself with the Lady Zavilla of House Gorni, who presented him with a great fortune and an heiress before considerately removing herself. It is rumored that the neglect and undisguised contempt of her husband greatly hastened the Lady Zavilla's death, and this I can well believe."

"How dare you?" Jianna felt the color burn her cheeks. Aware that an angry reaction would only please her tormentor, she strove to hold her temper and failed. The fear-fueled indignation came boiling out of her. "How dare you speak that way of my parents? You know nothing of them. You and your people are nothing but outlaws sneaking around out here in the middle of nowhere. You're a liar and that son of yours is an animal, a murderer, and a coward."

"Stay where you are, Onartino." Yvenza halted her son before he moved. Her attention returned to the prisoner, of whom she inquired lazily, "Well, maidenlady, where are your manners? Is that any way to address your future mother-in-law, or your husband-to-be?"

For an instant Jianna doubted her ears. Confused, she studied the other's face, which communicated nothing beyond pleasurable amusement. At last she answered, "I've already told you that I don't know the rules of this game."

"Perhaps because you've not yet heard the end of the tale. Listen and you'll learn everything you need to know. To finish, then—the years have passed, the innocent have suffered, while a villain enjoys the rewards of his crime. But there's a force of justice at work in the universe—this I firmly believe. Justice may be suppressed or circumvented for a while, but not forever. Your arrival, little niece, alters the situation at last. The schism dividing House Belandor is about to mend, and justice will be served. Is that not a rosy prospect?" The question must have been rhetorical, for she continued without pause.

"A union of House Belandor's sundered halves will heal ancient wounds. The marriage of Aureste Belandor's daughter to the Magnifico Onarto's oldest son serves this purpose splendidly. Upon Aureste's death or departure, his son-in-law will succeed to the title of magnifico. Thereafter, Onartino's issue will inherit. Who could ask for a simpler or more elegant solution to so vexing a family dilemma? Warms my heart just to think of it. Am I wrong to assume that your pleasure equals my own? Come, niece, tell me your thoughts." This time she seemed to expect a reply. There was none, and her voice lashed. "*Speak up.*"

Jianna started as if struck and spoke without thought. "You're criminal lunatics, and my father will give you all that you deserve."

"We are in full agreement upon that last point."

"He'll see that you're sorry for all that you've done. He'll—he'll string you up by the thumbs. For a start."

"Excellent," Yvenza encouraged. "And?"

"He'll punish you for making false claim to the Belandor name."

"False claim, when we, unlike you, are of the primary original stock? Amusing. And?"

"And you'll be sorry for killing my aunt Flonoria, my maid, my driver, and the guards. You'll regret your attack on our House; my father will see to that. You've made a big mistake, and if I were you I'd run away while I could."

"Now, that's what I call an honest reply." Yvenza nodded, entertained. "And I appreciate candor, if not impudence. No matter. Under our guidance you will very soon learn to govern your tongue."

"I hope I won't be here long enough to learn anything."

"Ah, Onartino." Yvenza favored her firstborn with a fond smile. "She will make you a delightfully spirited little wife, but you'll have your work cut out for you. I only hope you'll rise to the challenge."

"I'll rise," said Onartino.

"I believe you will. Maidenlady," Yvenza confided with a congratulatory air, "I think your husband-to-be likes you. He's a stout lad, as you've no doubt gathered, and you'll suffer no tedium in your marriage."

"Marriage? You keep speaking of that." Jianna struggled to conceal her rising dread. "It's a joke of some kind, I suppose."

"Is there not a certain school of philosophy that regards all human existence as a joke of some kind?"

"I don't understand your games. Speak plainly if you can, and tell me your intentions."

"I've already done so. My intention, little maidenlady, is to marry you to my oldest son. Is that plain enough for your understanding?"

"No, for it makes no sense at all." Jianna tried to speak very reasonably. "I know you're only amusing yourself, because you must know how impossible that is."

"How so?" Yvenza's brows rose. "You and Onartino are both young, healthy, of the best blood, and unattached. It's a perfect match."

"You cannot be in earnest."

"You'll discover otherwise."

"I'm already betrothed. My father has chosen a—"

"You will alter your plans. It's sudden, I know, but spontaneity possesses its own particular charm."

"You can't seriously imagine that I'd ever agree to such a thing."

"You'll agree to far more than that before we're done."

"Not in a lifetime."

"Oh, it won't take nearly that long. It would seem that you regard a respectable marriage to my poor son as the proverbial fate worse than death, but this is shortsighted. A moment's reflection will persuade you that far more unpleasant possibilities abound. You aren't convinced? Consider, then. As the legal wife of Onartino Belandor, heir to the family title, you will enjoy position, the prospect of wealth, and the legitimacy of your children. As his convenience, you are entitled to none of these benefits."

"His what?" Jianna inquired in simple disbelief.

"His convenience. You're unfamiliar with the expression? Your education has been neglected. It means—"

"I know what it means, but I don't understand what you're saying."

"I suspect that you understand well enough, but let's make certain. Know that your life has changed forever. Onartino has claimed you, and you are now his property to do with as he pleases. If you plan to argue the point on moral or legal grounds, I advise you to spare your lungs. Fortunately for you, my boy is the soul of integrity, and he is willing to make you his wife. For this he deserves your thanks. Should he encounter ingratitude, opposition, and obstinacy, however, he'll be forced to make the best of a bad situation, and who could blame him? He'll take what good he can have of you, and you'll suffer every indignity of matrimony while enjoying none of the advantages.

"One such advantage includes security. You are still young, but it's never too early for a woman to recognize the inconstancy of men, even so excellent a specimen as my Onartino. As a child, he tired quickly of his playthings. Once he wearied, he'd pass the unwanted item on to his younger brother, Trecchio, who'd entertain himself for a while before tossing the toy—by this time, usually much the worse for wear—out into the courtyard, where it would be snapped up by the guards, the stableboys, the spitboys, and others of that ilk, to be used by each in turn. When diversion palled or the mechanism broke, whichever came first, the plaything was discarded once and for all, and what befell the remains thereafter I can hardly begin to guess. Are you following all of this, maidenlady?"

"You're trying to frighten me." Jianna strove hard to make herself believe it. She took a deep breath. Her mouth had gone dry again, but her voice still sounded all right. "Perhaps you enjoy frightening people. But none of what you suggest is possible. I am a magnifico's daughter. That, if nothing else, makes me someone too valuable to subject to—to—the monstrous treatment that you suggest."

"Ah, but Aureste's daughter warrants special attention."

"We are strangers, and I've never done you or yours any harm."

"Nor did my husband do your father any harm."

"Even if all that you claim is true, it happened long before I was born."

"Unjust world, isn't it?"

"You're a civilized human being. You're a woman, and surely would never inflict such atrocities on another woman."

"Would I not? Think again, little maidenlady. If ever I possessed the womanly softness to which you direct your misguided appeal, your father cut it out of me years ago. I am not only capable of inflicting cruelty upon Aureste Belandor's daughter, but so willing that I long for the opportunity, even at the cost of self-interest. Do you know what I see when I look at you? I see Aureste Belandor's eyes, his face in female form, his surrogate self fallen into my power at last. Thus I hope to find you steadfast in your defiance. I yearn to encounter a strong will in need of breaking. In short, niece, I'm prepared to throw you to the dogs and return what's left of you to your father in a sack. Still want to describe me as civilized?"

The woman had not raised her voice, but the mask had slipped and hatred flashed for a red instant. Jianna curbed the impulse to step backward. *Madness,* she thought. She clasped her hands to disguise their trembling.

"Nothing to say, maidenlady? You've been quite talkative, until now. Fatigued from your travels, no doubt. You'll want to see your resting place."

"I'll take her," said Onartino.

"No you won't. No games for you yet, my boy. I want her intact for now."

"Now, later—what difference does it make?" Onartino demanded. "It comes to the same end."

"Don't argue with me. Your brother will take her. Trecchio, you meddle with her and I'll set the dogs on you. Understand?" Apparently his wordless shrug failed to reassure her, for she added, "Nissi, you go along and keep an eye on him."

Trecchio advanced to grasp Jianna's arm above the elbow. She pulled back, and his grip tightened painfully. The breath hissed between her teeth and her fingers curled into claws. Then her gaze jumped to Yvenza's face. She saw the anticipation there, and the urge to rebel subsided. Trecchio would hurt her if she tried to fight him; she saw it in his mother's eyes. He led her from the room, and she went tamely. The girl Nissi trailed a couple of paces in their wake. Jianna found the silent, insubstantial presence oddly reassuring.

Along a gloomy corridor he steered her, to the head of a narrow, steep stairway, where he paused briefly to pluck a lighted candle from a wall sconce. Then down into dim smelly dankness, a basement or cellar of some kind. Puddles lay underfoot, mineral deposits palely crusted the moist walls, and a sharp reek of mildew permeated the atmosphere. Jianna's reluctant footsteps lagged and Trecchio yanked her arm sharply, causing her to stumble. The cool touch of a small white hand steadied her, and she turned her head to encounter Nissi's lambent, colorless gaze. Nissi instantly ducked her head and backed away.

Trecchio never slackened his pace, but marched his charge straight to an alcove containing a low, heavy wooden door, which yielded with a shriek of rusty hinges. His gesture encompassed the darkness beyond. "In," he said.

Jianna swallowed her protests. With a lift of the chin she advanced, only to halt on the threshold as if her feet possessed their own will. A jerk of Trecchio's arm slung her forward into shadow. She staggered, then spun to face the doorway.

"I need a light—" she began.

The door slammed shut and the blackness caught her in its jaws. A vast weight seemed to crush her, and she gasped for breath. Tried to scream and, as if in a nightmare, produced nothing beyond an impotent mew. Heard the bar drop into place even as she sprang for the door; wrestled wildly with the unyielding latch, then gave it up and sank to her knees, racked with sobs.

It was inconceivable. She was not supposed to be here. She was supposed to be at the Glass Eye Inn, making ready to dine in the interesting common room. After dinner she was supposed to giggle and gossip with Reeni. She was supposed to sleep in a soft, clean bed and in the morning travel on to

Orezzia, where her noble prospective in-laws waited to welcome her to the great house of which she would one day be mistress. That was the future ordained by her father.

Her tears slowly dwindled. She rubbed her eyes and raised her head. Contrary to her initial impression, her prison was not entirely dark. A very small window—little more than a peephole, but fortified with heavy iron grillwork—admitted a current of chilly fresh air and a thin stream of moonlight by which she imperfectly descried her surroundings. She knelt beside the door on the stone floor of a chamber some six or seven feet square. Probably a storage closet, furnished with a narrow cot, a water jug, a bucket, and nothing more. No table or chair, no light, no fireplace, and the place was miserably cold; she was already starting to shiver. Rising to her feet, she stepped to the bed and found there a single woolen blanket. She wrapped herself in the musty-smelling folds, went to the tiny window, and peered out at moonlit dirt. The closet was partially subterranean, its sole window placed at ground level. She glimpsed a stretch of courtyard, presently empty; a section of some anonymous outbuilding; a patch of starry sky; nothing that told her much.

She turned from the window, rubbing her forehead. Her nose was stuffed from the recent crying, and her head ached dully. A touch of cool water on her face might help, if only that jug in the corner contained anything. It did. She dashed a little of the contents across her swollen eyes, then lifted the vessel to her lips and drank. Good. Cold and reasonably fresh. It was then that she realized for the first time that the closet contained no food. No matter. The mere thought of food sickened her. She felt as if she would never want to eat again. But she *would* want to eat again, common sense acknowledged; probably far sooner than she expected. And then what? Would her captors feed her, or did they mean to starve her into submission?

Her headache was gathering strength. She went to the cot, lay down, and shut her eyes, but with little hope of slumber.

Fear and confusion whirled about her mind, while the intolerable images burned behind her tightly closed lids. Aunt Flonoria, and her astonished dead face. Reeni, hurt and disfigured before she was murdered. The driver, the guards . . . Fresh tears scalded her cheeks.

There had to be a better image, one to drive the others away. Something shining, powerful, and benevolent to sustain her now. She blinked, and there it was—her father's face, so clear, perfect, and alive that she felt she could stretch forth her hand and touch him. Her hurried breathing eased then, for she knew beyond question that he would find her and save her. He would succeed because he always succeeded, and once he learned of her abduction, nothing would stop him.

She could almost pity the lunatics who had dared to lay hands on her.

"Father," she whispered into the night, "please hurry. Hurry. Hurry."

• • •

Hurry. They were taking an unconscionably long time about it all. The Magnifico Aureste stirred impatiently. His seat on the third-floor balcony of the Cityheart, formerly known as Palace Avorno, was comfortable and well situated, sheltered from the sharp chilly breeze yet affording a clear view of the straw-strewn scaffold set up in the Plaza of Proclamation below. The scaffold supported a block, beside which waited a masked headsman. The plaza was filled with spectators whose true mood was difficult to gauge. With a few conspicuous exceptions, there was little display of boisterous merriment. Similarly absent was any overt sign of the resentment or disapproval whose free expression would have sparked the wrath of the Taerleezi guards ranged about the scaffold. A good thing, too. But for the presence of those steel-edged guards, the angry tongues would be wagging, the fists and rocks would be whizzing. Certainly some of those rocks would fly high, even so high as the third-story balcony accommodating the unbeloved Governor Anzi Uffrigo, his lady wife, and a few favored friends, including a single handsomely attired Faerlonnish noble: the Magnifico Aureste Belandor.

Aureste cast a sidelong glance at the governor, whose gravely contemplative gaze anchored on the scene below. Uffrigo possessed a long, sensitive, melancholy countenance, with a fine thin nose and mournful melting eyes—the face of a poet or a mystic. Nothing there to suggest cruelty, lust, greed, or malice. Nothing at all to suggest the qualities that had won Governor Uffrigo the popular cognomen of the Viper.

"Tedious, eh?" inquired the governor in his light, melodic voice, without turning his head.

Apparently he had sensed the pressure of Aureste's regard. His instincts were as keen as his namesake's.

"They take their time," Aureste conceded with a humorous air.

"I trust the spectacle will justify the inconvenience." Uffrigo beamed his radiant, gentle smile. "They say this new headsman is an artist of matchless skill. We shall soon judge for ourselves. If he fails to please, I'll hand him over to his own successor."

"There is a pretty symmetry to that notion, Governor, and the possibility of limitless continuity. I envision a crimson progression from executioner to executioner, extending indefinitely into the future. Each heir to the title of Master Headsman is literally linked by blood to the progenitor of his line—inheritor of a proud tradition and member of a unique dynasty."

"Ah, Aureste." Uffrigo rippled a musical laugh. "If only more of your compatriots shared your drollery. So many of you Faerlonnish seem so lamentably dour."

So many had been given such good reason. But the Magnifico Aureste did not number among them, and he replied easily, "It is our national talent to discern the darkness impinging on every patch of sunlight, but a sanguine nature impairs my own vision. This is a serious disadvantage."

"You are such an amusing fellow, I don't know how we should do without you."

As always, it was difficult to know whether Uffrigo's approval carried an intentional barb. Swallowing his own flash of irritation, Aureste inclined his head smilingly.

"Yet I gather that we must now do without that pretty daughter of yours," the governor continued. "What is the child's name again? Jianna, is it?"

"Jianna, yes." Aureste's smile remained fixed in place. His daughter's mere name upon the governor's lips offended his ears, but by no external sign was his anger evident.

"A charming young creature. You've promised her to an Orezzian, I hear."

"You are well informed."

"So I endeavor to be. A pity she could not remain among us to delight all eyes here in Vitrisi, and I daresay she wept to depart her home. Ah, well. No doubt the match you've chosen for her offers many an advantage."

"Many," Aureste agreed, smiling on. Inwardly he wondered, once again, if the governor deliberately sought to bait him or touched raw nerves by sheer chance. He strongly suspected the former, for Uffrigo possessed a certain feline quality of playful cruelty. Irritating, but unimportant. In any event, a Faerlonnishman among the Taerleezi conquerors could hardly afford to take offense.

"The Orezzians are a warmhearted folk, devoid of prejudice, I'm told. They'll accept her without reservation," Uffrigo suggested.

Despite her father's infamy, he meant.

"Her countless delightful qualities are certain to purchase the child the warmest possible welcome," the governor continued cordially.

The massive dowry that she brings buys a measure of their tolerance.

"And she'll soon accustom herself to the unfamiliar habits and manners of her new family."

She'll always be an outsider in an Orezzian household.

"For all of that, my dear fellow, I daresay you will miss her?" the governor probed.

The fresh wave of anger that swept the Magnifico Aureste's mind was not easily mastered. This Taerleezi viper's interest in Jianna was a profanation of something immaculate. Across his mind flashed the image of a dagger slicing the offensive tongue from the governor's mouth. A pleasing concept. Face and voice were perfectly controlled as he replied with a light shrug, "It is not as if I had lost a son." Before the other could reply, he added, "Governor, I believe the festivities commence."

An open wagon flanked by mounted guards had reached the foot of the scaffold. Its passengers included a quartet of battered prisoners, their bruises black in the sunlight, their rags stirring in the hard breeze. One of the four doomed faces was known to the Magnifico Aureste. Without surprise he recognized the fugitive he had handed over to the Taerleezi authorities some weeks earlier. Faint satisfaction tingled across his mind.

The prisoners were conveyed from the wagon to the scaffold. The list of their crimes was read aloud—all four were convicted saboteurs, members of the resistance—and the executioner went to work.

Perhaps he might have been called an artist; a highly accomplished craftsman at the very least. The dexterity with which he divested each prisoner of hands, feet, and genitalia prior to the final decapitating stroke was wonderful to behold. Yet the Magnifico Aureste took little pleasure in the spectacle, which struck him as unattractive and uselessly prolonged. The offending parties were to be eliminated—an excellent objective. The bloody preliminaries were so much pointless embellishment.

The majority of spectators appeared not to share his sentiments. The acclamation greeting each precise stroke of the headsman's ax rang through the Plaza of Proclamation. The screaming voices offended his ears, seemed somehow even to offend his nose; the very atmosphere lay rank and heavy in his lungs.

Aureste drew a deep breath, and his nostrils twitched. An acrid reek all too perceptibly rode the breeze. Smoke, and plenty of it, tinged with the scent of charred meat. He looked up from the plaza to behold dark clouds of the stuff sweeping in from the east, and knew the source at once. In the slums known as the Spidery, great bonfires had been kindled to consume the victims of the plague. So swift had been the recent spread of the pestilence, and so luxuriant the proliferation of corpses, that the public pyres now blazed no less often than thrice weekly. Ordinarily the smoke drifted out to sea, but today the fickle breeze carried it straight to the Plaza of Proclamation.

His throat tickled. His lungs drank the airborne remnants of the nameless dead. Aureste coughed discreetly and wished himself far away.

"Note the power and precision. He is an artist as promised." Governor Uffrigo's soulful rapt gaze never strayed from the scaffold.

Aureste breathed a sigh and settled back in his seat. The choreographed carnage continued, and he willed himself to watch. Presently he found himself mentally superimposing the face of the Magnifico Vinz Corvestri upon the faces of the headsman's victims, and the spectacle acquired charm. The pleasant scene filling his mind's eye was less fantasy than foresight. For weeks his agents had woven their secret nets about Corvestri Mansion, and the culmination of their efforts was imminent. It would come any day.

FOUR

The workroom was discreetly situated in a cellar beneath the
kitchen behind Corvestri Mansion. The kitchen's separation
from the house reduced the risk of fire. The windowless workroom below, similarly distanced for corresponding reason,
was accessible only by means of a subterranean corridor
whose entrance was guarded when the chamber was occupied.
It was occupied now by three human beings, two of them living and one of them undead.

The Magnifico Vinz Corvestri, illicit arcanist and head of
his House, was deeply immersed in his work—with good reason. The plague-stricken object of his attention displayed the
rebellious tendencies so characteristic of his puzzling malady,
and effective control demanded effort. Control was essential,
however. Should the undead visitor escape the net of sorcerous restraints presently hemming him in, then the plague must
surely take hold in Corvestri Mansion, starting with the master and his only son.

Vinz's eyes shifted for a moment to the boy standing beside
him, heir to his title and his talent. Even in the midst of the
most strenuous mental endeavor, he experienced the usual
thrill of pride. Young Vinzille Corvestri, only thirteen years of
age, already demonstrated a precocious arcane ability that
more than qualified him to serve as his father's apprentice and
assistant. And an admirable assistant he was—careful, accu-
rate, diligent, yet at the same time imaginative, boldly original, blessed with flashes of insight that sometimes seemed
inspired. A genius, perhaps, gifted with powers destined to
outshine his father's.

Much of the gift resided in the lad's intense concentration, his exclusion of all distraction. He was doing it now, Vinz observed with approval, shutting out the world and everything in it beyond the plague-ridden prisoner before him. His face was still and almost eerily empty—a youthful, incompletely formed, but very excellent face, Vinz noted at some cost to his own focus. Vinzille Corvestri bore little external resemblance to his soft-bellied, round-visaged, nondescript father. Happily, he favored his handsome mother, from whom he had inherited his fine features, his slender height, and his chestnut-haired autumnal coloring. Yes, altogether an ideal son.

The moment's self-indulgence had taken its toll. The sorcerous net enclosing the undead visitor gave way, and a bony arm clad in dark rags thrust through the rent. That groping arm would spread pestilence unless promptly contained. Vinz Corvestri came within a breath of exerting his power and then held back, allowing his son to take command.

Vinzille rose to the challenge. Without hesitation he reshaped his mental construction, shifting the complex lenses of his mind to bend the energy of the Source in a new direction. The questing arm of the undead froze for an instant, then drew back through the rent in the sorcerous net, which promptly mended itself. The plague victim—a tattered former denizen of the Spidery gutters—pushed vaguely at the surrounding intangible walls, turning in aimless little circles within the confines of his prison. A flex of Vinzille's intellect seized and immobilized the undead, whose facial contortions expressed unidentifiable emotion.

"Name yourself aloud," the boy commanded in tones of adult authority.

Vinz Corvestri caught his breath. Direct verbal solicitation of the force inhabiting the ruined body of the plague victim had formed no part of his plan; had not, in fact, occurred to him. This novel approach offered further evidence, if any was needed, of his son's uncommon talent. A fresh wave of pride threatened to rock his concentration.

The undead's milky eyes rolled. His jaw shuddered and

dropped. A yellowish tongue protruded. It quivered and a low, unintelligible mutter emerged, something between a rumble and a moan. Scarcely a human utterance.

"Name yourself," Vinzille insisted.

Successive spasms convulsed the undead's body. A froth of reddish foam appeared upon his lips. *"We,"* he replied in a voice scarcely tolerable to human ears.

"Again," Vinzille directed quietly.

The undead's jaw clamped. His head thrashed in a recognizable gesture of refusal.

Linked to his son by the shared current of arcane energy, Vinz felt the sudden surge of the boy's will, the intensity of which would probably have achieved success had not a sharp knock on the workroom door blasted all concentration. He briefly sensed the heat of Vinzille's frustration, and then the connection lapsed.

Vinz contained his own annoyance. His servants, those few that he could still afford to keep, were well trained. None would presume to disturb the magnifico in his workroom without good cause. Stepping to the triply bolted door, he applied his eye to the peephole and spied the familiar outline of a Vitrisi resistance activist known to him and his household members only by the alias Lousewort. The Corvestri servants were under orders to admit Lousewort at any hour of the night or day. Vinz unbolted the door at once.

"Wait," he instructed his son.

"No." Vinzille shook his head. "We had it, I can get it back. Don't stop me now."

"Only for a moment."

"Please, Father. I can do it."

He probably could; he was already that accomplished. But no adolescent, however gifted, should be left to pursue so dangerous an endeavor unsupervised.

"Not alone. I'll return shortly. Wait." Vinz stepped out into the corridor, shutting the workroom door behind him.

Lousewort stood there, bland visage all but lost in the

shadow of a broad hat. It crossed Vinz's mind fleetingly that he had dealt with this man for years and still possessed no very clear mental image of the face beneath the hat; probably that natural or cultivated anonymity offered a valuable asset to the local resistance movement.

Vinz wasted no time in preliminaries. "I heard that Pesq and Fovi were taken in Mouse Alley. You're in trouble?" he asked.

"No, but you may be," Lousewort replied succinctly.

"There's not much they could tell the Taerleezis about me. Fovi doesn't even know—"

"I'm not talking about Pesq and Fovi. The Taers won't get anything out of them. But that maidservant of your wife's might be another matter."

"Brivvia, you mean?"

"I wouldn't know her name. Not so young, medium figure, brownish cloak."

"Brivvia. What about her?"

"How much does she know?"

"Nothing about the group."

"You sure? What could she pick up from the magnifica or the other servants?"

"They know next to nothing." So far as he knew, this was true. For reasons that he chose not to examine too closely, he had never confided in his wife. Her ignorance protected her, he had told himself on the rare occasions that he considered the matter at all.

"Let's hope so. Otherwise, no telling what your Brivvia may be carrying to the ears of Aureste Belandor."

Vinz stared at him.

"No mistake," Lousewort asserted, correctly interpreting the look. "She was spotted entering Belandor House around noon today. She stayed about twenty minutes, then went to a confectioner in Searcher Street, made a couple of small purchases, and came home. Any idea what your wife's servant has to tell the Kneeser King?"

"How can you know that the woman contacted Belandor himself?" Vinz demanded. "Perhaps she simply visited some servant of the household."

"Corvestri and Belandor retainers call on one another?"

"I couldn't say. It's not impossible."

"Nor is it impossible that she carried intelligence to the Viper's pet swine."

Or a note. The thought struck Vinz Corvestri with the force of a meteor. A note from her mistress, his wife, the Magnifica Sonnetia, to Aureste Belandor. His wife's former betrothed.

It had been a rare love match between Sonnetia Steffa and Aureste Belandor. That unflinching honesty of hers had impelled her to admit as much to Vinz Corvestri upon acceptance of his proposal. At times Vinz felt that he might have made do with perhaps a little less candor. On the other hand, but for her proud integrity, Sonnetia would never have broken off the betrothal to that walking cesspool Aureste. And had it not been for Vinz Corvestri, with his impeccable lineage and his offer of a marriage deemed fine by the most stringent of traditional Faerlonnish standards, she might never have been permitted to break it off, integrity notwithstanding. For then, as now, in the aftermath of the wars, the Steffa family coffers had been nearly empty and the continuing maintenance of an unwed daughter problematic. She might have run away or committed suicide; instead she had elected to wed the awkward, earnest young Vinz Corvestri. Her resigned acquiescence had hardly fueled his vanity, but so eager had he been to acquire the beautiful Sonnetia that he had willingly accepted her without dowry.

And so they had married, and she had scrupulously kept her end of the bargain. She had managed his household with care and skill, freeing him to fix his attention upon his arcane investigations. She had presented him with the best son in the world. Throughout the course of nearly twenty-four years together, she had rarely failed to treat him with kindness, courtesy, and at least the appearance of respect. And at night in the bedchamber? There, too, she displayed kindness and courtesy. And tolerance. About as much as any lawful husband had the right to demand, Vinz supposed, but sometimes he could not help but wonder whether Aureste Belandor would have received different treatment.

"Belandor has plans for you, I suspect," Lousewort offered. "You'd best take action."

Vinz nodded, frowning. Action. Never his forte. He preferred contemplation, experimentation, analysis. He was happiest and most at ease in his workroom, either alone or with his son at his side. Within that comfortable space, he could operate effectively. But the outside world was alien. There he was uncertain and accident-prone, hardly a match for such a natural-born predator as Aureste Belandor.

"You'll question this Brivvia, eh?" Lousewort prodded.

Yes, he would have to do that, and the prospect was unappetizing. The woman was likely to prove recalcitrant, severe measures would be needed to loosen her tongue, and he hadn't the stomach for violence. Well, perhaps it was time to master his own lifelong squeamishness. Or maybe the ugly task could be entrusted to a servant. Vinz became aware that he was nervously clenching and unclenching his fists.

"Whip the truth out of her," Lousewort advised. "And when you've got it, you may find yourself obliged to hit Belandor before he hits you."

The words had been spoken. Vinz felt his stomach roll over.

"Not an easy target, but with your abilities not impossible," Lousewort continued conversationally. "And a project my group would support. We've wanted to nail that whoreson for years."

Nail that whoreson. A faint sense of warmth began to well within Vinz. *Nail him.* Finally. Possible?

"You want me to—" he began, and a cry from the workroom cut him off. Hearing terror, Vinz turned, threw wide the door, and checked on the threshold, transfixed by the sight of his son wrapped in the embrace of the undead.

The protective web of magic hung in radiant shreds. The prisoner had torn free and now, attracted to vitality, sought to draw young Vinzille Corvestri into the twilight realm of death-in-life. Vinzille lay limp and insensible in the other's arms. The undead's lips pressed his in a devouring kiss.

Vinz was unaware of the cry that escaped him. He took a step forward and halted, recognizing the futility of physical intervention. Should he touch the undead, he would accomplish nothing beyond his own infection. At such a moment, arcane force was his sole weapon. A calmness fell over him then, a profound inner silence, the crowning achievement of a lifetime's study and practice. Beside or behind him, Lousewort was yelling, but he did not hear the words. He drew the air deep into his lungs and let the stillness claim him. At the center of that hushed inner universe glowed the ember that was his gift, and now he breathed the ember into flame. The familiar power blazed through him and he never faltered, never hesitated or groped for the words and gestures that tapped the wellspring. He was one with the Source and its vastness. He was absorbed, yet still himself—a self given over to absolute purpose. His will resonated, bending the power of which he was now a part upon the surrounding world.

The intangible net mended itself, binding the undead tightly and compelling him to release his prey. Vinzille dropped to the floor. Vinz tightened the strands, reducing the prisoner to compressed immobility. Without pause, almost unconscious of his own words and gestures, so deeply ingrained were they, he wove a second such web to encase the body of his son, containing all contagion.

It was now comparatively safe to touch the boy. Vinz let his sorcerously stimulated awareness sink back to the mundane level, and the world came rushing in. His mind rocked under the impact, and the tide of exhaustion always following significant arcane endeavor threatened to overwhelm him. He pushed fatigue away and issued instructions. Together he and Lousewort carried Vinzille from the workroom, and along the passageway back to the main house. Then up the servants' narrow stairway to the third story, and along another bare corridor whose splendid mirrors had been sold off years ago to pay Taerleezi taxes, to the boy's own bedroom.

Through it all Vinzille slumbered palely. But when they laid him on the bed, he woke and glanced about in confusion. His eyes found his father's face, and he whispered, "Wrong."

"Don't speak," Vinz advised.

"Wrong," Vinzille repeated.

"Wrong move?" Lousewort inquired, keenly interested. "Arcane error?"

"*Wrong.* Impossible."

"Explain, boy. I don't quite—"

"He's in no fit state to speak," Vinz interrupted curtly. "He should rest. You'd better go."

"Our conversation remains unfinished, Magnifico."

"We will finish it another time."

"I'll await word from you. I advise you not to delay." So saying, Lousewort retired with his hallmark inconspicuousness.

Vinz turned back to his son, who was trying once more to speak.

"Sorry." Vinzille struggled for breath.

"Not now." Vinz ignored something akin to physical pain.

"Do it alone. What happened couldn't."

"You've been exposed and infected, son. I can mend matters, but I must begin work. Don't distract me."

"More important."

"What?"

"This. Impossible. All laws—everything. Wrong."

"You're ill. Don't waste your strength."

"Currents ran backward—progressions inverted—couldn't happen—"

"Quiet, son."

"Natural law broken. *Believe me.*"

"I do. I know. Now lie still, else I'll have to drug you."

Vinzille closed his eyes, relapsing into silence or unconsciousness. Vinz stood a moment, then slipped a green lozenge from the pocket of his robe into his mouth, where it dissolved swiftly. The usual nausea assailed him, and he suppressed it. A few swift mental exercises completed his preparations, and he went to work. The task he confronted was arduous, necessitating supranormal investigation of the boy's interior, including every minute refuge wherein the agents of the plague could have sought concealment. It might take hours, even days.

Vinz commenced the search and was almost immediately interrupted, yanked from his sorcerous trance by the arrival of his wife. By some mysterious means she had learned of Vinzille's misfortune—probably some servant had spotted the boy being carried through the house—and now she wanted to be with her son. Understandable enough, but not a good time. He would have to tell her as kindly as possible that she was in the way, and she was likely to argue.

"What happened?" Sonnetia Corvestri asked, her voice low-pitched and well controlled as always.

Vinz looked at her. Her face—fine-boned, strong, and still almost untouched by age—was calm as a tomb. Her eyes—green, flecked with brown, like her son's—were fixed on Vinzille. A few uncharacteristic tears sparkled the lashes.

"Accident in the workroom. He'll recover, but he needs arcane assistance and he needs it now."

"I'll stay."

"No, madam. I must be alone with him for now. It is the only way I can work."

Her eyes shifted to his face. To his surprise, she nodded. "You'll let me know when I can come back?" she asked.

"I'll send word at the earliest opportunity. I promise."

"Thank you." She glanced away, then back at him, asking as a manifest afterthought, "You are unhurt in this accident, Magnifico?"

"Completely unhurt. I wasn't even in the room."

"You left him alone in such a place?"

She was staring at him, and a sudden sense of guilty responsibility flooded his mind. He could not afford such a distraction. "I must work," he reminded her. "I'll send for you when I can."

For an intolerable moment longer she gazed at him, then turned and swept from the room. He watched the tall; slim, straight-backed figure retreat, and found that all the old feelings of longing and inadequacy were still there inside him, strong and galling as ever. Not the moment to think about them.

The door closed behind her. He was alone again with his son. Vinz shut his eyes. It took all the discipline of devoted decades to clear his mind and resume his former heightened mental state, but he did it and the interrupted search resumed.

This time he was fortunate. Following a mere four hours of effort, he found what he sought—a vicious anomaly hidden deep within the recesses of Vinzille's sleeping brain; a distinctive invasive entity, all but devoid of physicality. He might have called it a parasite, but for its lack of substance.

It took the highest skills at his command to perform an extraction without damage to the host. Eventually he succeeded, but his victory was incomplete. He had intended to isolate and preserve the invader for further study. Immediately upon removal, however, the elusive entity dissipated; nor could all his skill call back so much as a ghost of its existence.

The loss was significant but hardly seemed to matter now, not with Vinzille lying there on the bed, white and motionless, but free of disease. The arcane net enclosing the boy's weedy frame could be dispensed with now. Vinz let the protective barrier slip, then collapsed into a chair beside the bed. For a while he simply slumped there exhausted, thinking of nothing. Presently he opened his eyes and watched his sleeping son. At last recalling his promise to his wife, he dutifully rose and tugged the nearest bellpull. A servant answered the summons, and was dispatched with a message to the magnifica.

Perhaps he fell asleep for a few minutes, for she seemed to materialize instantaneously, looking much as she had hours earlier. But not exactly the same. Her eyes were puffed. She had been weeping, an indulgence she rarely permitted herself. She was not weeping now, however. Her eyes were dry, her face set and white.

He answered before she asked. "He will recover. He is safe now."

Her lips quivered and for a moment he thought she might give way to emotion, but she did not. Silently she went to the bed and stood looking down at the insensible boy. Very lightly she touched his cheek with her fingertips. Vinzille did not stir.

Vinz thought she had forgotten his presence and was taken by surprise when she turned to face him.

"Why was he left alone in your workroom?" she asked quietly.

There was no hint of accusation in her voice or manner, yet the guilt stabbed, and with it came anger. *Because I was called away to be told that your personal servant has been seen entering Belandor House,* he wanted to shout. *Because that Brivvia woman you're so thick with is a spy, or maybe a messenger between you and Aureste Belandor. Because that collaborator you were once so eager to wed is probably plotting to ruin or kill me. Or do you already know that?* He said none of these things aloud, answering only, "I was called away briefly. I told him to do nothing until I returned. He disobeyed."

"Of course he disobeyed. Do you not know your own son?"

Vinz said nothing.

"He's still too young, that's all." She spoke with careful self-restraint. "He's very talented, but still only a boy. Please try to make allowances for that."

She blamed him for the accident; she blamed him for leaving an adolescent unsupervised in a dangerous place. She wouldn't utter a syllable of reproach, but he could see it in her eyes and that was rich, coming from her, whose closest personal servant had been spotted sneaking around Belandor House.

Scarcely trusting himself to reply aloud, Vinz inclined his head.

She bent a small, lackluster smile upon him before turning back to her son. For a moment Vinz stood watching them both, then let himself out of the room. He closed the door behind him with an audible thud, but his departure went unnoticed.

He went to his bed where he lay fatigued but wakeful, suspicions simmering. At twilight time he rose and made his way to the north wing, shut down these twenty-five years for the sake of necessary economy. Climbing countless stairs to the top of Corvestri Mansion's tallest tower, he placed a lamp in the window. The signal did not go unnoticed. When Vinz ventured out later that evening to a certain wineshop just behind the Plaza of Proclamation, Lousewort was there to meet him.

The place was busy and crowded. The atmosphere was hazed with smoke and the light was low, both attractive attributes under the circumstances. The two men faced each other across a small table. Vinz Corvestri hid in the shade of a wide hat chosen to preserve his anonymity. Lousewort was his usual highly nondescript self.

A serving girl brought them wine. Vinz waited until she withdrew, then announced with a resolute air, "I've considered all that you told me, and I've decided to defend myself. It is time to remove Aureste Belandor."

"More than time." Lousewort nodded.

They touched beakers and drank.

• • •

Jianna opened her eyes on cramped, dismal surroundings, which she regarded for a moment without recognition before yesterday's events came crashing back.

Early-morning light pushed greyly through the tiny window of her cellar prison. The iron grillwork looked solid enough to resist cannon fire. The oaken door was similarly substantial, and she did not waste her strength on it. It was not without reason that rural residences such as this one, built to withstand attack, were known as stronghouses.

Rising from her cot, she freshened herself as best she could. Ordinarily Reeni would have been there to help. Her eyes stung. No, she would not think of Reeni. There was still plenty of water left in the jug. But now, despite all horrors, her healthy young body craved food, of which there was none.

They could not possibly mean to starve her to death. There would be no point.

Vengeance was the point. That madwoman Yvenza wanted to drink blood, preferably Aureste Belandor's, but his daughter's would do. But no, she reminded herself. Yvenza had something far worse than starvation in mind.

Jianna shivered a little and wondered why her father did not appear. He would rescue her, certainly, but when? How long—the thought came unbidden—before he would learn that she had been abducted? It might be days—weeks . . .

She went to the window and looked out at the courtyard, where a servant threw feed to a flock of geese. Her stomach rumbled. She could gladly have done with a handful of that feed. After a while the servant retired and then came another bearing a flattened featherbed, which was beaten until the dust rose in clouds. The scene was prosaic to the point of boredom; her own plight all the more improbable by comparison.

Jianna thought of calling out to them, but suppressed the impulse. There was nothing they would do for her, no interest or point in watching them, but it was better than watching bare stone walls and floor. She stood staring out the window until the scrape of a bolt spun her around to face the door. It opened and her breath caught as Yvenza Belandor stepped into the room.

"Good morning, niece." Clad in last night's plain dark dress, Yvenza appeared formidably vital by the light of day. She bore a tray with a bowl of gruel, some bread, and fried lumps of unidentifiable composition. Beside her paced a gigantic brindled boarhound. "You spent a quiet night, I trust. Peaceful and undisturbed?"

Jianna nodded warily.

"Excellent. I told those boys of mine that I'd whip them bloody if they dared lay hands on you as yet. Good to see that a maternal admonition still carries some weight with the lads. Well, then. I imagine you must be hungry by now." She advanced to place the tray on the cot, presenting her back to the prisoner.

The door stood open. Jianna took a step toward it and a subterranean growl rumbled from the boarhound. Its head was lowered, fangs bared. She froze.

"Grumper will take you down if you try to run." Yvenza turned without haste. "And if you raise a hand against me, he'll tear you apart." She looked the other up and down. "Not that I'd need his help, as far as that goes. There's not much to you. I could break your arm or your neck with ease, and I doubt that you could return the compliment."

"Probably not." Jianna arched a fastidious brow. "I'm not much of a brawler."

"No, I don't suppose your father ever foresaw any need to teach his wee flower the rudiments of self-defense. Now, what would Aureste Belandor regard as suitable subjects? Dancing, perhaps? A little music, a little embroidery?"

"Among other things—mathematics, natural philosophy, languages, and literature, to name a few. Above all, I've been taught how to manage a large household, which is more than can be said for you, if I'm to judge by what I've seen of this place." *Idiot.* She should have kept her mouth shut. Now this virago would probably set the dog on her.

Yvenza, however, merely appeared amused. "Quite the little spitfire, aren't you, maidenlady? But I advise you to curb your wit in Onartino's presence. My boy is somewhat hasty of temper, as you may have observed, and far less tolerant than his mother. For your own sake, you'd best learn to avoid provoking your future lord."

This time Jianna managed to hold her tongue.

"Which brings me to the true topic of discussion." Yvenza produced a benevolent smile. "You've had an entire night to consider matters, niece. I trust you've used the time wisely."

"I've used the time to think," Jianna returned with spurious composure. "I hope you've done the same. If you have, then perhaps you'll avoid a serious error. Set a ransom on me, my father will pay it without hesitation, and you'll live to enjoy the profit. But if you harm me, he'll have his vengeance. You may be certain of that."

"Who speaks of harming you? You are offered a fine marriage. Most girls would be delighted."

"You've threatened me with violence and dishonor. You've promised me that you won't hesitate to carry out those threats, and I believe you. But if you do, then my father will retaliate. He'll raise a small army, he'll find this place, and stronghouse though it may be, he'll burn it to the ground. You and yours will die, else be left homeless and destitute. A high price to pay for the pleasure of ruining a girl who's never harmed you, wouldn't you say?"

For a moment Yvenza Belandor regarded her in silence, then curved a genuine smile. "Clever, like your father," she observed. "And no coward. But still young and apparently not yet much the strategist. Stop and think, maidenlady. How likely is it that Aureste will attack and raze our Ironheart while you lie here within its walls? He'll never place your precious little life at such risk."

"Depends on how greatly he's provoked. Push him too far and he'll strike back, no matter what."

"I think not. In any case, I can deal with your father should the occasion arise."

"Don't be too sure of that. He knows how to fight. He—"

"His martial prowess, should he actually possess any, is unlikely to display itself. Unless I am much mistaken, the next intelligence he receives will confirm his daughter's marriage to my son."

"Yes, you *are* much mistaken if you think I'll—"

"What I think is that you'll consider the consequences of refusal. I will leave you now. I will return in one hour with my oldest son. If at that time you accept his offer of marriage, I shall embrace you as a daughter, and you will be treated as such. If you refuse, I'll regard our conversation as concluded. Containing my disappointment as best I may, I'll withdraw, leaving you alone with Onartino. What happens thereafter will be a matter entirely between you and him."

"I don't believe you," Jianna lied. She had gone cold inside. She tried to moisten her dry lips and failed. "You're not a monster. You won't do this."

"You've a great deal to learn, maidenlady. I shall enjoy observing the progress of your education." Yvenza sauntered from the room, trailed by the dog. The door closed behind them, and the bolt scraped.

Jianna stood staring at the locked door. Presently her vision blurred and the hand she raised to her eyes came away wet with tears. She dashed the droplets away. No time for tears now; she needed to think. If Aureste Belandor found himself imprisoned and endangered, he wouldn't weep; he'd find some way of besting his enemies. His daughter would do the same. She drew a ragged breath and strove to focus. But her mind was clogged with bewilderment and terror; there was no room left for strategy. No room, *no time*. Yvenza had promised to return in one hour, together with her subhuman son. One hour, and they would be here, and she did not let her mind touch upon what would happen then.

The cellar air was chilly, but the sweat prickled under her arms and the palms of her hands were clammy. Her eyes ranged the trap of a room, found no escape, and shut—but that only worsened matters, sharpening the mental images. She saw Onartino, his muscular bulk, his dead eyes, and there was no weapon with which to fend him off, nothing to hide behind, nothing to stop him except a promise to place herself in his power forever, and even that ultimate concession could only postpone the inevitable for a little while.

How little?

Any respite, however brief, might offer an advantage. That's what Aureste Belandor would say if he were here. He would tell her how to outwit her captors, how to lie to them and purchase herself a little time. Or perhaps he didn't need to tell her; the answer seemed suddenly clear enough. Why had it taken her so long to see it?

She would promise to marry Onartino. Some indeterminate interval would elapse before a legitimate magistrate empowered to perform the ceremony could be secured. During that time she would be treated decently—Yvenza had said so. They would surely let her out of the cellar. If she played her part well, they might even come to think her resigned to her fate. They would relax their vigilance, but she would not relax her own. She would watch continually, and sooner or later her chance would come. She would escape Ironheart, make her way back home, tell her father what had happened, and then he would order this entire nest of outlaws exterminated. Maybe he would let her watch the executions.

It was all there, whole and complete in her mind, the fruit of desperation. But Aureste Belandor's daughter would make it work.

She became aware that she was trembling. She would have to control that.

Wrapping her arms tightly around herself, she bowed her head and willed herself to think of Vitrisi and the people she had left there. Her father. Uncle Innesq. Even prissy Uncle Nalio. They were not lost to her; she would see them all again, and soon.

The diversion was effective. Her breathing eased, and her pulse steadied. When the door opened again, she was almost calm.

"Time's up." Yvenza, intolerably casual, stepped into the room.

Beside her Onartino loomed like a monolith. His eyes, although pale in color, somehow seemed to reflect none of the morning light.

At sight of him, the hatred and terror swept through Jianna in fresh waves. She concealed both, resisting the natural impulse to back away. Her face was as expressionless as Onartino's own as she informed her jailer, "I will marry your son on one condition."

"No conditions." Onartino's opaque gaze never flickered.

"You pique my curiosity, maidenlady," Yvenza conceded. "I will allow you to state your condition."

"If I'm truly to wed, then the marriage must be legal and as decent as possible under the circumstances," Jianna returned steadily. "The ceremony must be properly performed by a magistrate or some other equivalent authority."

"We'll decide who does the mumbling." Onartino shrugged. "You'll take what comes."

"It must be done right. That's the only way I can ever in good conscience consent."

"Your consent isn't required," he reminded her. "Haven't you gotten that through your head yet?"

"Softly, son," Yvenza advised. "Your bride makes a good point. Nothing must compromise the legitimacy of the next Belandor heir. My grandson will be conceived safely and solidly within the confines of matrimony. I'd keep that in mind if I were you."

"Well, you aren't me, and you're pitching a silly female fit over nothing."

Yvenza backhanded him across the face so hard that he staggered. Onartino pressed a hand to his reddening cheek. For an instant his eyes came to glaring life, then went dead again.

"That's no way to speak to your mother," Yvenza pointed out.

"Sorry, Mother."

"That sort of talk makes me feel that I haven't trained you well. Am I right about that? Is additional schooling called for?"

"No, Mother."

"I truly hope not. Now listen to me. Aureste's girl here transparently plays for time, but she happens to be right. Your son and heir must be legitimate."

"And who's to judge that? I'll take the title of magnifico by double right as Onarto's oldest son and Aureste's son-in-law. My own son by this one"—he jabbed an indicative finger—"inherits, no questions asked. When that time comes, you really think anyone will be asking who performed the marriage ceremony, maybe decades earlier?"

"Stranger things have happened," Yvenza observed serenely. "It is a chance we are not going to take."

"That should be my decision."

"Yes, it should, and it grieves me to find you unequal to the challenge."

"You should know better. All right, Mother. What do you mean to do? Lead this stolen cow into Orezzia to stand up before a justice of the peace? I wish you well with that."

"Are you attempting sarcasm, my son? You've no talent for it. Spare yourself and your listeners," Yvenza advised. There was no reply, and she continued, "The East Reach Traveler is an official representative of the Orezzian courts—"

"Appointed by a turd of a Taerleezi governor," Onartino observed.

"No matter. He's a magistrate with authority to perform marriages. We'll intercept him."

"That could take weeks."

"A few days, more likely."

"Too long to sit around waiting. No need, anyway. Look, we rule this stretch of countryside. Let's just declare her my wife on our own authority and get on with it."

"You'll have to restrain your ardor, my young gallant."

"That won't be hard." His contemptuous glance raked Jianna's body. "But I don't like wasting time."

"Your consent isn't required." Yvenza favored her son with a steely smile. "Haven't you gotten that through your head yet?"

He shrugged.

Turning to the prisoner, Yvenza remarked, "You've made a sensible decision, daughter, and your title of maidenlady is safe for a little while longer. I am already planning the wedding, however. It will be small and modest, but deeply satisfying to some of the parties concerned."

FIVE

"Downstairs? Taerleezi soldiers in the reception gallery?" Aureste Belandor demanded.

His informant puffed her air sacs. Distended membranes quivered, and croaking affirmation emerged.

"In Faerlonnish," Aureste directed. Confronting empty golden eyes, he repeated the command sharply. These Sishmindris often feigned linguistic limitation, but almost all of them had mastered the language of their masters to some degree. He bent a piercing gaze upon her.

"Yes. Two," she replied in her hoarse inhuman voice, adding with palpable reluctance, "and other."

"What other?"

She flexed her brow ridges, the Sishmindri equivalent of a shrug. The impertinence deserved punishment, but he was pressed for time and therefore dealt her greenish face the most perfunctory of slaps—more of a threat than a real blow. Even such fleeting contact with the cool, slightly moist flesh of the amphibian was distasteful. He drew his hand back quickly. She neither flinched nor uttered a sound. Her silent impassivity was appropriate but annoying, and he found himself wondering whether the stroke of a riding crop across her shoulders would draw some livelier response. Before he had made up his mind to perform the experiment, she bowed deeply and withdrew.

Aureste descended to the reception gallery, there to encounter a brace of Taerleezi guards, one of them an underofficer. With them waited a travel-stained civilian of Faerlonnish aspect.

"Gentlemen." Aureste inclined his head to the angle precisely calculated to convey the obligatory respect due Taerleezi authority while maintaining the superior dignity of a Vitrisian magnifico.

The Taerleezi guards saluted correctly, in minimal acknowledgment of their host's rank but without the vigor or deference undeserved by a member of the conquered Faerlonnish.

"Communication from the Eleventh Section Watch Station, Magnifico," announced the underofficer. "This traveler here— what did you say your name is?"

"Rivviu Chelzo, in service to His Lordship the Magnificiari Abbevedri of Orezzia," the civilian replied.

"This Chelzo here brings news that concerns you, Magnifico," the underofficer continued. "You'd best hear it."

"Speak, then," Aureste directed.

"According to your will, Honored Magnifico." Chelzo bowed in typically gauche Orezzian style. "I was traveling upon my master the magnificiari's command to the city of Vitrisi, along the VitrOrezzi Bond. Scarcely halfway to my destination I paused along the way, and in a clearing a few paces from the road happened upon a scene of destruction. A fine carriage stood there. The horses were gone, but the passengers remained—two women, both dead by violence. Seven men liveried in grey and silver likewise lay dead on the ground, together with one other corpse, plainly dressed, a kerchief hiding his face. It was clear that the carriage had been attacked by a gang of highwaymen. Alone I could do nothing for the dead, nor would I entrust the news of the massacre to the folk at the wayside inns, for fear of looting. Thus I continued on to Vitrisi, where I told my tale to the authorities at the first Watch station I could find. And they have brought me here to you, Honored Magnifico."

"This Orezzian has described the arms on the carriage door," the underofficer clarified unnecessarily. "Three wheels of black fire upon a silver field. These are the arms of House Belandor."

... the passengers remained—two women, both dead by violence.

Aureste Belandor scarcely heard his own roar of furious anguish. The surrounding atmosphere seemed to boil and burn. He struck out reflexively and only dimly sensed the impact of his fist on flesh and unyielding bone. The reddish haze momentarily clouding his vision cleared, and he looked down to behold Rivviu Chelzo stretched out on the floor, blood streaming from a split lip. The luckless messenger coughed and spat out a tooth. The two Taerleezi soldiers stirred a little but made no move to interfere.

Aureste restrained his impulse to kick the fallen man. The blood was thundering in his ears and a feverish heat possessed him, but he could not afford to give way entirely to rage. Two dead women, only two, when three had embarked from Vitrisi. A constriction in his throat threatened to muffle his voice, but he managed to command steadily enough, "Get up."

Rivviu Chelzo cowered. His eyes jumped to his Taerleezi companions in vain search of assistance.

"Come, man, I won't hurt you," Aureste promised impatiently. "Get up."

Chelzo obeyed with reluctance.

"Describe the two women."

Chelzo's gaze wandered anew in search of help or escape, found none, and returned to his interrogator's ashen face. Wiping the blood from his mouth with the back of his hand, he answered, "One inside the carriage, of middle years with greying hair piled up in a tower, generous girth, fur-trimmed cloak, a lady. The other on the ground, much younger and smaller, hard to judge what her face might have been, light brown hair all in curls, ordinary clothes, not a lady. Maidservant, I think."

"And what of another—young, slender, well garbed, very beautiful, with dark hair and black brows?"

"No. Nobody like that."

"If you are lying to me, pig, I'll exterminate your entire family down to the newest suckling."

"I speak the truth, Magnifico." Chelzo swallowed fervently. "There were only the two women, neither as you describe. Believe me, Magnifico."

Believe him. He burned to believe. Jianna, still alive out there. She was clever and resourceful. Somehow she had managed to escape. She had run off into the woods, eluded her assailants, gotten clean away, and soon she would send word to her father. She would easily find help—anyone she encountered should consider himself privileged to serve her—and very soon a messenger would arrive, any minute now—

Or perhaps she had not actually escaped, maybe that was too much to expect. They had taken her prisoner, but they wouldn't harm her, not when they discovered her identity. Jianna would have sense enough to name her father, or else they would simply recognize the Belandor crest on the carriage, and they would demand a high price for her safe return, but he would pay gladly, anything they asked, and then they would send her home.

But he should have heard from them by now. The demands of the kidnappers should have flown on the wings of greed, easily preceding this ordinary traveler Chelzo to the door of House Belandor. Where was the ransom note?

Could there be some forgotten enemy out there whose lust for vengeance exceeded the lust for cash? Someone who would kill Jianna and relish her father's agony above money? Had he ever crossed paths with anyone that unnatural?

Aureste did not take time to review the long list of potential nemeses. Turning to the Taerleezi underofficer, he commanded, "You will dispatch a party of your men to the site of the attack. This Orezzian will guide you. You will search the area for my daughter, the Maidenlady Jianna Belandor."

"Outside our jurisdiction," the other informed him. "Go to Orezzia and try your luck with the commandant there. As for the gathering of your Faerlonnish dead, that's no concern of ours."

For one moment, the urge to kill almost overpowered Aureste. He wore a dagger at his waist. A single quick, enjoyable thrust would wipe the look of cold contempt off that Taerleezi face forever.

And then he would be tried as a partisan murderer, noble rank notwithstanding. A Faerlonnishman convicted of killing a Taerleezi soldier would suffer public execution by torsion, and his friendship with the governor, expensive though it was, would not save him. He would die horrifically and then there would be nobody to rescue Jianna—at least, nobody as capable as her father. No, he could not afford to indulge his appetites. Someday the opportunity would arise, but not now.

"You waste time." Aureste charged his restraint with precisely modulated menace. "The governor will confirm my orders. The delay will displease him."

"I can't speak for the governor." *And neither can you, Faerlonnish kneeser.* The underofficer's silent postscript hung in the air.

"You will be hard-pressed to speak for yourself when your superiors are informed of your conduct. You may go," Aureste decreed. "This Orezzian will remain."

"I cannot stay," Chelzo objected. "My master the magnificiari expects me. My master—"

"Must survive without you for a time," Aureste advised him. "You have now entered my service, where you remain until dismissed."

"Truly, I cannot," Chelzo mourned. "You must understand that my master the magnificiari will not endure it. My master the magnificiari is of a choleric disposition. Should I fail to complete my errand promptly, I shall suffer the magnificiari's extreme displeasure."

"Should you prove obdurate, you will suffer mine."

"But—"

"Your master the magnificiari is far away," Aureste suggested pensively. "He is in no convenient position to express his disappointment. The same cannot be said of me."

The Orezzian had no answer.

"I have dismissed you." Aureste's attention returned to the Taerleezi guards. "You are unwilling or unable to address the situation, and your incompetence offends me. Remove yourselves."

Such insolence from a member of the subject population might ordinarily have warranted a beating or worse, but the governor's marked favor offered unusual privileges.

For a moment the underofficer stared, then sketched an ironical salute and withdrew, followed by his lividly silent subordinate. The luckless Chelzo remained.

"You will lead me and a band of my servants to the site of the attack," Aureste informed his captive.

"Please, Magnifico, you don't need me for that," the other appealed. "I can tell you where it is. There are landmarks; you won't have any trouble."

"I anticipate none. Prepare to leave within the hour."

"Magnifico, pity me. I am weary with travel. I've not rested, eaten, or performed my master the magnificiari's bidding."

"I am your current master and my bidding is your sole concern. You may go to the kitchen, eat, and refresh yourself as best you can in the time that remains. Do not commit the blunder of attempting escape. My fund of good nature is not inexhaustible."

"But—"

"Do you argue with me, fellow?"

"Never, Honored Magnifico. Not at all. No."

Aureste tugged the bellpull, and a human lackey appeared within seconds. Orders were issued and the servant withdrew, trailed by the despondent Orezzian.

Despite his fifty years he was still fit, capable of riding hard and living sparely. This so, preparations for departure could be completed within the space of minutes. In the meantime, there was another potential source of assistance awaiting consultation, and that one probably the best.

A quick march brought him to the second-story salon, with

its carved dark paneling and its hidden doorway standing wide open. He went through into the workroom beyond, where he found his brother closeted with a pair of the household Sishmindris. The creatures were croaking and peeping away in their barbarous tongue, while Innesq Belandor leaned forward in his wheeled chair, listening with the closest attention. Fresh anger scalded Aureste. Jianna was missing and in danger. In the midst of such crisis, what right had Innesq to squander his attention on chatty amphibians?

The unintelligible conversation cut off as he entered. Silence smothered the workroom. Aureste confronted three sets of eyes whose shared inscrutability heightened his rage. It was almost as if they resented the master's intrusion. Addressing the amphibians, he commanded harshly, "Get out."

The golden mottled eyes remained as expressionless as ever, but both Sishmindris cringed in expectation of a blow and sidled for the exit. Aureste did not trouble to watch them go. His gaze sought his brother's calm pale face.

"What has happened?" Innesq inquired at once.

"The Belandor coach was attacked en route to Orezzia. Flonoria and the servants were killed. Jianna has disappeared. There is no corpse, no ransom note, no word from her. What can you tell me?"

"Flonoria killed?" Innesq appeared stunned. "There can be no mistake? Our sister is dead?"

"So I've been told, and the messenger has neither wit nor motive to lie."

"It is almost inconceivable. She was kind and harmless. Who would have the heart to lift a hand against her?"

"I don't know, and can't concern myself at the moment."

"Can't concern yourself? What are you saying? She was our sister, and a Belandor."

"An insignificant one."

"You cannot mean that. I hope you are not truly as callous as you seem."

"Enough of this. It's absurd at such a time. Did you not hear me, Innesq? Jianna is missing. Nothing else matters until she is restored to me."

"I understand. I share your grief and concern."

"Then prove it. I need your help. You must use those arcane skills of yours to find her. You must do it now, without delay. I'm relying on you."

"Aureste, compose yourself. You speak wildly."

"I am perfectly composed. I've requested your assistance. I'm your older brother and the head of House Belandor. Will you deny me?"

"Never while it lies within my power to serve you, but I am not certain that you know what you ask. Do you take me for a god or a demon, fit to deliver miracles upon demand?"

"*Yes.* Oh, I know you're neither god nor demon. But you have the knowledge that grants power—the talent, the intelligence and self-discipline, all that's needed to perform marvels—combined with the affection that you bear your niece. All of these are in you, and therefore I know that I don't ask more than you can give."

"You do not ask more than I am willing to give, but I fear that you overestimate my powers. I cannot flourish a magic wand and bring Jianna home."

"I know. But you can tell me where she is. You've done it often enough."

"Yes, when she was a child lost in the cellarways of Belandor House. But—"

"More recently than that, and your vision doesn't confine itself to this house. There was the time she ran off to see some rope-dancer, and you located her within minutes."

"Barsudio the Boneless performed in Vitrisi that day, almost within sight of the Clouds. The search commenced within two hours or so of Jianna's departure, and the imprint of her passage lingered upon the epiatmosphere. Her whereabouts all but proclaimed themselves to the trained observer. The present circumstances are quite different, and I fear—"

"Don't fear. And don't tell me you can't succeed; I won't hear it."

"You won't hear. As always." Innesq shook his head. "Aureste, you do not stop to consider the element of time."

"Have you not listened?" Aureste's frustration threatened to slip restraint. "I've already told you that I need your immediate assistance. Why do you waste priceless minutes in argument?"

"You've demanded instant results, but your expectations are unrealistic. It is possible that an arcane investigation will yield some clue concerning Jianna's fate, but the project requires hours of effort—perhaps days."

"That won't do. You must work faster."

"Impossible."

"Not for you. Don't sit there dreaming up objections. Just do it. Now."

"You imagine that sheer force of will overcomes all obstacles. Perhaps for you it does, but my world is quite different. There are supradimensional exigencies to consider."

"I don't know what you're talking about and I don't care. I only know that you can help Jianna if you choose. Will you not try, Innesq? Is that too much to ask for your niece?"

"I will do all that I can for her. But understand that the process may be protracted, and there is no help for that. Moreover, your presence will be required."

"Mine? Why?"

"The bond between you and Jianna is always strong and particularly powerful now, in view of your heightened emotional state. When you have been properly prepared, your consciousness set to rest and your logical faculties disabled, then those alternative forms of perception of which you are not ordinarily aware will operate freely. By their agency, if we are fortunate, we may perhaps trace Jianna's path."

"Consciousness set to rest? You speak of a sleeping draught?"

"Not in the sense that the term is generally used. Your body will remain active, perhaps excessively so. But your awareness of your surroundings must be disengaged and your power of reason suppressed. Throughout this interlude, your freedom of movement must be restricted."

"Are you suggesting that I should be—"

"Tied down to a chair. Regrettably so. I am sorry, but it is for your own protection as well as the household's. The procedure I offer jeopardizes body and mind. There is no predicting its duration and no assurance of success at the end. Perhaps you would do best simply to assemble and dispatch a search party, or even lead the hunt yourself. You would prefer to take charge personally, would you not?"

"That was my first thought. In fact, I've already issued orders to that effect. But tell me truly. This procedure of yours—if successful, does it offer the best hope of locating Jianna quickly? Or at least of knowing that she lives?" Aureste took care to maintain a dispassionate tone.

For a moment Innesq regarded him and then replied with palpable reluctance, "That is possible. But the risks are real, and I advise you to consider them. You will hardly be fit to assist your daughter if you are left physically or mentally impaired."

Impaired. Crippled or paralyzed. Mad or simple-minded. An ugly, vivid image filled Aureste's mind. Himself, some years hence, squatting half naked in some rainy alley deep in the Spidery. Starved old body covered with welts and bruises visible beneath a scant covering of filthy rags. Long, sparse wisps of white hair. Slack jaw, toothless gums, sunken cheeks. Dull eyes, vacant, mindless, dead.

Aureste blinked, and the image faded. His jaw was set and his armpits tingled with sweat. Meeting his brother's eyes, he unclenched his teeth and proclaimed, "I've complete confidence in your abilities."

"That is a lie," Innesq returned serenely. "No matter, I see that you are resolved."

"Let's get on with it."

"Seat yourself, then." The chair that Innesq indicated was plain and heavy. Its four legs were strongly bolted to the floor.

Aureste obeyed. "And now?" he prompted with a false air of confidence.

"And now I must ask you to wait while I prepare a draught."

"How long will it take?"

"Not above an hour."

"Too long. You must do it in half that time."

"Once again you demand the impossible."

"Isn't the impossible exactly what this magic of yours is designed to accomplish?"

"That is a commonplace misconception. Just now, you expressed your faith in my abilities. If you spoke truly, then you will trust me to work at the best speed allowing for safety."

"I don't care about safety."

"We do not all share in your fine disregard for life, limb, and sanity. Be still, Aureste. Hold your peace and wait."

Here in this workroom, within the realm of the arcane, his brother ruled. Biting down on his frustration, Aureste obeyed. Innesq busied himself with flasks and vials, powders and granules, weighing and mixing. The interminable minutes expired one by one. Surely the full hour and more had elapsed. Innesq was dawdling. An angry complaint rose to Aureste's lips. He held it in. Time crept on.

A froth of black bubbles at the top of a beaker, accompanied by the release of an indefinably sullen odor signaled completion.

"It is ready." Innesq approached, bearing the beaker. "I cannot allow you to drink before you consent to accept to restraint."

"Unnecessary. I give you my word that I won't stir from this chair. That should suffice."

"It does not. It is not that I doubt your sincerity," Innesq forestalled his brother's irate rejoinder. "But you do not understand the nature of the journey you undertake."

"Must you sound so damned mystical?"

"Sometimes it is unavoidable. Listen to me. When you swallow this draught, your world will change for a time. Your perception of physical surroundings will fade, but your inner eye will sharpen. Please do not ask me what I mean by the term 'inner eye'—you must accept the fact that it is there and that it is perhaps capable of discovering the lost Jianna. It is the—how shall I put it?—the rational consciousness, the controlled orderly intellect, that must yield its sway and transfer its power to another aspect of the mind. Do you understand me?"

"No. Let's just do it."

"Will you submit to restraint?"

"If that's what it takes to persuade you to continue."

"It is. Drink, then." Innesq proffered the beaker.

Accepting the vessel, Aureste gulped the contents without allowing himself to look, smell, taste, or think. The liquid burned its way down his throat. His eyes swam, and he blinked.

Innesq reclaimed the beaker and put it aside, then set about fastening his brother to the chair with leather straps. Aureste watched bemusedly. Soon he found himself bound fast at wrists, ankles, waist, and chest.

"How do you feel?" asked Innesq.

"Restricted. I don't like it."

"Vision? Hearing? Sense of solidity?"

"Perfect. This potion of yours isn't strong enough to overcome the strength of a Belandor mind. We are hardly common clay, a point you have perhaps overlooked."

"You are not in pain?"

"Certainly not. I'm unaffected. It isn't working."

"Patience. Wait."

"I've waited long enough. You'll have to try something else."

"It is too late for that."

"Unfasten these straps and turn me loose."

There was no reply. Innesq's attention seemed fixed on distant vistas. Aureste strained uselessly against his bonds, then subsided with a muted snarl. The anger and frustration boiled within. An indeterminate span of time elapsed and gradually the heat subsided, its fury giving way to unquiet warmth. The workroom and its contents fell away, and by some agency that he neither trusted nor believed in, he found himself in another place, a region of distorted vision, half-heard echoing voices, devouring atmosphere, and faded recollections. He did not know where he was, but he was not afraid; somehow it was right and even essential that he had come. He was not walking, but somehow he was moving through live slithering shadows, and it seemed that he was searching for something or someone, while someone or something followed close upon his heels.

What heels? He had no limbs, no flesh; his corporeal self was gone. His disembodied intellect quested through dim space filled with misshapen old memories that whispered and tittered in passing. He saw and heard them indistinctly. His perceptions would doubtless sharpen if he could locate his eyes and ears. Surely his body could not be far away, it would not have gone wandering off on its own. He could probably find it, find something, find someone, if he reached out through the shadows.

Reach out with what? No arms, no hands, but he tried anyway and a kind of convulsion rocked his mind; he thought he caught the sound of distant screaming. For a while he fought and floundered, the screams shrilling eons away, but his body remained elusive, reintegration unobtainable, and presently he abandoned the struggle. It was easier then, less infuriating, even comfortable to drift on alien currents of disembodied sensation. He might have allowed himself to relax into slack acquiescence but for the prodding sense of purpose. He could not rest; that much he knew on some unassailable level, and it was all that he knew.

On he went, and the memories cavorting about him burst into flame that overran the universe. The atmosphere was the color of molten steel, and he had no flesh but he burned. He would have turned back then, but the place he had come from was lost beyond hope, and there was still that nagging sense of purpose.

The fiery atmosphere extinguished itself and the hot light yielded to immeasurable darkness. He could see nothing, hear nothing, but perceptions that he did not recognize guided him and he moved with confidence, still seeking something, someone. He did not remember what or who, but he would recognize it when he found it. *Her.* When he found her.

A sense of urgency grew in him. Something was drawing him on through the dark, its strength increasing as he advanced, and he gave himself over gladly to that power, recognizing the imminence of revelation. The unseen presence was still close behind him, but he did not fear it, perceiving only reassurance there.

The absolute darkness darkened impossibly and the deep places in his mind, slumbering undisturbed throughout a lifetime, stirred to reluctant life. The impressions seeped in and he could neither sort nor comprehend them, but knew that they would guide him.

They did so. His disengaged self rode intangible tides. Then he caught the first flutter of identity somewhere in the void, and he strained toward it.

The object of his search was drawing near, the shape and texture of her mind clarifying by the moment. The clean vigor of her thoughts reminded him of green growth in springtime. Nearer yet, close enough to catch the fragrance of youth, close enough to catch her intelligence, her fears, and finally her awareness of his approach. She knew him, she was reaching toward him. She wanted and needed his help.

As soon as he could find her.

She was very close now, so close that he caught the essence of her surroundings, the persistence of stone, the obstinacy of iron, the warm solace of aged wood. He could taste it all in the echo of her thoughts.

What was left of his consciousness impinged on hers and a

sense of familiarity thrilled deeply through him, but he still could not identify her. He knew only that the sum of his hopes resided in her deliverance. His need flung him wildly through the dark, where he lost his way, lost all contact with her mind, and found himself alone in black nothingness.

But not quite alone, for that silent presence with him from the start was with him still, its mute reassurance calming his angry confusion. Perhaps it could guide him back to her. He reached out toward the other, but the darkness was impenetrable, its weight intolerable, and now it absorbed him into itself.

. . .

He woke to find himself slumped in a chair, the restraints gone, his brother patting his face with a cold, wet cloth. Water trickled down his cheeks.

"Stop that," he commanded, distantly surprised to hear his own rich voice emerge small and dull.

Innesq obeyed. "Sit still. Rest," he advised.

"What did you learn?"

"Presently."

"Now." His voice was still too weak, and he repeated more forcefully, "Now."

"Very well. She is alive. You caught a distinct resonance of her existence, which I was able to interpret."

Alive. Aureste expelled a sigh and allowed his eyes to close. The surge of relief that swept his mind failed to renew his strength. He was indescribably tired, and a headache throbbed behind his left eye. He longed for sleep, and there was no time for it.

"She's safe, then?" he demanded. Silence, and he opened his eyes to search his brother's still face. "Well?"

"She does not perceive herself as safe," Innesq admitted.

"What do you mean?" Frustration generated internal heat. "Why don't you speak plainly? Has she been hurt? Is she in danger?"

"That is unclear."

"Inadequate. I want an answer. What good is this precious art of yours if it can't serve Jianna?"

"Aureste, you condemn without understanding. You would do better to hold your peace and allow yourself time to recover."

"Unlike you, I don't enjoy the luxury of time. I've a daughter in need of rescue, a matter that hardly seems to rouse your concern. Return to your experiments, then. It's clear that the life and safety of your niece count for nothing."

"You do not mean that. It is only your fear and anger speaking."

"Have you added mind reading to your little repertoire of magic tricks? Next summer you might set up a booth at Three Islet Fair."

"Perhaps," Innesq agreed without rancor. "Have you any more insults burning for utterance, or are you ready to listen?"

"To what? You've already told me that you have no answers. I've wasted enough time here. Now I'm going out to find her." Aureste rose to his feet. A wave of dizziness rocked him, the workroom spun, and he dropped back into the chair.

"You will not go anywhere just yet," Innesq observed.

Aureste blinked. His sight was curiously dim, but he could still make out his brother's face, grave and composed as always. "How long—" he began.

"Hours have passed. It is night."

"No matter. I can—"

"Hush. Listen to me. Jianna is alive. Your mind touched hers, and that contact furnished certain images—clouded, to be sure, but—"

"What did you—"

"Do not interrupt. Sit still for now or you will make yourself ill. Jianna is alive and probably uninjured; or at worst, not seriously injured. Her position is perilous, however. She is certainly held captive somewhere in the wilds of the Alzira Hills. She is just as certainly threatened with harm of a serious nature, but I do not believe that her life is in any immediate danger. There is no point in demanding particulars—I am unable to furnish any but one, which pertains to the nature of her prison. She is held in a rural dwelling of no vast size, but solid and impregnable as a fortress."

"A stronghouse, you mean?"

"Probably."

"Is there anything more you can tell me?"

"Not at this time."

"Well. A stronghouse," Aureste mused. "Somewhere in the Alzira Hills, between Vitrisi and Orezzia. That shouldn't be so difficult to find."

"And then?" Innesq inquired. "You know better than I what would be needed to breach such defenses."

"A small army." Aureste nodded. Renewed purpose lighted his mind, and his weakness began to recede. "Very well. I'll raise one."

SIX

"Pick only the purple ones with yellow stripes," Yvenza Belandor directed. "If the leaf is still green or the stripes have gone to brown, I can't use it. You understand me?"

Jianna inclined her head.

"Then say so."

"I understand you," Jianna mumbled, eyes glued to the ground.

"Speak up, girl. You have a voice. Are you too frightened to use it?"

"I said I understand you." Jianna's head came up. "And you'll be the frightened one when my father hunts you down."

"That's better." Yvenza's smile bared a white palisade. "A small flare of honest defiance. Always preferable to a sullen humor. I can't abide the sight of moping, sulky faces about me."

"I should think you'd be accustomed. You appreciate honest defiance? Enjoy this, then. No matter what you do, you'll never get the better of Aureste Belandor. You're no match for him, you can't reach high enough." *Shouldn't have said that.* She was in no position to provoke her captor, who might easily order her beaten, maimed, or killed; or worse, might hand her over to that hulking brute of a son. It was impossible to view Yvenza's iron-jawed face without seeing Onartino there as well; and impossible to think of Onartino without reliving the moment of Reeni's murder. The fear and hatred flooded Jianna's mind. Allowing nothing beyond false confidence to show on her face, she added, "And such power as you hold over me doesn't matter. You may force me to work like a servant, but you can't make me forget who I am."

"Rest assured, Aureste's daughter, nobody forgets your identity. As for your complaints, they're misplaced. Time you learned how to make yourself useful. Your days as a pampered pet have ended. Not every branch of the Belandor family tree is rotten and blighted as yours."

Liar! Father works hard in the family interests; he's kept our House safe and successful through all the times of trouble. And Uncle Innesq mews himself up in his workroom for days and nights on end. What do you suppose he's doing in there, playing at solitaire? Jianna said nothing.

"Here you will work," Yvenza continued, "as I would expect of any prospective daughter. No doubt the concept is foreign, but you'll learn, else go hungry."

Jianna replied with an indifferent shrug.

"Cheer up, maidenlady. The work may seem menial, but you toil nobly in the service of the Faerlonnish resistance. What better means than that to atone for the crimes of your kneeser father?"

Stifling the angry denial that would only amuse her tormentor, Jianna merely asked, "What do you mean?"

"We here at Ironheart offer all possible assistance to the soldiers of the Ghost Army. As the newest member of our household, you will do likewise."

"I see." "Ghost Army" was a popular term for the loosely knit bands of guerrilla marauders sworn to the expulsion of the Taerleezi occupying force. As far as Jianna was concerned, the Faerlonnish resistance comprised a gang of misguided zealots idiotically dedicated to a hopeless cause, but one consideration offered consolation. Sooner or later, her kidnappers' ill-chosen loyalties would bring them all to execution. She might even witness Onartino's public torsion.

"You are looking quite pleased." Yvenza favored her prisoner with a hard glance.

"Well, wouldn't any right-thinking Faerlonnishwoman?" Jianna inquired guilelessly.

"Patriotic sentiments upon the lips of Aureste Belandor's

own child. That is heartwarming. I trust we may expect your best efforts, then."

"With what? Plucking little purple leaves for the resistance?"

"You haven't troubled to ask the use of the little purple leaves."

Planning to work them into funeral wreaths? Jianna assumed an expression of polite inquiry.

"They're called kalkrios, and they possess narcotic properties," Yvenza informed her. "When seethed and reduced, they yield the elixir kalkriole that offers painless sleep."

"You brew this elixir and somehow carry it to the Ghost Army?" Jianna inquired, her interest captured.

"From time to time. More often the Ghost forces of these hills send their wounded to me."

"You mean that you harbor resistance people right here within your own walls?" Jianna's surprise gave way to comprehension. *She thinks she can say anything she pleases because I'll never get out of this place to report it. We'll see.* Aloud she observed, "You must have them pretty well hidden."

"Astonished that Ironheart hasn't yielded quite all of its secrets to your eager young eyes? Don't worry, you'll see them soon enough."

The promise was not intended to convey reassurance.

"In the meantime, you've other concerns," Yvenza continued. "The kalkrios. Work your way through the garden and pluck the leaves that are ready. Bring them to me when you're done. I expect a full basket. Don't take all day about it. And don't try to stray from the house—Grumper won't like it. Guard her, boy," she instructed the dog, then turned and walked away. Grumper remained.

Jianna stood watching her go. Evidently confident that the prisoner would attempt neither flight nor attack, Yvenza never bothered with a backward glance. Her casual assurance was insulting but justified. Only a few yards of weedy, uncultivated ground separated the garden from the edge of the woods surrounding Ironheart. Between Jianna and those woods sat Grumper.

She studied the huge boarhound. Usually she was fond of dogs, and this one was quite regal, even beautiful, with his proud carriage and his deep, intelligent eyes. Under other circumstances she would have hoped to befriend him. Well, perhaps he was more susceptible than he appeared. It was worth a try.

"Grumper. Grumper, boy," she coaxed melodiously. "Here, Grumper."

His ears twitched.

"I'm Jianna. I'm not a bad person, I mean no harm, you can trust me."

He cocked his head.

"Come on, come over here, it's all right."

He stared at her. She extended a cautious hand, which he ignored. His mournful eyes never strayed from her face. At least he wasn't trying to rip her throat out.

"I'm going to step into the woods for a moment." She let her hand descend slowly. "Won't be gone a moment. Nothing for you to worry about. There's a good dog." She dared a gliding step toward the trees.

Grumper lowered his head and growled. Jianna hesitated.

"Good dog," she repeated without conviction. "Gooddog-GooddogGooddog." She took another step.

He made a snapping lunge, and his teeth clicked within a breath of her wrist. She gasped and shrank back. Grumper sank to his haunches, eyeing her alertly. Beyond doubt he could have bitten her had he wished.

"All right," she said. Her heart was pounding, and she wondered if the dog could hear it. "All right. For now. Next time I'll try offering you some food. We'll see if you're really as incorruptible as all that." Turning her back on him, she contemplated the shrubbery. Purple leaves with yellow stripes, Yvenza had told her. Resentfully she began to pick, dropping the small harvest into the wicker basket furnished by her captor.

The leaves, she soon discovered, were guarded by needle thorns easy to overlook by reason of their extreme fineness. She could avoid them if she placed her hands with care and for a time she did so, pinching individual leaves between thumb and forefinger, plucking with great delicacy. The purgatorial minutes passed. At the conclusion of a minor eternity she looked down to find the bottom of the basket barely covered with a thin purple layer. At this rate she would hardly finish before nightfall.

Her stomach rumbled. The hour was early but she was already hungry. There would be no food until Yvenza's demands had been met, and Yvenza wanted a full basket. Jianna willed her hands to greater speed. The basket began to fill, but soon she felt the jab of thorns and presently her fingers were dotted with red.

An angry exclamation escaped her. Grumper stirred at the sound.

"This is your mistress' doing," she told him. "I'm surprised she hasn't stayed to enjoy the spectacle." But Yvenza had not troubled to watch, had not even posted a human guard, evidently deeming a single boarhound quite equal to the task of controlling the prisoner. It was downright offensive.

"She's underestimated me," Jianna assured the dog. "She'll find that out soon enough. So will you, fleabag."

Grumper yawned.

"I loathe you," she announced, and resumed her labors.

A chill autumn breeze punched through her garments, and she shivered. Her stomach rumbled. She was hungry, and the basket was nowhere near full. Her hands flew, the thorns stabbed, and her blood welled from fresh punctures. Her anger deepened. Absurd and outrageous that she should endure this, when the only thing standing between herself and freedom was one ordinary dog. She was scarcely worthy to call herself Aureste Belandor's daughter if she couldn't manage to outwit Grumper.

Breaking a twig from the nearest bush, she threw it toward the house.

"Go. Fetch," she commanded. "Fetch!"

Grumper lay down, tongue lolling. If she had not known better, she might almost have imagined that he was laughing at her. If only she could lay hands on a good-sized stick or rock, she would knock the smirk right off his canine face. Her eyes ranged the ground and found nothing. Brute force probably wouldn't serve, anyway—not against fangs of such length and whiteness. Force of will, then. The power of the superior human intellect.

"Grumper," she commanded with an affectation of calm authority. "Stay. You understand me? Stay." She edged toward the woods.

Instantly he was on his feet. A warning growl rumbled.

She did not let herself hear it. "Stay," she repeated firmly. Her air of confidence remained intact as she moved away.

Too swiftly for her to attempt evasion, he sprang forward, seized a mouthful of her skirt in his jaws, and tugged powerfully, throwing her to her knees. Before she could rise he was on her, his weight bearing her to the ground.

Jianna lay flat on her back, the boarhound looming over her. For an endless dog-scented moment, he stood staring down as if considering her dismemberment, then withdrew a few paces and seated himself nonchalantly.

Jianna sprawled paralyzed until the cold from the ground began to seep through her clothing, and then she sat up. Grumper watched steadily, but left her alone. She had not been hurt, but she was covered with dirt and her skirt was ripped. She was conscious less of alarm than acute embarrassment, coupled with the hope that human eyes had not witnessed her defeat. The wicker basket lay on its side a few feet from her, its contents scattered. Even as she watched, the wind sent the kalkrios traveling. On hands and knees she scrambled in pursuit. Only a few escaped. Barring dirt and discomfiture, she was not much worse off than she had been some twenty minutes earlier. Twenty extra minutes without food.

She stood up. Her supply of initiative was depleted, but only temporarily. Turning her back on Grumper, she went back to work. Fresh blood beaded on her fingers, and the basket filled. When the contents approached the rim, she fluffed the leaves artistically and the job was done.

"Finished," she informed her guard. "I'm going back now. If you don't mind." And it seemed that he understood her well enough, for he made no threatening move, but paced gravely at her side as she made her way from the garden to the nearest gate in the solid stone wall girdling Ironheart.

A sentry stood at the opening, a sentry of sorts, but certainly not a person that her father would have allowed to hang about so much as a back entrance to Belandor property. Here was no smartly liveried retainer agleam with polished steel. She beheld a slack-jawed, round-shouldered—*menial* was the kindest term to apply to the lout—bundled in drab homespun.

He might be sharper than he looked, though. She would soon find out. Marching straight up to the sentry, she halted and offered her most winning smile, the one her father could never resist.

"A word with you," she suggested sweetly. "Your name?"

He stared at her. Perhaps he was deaf. She repeated the question.

"What for?" he demanded, narrow-eyed but not deaf.

"Well, it's easier for me to speak to you if I know your name," she returned, sweetness carefully maintained.

"No need for talk."

Surly oaf. At home, her father would have ordered him beaten for such impertinence. Here she could not afford to take offense. "Only listen for a moment, then," she urged softly. "I'll be brief. Do you know who I am?"

"You're the Great Kneeser's daughter," he returned without hesitation.

"The Magnifico Aureste Belandor is my father," she told

him, containing the impulse to slap his face. "By this time, he has probably learned of my abduction. He'll begin searching, and he'll never rest until he finds me. When that day comes, those who have wronged us will be punished. They will pay dearly for this outrage."

"That so?" inquired the sentry.

"Yes, that is so. My father will tear this place apart stone by stone. The guilty will perish by fire and sword. Those wretches who survive will be dragged in chains back to Vitrisi for execution. Painful, public, *prolonged* execution."

"Big talk for a little girl. You get that out of some book?"

"It's more than talk, you may be certain. My father is a man of rank and influence, trusted adviser of the Governor Uffrigo—"

The sentry spat eloquently.

"Possessing power to punish his enemies, and wealth to reward his friends," Jianna instructed. "Be his friend now, and you'll never regret it. Help me get away from this place, take me back to Belandor House, and my father will give you money—position—anything that you want. Take this opportunity, and be a prosperous man."

Accustomed to having her own way, she did not anticipate refusal, and was taken by surprise when he vented an explosive exhalation, something between a grunt and a snort of derision.

"Good one," he said.

"Do you not believe me?" she asked, frowning. "Truly, I am in earnest. Conduct me back to Vitrisi, and the Magnifico Aureste Belandor will pay you whatever you ask."

"Then he won't pay nothing. And the only place you're going is back inside. Move it."

"I don't think you understand. I tell you, my father the Magnifico Aureste will set you up in comfort for the rest of your natural life."

"Which won't be good beyond sundown if I cross the Lady Yvenza."

"You needn't fear that woman. My father will protect you. My father—"

"Wouldn't be no use to me. You don't know our Lady Yvenza, that's plain. I'd pit her against your kneeser any day."

"She has no power in Vitrisi. My father—"

"The thing about our Lady Yvenza is, she's not like other women," the sentry continued appreciatively. "No softness, no nonsense about her. You bump that one, she'll crack your nuts. She's good as a man, that way. You know what she did once to some fool servant caught pilfering salt pork from the stores?"

"It doesn't matter. My father—"

"Had the thief's hand cut off, for starters. Then what do you suppose she does?"

"I don't want to know. Listen, you can be a rich man, or else a dead one when my father—"

"She has that cut-off hand salted down and stowed away in the larder. Says that she's just replacing the pig meat that was stole. Now, there's real wit for you."

"That's disgusting. You're making it up."

"That's what you think. So I ask you, what kind of fool would I be to go thumbing my nose at our Lady Yvenza?"

"Bah, you'd be perfectly safe, my father would see to it. I give you my word."

"*Your* word?" He blasted another snort. "You're funny as a dancing dwarf. Who are you to be throwing your *word* around so large when you can't even best a dog, much less the dog's mistress? Yes, I saw it all, and a rare sight it was. Thought I'd die laughing when Grumper took you down. He's a right lad, Grumper is. Aren't you, boy?" He clicked his tongue approvingly. "Good lad!"

Grumper wagged his tail.

Jianna's cheeks warmed, and she knew she must be blushing like an idiot. This insolent, unspeakable oaf was actually laughing at her. Insulting her. Drawing herself up, she assumed the expression of cold displeasure that she had so often seen her father use to such potent effect on others—never on her.

"You have made a poor decision," she informed the sentry ominously. "You will discover your error when you come face-to-face with the Magnifico Aureste Belandor."

"Face-to-face, eh? Heh. Will he get up off his knees for that, or will I have to get down on mine?"

Jianna's jaw clamped on a furious reply. She would not lose her temper or her dignity; she would not. Head up and spine straight, she turned and swept away in regal silence, closely trailed by Grumper. Behind her swelled the sentry's unrestrained guffaws.

He'd be sorry, *so* sorry one day. Soon. They all would.

Nothing for it but to go back inside. At the moment there was nowhere else to go, and surely they would feed her now.

The surrounding atmosphere dimmed but did not warm as she reentered Ironheart. She made her grim way along the ground-floor rear hallway. She was not alone, there were servants here and there, but they scarcely heeded her. All of them human, she noted. Not a Sishmindri in sight, which was regrettable, for at least the amphibians demonstrated proper respect. They never laughed. Come to think of it, she did not know if they could laugh.

Nor did she know where to find Yvenza Belandor. She paused to inquire and was directed to a closet adjoining the kitchen. Jianna rarely if ever set foot in the kitchen at home, but she was ready to change her habits now. There was, after all, food to be found in a kitchen.

She went in, and the perfume of baking bread drew growls from her stomach. Beside her, Grumper shifted weight. She glanced down and followed his devoted gaze to an arched doorway. She went to it, knocked, heard a woman's voice answer, and entered a humid old stillroom furnished with floor-to-ceiling wooden shelving. The shelves were crammed with urns, vials, flasks, bottles, boxes, sacks, and casks. A fire burned on a small hearth. An iron pot hung above the blaze, and Yvenza Belandor stood stirring the contents with a withered stick. The ruddy light from below threw every facial crag and furrow into cruel relief.

Witch, thought Jianna. Wordlessly she extended the basket.

"You took your time." Yvenza made no move to accept the offering.

"Well? Is it all right?" Jianna felt like a fool standing there with the little basket dangling from the end of her stiffly outstretched arm.

"It will do. Dump those kalkrios into the pot."

Jianna obeyed. The warm aromatic vapor rising from the cauldron bathed her face, not unpleasantly. For a moment, her eyes misted and her head swam.

"Take care," Yvenza advised with amusement. "Else those fumes will lay you out senseless on the floor for the rest of the afternoon."

"I may be a trifle weak with hunger," Jianna suggested. "I've not eaten today."

"Nor will you, before your work is complete."

My hands look as if I'd stuck them into a beehive, thanks to those miserable thornbushes of yours. What more do you want? Jianna stifled her indignation.

"Simmer the kalkriole broth until it's reduced by half. Strain it three times through gauze, funnel what's left into a dark jug, stopper it tightly, wrap it in a towel, then report to me for orders."

Orders. As if she were speaking to a kitchen maid.

Jianna refused to react, allowing herself only the neutral query, "Anything more?"

"Yes. Here." Yvenza handed her the stick. "Stir. Often."

The stick was too flimsy to serve as a weapon.

"You might try breaking off a jagged end and going for the eyes," Yvenza offered pleasantly.

Jianna repressed a guilty start. Evidently her face had given her away again. "I couldn't do anything so vicious and pointless," she murmured, keeping her own too-revealing eyes earnestly downcast. "I know I can't escape this stronghouse."

"But it would entertain me to watch you try. I trust you won't deprive me of that pleasure." Yvenza exited, trailed by Grumper.

"And it would entertain me to see you brought to Vitrisi in chains," Jianna answered, alone in the stillroom with no one to hear. And she would see it, she would see that woman and her detestable brood handed over to the Taerleezi authorities for trial and execution. Soon.

In the meantime there was stirring, straining, and funneling. Jianna hurried competently through the work. When she had finished, she took up the stoppered earthenware jug, stepped toward the door, and hesitated. Her eyes traveled the surrounding shelves, skimming flasks and casks, lingering on handwritten labels. Most of the names were unfamiliar. Nothing useful there, or at least nothing that she knew how to use.

She went out into the kitchen, and Yvenza was not there. A pock-faced potboy toiled at a washtub. He sneaked a quick glance at her, then looked away. Ignoring him, she surveyed the kitchen table, upon which half a dozen big loaves of new bread stood cooling. Beside them, a bowl of pears. *Food.* Setting the jug aside, she grabbed a loaf, ripped off a chunk, and wolfed it down. And another. As hunger subsided, she became aware that the potboy was staring. Well, he could goggle all he liked, but if he dared to interfere, she would dig new craters in that pocky face of his.

The potboy attempted no interference, merely stood watching openmouthed as she seized a pear and tore into it. The fruit was green and granular, but she devoured three pears in quick succession before the pace of her chewing slowed. Only then did she pause to consider consequences. She had disobeyed Yvenza. There could be disciplinary action.

A queasy little qualm rippled through her, and she was instantly furious with herself. These homespun criminals would not intimidate her. She was her father's daughter. Squaring her shoulders, she took up the jug and marched off in search of Yvenza. As she went her eyes ranged, taking in the ground-floor fenestration, completely unguarded and completely useless. The stronghouse architecture of Ironheart dictated narrow, deep windows armored in iron grillwork. No exit there.

On she went, and now she knew where she was, back in the front ground-floor gallery. Ironheart was not so difficult to learn. It wasn't nearly the size of Belandor House. Even so, she had to ask directions that sent her up to the second story with its tiny chambers and its puzzling absence of corridors; through the warren to the northern corner of the building, where a cramped old stairway wound its narrow way up to a square room at the top of a tower. The deep slits piercing all four walls suggested defensive intention, but the place was currently serving another function.

Infirmary, Jianna realized.

The room was furnished with cots and pallets, four of them occupied. A quartet of bandaged young men lay there and she eyed them with interest, for it was the first time to her knowledge that she had ever come face-to-face with authentic Ghosts of the resistance. They did not meet her expectations, which involved hulking hirsute ruffians of burningly fanatical demeanor. These lads appeared neither crazed nor vicious. They looked quite ordinary, surprisingly young, even appealing in a sad and sickly sort of way. One of them was white and still, either asleep or comatose. One tossed and muttered in the throes of delirium. Two were awake and aware, their faces pinched with pain. Yvenza was present as well, on her knees beside a cot, feeding soup to one of the wakeful tenants. She turned as Jianna entered and rose to her full height.

Yes, I already know you're bigger than I. Jianna met the other's eyes straightly.

"Give me the kalkriole. You take over feeding."

Take over feeding? Jianna stared. This woman expected her to come within smelling distance of an ailing male stranger, an outlaw Ghost no less, dangerous, possibly diseased, probably dirty—and feed him? With her own hands?

"Now," Yvenza commanded.

No help for it. Approaching with reluctance, she handed the jug to Yvenza, received a soup bowl in exchange, and knelt beside the cot, too close to the criminal invalid, far closer than she wanted to be. Yes, he *was* dirty, her eyes and nose registered. Grubby, smelly, and unkempt, with a sandy stubble of beard prickling his chin.

"New girl. Fetching." He inspected her appreciatively. "What's your name, honey lips?"

Insolent lout. Wordlessly she extended a spoonful of soup.

"Shy one, eh?" He gulped the soup. "Don't be afraid. It's all right, I'm friendly."

Far too friendly. Glowering, she offered another spoonful.

"Come, you can tell me your name, can't you? Or d'you want me to guess? Let me see—is it Netta? Zeev? Kitzi?"

She kept her eyes down and her lips compressed.

"Ho, this beauty is a mute. Maybe not such a bad thing. Most girls talk too much."

He was the one talking too much.

"All right, sweet Silence, if you won't give me words, at least give me soup. Let's have it."

She offered the spoon and as he leaned forward he grasped her wrist, ostensibly to steady it, although there was no need. The unwelcome, unnecessary contact took her by surprise. She started and dropped the spoon. The hand holding the bowl jerked, sloshing soup across the bed and its occupant. A sharp curse escaped him.

Yvenza turned at the sound of it. "What are you yowling about?" she inquired.

"This sullen slattern of yours is trying to drown me," the invalid complained. "Or maybe starve me."

Outraged, Jianna cast about for a suitably crushing retort.

"She's new," Yvenza observed with amusement. "A little awkwardness is only to be expected. I've no doubt that she'll strive hard to improve herself."

Jianna felt the angry color mount uncontrollably to her cheeks.

"In the meantime, do we all wallow in spilled soup?" the Ghost demanded. "Is there no able body about? Where's Rione? He knows what he's doing."

"Off in the hills, tending to your comrades. He'll be back within a few days."

"It can't be too soon."

"I agree."

Their discourse mystified Jianna. Rione? The name was unfamiliar. One of the servants? She would have assumed so, but for a certain fleeting alteration in the quality of Yvenza's voice. There was something present for an instant—approval? Satisfaction? Esteem? And in that moment as well, a change in expression, a brief softening or corrosion of the customary iron.

"Because Rione has got a kind of native wit about him," the Ghost expanded. "Like he was almost born knowing just what to do and how to do it. It's something just there in him."

"You have the good sense to see it." Yvenza nodded.

Still that indefinable note in her voice. Respect?

"And if it isn't there to begin with, chances are it never will be," the Ghost continued. "Like this one." He jerked a thumb at Jianna. "Born clumsy, that's clear, and nothing will change nature, I always say. Born a clumsy calf, grows into a clumsy cow, clumsy from start to finish—"

"That's enough!" Jianna finally found her voice. "You hairy, smelly, lying piece of garbage, how dare you blame me for an accident that you caused all by yourself?"

"So she *can* talk," the Ghost approved.

"Yes, I can talk and, unlike you, I can tell the truth. You made me spill the soup because you couldn't keep your hands to yourself."

"What? Me? Have you forgotten that you're talking to an invalid?"

"Nothing would've happened if you hadn't been pawing me."

"Girl's confused," opined the Ghost.

"I am not. Are you going to deny that you grabbed my wrist?"

"Grabbed? You say *grabbed*? The smallest touch, meant only in kindness, and you dare say *grabbed*? I can't believe my ears. Aren't you ashamed, girl?"

She considered dumping the remainder of the soup over his head. Before she had made up her mind, Yvenza reentered the discussion.

"Even the smallest touch, meant only in kindness, can be a tricky business," she observed drily. "Our little neophyte here is promised to Onartino. I'd consider that, my lad."

"Promised? You mean—"

"I mean that my son plans to marry this girl at the first opportunity. She'll be his wife and my daughter."

"I didn't know, lady." The Ghost appeared to dwindle in size. "No offense meant, I vow and swear."

"If I thought otherwise, I'd take appropriate action," Yvenza assured him serenely. "So, too, no doubt, would Onartino. My boy is touchingly devoted to his betrothed. Their mutual affection is a rare treasure, an example and an inspiration to us all."

"A treasure." The Ghost nodded vigorously. "I can respect that. I hope the young lady took no offense, for none was meant."

Jianna replied with a distant nod, hardly noting him, for the allusion to Onartino had recalled her to the reality of her position in this household. Sometimes it was possible almost to forget for minutes or even longer at a time. Since the morning she had consented to wed Yvenza's oldest son, her circumstances had altered, much for the better. She had been liberated from her cellar closet and given a modest room of her own near the top of Ironheart's southwest turret. True, the chamber door was bolted from the outside every night from sundown until dawn. True, the two windows were barred. The furnishings were rudimentary, and cold drafts swept the bare floor. But the place offered an illusion of privacy. There she slept alone and unmolested. Occasionally she was even permitted to dine in blessed solitude. More often, however, she was obliged to take her meals with the family, as befit her new status.

The company of her captors was always distasteful, but at table she suffered no greater degree of abuse than they habitually inflicted upon one another. Beneath Yvenza's watchful eye, no one attempted outright indecency. So long as she labored to the matriarch's satisfaction, she was fed. She was permitted to bathe occasionally, unobserved so far as she knew, and she was allowed to wash out her own garments. Not that she had many. The boxes containing her massive, exquisite trousseau had been left with the carriage and carnage at the site of the attack. But she had been given a length of linen, needle, and thread with which to fashion a serviceable set of spare undergarments, and thus equipped she contrived to keep herself reasonably clean.

She was free to walk the corridors of Ironheart during the day, to venture out into the courtyard when she wanted fresh air, to converse with anyone willing to answer. All in all, not the worst species of captivity imaginable. At times she might almost have resigned herself to wait in patience for her father's arrival at the head of a rescue party—save for the presence of Onartino.

The mere sight of him dried her mouth and roiled her stomach. With disgust and contempt, she assured herself. Not fear, never that, for she was Aureste's daughter and she feared nobody; certainly not some hulking, ham-fisted backwoods bully.

A killer who likes to hurt women.

Reeni's blood drenched her imagination. The familiar

dread and hatred stirred. She realized that her teeth were clenched, and deliberately she relaxed her jaw. She was safe from Onartino for the present, safe until such time as the East Reach Traveler arrived to perform a marriage ceremony, and that delay could last for weeks.

Or days. Maybe only hours.

Long before the magistrate reached Ironheart, Jianna promised herself, she would be safe at home in her father's house. But the days were passing and Aureste had not appeared. She never doubted for an instant that he would come for her. But of late the first suspicion had surfaced that he might come too late.

"She narcoleptic or something?" inquired the Ghost. "No disrespect intended."

"I believe she has lost herself in visions of impending wedded bliss, as young women will," Yvenza explained. Her voice sharpened to penetrate her captive's unpleasant reverie. "Wake up, girl. Make yourself useful. Take the dirty dishes back to the kitchen. Return the kalkriole to the stillroom. Leave it on the table there. Then you'll start an inventory of the household linens. You can write, can't you? Check the linen presses, list the contents, and don't forget to look in on the laundry. You understand me?" Without awaiting confirmation, she commanded, "Get to it."

Jianna permitted herself one brief, defiant glare, then set to work, gathering dishes and spoons with the obedient efficiency of a trained servant. As she moved about, she noted that one of the wounded, awake when she had entered the room, was now deeply asleep. He had swallowed Yvenza's kalkriole, and the soporific was evidently potent. Stepping to his bedside, she stared down into his sleeping face, then cast a surreptitious glance back over her shoulder. Nobody was watching her. Yvenza and the loquacious Ghost were still mutually engaged, still celebrating Rione, whoever that was . . . *When everyone had given him up for dead, Rione managed to draw the venom out . . .* Physician? Apothecary? No matter.

She bent and poked the sleeping man's midriff sharply. There was no response. He slumbered on serenely. Yes, that kalkriole was powerful indeed. She eyed the stoppered jug with new respect and some speculation.

Scooping up the last of the empty soup bowls and adding it to her tray, Jianna departed the infirmary. She made her way down the narrow stairs to the second story, moved confidently through a communal dormitory that she remembered, through a connecting closet, into a dark storeroom with doorways punctuating each of its four walls, where her assurance flagged. She thought she recalled walking the length of this rectangular space on her way to the north tower, and therefore did so now, choosing the exit at the far end of the room. She went through into a cubby that she did not recognize and then into a tiny, bare place with a hole in the floor and the unmistakable stench of a latrine.

She had chosen wrong and lost her way—all too easy in this second-story maze of nested chambers. Inwardly berating the mutton-headed architect who had planned an interior devoid of corridors, she began to retrace her steps. Of course, it might not be the architect's fault. Probably his design had been butchered by generations of residents partitioning the chambers into smaller and smaller cubicles. She was still pondering the issue when she came to an oaken door whose height and solidity suggested significance.

Jianna went through into a bedchamber occupied by Onartino and a very young serving girl. The girl stood trapped in a corner. Her skirt was up, her face wet with tears. Onartino's large bulk pressed her against the wall. His hands were busy.

For a moment Jianna froze, astonished and almost incredulous. She stood behind Onartino, who did not notice her presence. But the servant girl saw, popped wild eyes, and loosed a desperate squeal. Onartino turned and Jianna gasped. His breeches were undone, his erect member exposed. She had never seen one before, and though she had wondered and sought information often enough, she knew at once that she did not want to see his. Someone else's possibly, but not his. Despite all alarm and revulsion, she could not look away.

Recognizing providential opportunity, the servant girl tore herself loose and bolted for the exit. She was through and gone in an instant. Jianna stood staring. When she finally managed to lift her gaze to Onartino's face, she found that his eyes, as always, expressed nothing at all. He did not trouble to do up his breeches, but remained as he was, mutely surveying her.

She had no idea what to say or do. Confusion and humiliation paralyzed her tongue, and it wasn't fair, for he was the one with cause for shame. *You're a disgusting pig and someday you'll pay,* she wanted to shout, but did not dare. Aureste Belandor's daughter had never feared another human being in all her young life, had never even imagined that she could, but lately that had changed. No need to let Onartino know it, however. With a lift of the chin, she turned to go.

"Stay where you are," he directed.

She meant to ignore the command, but her feet seemed to stop moving of their own accord.

"You're the cunning little piece, aren't you?" he observed. "You play the milk-and-water virgin, but the first chance you get, you come creeping to my room."

He deluded or else amused himself. She did not know which.

"Don't worry, I have what you want," he assured her.

"I came in here by accident. I lost my way." Jianna found her voice—a small, thin voice, but tolerably steady. "I'm going to the kitchen."

"Not just yet. Shut the door," he ordered.

Her heart lurched. Something terrible would happen if she defied him, and even more terrible if she obeyed. She did nothing.

"I won't be happy if I have to tell you twice," he informed her. "You should have learned that by now. Since you're so clever."

If she made a run for it, she might elude him in the second-story maze. With any luck she might find her way to the stairs.

Perhaps her thoughts showed on her face, for he closed the distance between them in three long strides. She would scarcely have imagined a man of his solidity capable of such speed. He had slammed the door shut and placed himself in front of it before she had taken a single step. Now he stood looking down at her, still utterly expressionless, and she was struck once again by his sheer size and bulk. The fear that she was coming to know so well was rising, accelerating her heart and knotting her innards. She could not suppress it, but still she strove to conceal it.

The face that she turned to him was blank as his own, her voice cold as she reminded him, "I'm on my way to the kitchen, at your mother's request."

"It will wait. Put that tray down."

"Why?"

"You scared off the better game, so I suppose I'll have to settle for you."

"Please stand aside and let me pass."

"Back to playing the prim maidenlady?" He cuffed her face, quite lightly, but hard enough to rattle her teeth and the dishes on the tray. "Don't trifle with me and don't argue. Arguing is a mistake."

The tears scalded her eyes but a rush of hatred burned them away before they fell. For a moment anger conquered fear, stiffening her spine. "You let me out right now or I'll scream the roof down."

"Scream all you like, you stupid sow. Nobody will care. Want something to scream about?" He slapped her again.

She staggered, and one of the soup bowls slid off the tray to shatter on the floor. The taste of blood filled her mouth. She must have cut the inside of her cheek on a tooth.

"Careless. Unthrifty. Destroys household property. What sorry sort of useless wife is that? Well, maybe there's one thing you're good for." He shoved her and she stumbled backward a couple of paces. Another bowl hit the floor. "I don't hear you screeching. Aren't you going to make some noise? Or have you gotten it through your thick skull that nobody will give a shit?"

"Your mother might," she reminded him.

"I don't see her about. And you won't go blabbing tales."

"You think not?"

"I think you don't want to find out what will happen if you stir up trouble."

"I will stir up trouble, though," she assured him, astonished by her own tone of cool conviction. "Lots of trouble. I'll go to your mother and let her know that you disobeyed her direct orders. I don't think she takes kindly to disobedience. But you probably know that better than I."

"She won't hear about it. And if you think I'll put up with these feeble little threats you're trying on, then you have a lot to learn. Your training starts here and now." He came at her.

Jianna did not allow herself to retreat. If she retreated now, she was lost. In any case, there was nowhere to run. At that moment she found herself almost beyond terror, her blood ablaze with loathing akin to exhilaration. Her father's face was there in her mind, and she knew what he would counsel.

"Touch me now and I'll tell your mother everything. No threat or force in the world will stop me. The only way you'll silence me is by killing me outright and if you do that, then all your plans fail. You lose everything." She locked eyes with him. He stood towering above her, so close that she caught the reek of his breath, but she resisted the urge to turn her face away. She took a deep breath and continued, "But you can make things easy for yourself. You can spare yourself all that trouble and bother by just standing aside and letting me walk out."

Almost impersonally she wondered if he would now kill her or worse. She might fight, but she would not be able to stop him. And afterward, even if she continued to breathe, her life would be over. She did not let her eyes flicker.

His face was a void as broad as the polar seas. He stood there looking down at her for centuries. Then he reached out and grasped her arm above the elbow, so hard that the pain squeezed her eyes shut for a moment.

"You're right about the bother," he told her. "You're worth none. It will be no hardship to wait a few more days for that Traveler fool to make it legal. And when he does, you may find that you'll regret today's business. Trust me, girl, we'll have ourselves a merry dance, you and I." His grip tightened. "Until then, stay out of my room and out of my way." Opening the door, he swung her around and thrust her through.

The big oaken door slammed shut behind her. For a moment she stood as if stunned, then hurried away. She still clutched the tray, but her hands were shaking badly, clattering the dishes. Now that she was alone, the sobs burst forth and the tears streamed. She had no idea where she was or where she was going, but wandered at random through a succession of alien chambers until by chance she came upon a stairway. She descended to the first story and once more had her bearings.

She paused briefly to compose herself, wiped her face on her sleeve, then made her way to the kitchen, where she rid herself of the tray and what remained of the crockery. And then, into the stillroom.

She placed the kalkriole on the table as Yvenza had commanded, began to turn away, then turned back to eye the jug. Her pulses still raced and her breathing was ragged—souvenirs of the recent exchange with her betrothed. If she remained in this place, she could look forward to many more of the same. But no, she reminded herself, not the same. Today she had escaped almost unscathed. She was unlikely to enjoy such good fortune a second time. Should the threatened marriage ceremony actually take place, then she would become his property, to do with as he pleased for the rest of her life, which was likely to prove agonizing and short. All of this would happen unless her father arrived in time to rescue her, *and he was taking too long about it.* She could wait no longer. She would have to rescue herself.

She needed a plan, and quickly. There was already a germ of an idea.

Her eyes traveled the surrounding shelves, skimming countless containers. *No good, no good, no good.* Then she spied a well-corked vial, tiny enough to suit her purposes. It contained a quantity of nameless grey powder, which she poured out onto the floor and blended with the dust in the corners. Kalkriole from the jug replaced the original contents. She jammed the cork in tightly, slipped the vial into her pocket, and felt indefinably comforted, as if she had found a weapon.

She did not know quite how or when she would use the soporific, but she would surely find a way.

Soon.

SEVEN

She needed cheese. Meat might have been better, but meat was hard to come by and quick to spoil. The cheese would work almost as well, and presented several practical advantages. She had secured the necessary bread the previous day, and if it was growing stale, that was actually all to the good.

The cold-closet containing perishable foodstuffs adjoined the kitchen, which was never unoccupied. But the closet possessed a second doorway giving onto the courtyard, allowing convenient delivery of the assorted furred or feathered woodland creatures that Onartino and Trecchio managed to kill during the course of their sylvan rambles. The courtyard door was barred at night but remained unlocked during the daylight hours, for the Lady Yvenza hardly feared pilfering. Her confidence was well founded. With the sentry's tale of the mutilated wretch caught stealing salt pork still fresh in her mind, Jianna would rather have avoided the cold-closet altogether. But there the cheese was stored. And she needed cheese.

Most of the time Yvenza kept her busy drudging away at one domestic duty or another. Around noon, however, after she had finished inspecting a massive batch of mending, there came a lull in the rhythm of her labors and she managed to slip out into the courtyard.

The air was raw and the sky was drab. A wedge of black birds cleft a passage through the clouds overhead. Autumn was sharpening; time was passing. One of the servants, busy recaning the seat of an old chair, seemed wholly absorbed in his work and unaware of her presence. Another, working the tangles out of an enormous length of rope, appeared equally oblivious. They had not noticed her as yet, but she was scarcely invisible. One or the other need only lift his eyes. She hesitated.

Audacity possesses its own particular utility, her father had often advised her. *Assume a confidence of demeanor and you will go unchallenged more often than not.*

So be it, then. Audacity. Drawing a deep breath, she marched straight across the open space at an unhurried pace designed to create an aura of legitimate purpose. If anyone accosted her, she would claim that Yvenza had dispatched her upon an errand.

That necessity never arose. Neither of the servants glanced up from his work. Her presence went unmarked or else ignored. The cold-closet door, unlocked as expected, yielded without protest, and she slid through.

The place was windowless and dark. The air was still and thick with edible odors. Jianna waited and let her eyes adjust. Presently she spied a linear luminosity at floor level—light leaking in under the door from the adjoining kitchen. There were voices and clattering on the other side of that door, and she wondered briefly what she would say if someone entered and discovered her here. *Assume a confidence of demeanor . . .*

Something rustled nervously in the dark. *Mice.*

Her surroundings lightened into dim view. The cold-closet was sizable, its walls draped in shadow. She spied wooden barrels large and small, baskets of fruits and roots, hanging garlands of sausage, pale cylinders and blocks wrapped in coarse fabric. She went to work on one of the cylinders, and her nose confirmed her success even before the coverings fell away to reveal a substantial round of firm-textured cheese. Exactly what she wanted.

Her fingers danced, worrying fragments off the edge of the cylinder. A few crumbs found their way to her mouth. Most went into her pocket. When she judged she had taken enough, she stopped. The big cylinder was visibly pocked, as if nibbled by mice. With luck, anyone seeing it would assume that such was the case. For the cold-closet was surely infested; she could still hear those furtive little rustlings in the gloom. For some reason the hairs along her forearms rose.

Time to go. She had managed to escape detection so far, but her good luck could not continue indefinitely. She took the time to rewrap the cheese neatly, then turned and made for the exit.

Her hand was on the latch when she heard another little rustle and then a whispery voice.

"Yes."

Jianna drew a startled gasp, too spontaneous to suppress and sharply audible in that confined space. No point now in trying to hide. The unseen other, whoever it might be, was certainly aware of her presence.

"That, too." The small whisper thrilled. The speaker's age and gender remained obscure. There was a long pause, and then as if in reply to a silent query, *"They do not tell me."*

Her curiosity almost outweighed her alarm. Stepping resolutely to the rear of the cold-closet, she discovered the owner of the voice lodged in the narrow space between the wall and a barrel. There in the shadows crouched a diminutive, skinny form crowned with straggling locks fair to the verge of whiteness. She descried a little peaked face and pale lambent eyes that seemed alien as a Sishmindri's.

"Nissi?" There was no response, no sign that the other had heard.

"I will . . . try . . ." The alien eyes were inexpressibly distant. Apparently unaware of Jianna's presence, she was speaking to herself or else to some unseen listener.

Automatically Jianna glanced about in search of the invisible audience, then recognized the absurdity. This pallid wraith of a girl was mad or moonstruck.

"Nissi," she repeated more insistently, and this time she was heard.

Nissi's luminous gaze focused. "He says, 'Ask them,'" she confided in her tiny voice.

"Ask whom? Ask what? Who says?" The questions were no doubt pointless, but Jianna could not contain them.

"He does. The nice one."

"The nice what?"

"They are not all nice."

"Who or what aren't?"

"Sometimes they get angry. Because I go too fast. Or else they just fade away. But he doesn't. He keeps up and he's nice."

"But who?"

"He tells me not to be afraid in the woods when the world isn't real anymore. Are you afraid when that happens?"

"Are you all right?"

"Yes, thank you." The enormous eyes widened. "Are you all right, too?"

"Well enough." *As long as you don't go telling the world that you've seen me in here.* Jianna eyed the other narrowly. What would this peculiar, inscrutable creature choose to do? A word in the wrong ear could bring punishment ranging from the unpleasant to the unspeakable. How best to silence Nissi? Enlist her sympathies, perhaps? Assuming a woeful expression, she elaborated, "Only—well, I've just been so *hungry,* so sick and faint for lack of food, so *desperately* famished, that I finally felt I'd surely die if I couldn't just—if I couldn't somehow—"

"Please," Nissi interrupted almost inaudibly. "Please promise."

"—find something, maybe just a handful of dried beans or an old root—"

"Please promise that you won't tell."

"Tell what?" Jianna inquired, her rush of creativity momentarily diverted.

"That you saw me here. That I did the Distant Exchange."

"Oh. *Oh.*" So the white girl wasn't supposed to be in the cold-closet, either. Jianna's confidence rose and her curiosity bloomed. "The Distant Exchange—I've heard of that. It's something arcane, isn't it?"

"They would not like it. Lady Yvenza—Master Onartino . . ."

"Why not? Are they worried about the Taerleezi ban?"

"They . . . would not like it."

"I see. Well, then." Jianna considered. Her prospects had brightened. "In that case, I give you my word. Your secret is safe."

Nissi regarded the floor.

Jianna studied the huddled figure. At last, she ventured to ask, "You have the talent?"

The colorless head bobbed.

"And the Distant Exchange lets you communicate with others like yourself?"

Another silent nod.

It was not so surprising. Power ran in the Belandor blood and always had. Nissi might not be the legitimate product of a lawful marriage, but talent made no social distinctions.

"Well, then—" Jianna swiftly reviewed possibilities. "Perhaps you could send a message from me to my Uncle Innesq in Vitrisi? He has the talent, too, you see."

Nissi stared mutely.

"Just a short message, only to tell him that I'm alive and unhurt," Jianna urged. "He doesn't know what's become of me and he must be sick with worry. All of them would be." It was her father's state of mind that most concerned her, but an appeal on Aureste Belandor's behalf was hardly apt to rouse sympathy within the confines of Ironheart, so she concluded, "Uncle Innesq could let the rest of the family know that I'm alive. It would be a great kindness."

The ensuing silence suggested that the request had gone unheard. At length Nissi murmured, "Family . . ."

"Yes. They probably think that I'm dead."

"They would . . . grieve?"

"Very much so." Some of them, at any rate. "They've offended no one, they shouldn't have to suffer. Will you help me?"

Silence resumed.

"I think you want to," Jianna essayed.

"They would not like it," Nissi repeated.

"They'd never know."

Nissi shook her head.

"They wouldn't find out, you've nothing to fear." This last was probably untrue, but Jianna did not let herself think about it.

Nissi rose to her feet and drifted noiselessly toward the exit.

"Wait, where are you going? Nissi, please wait, won't you even send the smallest message to my uncle? Just enough to tell him that I'm still—"

"I am leaving now," Nissi announced.

"No, wait, you can't go yet, not if you don't want to be seen. There are servants out there in the courtyard."

"They will not . . . notice me. I am easily overlooked."

"But shouldn't you at least—"

"I am leaving now."

The door opened briefly and Jianna blinked against the stab of daylight. During that blink, Nissi vanished and the cold-closet sank back into comforting shadow.

If otherworldly little Nissi could wander the courtyard at will, then surely Aureste Belandor's daughter could do at least as well. Chin up, Jianna departed the cold-closet and made her way back into the house without incident. Once inside, she was obliged to sit rolling bandages for hours, and after that she transcribed the notations on countless crumpled paper scraps into the household ledgers, copying each entry in her neat, fine hand. The afternoon slowly spent itself. In the early evening she endured dinner with the family, and after that she was free to seek the sanctuary of her own room. She heard the scrape of the bolt locking her in for the night, and then she was finally alone.

The room was cold. Despite the advancing season no fire

burned on the grate, for the matriarch of Ironheart deemed such comfort superfluous. A tiny oil lamp furnished the sole illumination and by that feeble light she worked, sprinkling absorbent bits of stale bread with the kalkriole elixir, rolling the bits into tiny balls, enclosing each moist ball within a layer of cheese. Presently she had molded a dozen neat spheres, which she wrapped in her only handkerchief. The small bundle disappeared into the pocket of her gown. This done, she stripped down to her linen, blew out the lamp, and slipped into bed, where she lay taut and wakeful well into the night.

· · ·

Two more days trudged by without incident before Jianna's unspoken hope was fulfilled and she was dispatched to the garden.

Once again she stood amid the thorny shrubs without the wall of Ironheart. Once again she bore a wicker basket that she had been commanded to fill with kalkrios leaves, the last harvest of the year. Once again the woods beckoned and once again Grumper barred her path to freedom. But this time it was going to be different.

Jianna worked her way along the row of bushes at an unhurried pace, the boarhound close on her heels. Practice had improved her skills and now she easily avoided the thorns. Her fingers flew unbloodied, and the basket filled quickly. When she reached the end of the row, she paused to shoot a glance at the gate in the wall. There slouched the homespun sentry, his attention fixed upon the lighting of his clay pipe. He did not trouble to look her way. The dog could be trusted to control her, and her value as a source of amusement had lapsed days earlier.

She was unobserved by all save Grumper. Turning to face him, she remarked, "We need to talk."

He stared at her.

"Perhaps we started off on the wrong foot," Jianna continued earnestly, "but I hope that it's not too late for the two of

us to establish a relationship built on mutual respect and courtesy. Wouldn't you prefer that, Grumper? I know *I* would."

His ears twitched at the sound of his name.

"There's been a certain uneasiness, even antipathy between
the two of us in the past," she conceded sadly. "There was an
incident that we should doubtless both prefer to forget. I'm
sure that I was at least partially to blame for that, and I want
you to know that I regret it."

He cocked his head.

"I want to make amends and start over, Grumper. Would
you like that, you handsome boy?"

A low growl rumbled from the depths of his throat.

"Oh, I don't believe you really mean that. You'd really like
to be friends, wouldn't you, Grumper? Well, so would I, and I
can prove it. Just to demonstrate my good intentions, I've
brought you a gift. Something good, something delicious, es-
pecially for you. See, look at this." She drew the small linen
package from her pocket and opened it, exposing the cheese
balls.

Grumper's nostrils quivered.

"Yes, you're interested, aren't you? And you should be,
they're lovely. And all for you, good doggy, all for you. Here,
boy, catch." She tossed him a tidbit, expecting him to catch it
in typically voracious canine style.

Grumper, however, allowed the offering to hit the ground.
He eyed it with interest, even longing, but made no move to
touch it.

"Clever dog," Jianna acknowledged sourly. "Well trained.
But let's see how untouchable you really are." She set to work
on one of the balls, peeling away the exterior layer of cheese
but leaving the doctored bread center intact. When she had
stripped off a sizable morsel, she chirruped enticingly, and
Grumper dragged his eyes from the food on the ground to her
face.

"Look, Grumper," she invited. "Look at this beautiful
cheese. So rich, so satisfying, so luscious. Can you smell it? I

hope you can, because it's wonderful. I'm telling you, I can't resist it myself. See, Grumper? I'm eating, I'm just *feasting*." She popped the cheese into her mouth and savored it at length. The flavor was unremarkable. Closing her eyes, she loosed a moan of pleasure. *"Uuummmmmmmmmm. This is so good.* I think it's the best cheese I've ever tasted, the best cheese *any-one's* ever tasted. This is the high point of my entire *life.*" For some seconds, she radiated ecstasy, then opened her eyes. Grumper stood transfixed, rapt gaze fixed on her face. A thread of saliva dangled from his lips. Good. "You really ought to taste this, boy. You owe it to yourself. And mind you, I understand that this places you under no obligation whatso-ever. I expect no special consideration in return." Kneeling, she proffered the remainder of the cheese ball on an open palm.

Grumper sniffed yearningly. A moment longer he hesitated, then his will buckled and he accepted the food from her hand. He wolfed it down in a single gulp, made similarly short work of the ball on the ground, then stood waiting for more.

"Yes, you love that, don't you? Of course you do. Here, have another." She tossed him a cheese ball, and this time he caught it in midair. "Oh, yes, good. Eat up."

Grumper complied, and the cheese balls vanished. When he had finished eating, he licked his chops, lay down, sighed deeply, and went to sleep.

Jianna watched in disbelief. It had been so miraculously quick and easy. Almost she suspected the hitherto invincible Grumper of indulging in some canine version of a practical joke. If she made the wrong move now, he would surely spring to his feet and knock her down, and then the sentry would laugh at her again. But when she spoke his name he did not stir, and when she ventured to touch him, he remained quiescent. She prodded his ribs, as she had not long ago prodded the sleeping Ghost in the infirmary, and like the Ghost, Grumper slept on.

She had done it. She had outwitted her enemies in a manner

befitting the daughter of Aureste Belandor. There remained only the mechanics of actual departure. Jianna, crouched low to the ground beside the unconscious boarhound, cast another hostile glance back at the sentry. Tobacco occupied his full attention. He was not watching her. The moment had actually come. Briefly she considered her situation—poised on the verge of solitary flight into the wilderness, devoid of provisions, money, weapons, friends, or knowledge of her surroundings; devoid of anything likely to ensure her survival. It seemed like a leap off a cliff, but the alternative was worse.

Almost before she realized that she had made up her mind, she found herself creeping on all fours toward the shelter of the woods. The height of the shrubbery would conceal her flight, for a while. Should the sentry happen to look her way, he would probably assume that she had paused for rest, seating herself out of sight on the ground among the bushes, her actions observed by the watchdog. With any luck, he wouldn't note her absence for long minutes to come.

She hardly expected luck. Her ears all but tingled in anticipation of a shout from the guard or a growl from a revived and vengeful boarhound. But nothing interrupted her progress, and moments later she reached the dank shade of the woods. Springing to her feet, she began to run. The woods were completely unknown territory. She had no idea where she was going other than away from Ironheart.

The ground was deep in fallen leaves. No path or trail was visible. She ran blindly. The low branches and brambles slapped and grabbed at her in passing, but she scarcely felt them. She ran for what seemed a very long time, ran until her breath came hard and her steps faltered, and even then she did not stop, but only unwillingly slowed to a walk. On she pushed at the best pace she could maintain, until at last she grew certain that she had put miles between herself and the stronghouse, losing herself in a trackless wild beyond reach of the outlaw Belandors.

Jianna paused and looked around her. There was nothing

to see but the countless grey trees, their boughs thinly clad in the last clinging leaves of autumn, their tops half lost in the persistent fog of the Veiled Isles. She could hear the rustle of branches, the occasional birdcall, the scratch of a squirrel's claws on bark, and little more. She sensed no human presence; she had never felt more completely alone. The muted scene breathed tranquillity. Surely she need not fear pursuit; they would never find her here.

A brief blaze of passionate gratitude swept through her, and then the mind of Aureste's daughter resumed functioning. By this time the sentry back at Ironheart would have noticed her escape and sounded an alarm. They would pursue her; perhaps the chase had already begun. Unlike the fugitive, the Belandors and their creatures knew these woods well and would probably hunt her down with ease. She needed to find help before they caught up with her. A town or village, even an ordinary cottage, someplace with men of decency willing to protect her. Or if she could find her way back to the road, she might meet travelers, a carriage or coach to carry her off to safety and civilization, either in Orezzia or Vitrisi.

Vitrisi. Home. Father and family. Belandor House. And beyond them, the sights and sounds of the city that she loved. *Home.* If only she could get back there, she wouldn't be pushed out again, no matter what her father had to say about it. *If only . . .*

Which direction? She had no idea, but it did not matter. The Alzira Hills were wild but hardly uninhabited. Sooner or later she would encounter humanity.

She resumed walking, choosing a route that took her downhill. The way was easy, but the ground was stony and she still wore the same fashionable, insubstantial shoes in which she had traveled by coach from Vitrisi. The only pair she owned, now.

Presently her feet began to hurt. The pretty shoes were chafing her heels, no doubt raising blisters the size of inflated bladders, but there was nothing to be done about it now. On she went, but soon her attention shifted from the pain in her feet to the sharpening pangs in her belly. She had not eaten since daybreak, and now her stomach was making its dissatisfaction known. She should have brought some sort of provisions with her, she realized belatedly. It dawned on her that she really had not planned particularly well.

She had been resourceful and inventive enough in creating the cheese balls, but her imagination had not carried her beyond the moment of escape from Ironheart. She had never considered her course of action once clear of those stone walls. She had not done so, she now perceived, because on some level she had not truly expected the trick with the drugged tidbits to work. Even now, her success seemed unreal. And it would be unreal indeed if she eluded her hunters only to die of hunger and exposure, alone and lost in the woods. On, then. And never mind the blistered feet.

People found all sorts of roots and fruits to eat in the wild, did they not? And water? People found edible greens and delicious wild mushrooms. Honey in hives. Nuts and seeds. The woods were absolutely crammed with food, were they not? *And water?*

Nothing recognizably edible presented itself, but the question of water was answered with rainfall; a light sprinkling at first that swelled and settled into a steady downpour. The trees offered little protection, and Jianna's garments were soon sodden. A grim little breeze punched through to punish her flesh and she shivered miserably. The breeze hit harder, driving cold rain into her face, and her teeth chattered in response.

But now, at last, an encouraging sign. She had come upon a forest trail—narrow, overgrown, and showing little evidence of use, but undeniably a trail that must lead to something or someone. For another twenty minutes she followed the twisting path down a long, gradual incline, at the foot of which she found her way blocked by a stream. Running to the water's edge, she dropped to her knees, dipped her cupped hands, brought them forth brimming, and drank deeply. The water was cold, muddy, and more than likely to make her sick, but for the moment she did not care. Repeatedly she dipped and drank until the ferocious thirst born of much exertion coupled with nervous tension began to abate. She wiped her mouth with the back of her hand, despite the manifest futility. The rain was pouring down, soaking her to the skin and chilling her to the bone.

The stream, already swollen, ran swift and brown. On its far side a break in the underbrush marked the continuation of the trail. There was no bridge. A succession of big stones bulging above the surface of the water offered the obvious means of crossing. The first of the stones stood no more than a yard or so from the bank. Jianna effortlessly stepped across onto the broad, flat surface. On to the next, with equal ease. Two more, and now she had reached the middle of the stream, where the water ran its deepest and the wet rocks were slimed with dark algae. Pausing briefly to wipe the rain out of her eyes, she took a long hop and landed atop a humpbacked algal plantation. The slick, rounded surface offered no purchase to her smooth-soled shoes. Her foot slipped, her ankle turned, and she fell sprawling into the stream.

A shocked squeal escaped her. The water was shallow, only a few inches above knee level, but it was shudderingly cold. Thrashing, she struggled to stand up; half rose, slipped again on the rocks of the streambed, and sat down hard; tried again, and this time managed to find her footing. Pain shot through her ankle; beyond question it was twisted or sprained. *Or broken.* No; if it were broken, she would not be standing on it.

Gathering up the burden of her drenched skirts, she limped the rest of the way across. By the time she reached the bank, the ache in her ankle was fierce and steady. She paused to inspect the damage. The joint was already starting to swell, despite the frigid bath; soon it would be worse. Impractical to continue walking on it. Impossible not to. She glanced about in search of a good stick or fallen branch to use as a cane, but there was none to be seen. Her eyes stung and, rather than giving way to tears, she spat an expletive, one that she had sometimes caught upon the servants' lips when they did not know that the magnifico's daughter overheard them. Setting her chin, she made haltingly for the gap in the underbrush.

• • •

The sentry sat on the ground with his back resting against the wall. His lungs were pleasurably filled with tobacco smoke, his mind pleasurably empty. The jolt of a hobnailed boot striking his ribs roused him from his reverie, and he looked up to find Master Onartino standing above him. As usual, Master Onartino's eyes expressed nothing at all, but his face was flushed and his breath alcoholic. The sentry scrambled to his feet. Removing the pipe from his mouth, he stiffened in anticipation of a reprimand, probably accompanied by a blow. He received neither.

"Where is she?" demanded Onartino.

"Sir?" mumbled the sentry, surprised.

"The girl. The hothouse flower, the rare bird, the princess. Where is that little slut?" Onartino neither raised his voice nor slurred his words, but the red stain suffusing his face darkened as he spoke.

"Kneeser's daughter?" The sentry's surprise deepened, luring him into imprudence. "What d'you want with her, then?"

He had gone too far. His mistress' son struck him, and he staggered a little but stayed on his feet.

But the alcohol must have loosened Master Onartino's tongue, for—having expressed his disapproval—he deigned to answer the question, after a fashion.

"Anything I like," muttered Onartino, almost to himself. "She's mine."

He was a little premature, but the sentry voiced no objection, merely extending an indicative finger toward the kalkrios bushes. "Picking," he explained.

"I don't see her."

"Then she must be down on the ground going for the low leaves. She's coming up a pretty fair picker."

"You let her out of your sight, clodpoll?"

"Grumper's there, sir. He'll hold 'er, right enough."

"You'd better pray that he does." So saying, Onartino turned and made for the shrubbery. At the end of the longest row, where the bushes grew high and thick enough to furnish adequate cover, he found the brindled boarhound alone, fast asleep on the ground. An angry exclamation drew no response. Bending low, he shouted the dog's name, but Grumper slept on. Two or three light kicks availed nothing, and a heavier one proved equally ineffectual. Onartino's red face went purple. A short cudgel materialized in his hand, and blows rained down on the unconscious dog. Grumper stirred and whimpered, but never woke. Eventually his stirring ceased and he lay very still. Blood spotted his head and muzzle.

Onartino drew back a step. His face was expressionless as ever, save for the small vertical line that dented his brow. His mother set great store by that dog. For some seconds, he stood staring down at the motionless animal, then appeared to reach a decision.

"It's her," he announced aloud. "No matter. There's nothing I can't track." His proven prowess as a hunter supported this claim. He glanced up at the sky, whose grey uniformity threatened rain. All to the good. Her feet would leave deep prints on moist ground. "Nothing I can't track," he repeated, and set off into the woods at a smart pace.

• • •

Jianna was soaked and freezing. Her ankle throbbed cruelly. She yearned beyond expression to stop and rest. But they might be close upon her trail, for they were surely hunting her by now. Servants from Ironheart—perhaps even Yvenza herself; Yvenza, who would welcome the opportunity to punish her. She could not afford to linger.

There was no human help in sight, but her searching eye fell upon an object of potential value—a big fallen branch, long and sturdy enough to suit her needs, lying beside the trail. She picked it up, took a moment to strip off a few twigs, then tried leaning her weight on the new staff. Yes, it offered good, solid support. And when she attempted a few careful steps, she found herself favoring the bad ankle in a way that distinctly diminished the pain. With the aid of the staff, she could walk for at least a while longer.

On she hobbled through a dim, wet world. The trail was softening beneath her feet, and she sank into the mud with each step. Her heavy, sopping skirts and cloak weighed her down without excluding the cold in the least; her teeth chattered, and she was shivering. Deliberately she filled her mind with warming images—home, family, defeat and capture of the outlaw Belandors, the magnifico's vengeance upon the abductors of his daughter . . . happy thoughts.

The trail leveled and widened. A thick carpet of fallen leaves covered much of the mud. Here the way was not so difficult, but Jianna's spirits hardly rose, for every instinct shouted that pursuit was gaining on her. And how should it be otherwise, when ill luck and injury held her best pace to a hobble? She glanced back over her shoulder for the thousandth time. Still nobody there. *Yet.* Help, she needed human help. *Immediately.*

She tried to push herself to greater speed, but her ankle rebelled. Such a fierce pang smote her that she cried out and halted, jaw clenched. When she resumed progress moments later, her pace was slower than ever and she leaned heavily on the staff.

The trail curved to circle a granite outcropping, and it took her centuries to toil her way around the great rock. An eon expired, and then the path unbent itself to push straight on through an endless soggy wilderness empty of human life.

But not quite empty. The curtains of pouring rain seemed to part slightly, allowing passage of a large, dark shape of indeterminate species, which presently resolved itself into a human on horseback. A rain hood and an enveloping cloak obscured all details of face and figure, including gender. Jianna cared nothing for details. What mattered was that this rider clearly had not pursued her from Ironheart. Relief and intense gratitude filled her. She called out and the hooded head lifted, but she still could not make out a face. She struggled forward at her fastest limp, and the stranger advanced to meet her. Presently they confronted one another and now she could see that the face beneath the dripping hood was masculine and mature but not elderly. The eyes were light in color and intent in expression.

"Help me, please help me," Jianna appealed.

He dismounted at once. "Lost?" he inquired.

"Very. And worse. I was abducted, held prisoner." The words tumbled out. "I managed to escape only a little while ago and I ran away, but slipped while crossing the stream and hurt my ankle, and now I can barely walk, much less run, and they're sure to be hunting me. They know these woods, they can travel much faster than I can, the dog may have awakened, they may be using him to track me, and they could catch up any second now. If they find me, they'll drag me back to that place and I know I'll never get away again, never. I can't let that happen, they're vicious demented criminals and they've got horrible plans for me. Please, please, help me get home. My father will be so grateful, he'll reward you well, really well, I promise. But we need to go *now,* right *now* before they find me—"

"Stop. Take a deep breath," he advised.

His voice was low-pitched and possessed of a singularly soothing quality. Her breathing eased at the mere sound of it, and she followed his instructions without thought.

"And another."

Again she obeyed.

"Good. Now calm yourself, there's nothing more to fear. You've been found and you are safe. First we'll tend to your injured ankle, and then we'll see about returning you to your friends and family."

So compelling and reassuring was his voice, so gentle his manner, that it took her a moment to notice that he had simply disregarded her attempted explanation. And why wouldn't he? Her own voice echoed in her mind: ... *abducted, held prisoner ... sure to be hunting me ... the dog ... horrible plans for me* ... It all sounded absurd, a fever dream or the outcry of a hysteric. If she wanted him to believe her, she had better control herself, moderate her language and her tone.

"Thank you. I am very eager to return to my family," she returned quietly. "My father is in Vitrisi. Will you please escort me back to him?"

"That is hardly practical."

"It isn't? Why not?" Jianna was nonplussed. Perhaps his voice had misled her, for he spoke with the accent of an educated Vitrisian and she had unconsciously classified him at the first sound of it. She was a lady of Vitrisi in distress; as a gentleman of her city, he should stand ready to assist her by any and all means within his power.

"Vitrisi is days distant, and I am wanted here."

"But what am I to do? I tell you I must go home to my father! He can protect me from those criminals. Do you not understand?" Her voice was rising again, despite her efforts to control it. "I'm in danger, they're hunting me, they're depraved lunatics with a grudge against my father, and I need your help!"

"You shall have that," he assured her. "Let us see first to your ankle and proceed from there. Come, seat yourself."

Once again his low, unhurried voice exerted a curiously calming effect, and without argument she sat down on a rock and waited a moment while he tethered his horse, then extracted a small leather pouch from one of the saddlebags. This done, he knelt before her and paused courteously. "With your permission."

He was a stranger and they were alone in the wild, but somehow she did not hesitate a moment to draw her skirts back a few inches, exposing her foot and swollen ankle to view. His brows rose at sight of her delicate, waterlogged shoe. He removed it and set it aside. Then he took her ankle in both of his hands and still, such was the power of his voice and manner, she was not frightened or offended in the least. His touch was warm, light, and sure. Exploratory pressure here and there produced only the mildest of twinges. A brief examination sufficed to satisfy him.

"You've strained your ankle," he told her. "No doubt it's painful, but the injury is minor. A few days of rest should effect a cure, although I'd recommend favoring the ankle for another month or so thereafter. In the meantime—" The leather pouch yielded a roll of spotlessly clean bandages. One of these he wound around her ankle and fastened with a small metal clasp, his movements so deft and precise that the operation was painlessly completed within seconds. He slipped the shoe back onto her foot and stood.

"I've never seen anything quite like that before." Jianna studied her well-wrapped joint in wonder. The bandage was fashioned of some subtly lustrous fabric that seemed to offer support without bulk or binding.

"That is my own invention. It's made of silk for lightness and strength, knitted for elasticity."

"You can knit silk?"

"Not personally," he admitted with a slight smile that transformed his face, lighting up the grey-blue eyes. She saw then that he was considerably younger than she had at first supposed. The gravity of his expression had misled her, but he was probably no more than seven or eight years her senior.

"Surely you must be a physician?"

"I am."

"But how fortunate for me. Whom shall I thank?"

"I'm called Falaste."

"That's a Vitrisian name. And you speak with the accent of the city, too. You are a long way from home, Dr. Falaste."

"The city isn't my home. I am of Vitrisian descent, but I don't live there."

"Orezzia, then?"

"I'm nomadic. My practice carries me throughout the range of the Alzira Hills."

"Couldn't your patients spare you for just a few days while you conduct me back to my father's house? You've done me a great favor, and my father will be eager to reward you."

"You'll not be starting any long journeys before that ankle of yours has had a chance to mend," he informed her. "A week's rest and then you should be fit to travel. Fortunately, you're not far from comfortable shelter. Only a few miles from here stands a stronghouse whose owners can certainly be persuaded to take you in."

"You're not speaking of Ironheart?" she cried.

"Ah, you know it?"

"Yes, I know it! That's the place. Those are the people. That's where they took me and held me prisoner. In a locked closet in the cellar! And threatened me and set the giant dog on me! There's a family of monsters living there and if they recapture me, there's no telling what they'll do!" Her voice had risen again, but for the moment she could not master it. "I'm not exaggerating. They're highwaymen and murderers. They killed my aunt, my maid, and the guards. There's nothing they won't dare!"

He pressed his hand lightly to her brow for a moment then withdrew it, remarking, "You do not seem feverish, but perhaps your ordeal has—"

"I'm not feverish, and there's nothing wrong with my mind! And I'm not lying to you!"

"I don't suggest that you lie. But you've been injured and frightened. Under such circumstances a little confusion is often present, and misinterpretation is possible."

"I'm not misinterpreting my dead aunt and maid! I'm not misinterpreting my own abduction, or the threats and blows I've received! Above all I'm not misinterpreting the ruin that I face if they lay hands on me again!" She managed to get her voice back down again, concluding on a calmer note, "Dr. Falaste, you must believe that everything I've told you is true."

For a moment he studied her, his clear eyes seeming to plumb the depths of her mind. At last he suggested, "Let's consider, then. You are a young woman—scarcely more than a girl, really—very well spoken despite your agitation, bedraggled but elegantly clothed, unmistakably of good background and probably high family. At your stage of life, you can hardly have acquired mortal enemies. And yet you accuse the residents of Ironheart—I know them, by the way—of the worst imaginable crimes. These people can't quite be considered exemplary, granted, but they're not lunatics and I assume you've committed no unpardonable offense against them. What possible reason could they have, then, to use you with the cruelty you describe?"

"My father," she returned at once. "They hate my father bitterly. They imagine that he's wronged them, they hold him responsible for all their misfortunes, and they mean to strike at him through me."

"Indeed. You've a dramatic turn of phrase."

"I am not making this up!"

"And who is this father of yours that stirs up such commotion?"

"My father is the Magnifico Aureste Belandor, of Vitrisi. I am Jianna Belandor."

He did not change expression, but it seemed to her that his eyes darkened at the sound of the name.

"I hope," he observed slowly, "that this is fantasy or theater. You allow a lively imagination free rein, perhaps?"

"I do not. And I'm not delirious, either. I am Jianna Belandor, daughter of the Magnifico Aureste. Why are you looking at me like that? I hope you're not another of those bigots filled with prejudice against my father?"

"Maidenlady, I fear that you'll find an entire world populated with just such bigots."

"Then ignorance is everywhere, and it's so unjust. My father is a fine man, a kind and warm and generous man. The world doesn't know him."

"Possibly the world knows him better than you realize. But I will confess, his daughter's loyalty speaks well for the magnifico."

"You're beginning to believe what I tell you, then?"

"I'd prefer not to believe, but you are persuasive, and your story possesses its own logic. If you are truly Aureste Belandor's daughter, then the treatment you claim to have received at Ironheart becomes understandable. It is possible."

"It's more than possible, it's fact," Jianna declared. "You say that you know those people. If so, then you must have a good idea what they're capable of doing to me. My life is over if you don't help me to get away from them. Please, please, take me back to Vitrisi!" She gazed up at him with enormous pleading eyes. His face was still, but instinct told her that she was making progress.

"There are other considerations," he observed at last.

His objection, whatever it might be, could surely be overcome. Jianna looked up at him. Her lip quivered and her eyes filled with tears, which she made no effort to suppress. She did not let a sound escape her, but stood bravely and piteously silent, tears coursing down her cheeks. This tactic almost never failed to conquer her father.

And it seemed that Dr. Falaste was similarly susceptible, for his face softened and he looked young again, if somewhat troubled.

"Maidenlady—" he attempted.

She turned aside as if ashamed of her tears, but in reality offering him a good view of her pretty profile. She let her shoulders shake a little with silent suppressed sobs. Aureste could rarely resist silent suppressed sobs. She glimpsed the physician's face out of the corner of her eye and saw uncertainty there. Good. In her imagination she approached the gates of Belandor House, with Dr. Falaste at her side. She would introduce the doctor to her father. Falaste would instantly perceive the magnifico's essential goodness. Aureste in turn would immediately recognize the physician's talent and intelligence. With the magnifico's assistance, Falaste would remain in Vitrisi to establish a fashionable, highly profitable practice. He would be a frequent guest at Belandor House, and she would see much of him. There was something so agreeable in this mental exercise that her lips almost started to curve into a smile. She compressed them firmly and stole another glance at him.

He seemed lost in frowning cogitation, and she took the opportunity to study him: face long but not excessively so, complexion pale but not unhealthily so, straight features, stubborn chin, an indefinably scholarly look. Hair presently invisible beneath the rain hood. Medium stature. Probably slender in build, under that voluminous rain cloak. A fine, intelligent, and thoughtful face. Its owner was sure to help her.

Falaste's head jerked slightly, as if he had reached a decision. Confidently Jianna awaited his reply.

"I'll help you to shelter," he told her.

"In Vitrisi," she prompted, a little confused.

"No. That's not possible. But I'll bring you to some cottage or campsite, where you'll find assistance and a place to rest safely until you're fit to travel."

"No, that isn't what I want." Her surprise equaled her disappointment. She had been quite certain, moments earlier, that he would succumb. "If you won't take me back to the city, then at least bring me to some inn or posting house along the VitrOrezzi Bond."

"The nearest is a good day and a half from here."

"Well? Can you not spare the time to assist me?" She had

not yet given up hope. Perhaps he could be shamed into compliance. "Are you not a gentleman?"

"Maidenlady, if you are truly Aureste Belandor's daughter, be certain that I offend family, friends, and allies by offering you the smallest aid, even so much as a bandage for your ankle. Nevertheless, I will conduct you to the nearest cottage, where I'll exert such influence as I own to gain you admittance."

"Oh," she exclaimed, "you might just as well throw a rope around my neck and drag me back to Ironheart behind your horse!"

"Good idea." A flat new voice entered the discussion.

Jianna's heart missed a beat. She wheeled to discover Onartino Belandor standing a few paces behind her. In the midst of the debate and the downpour, she had failed to notice his approach, and in that moment it seemed unbelievable that she had sensed nothing, because he was so extraordinarily large, looming there as huge and impervious as a rain-soaked colossus. The cold terror and hot hatred flared inside her and every nerve urged flight. She started to rise and the flash of pain from her ankle reminded her that she could barely walk, much less run. A rush of defeat and sick despair all but overwhelmed her. For a moment her eyes shut. Then she drew a deep breath, picked up her staff, and with its support stood up straight to face her hunter.

Onartino snapped his fingers sharply. "Heel," he commanded.

Her eyes widened a little in disbelief. She did not stir.

"Not trained yet?" Onartino inquired. "We'll fix that." One of his pockets yielded a small rawhide quirt. He gave it a flick, and the braided lash answered with a pert pop. Educational aid in hand, he started for her.

This time, she sensed, he truly meant to hurt her, and there was nothing she could do to elude him or to hold him off. Without conscious volition, she threw a glance of anguished appeal into the eyes of Dr. Falaste. His response was all that could be desired.

Without apparent haste he stepped in front of her, blocking Onartino's way. "Softly," he suggested in pleasant tones.

"Keep out of it, Rione," Onartino advised, finally acknowledging the other's presence.

Rione? The name was familiar. She had heard it spoken more than once, not long ago. At Ironheart? Yes. The memory clicked into place. Of course. Rione was that mysterious genius whose praises were sung in the infirmary. Why had he lied to her about his name? Or perhaps he hadn't lied. Maybe *Falaste* was simply his given name. All of this shot through her mind in a fraction of a second.

"Glad to keep out of it," Falaste or Rione or Falaste Rione returned in his uniquely calming voice, "so long as it's understood that there will be no violence here."

"Just a little instruction," Onartino assured him.

"With a whip? I think not."

"You *think* all the time, boy, and it doesn't amount to much. It never did. Step aside."

"Put the whip away. You'll not be using it on this girl."

"Do you know who and what she is?"

"She told me her father's name."

"Did she remember to mention that she belongs to me?"

"If I'm not mistaken, the institution of human slavery has been abolished."

"The institution of human marriage hasn't."

"You claim that she's your wife?"

"As soon as the East Reach Traveler turns up to make it legal. Me, I see no reason to wait, but Mother wants it done up in pink ribbons."

The doctor hesitated, then turned to Jianna and asked, "Is this true?"

She looked into his clear eyes and somehow never even thought of lying. "There's some truth in it. The fact is that they abducted me and then used threats and terror to force my consent. I did agree to wed this—this person here, but much against my will, and only to avoid immediate injury and dishonor."

"There, she confesses, she's plighted her skinny little troth. Still questioning my rights?" Onartino demanded.

"This is Magnifica Yvenza's desire?" the doctor inquired.

"Her plan. She's set on the match. You know how she is."

"I do. I see the evidence of her mind at work."

"You mean to cross her?"

The doctor answered with an infinitesimal shake of the head.

"Then you can go on ahead and tell them that I'm whipping my little bride back home to Ironheart. Run along, boy."

"Wait!" Jianna felt the stirring of incipient panic. "Don't go! Dr. Falaste, you can't let him take me back to that place. For pity's sake, help me!"

"Maidenlady, I've already violated loyalties for your sake. I can do nothing more."

"I thought you were a kind man, a decent man. Was I wrong? Look at Onartino Belandor standing there with his whip. Do you know what will happen if you leave me alone with him?"

"By your own admission, he is your betrothed. What passes between the two of you is a matter of family."

"He's not my betrothed; I was already promised to someone else. I was on my way to Orezzia to be wed when they attacked my carriage. This man and his people aren't family, they're just kidnappers. If you leave me in his hands, he'll kill me or worse."

"I don't mean to kill her," Onartino observed with the faintest hint of enjoyment. "Not before she's tasted the joys of motherhood, anyway. You're in the way here, Rione. Run along home."

"Please," Jianna whispered, eyes fixed on the doctor's face.

He glanced at her so briefly and indifferently that it seemed as if her plea had gone unheard, then informed Onartino, "I'll accompany you and the girl back to Ironheart."

"I told you to get out of this."

"We've two hours or more of walking before us," the doctor observed serenely. "Best waste no more time. Put the whip away. You've no use for it today."

"Sure about that?" Onartino stared down at the doctor, who stood some inches shorter than himself.

"Quite sure, as I know you're no fool, appearances occasionally notwithstanding."

Jianna stiffened. To her surprise, Onartino replied with a mere twist of the lips, a small grimace of contemptuous amusement. In silence he returned the quirt to his pocket. He was not going to use the lash on her. He was not going to use anything on her. She swallowed a sob, her relief tempered by recognition of the reprieve's probable brevity.

"Maidenlady, you'll ride," the doctor declared.

"She'll walk," said Onartino.

"She's injured her ankle."

"She'll survive."

"She'll delay us if we're held to her best pace," the doctor observed easily. "Unless, of course, you'd prefer to drag her by the hair."

"She deserves a lot worse than that, after what she did to Grumper," Onartino told him. "Fond of Grumper, aren't you, Rione? Well, I think she's killed him. He was guarding her. Somehow she got the better of him, beat the shit out of him. Probably used a rock. That's how she got away."

Jianna stared at him, dumbfounded. He met her gaze blandly.

"Grumper is dead?" The doctor was taken aback.

"I think so." Onartino shook his head. "Mother will be seeing red. That was her best hound."

"It's a lie!" Jianna found her voice. "I never struck the dog. Even if I wanted to, how could I? He'd have torn me apart if I'd tried it. If he was beaten, then somebody else did it."

"Who else had reason?" With a shrug of his heavy shoulders, Onartino addressed the doctor. "There you have it. Don't let the big eyes fool you. She's her father's daughter."

"I swear I never hurt Grumper." Jianna spoke urgently to the doctor, who was scrutinizing her face as if striving to read the mind and character behind it. For reasons that she could hardly define, it seemed essential to convince him. She did not want to watch the expression in his eyes transmute to hostility and disgust. "I wouldn't do such a cruel thing, I've never so much as slapped a Sishmindri. Please believe me."

"Maidenlady, I should like to believe you," he returned quite gently, "but I'm in no position to judge. Come, it's time to leave."

She gazed up at him, unable to comprehend how this man could offer kindness and assistance, then turn around and hand her over to her enemies. Passionate entreaty shone in her eyes. She saw compunction in his, but no yielding. In miserable silence she stood and limped a few paces to the horse. She could feel the weight of Onartino Belandor's regard as she went, but did not glance in his direction. The doctor boosted her into the saddle, then loosed the tether. For a wild moment she thought of clapping her heels to the horse's flanks and galloping away; but it was impossible, he held the reins firmly.

They moved off along the path, back the way that she had come, with the doctor leading the horse and Onartino bringing up the rear. Neither man could see her face. Jianna's shoulders slumped. She bowed her head and her tears flowed, invisible in the falling rain.

EIGHT

"I will add another five hundred diostres if they can be transferred to my command within twenty-four hours," Aureste Belandor offered.

"Impossible," declared the Governor Uffrigo.

"A thousand, then."

"My dear fellow, ten thousand wouldn't suffice." Uffrigo beamed his gentle smile. "It is not a question of money."

"It is always a question of money."

"Upon my honor, I never knew you for such a cynic." The governor did not trouble to conceal his amusement. "It is enough to shake my faith in human nature, just listening to you."

"Governor, I haven't come here to fence. The matter is pressing. Name your price. I will pay it."

"Ah, you mean that, don't you? I recognize desperation when I see it." The radiance of the gubernatorial smile dimmed, giving way to limpid candor. "Then let us speak openly like the true, close friends that we are."

The two true, close friends sat in the governor's private sitting room situated on the second story of the Cityheart. Here the atmosphere was lusciously warm, and the classical simplicity of the architecture warred with the Taerleezi governor's appetite for magnificence. Uffrigo's taste ran to massive furnishings heavily crusted with gilt carving. The walls glittered with vast mirrors ornately framed, the ceilings glittered with chandeliers dripping crystal, the brocade draperies swathing the windows glittered with thick golden fringe. The marble floor was polished to a hard gleam, and the Taerleezi emblem gracing the central medallion of the deep carpet glinted with golden thread.

The governor and his visitor occupied vast overstuffed armchairs. Between them stood a low table freighted with expensive edibles—out-of-season fruits, aged cheese, new bread, and a jeweled assortment of glazed sweets—all laid out in insistent profusion, for Uffrigo was nothing if not hospitable. The governor—faultlessly groomed, attired in handsome robes of tawny velvet—sat comfortably at ease. Aureste Belandor—carelessly dressed, eyes shadowed, and face haggard with sleeplessness—recognized the strategic disadvantage of his own position and for once did not care.

"Aureste, you shall have your Taerleezi troops in good time," Uffrigo promised melodiously. "That is certain. But I cannot spare them yet; they are needed here in the city. You must wait a little."

"I can't wait." Aureste took care to speak calmly. "Too much time has passed already. I'll increase my offer substantially, but that increase is contingent upon immediate delivery. You understand the reasons. I've explained the situation."

"Not entirely. It's my understanding that the Belandor carriage carrying your daughter was waylaid en route to Orezzia. The passengers, driver, and guards all died, but your daughter vanished without a trace. No one has seen her and there's been no demand for ransom, but you are convinced that she is still alive, held prisoner somewhere or other in the Alzira Hills. Correct so far?"

Aureste nodded.

"Is this conclusion based upon anything more than wishful thinking?"

"It is. I've access to certain intelligence whose source I can't divulge."

" ' . . . Whose source I can't divulge.' I've always admired that phrase, it has such a ring of righteousness. Despite your reticence, my dear fellow, I believe I can guess. As I recall, you've a rather gifted brother. But come, we'll say no more of that." Uffrigo chuckled warmly. "As always, you may rely on my discretion."

He was paid handsomely for that discretion. Aureste did not allow his expression to alter.

"Let us grant for the sake of argument that your intelligence is correct," the governor continued. "I don't understand the silence of her captors or the absence of a ransom demand, but let that pass for now. Do you have any idea of her exact location? If you had those troops you so much want here and now, would you know where to lead them?"

"I believe so. I've been given to understand that she's held in a stronghouse—a distinctive, recognizable style of construction. One of my agents has located just such a stronghouse buried in the woods of Alzira above the VitrOrezzi Bond, not far removed from the site of the attack. This is my target."

"Really? You are so certain? The right sort of architecture, convenient location, and that's enough to justify so costly an undertaking? There's nothing more? Have you any idea who inhabits this stronghouse?"

"I do." Aureste paused, disinclined to continue, but the governor sat watching with a bright-eyed expression of innocent curiosity that somehow managed to suggest the unhappy consequences of recalcitrance. "I know the inhabitants; it's an old association. There are mutual grievances."

"*Are* there indeed? The plot thickens." Uffrigo was patently charmed. "Then I must suspect that the assault upon your Belandor carriage was no random occurrence."

"I think not."

"Confide in me, my friend. Exactly who are these mysterious enemies of yours?"

The familiar anger boiled up inside him, but as always Aureste concealed every trace of it. He knew from hapless experience that the governor's seemingly idle curiosity was not to be denied—evasion was useless, and he attempted none. Inwardly cursing the fates that subordinated him to a playful

Taerleezi viper, he confessed, "They are family and retainers of my predecessor."

"Come again?"

"The surviving members of Onarto Belandor's household. The traitor Onarto, as you may recall, held the title of Magnifico Belandor before me."

"I wouldn't know. You were already magnifico by the time I was appointed to the Vitrisi post. Ah, never shall I forget the warmth of your welcome. A pity so few of the Faerlonnish share your sense of generous hospitality."

As usual, it was difficult to know whether or not the barb was intentional. Aureste said nothing.

"And this naughty Magnifico Onarto was executed as an enemy of Taerleez?" Uffrigo delved.

"No. He and his immediate family fled Vitrisi. Presumably he was warned of impending arrest in time to make good his escape. He took refuge in the woods for a time, I was told. But I've heard nothing of Onarto or his people in decades, and I'd imagined that branch of the family extinct or emigrated years ago."

"But the branch, as it were, has taken root and flourished. Perhaps Onarto lives on yet in sylvan splendor, cozily at one with nature."

"Perhaps," Aureste agreed blandly.

"So you suspect disgruntled kinsmen of stealing your fair daughter. But this is pure conjecture, is it not? Has your agent reported any sightings? Anything even to suggest, much less confirm her living presence in this stronghouse?"

"No."

"No. Well, then, I can't help but observe that your proposed expedition is highly speculative in nature. Only consider, my dear fellow. Why should your enemies abduct and hold pretty little Jianna in silence and secrecy? Where is the satisfaction in that? If they have her, wouldn't they want you to know it? Would they not, in fact, delight in tormenting you with all sorts of colorfully gruesome threats? If vengeance is the motive and your suffering the aim, they cannot remain silent."

"Unless they mean to plague me with uncertainty."

"There's an exquisite refinement. Are these people capable of such restraint?"

"I couldn't say." Aureste spoke the simple truth. He had revolved these same questions ceaselessly for days without reaching a satisfactory conclusion.

"It's a sad truth," Uffrigo mused, "that the simplest and most obvious answers to knotty questions are too often correct. In this case, despite your mysterious informant's opinion, you must consider the possibility that you've heard nothing of your daughter because there's nothing more to hear. The poor child is gone."

The governor spoke with the voice of common sense, and ordinarily Aureste would have accepted it as such. But Uffrigo was no ordinary source. With his brows arching high above wide eyes, his tender solicitude, his burlesque concern, the man begged for dismemberment. As always, Aureste controlled his impulses, but the words, the questions and suggestions, could not be ignored. Jianna dead? Murdered—perhaps tortured first? The pain that struck him was almost physical, and sharper than any he had known in years. He had felt something like it when Sonnetia Steffa had wed Vinz Corvestri, but never since, and for an instant the sensation was all but unbearable.

He pushed it away expertly. Uffrigo was wrong, she was alive. He had touched her mind, he had met her in some realm beyond reason; she was alive. Composure restored, he was able to reply with assurance, "I've reason to believe otherwise and therefore, in the matter of those troops, can brook no delay."

"Well, you'll brook a few days' worth, at the very least. There's no help for it. And please don't wound my feelings with further offers of money." Uffrigo sipped his wine with appreciation. "My good cynic, you must believe that I am in earnest when I tell you that the soldiers are needed here in Vitrisi. There's a veritable riot going on in the Spidery. That is no exaggeration. The exuberant Faerlonnish guttersnipes of the neighborhood are busy burning, pillaging, and murdering. Ostensibly they protest the quarantine. In reality, they seize the opportunity to loot. The best efforts of my troops barely suffice to contain the unrest. I can spare none of them."

"Scarcely a serious menace." Aureste's negligent shrug dismissed the insurgents. "It's an insult to your stout Taerleezi men to suggest otherwise. Lease me a single squadron, Governor. I'll pay you five thousand and return them to you within days. You can surely do without them for so short a term as that."

"Ah, you tempt like an evil spirit, my friend, but I cannot give in. You know that Palace Bonevvi was torched within the past week. Neither Councilman Coscaa nor his lady wife made it out alive. The councilman's zeal in defense of Taerleezi interests will be missed. Then there was the massacre of the Scythe Street guardsmen. And the murder of the Watch at Frog Well. The explosion and destruction at Gate Blackshield. The Sishmindri immolation, not two weeks ago. The attack on the Oats Street Armory and the mutilation of the Taerleezi dead. Your Faerlonnish resistance people have whipped this city into a frenzy and if I cannot oblige you at the moment in the matter of the troops, then you must lay the blame at Faerlonnish doors."

"I do so, Governor. And if burning the Spidery and everything in it to the ground would halt the plague, disinfect the city, and free a squadron of your troops to recover my daughter, then I will personally supply the oil and gunpowder."

"Ah, Aureste, Aureste." Uffrigo warbled a laugh. "I could almost imagine that you speak in earnest."

"I do."

"Your spirit is admirable. And I must confess, the concept is pleasing. I'm much inclined to accept your offer, but for the small matter of containing the blaze. Once the pestiferous

Spidery and its plaguey inhabitants are consumed, what prevents the fire from spreading throughout Vitrisi?"

Vitrisi could burn, and welcome, if its destruction delivered Jianna. He could scarcely voice this sentiment and therefore Aureste replied, "I've every confidence in the ability of the Taerleezi authorities to protect and preserve the city."

"We Taerleezi authorities have enough to occupy our attention without the additional nuisance of controlling creative home-grown efforts at municipal replanning. Make up your mind to it, my friend. You must wait some few days for those troops, and no sum of money is large enough to alter matters at this time."

It was no ploy. Uffrigo meant what he said. Expecting to encounter the usual venality, Aureste was taken aback. When the greatest of all weapons, money, seemed to lose its power, he found himself momentarily at a loss. Moreover, a certain filminess of the gubernatorial eyes, a smooth blankness of expression, silently signaled his dismissal.

For one moment the anger that he so often suppressed threatened to burst restraint. For one moment he doubted his own ability to control it. Then the habit of decades came to his rescue and he contrived to incline his head with an air of good grace, although he did not trust himself to speak.

"Come, come, my dear fellow," the governor encouraged. "It is only a brief delay, and we may yet hope for a happy conclusion. But if it should happen that all does not end well, then here's a thought to console you. As you yourself once remarked, it is not as if you had lost a son."

. . .

He was back in the grand Belandor carriage again, the Cityheart behind him, the streets of Vitrisi before and about him. For a time he yielded to an uncharacteristic sense of weary defeat, and the city flowed by unheeded. His mind turned in upon itself, drawn to the past, and he found his memory swarming with unwelcome images a quarter of a century old.

Onarto Belandor with his foolishly trusting face; the Magnifica Yvenza, formidable even as a young woman; a couple of sullen, dough-faced little sons, their names forgotten; various visitors, retainers, and dependents at Belandor House in the wake of the wars. He had not thought of them in years. Long ago he had perfected the art of excluding uncomfortable recollections, but somehow they found entrance now. Onarto was gone, doomed by his own kindly simplicity, but some of the others lived on to plot vengeance. Now they had taken Jianna and her sufferings were likely to tax their powers of inventive cruelty, because she was Aureste Belandor's daughter.

His eyes were stinging. It took him a moment to recognize the urge to weep, something he had not experienced in nearly half a lifetime. He did not give way to it now, but minutes passed before he regained full self-mastery. Presently, however, the magnifico's pronounced quality of natural resilience reasserted itself, and he began to notice his surroundings.

The carriage was rattling along Harbor Way. The warehouses rose on either side, their eaves bright and noisy with Scarlet Gluttons. At the Box an auction was in progress, and he saw at a glance that the bidding was slow. Perhaps the object of sale lacked wide appeal—it was a female Sishmindri displaying the loose, sagging belly and emaciated limbs indicative of recent pregnancy. Or so such signs were generally interpreted, but nobody truly knew, for the creatures had never been induced to breed in captivity. Certain owners actually regarded this sterility as an expression of unspoken defiance, but Aureste knew better. The Sishmindris were incapable of deliberate design; they hadn't the intelligence. If in bondage they produced no spawn—or sprats, or whatever they begot when left to their own devices—then the reason was simply biological.

Whatever her recent past, the female's flapping gut, scrawny legs, and manifest apathy surely depressed bidding. But another consideration might have been equally responsible. It had long been known that Sishmindris were susceptible to the plague. It had long been suspected but only recently proved that the disease could pass from amphibian to human. This scientific advance had triggered a spate of Sishmindri slaughter throughout the city. Certainly the majority of owners were too sensible to sacrifice their valuable chattel. But even among the canniest, a newly delivered specimen of unknown provenance invited suspicion. The female on the auction block was likely to sell for a small handful of silver, and her merchant-owner would take a substantial loss. Such was the sad state of the market.

She had probably hit the Vitrisi docks within the past twenty-four hours, freighted by ship from one of the inland river ports. Aureste's mind flew to the wharves, where the stevedores unloaded cargo and the merchant seamen drank away their free time in the waterfront taverns. Hardy men accustomed to labor, discipline, risk, and privation. A wealth of potential muscle, there.

Perhaps he need not wait for those Taerleezi troops after all. The sweepings of the waterfront could hardly compare with Uffrigo's trained guards, but there was much to be said for immediate availability.

Aureste issued orders and the carriage changed direction, heading toward Renuvi's Row, which bordered the waterfront and boasted no fewer than five roaring taverns, the heaviest concentration in the city. Long before he reached his destination, he caught the tang of smoke on the breeze, with its too-familiar suggestion of charred meat. Another vast bonfire in the Spidery, another mass cremation of the plague's nameless victims. But there was something different today, something wrong, and it took the anomaly a moment to register. The smoke was floating in from the west. It did not originate in the Spidery, but the odor was unmistakable and the implications were disturbing. Aureste frowned. Ordinarily he did not much concern himself with the raging progress of the plague through the slums. But the blaze of pyres creeping west across Vitrisi into the decent parts of town suggested a certain pestilential presumption impossible to ignore. He would ignore it for now, however. There were more immediate concerns.

On toward Renuvi's Row, but at the bottom of Goatsgraze Street came an unwelcome discovery. The carriage halted with a jolt. Shaken from his abstraction, Aureste looked out to behold a knot of Taerleezi soldiers and, behind them, a barrier of upright wooden timbers blocking off the street. A gate in the stockade, wide enough to admit passage of a wagon or carriage, stood firmly shut. The gate was marked with a big letter X daubed in red paint: the emblem of the quarantine. Here? Aureste's brows rose in surprised displeasure. He snapped his fingers and one of the soldiers, attracted by obvious affluence, approached at once.

"How long has that thing been here?" Aureste's gesture condemned the barrier.

"Quarantine was slapped on two days ago, sir," replied the guard.

"It's in my way. Open up and let me through."

"No one but the vapor-men allowed in or out, sir."

"You'll make an exception for me." Aureste flashed a coin.

"Don't you understand? It's the plague."

"I'm protected." This was true. Aureste had recently taken to carrying a pomander packed with select herbs soaked in vinegar, tortoise urine, and spirits of ammonia, guaranteed by the governor's own physician to ward off infection. His driver was not similarly fortified, but the driver was replaceable.

"Can't do it, sir." The guard spoke with manifest regret, his eyes fixed on the silver in his questioner's hand.

Aureste considered the efficacy of threats and concluded that bluster would not serve him. "I've business in Renuvi's Row," he explained shortly. "What is the best route?"

"Quarantine perimeter includes the entire area as far west as Spigot Street, and north to the edge of the Mews."

"As large as that," Aureste murmured.

"You'll have to go around it, sir."

"That is a considerable distance." The drive would be

lengthy and the afternoon was already well advanced, but
there was no alternative; the Taerleezi guard was clearly not to
be swayed.

"When you're passing nigh the big smokes, a mask were
best, sir."

He did not need a mask. He had his expensive and doubtless reliable pomander, but there was little point in educating
the guard. "You wear no mask yourself," Aureste observed.
"Tell me, my friend, do you and your comrades not fear the
local miasma?"

"No, sir. I chew chicory and carry a Troxius medal. We all
do. I keep to the right side of the fence and see to it that other
folk do the same."

"Commendable. For your good work, then." Aureste relinquished the coin, and the guard withdrew. Leaning out the
window to instruct his driver, Aureste paused, caught by a
scene unfolding directly before him. The wooden stockade
blocking his passage extended the entire width of the street,
terminating on either side at the wall of a tall house or tene-
ment. Similar guarded barricades, probably scores of them,
defined the quarantined area. So long as the quarantine endured, there was no departure from the plague's domain save
by illicit means ranging from bribery to arcane device. By all
accounts, however, life within the proscribed territories was
nightmarish in quality, and inhabitants wild to escape often
resorted to desperate measures. One such inhabitant was
doing so now.

It was a woman, young and slim, poorly clad, with dark
hair streaming in disarray. Her facial features could not be
judged at such distance, but the slender figure and long hair
immediately recalled Jianna. She stood atop the roof of one
of the four-story tenements fronting Goatsgraze Street. Having somehow made her way to that height, she had managed
to affix a rope ladder to a bit of ornamental ironwork. Now
tossing the free end of the ladder from the roof, she began to
descend. She was nimble but apparently unhinged, for she

made not the slightest effort to conceal herself. Taerleezi guards converged on her at once.

"Go back," one of them called out. "Back into quarantine."

Pausing midway down the ladder to regard the speaker, the girl replied in clear and very reasonable tones, "Things keep fading in and out, back there. And then you can't hear or see good. It's get out or fade out."

Aureste could see her face more clearly now. She appeared less crazed than hugely obstinate, her eyes slitted, her jaw set in boundless determination. She displayed no sign of confusion or illness. After a moment, she resumed her descent.

"Forbidden to leave quarantine," a guard expostulated. "Go back! You understand me? Go back!"

She neither replied nor obeyed. Down the ladder she backed methodically, while citizens in the street, attracted in numbers by the novelty, yelled frantic warnings, all of them ignored. A command was issued and one of the guards advanced bearing the infamous Taerleezi Toothpick: a pike of exceptional length, designed to maintain suitable distance between executioner and potentially contagious victim. A final warning went unheeded and, amid the shouts of the spectators, the Toothpick plunged into the would-be escapee's back. She fell from the ladder, dead before she hit the stones of the street.

Aureste winced. Her generic similarity to his daughter inspired that response, but in fact his sympathies were hardly engaged. She had been suicidally stupid, or perhaps just suicidal. If the latter, then her plan had succeeded and all had concluded in accordance with her wishes.

A sizable contingent of citizens lacked the magnifico's consoling philosophy. As the guards tossed an oiled pall over their victim's body, the cries of protest intensified. When a smoldering splint attached to the end of the Taerleezi Toothpick was used to set the pall alight, the cries gave way to howls of wrath. The blaze mounted, the flames jumped, and the emotions of the spectators did likewise. The guards were only following standard procedure; a purifying bath of flame was believed to render a possibly plague-ridden corpse relatively safe for handling and prompt removal. The fire benefited all, but the citizens cared nothing for public safety; something in the spectacle of a young woman's slaughter and instant immolation seemed to have driven them beyond reason.

The furious outcry swelled and somebody threw a stone that grazed a Taerleezi brow, drawing blood. A pelting rain of rocks and refuse followed. The outnumbered guards drew forth their truncheons, ordinarily effective in subduing unruly Vitrisians—but not today. The citizens snarled and stood their ground. For once it was the guards who gave way, the small band of them retreating in tolerably good order. They were heading for the nearest Watch station. Within minutes they would return with reinforcements, but for now, remarkably, the day belonged to the Faerlonnish.

The elated citizens, their energies now unfocused, milled in aimless excitement until the arms blazoned on the Belandor carriage drew notice. The lone passenger was recognized and the familiar yelping cry arose: *Kneeser.*

A flying rock hit the carriage with a thump. And another. Yet another, better aimed, whizzed in through the window to miss Aureste's head by a hair. A quiet curse escaped him. He rapped the roof sharply, signaling the driver to depart. Goatsgraze Street allowed no room to turn the big carriage about, and therefore the driver whipped his team left toward the mouth of some nameless alley. The chorus of vituperation broke as citizens scurried to clear the path. Only one of them, a bold and acrobatic zealot, dared to fling himself upon the vehicle as it passed, thrusting head and upper body in through the window.

Aureste gazed into a swarthy young face ablaze with hostile excitement. Abuse foamed from its mouth. Almost before he recognized his own intention, he had drawn the dagger from his belt and slashed the face deeply from forehead to jaw. He had not lifted the dagger against another human being in years, but he had lost none of his skill.

The intruder howled and clapped a hand to his eye. Blood welled between the fingers. A vigorous shove thrust him from the window. The Belandor carriage rumbled on unhindered, pursued only by the imprecations of the witnesses.

His route was circuitous, and he did not reach Renuvi's Row before late afternoon. A quick reconnaissance informed him that two of the five taverns he sought were closed, their clientele doubtless reduced by the pestilence ravaging the area. A third was open for business but deserted save for an inert sprinkling of sodden inebriates. The last two were open and comparatively lively, but the patrons ran largely to aging tipplers and flush mariners disinclined to accept perilous employment. Aureste Belandor labored and haggled at length but his quarry resisted all blandishments and at the end of the day he had secured no more than three remotely acceptable recruits.

· · ·

The mists lay heavy on the northern hills. In the late afternoon, at that time of year, the daylight was already beginning to fail. The landmarks were shrouded, the peaks and skyline obliterated, the trail all but invisible. The ground underfoot was damp and yielding. From time to time, it trembled.

A lone traveler making his way on foot along the slopes heard the growl of subterranean thunder. The ground shook beneath his feet, throwing him to his knees. And as he crouched there, the shuddering world altered impossibly. The ground beneath him lost its solidity, even its reality. He did not sink in swamp or quicksand, but lost himself in the insubstantiality of a dream. A cry escaped him and his voice—immensely distant—seemed to echo through a limitless void. The surrounding mists clenched; the faint light filtering through them bent and warped, split and jumped, confounding vision. And behind those mists, or within them, resided a huge Awareness.

Terrified, he threw himself full length, clutching at the grasses beneath him—the rocks—the ground—fingers scrabbling in search of solidity that no longer existed. In an instant the world had become an alien realm wherein he had no place. Here he was lost, helpless, and deeply unwelcome.

It ended as abruptly as it had begun. The quivering ceased, the moment passed, and normal physicality resumed. For some minutes thereafter, he lay where he had fallen, body pressed hard to the chill, familiar ground, hands twined deep in the dead grasses. His emotions were manifold, but they did not include confusion. He knew what had happened, and why.

Bearded face pale, forehead sweat-dewed, he climbed to his feet and resumed his interrupted trek, nerves braced against a repetition.

On through the silent mists he trudged, the moist air darkening about him as he went, and now his path ascended sharply. Another tiny quake shook the hills, this one so minor that he kept his footing. A quarter hour of arduous climbing brought him to a broad flat shelf abutting a sheer perpendicular wall of granite. The path continued on through a narrow cleft in the wall, but the way was guarded. A pair of adult Sishmindri males stood there for all the world like human sentries. Both were fully mature and powerfully built, their brow ridges all but invisible, their skulls flat behind the bulging golden eyes. Their demeanor was singular: neither fearful nor servile. More surprising yet—they were armed, after a fashion. Faerlonnish law in every city forbade Sishmindris the use of weapons upon pain of death to the amphibian and heavy fine to the owner. But these two bore great clubs reinforced with spikes of chipped stone. Astonished, the traveler halted. Human and Sishmindris regarded each other.

He had no idea how long the mutual inspection continued. The huge amphibian eyes told him nothing. At last he ventured to speak.

"Greetings," he offered in the guttural Sishmindri tongue.

The golden eyes did not blink, but the air sacs fluttered, a sure sign of surprise. Not often did the Sishmindris hear their own language upon human lips. After a moment, one of the guards, if such they were, replied briefly, "Forbidden."

"I come in friendship," declared the traveler, with more courtesy than he would have shown any human blocking his path. "I seek the summit of the Quivers."

"Forbidden," the amphibian repeated.

"Why?"

"Ground of virtue," the other explained. "Ground of power."

"Yes, I know. That is what I seek."

"Not here. Forbidden. Ours."

"Yours?"

"Ours. Our people, our place. Our ground."

The traveler's astonishment deepened. Never had he encountered the like. Sishmindris did not claim ownership of territory, any more than frogs claimed ownership of a pond, so far as he knew. But then, he had never conversed with frogs.

"I do not challenge your claim," he returned. "I want only a small space for shelter."

"No. No men. Ground of virtue, sacred ground of power. Ours." The amphibian speaker lifted his club and puffed his sacs. "You go."

The traveler considered. The arcane technique at his command could undoubtedly win his way past the sentries. But the exercise would be lengthy, taxing, and certain to leave him depleted. He might ascend to the summit, there to set up residence upon a site richly infused with the energy of the Source; the Sishmindris could hardly stop him. But thereafter he would be their enemy. Their claim to ownership of the land was so hopelessly absurd and clearly doomed that it engaged his sympathies. Had humans barred his path, he would not have hesitated to deal with them as need dictated, but the amphibians were another matter.

"And what do you do," he inquired on impulse, "when the world becomes unreal?"

"Wait, and trust in ground of virtue. Our ground."

"I shall seek elsewhere, then," the traveler declared. "There are other possibilities." And so there were, provided the arcanists of the Veiled Isles remembered the ancient cleansing procedures.

"You go. Go."

"Farewell. Good fortune to you and your people."

Once again the amphibian air sacs fluttered in amazement and the hitherto silent member of the guardian pair now spoke up to inquire, "What is your name?"

"I am called Grix Orlazzu."

"Seek in the north, Grix Orlazzu. There are realms of virtue within the Wraithlands. Go north."

"I will do so. Good-bye." So saying, Grix Orlazzu took his leave. The mists swallowed him at once.

NINE

The boarhound lay motionless on the floor of his mistress' bedroom. His eyes were closed, his body limp. A threadbare blanket had been spread beneath him; no other covering softened the bare boards. A few feet away a generous blaze crackled on the grate, another rare concession to comfort in that ascetic space. The dog's external wounds had been bathed and dressed. A bowl of chopped meat sat inches from his nose, but the aroma did not wake him. Nor did the sound of his mistress' voice, although she called his name often.

Yvenza Belandor sat cross-legged on the floor beside the injured hound. She wore her usual plain dark gown, and her marbled hair was twisted into its usual knot. But her expression, comprising grief and anger, was uncharacteristic. Beside her knelt Nissi, colorless and insubstantial as fog, her face expressing nothing beyond trepidation.

"Please," Nissi whispered. "Please, Magnifica."

"No." Yvenza's eyes did not stray from the still canine form.

"Only today."

"No." Yvenza stretched forth a hand to scratch lightly behind the dog's ear. Grumper never stirred.

"Please. Please let me."

"I said no. Don't try my patience. In any case, it's too late. He's done."

"No." Nissi bent low and pressed her cheek to Grumper's skull. She remained so for some seconds, eyes shut and hands pressing the dog's muzzle, then sat up to announce almost inaudibly, "He is still here."

"Your fancy."

"His time is almost gone. The connection is like the ghost of a cobweb. But there is still something."

"If so, my voice will bring him back."

"He has strayed too far to hear. But he will hear me and perhaps he will come. If you let me call through the spaces that are not."

"You won't. I give you no leave." The other stared at her with enormous eyes, and Yvenza added sharply, "Don't speak of this again. The arcane ways are not for you."

There was a long silence during which Nissi's eyes sought the motionless canine form and remained there. At last, she ventured in the smallest of whispers, "But. I. Can."

"You will not." Yvenza's eyes and voice went steely. "You haven't the right. Do you understand me?"

The pale head bobbed. The pale eyes remained downcast.

"The talent resides in House Belandor. So it has always been. But you are not a true Belandor, not the product of any union recognized by law. You have no right to the name, the wealth, the power, or the talent. Your use of the arcane skills is presumptuous. It is impertinent."

"It is natural to me." Nissi's response was barely audible.

"And an insult to me. A reminder of something best forgotten. I do not suffer insults tamely, girl. You ought to know that by now." No response was forthcoming, and Yvenza pressed on. "You will respect my wishes. You will abstain from all practice of the art so long as you reside beneath my roof. You will give me your word on this."

Nissi replied with a seemingly unconscious, almost invisible shake of the head.

"In charity I have sheltered and fed you throughout the years. In return I am entitled at the very least to your respect and obedience. Should I fail to receive my due, I can't be faulted for turning you out to fend for yourself. How far, I wonder, would your talents carry you on your own in the cold world? Would you like to find out?"

Another tiny, voiceless negative.

"Then you will renounce the arcane art and its practice. I want your promise."

A couple of large tears spilled from Nissi's eyes.

"I don't hear you," Yvenza observed.

"Roof." The syllable seemed to fight its way past huge barriers.

"What?"

"Beneath your roof. Promise."

"I hope you aren't trying to be clever." The implied threat seemed almost an afterthought. Yvenza's attention had returned to the boarhound. Grumper lay limp and inert as ever. His mistress laid a hand upon him. "Are you still here?" she asked in a softened voice that few human listeners ever heard. "Grumper, lad?"

"No," Nissi said. "I felt him leave a moment ago. He is gone now."

"So I've known for the past half hour." Yvenza straightened. "That girl will smart for it."

"With . . . black eyebrows."

"Aureste's daughter, yes. When they bring her back, I'll hamstring her. That should discourage future excursions."

"She . . . likes cheese."

"Does she? Perhaps I'll ram three or four pounds of Westmarch Blue down her throat."

"She did not hit Grumper."

"What did you say?"

"She did not hit him."

"How do you know?"

Nissi studied the dead dog in silence.

"Look at me."

Nissi's lower lip quivered. Her small hands began to shake. Her ordeal was cut short by arrival of a servant bearing the news of Master Onartino's return, accompanied by Falaste Rione, with the kneeser's daughter in tow.

· · ·

The rain ended well before they reached Ironheart, but Jianna remained soaked to the skin and chilled to the bone. The chill deepened as she beheld the stronghouse rising in all its solidity before her. Once again the urge to flee swept through her and she eyed the reins, wondering if she might snatch them from the doctor's hand. But even as she watched, his grasp tightened, almost as if he felt or read her thought. The inexorable progress continued, bearing her to the side gate in the outer wall, through the gate and into the courtyard, across the courtyard and around the house to the front entrance, before which they halted.

There had to be something she could do. Impossible that she, the daughter of Aureste Belandor, could sit there so passive, so acquiescent.

The doctor helped her down from the horse. At least she did not have to suffer Onartino's touch. Falaste's assistance in climbing the low stone steps to the front door was actually welcome. Then they were through and she was back inside Ironheart, in the grim entry hall that was always dim even on the brightest of days, which this day conspicuously was not. And there was Yvenza advancing to meet them.

She had attempted escape. The boarhound was dead. There would be consequences, possibly horrific. Jianna's innards knotted, and she wondered if criminals facing death by torsion felt the same. The criminals were comparatively fortunate, however; they were not obliged to face Yvenza Belandor's wrath.

But Yvenza did not appear wrathful; quite the contrary, in fact. She was smiling as she approached, her eyes filled with hitherto unrevealed light and warmth. Never before had Jianna seen this woman display such natural maternal affection, nor dreamed that it was there at all. Then she saw that Yvenza was not looking at her son, had barely noticed his presence. Her radiant regard was fixed on the doctor.

"Falaste, lad. Welcome home." She extended both hands, which he took in his own, pressed lightly, and released.

"Magnifica." He addressed her with a mixture of warmth and deep respect.

"How long shall we have you here with us?"

"Several days at the very least."

"The more the better. You are needed. They're clamoring for you in the infirmary. No one else will do."

"Any new admissions?"

"Three within the past two weeks. Our Ghostly friends grow reckless and unlucky."

"Through anger, I think. I'll look in on them at once."

"No, you won't. Not before you've eaten and rested."

"Magnifica, that can wait."

"Ah, Falaste, that foolish large heart will be your ruin, one day."

There was something in Yvenza's expression, her smile and her eyes, that struck Jianna as extraordinarily familiar, something that she had seen countless times. Familiarity notwithstanding, it took her a moment to place the memory. The look in Yvenza's eyes as they rested upon the doctor was just the same expression that shone in her father's eyes when he looked at *her*. A pang shot through her then, but even as she watched, Yvenza's eyes shifted from Falaste to her biological son, and changed.

"Well, boy," the matriarch observed with a congratulatory air, "I see you've recovered the little runaway bride. Good work."

"Too easy," replied Onartino.

"Perhaps next time she'll offer more of a challenge."

"I doubt it."

"I suspect you underestimate your sweet soul mate here. Does he not, girl?" Doubling her fist, Yvenza struck suddenly and strongly.

Taken off guard, Jianna made no move to block or evade the blow, which stretched her full length on the floor. Shocked and dizzy, she sat up slowly, cradling her jaw.

"That's for Grumper," Yvenza informed her.

"Magnifica!" the doctor remonstrated. He took a step forward as if to intervene.

"You stay where you are, *Falaste, lad*," Onartino advised. Turning to his mother, he suggested, "Grumper deserves more. He was worth ten of her."

"No doubt. And he was worth ten of you into the bargain, so hold your tongue," she returned, then met Jianna's eyes and commanded, "Get up."

If she got up, Yvenza would probably hit her again. If she cowered on the floor, she would look craven. Before she had reached a decision, the doctor spoke again.

"Magnifica, you should know that this maidenlady has been injured. She's twisted her ankle and can scarcely walk."

"That's convenient. Maybe I needn't hamstring her after all. Perhaps a good whipping and a few days without food will do."

"You should also know"—Jianna ventured to enter the discussion—"that I did not beat your dog."

"Indeed." Yvenza considered. "In that case, how did you get away from him?"

In her eagerness to proclaim her innocence, she had failed to anticipate that inevitable question. Jianna felt her face flush. Her imagination churned uselessly. No remotely convincing lie or evasion suggested itself, and at last she replied, "I won't tell you that."

"I urge you to reconsider." Yvenza kicked her in the stomach.

Jianna gasped and doubled, clutching herself. When her distressed breathing eased, Yvenza repeated the question. "How did you get away from him?"

Jianna stared at the floor.

"That first kick was scarcely a nudge. The next one takes out your front teeth," Yvenza remarked conversationally. "A pity to spoil such pretty pearly whites, but I'll force myself."

"She's mine, I'll handle it. With a good leather strap," Onartino offered.

"Shut up, boy."

"Maidenlady," the doctor appealed, and his voice owned the power to draw her eyes from the floor to his face. "It is best by far to answer the magnifica's questions and to tell her the truth. For your own sake, believe this."

She did believe it. Yvenza would not kill her at present, but the woman was certainly willing and able to inflict serious injury. And what good would it do to escape and return to Belandor House, maimed for life? In such circumstances as these, Aureste Belandor would surely counsel compliance or at least the appearance thereof. Tossing the hair back from her face, Jianna shifted her gaze to Yvenza's eyes and answered coldly, "Very well. I drugged the dog with a sleeping potion."

"Kalkriole?"

"Yes."

"How did you get him to drink it?"

"I gave him doctored food pellets."

" 'She . . . likes cheese.' " Yvenza nodded to herself. "And then, when he was helpless, you picked up a rock and beat him to death."

"Then, when he was helpless, I ran for the woods." Jianna arose with care. Her jaw and her midsection ached; her ankle throbbed. "If you won't credit me with common decency, at least credit me with common sense. When I had the chance to get away, and every second counted, do you really think that I'd have tarried to beat an unconscious dog? Within a few yards of the household sentry, whose attention might easily have been caught by the sound of the blows? I'm not that stupid. As for the escape attempt itself, you can punish me if you will, but you can scarcely blame me. If you were in my position, Yvenza Belandor, you'd have done exactly the same."

They were all staring at her and Jianna wondered if she would be struck to the floor again or worse. At last, Yvenza inquired, with a certain sinister mildness, "And if you did not kill Grumper yourself, then whom do you accuse?"

Your murderous brute of a son, most likely. Jianna's eyes jumped to Onartino's face, which was empty and blank as unused paper. *He probably lost his filthy temper.* Aloud she replied, "I wasn't there, I didn't see. I accuse no one."

"Not directly, at any rate." For a glittering instant Yvenza's eyes shifted to Onartino. He sustained the scrutiny unmoved, and her attention returned to Jianna. "Let us give you the benefit of the doubt and assume that you tell the truth. Indeed, I suspect that you do. There remains the matter of your flight. The attempted desertion of your own betrothed, my poor devoted son. Did you mean to break his sensitive heart? We must see to it that such an act of cruelty is never repeated. My own thoughts lean toward your permanent disablement. Would that do the trick, I wonder? What do you think, niece?"

My father will tear the flesh off your bones if you hurt me. The threat rose automatically to her lips, but she held it in, for Aureste Belandor's name, a formidable charm throughout her life, held no power here.

"Look at those eyes," Yvenza suggested with a smile. "Her father's eyes, to the life. Notice the fire there. She'd burn me to cinders with those eyes—if only she could. In the interest of self-preservation, we'd best extinguish that blaze."

"Don't do anything to make her ugly, or I won't have her," Onartino warned.

"You'll have her with her face turned inside out, if you're told to," Yvenza informed him. "But now that you mention it, I perceive the difficulty. You are required to sire an heir upon this girl, and it wouldn't do to demand performance beyond your capabilities, my son. Very well, we shall not mar her beauty—today, at any rate. How best to damp a fire, then?" Yvenza affected to ponder. "Water usually serves. Yes. Our little runaway shall spend the next week cooling her heels in the subcellar, where the water on the floor rarely exceeds an inch in depth, except when the cesspit overflows."

"I'm not afraid of your subcellar." Jianna lifted her chin.

She knew that she ought to hold her tongue, but could not. "As for the cesspit, I feel that I've been living in one since the day I was brought here."

"Take care, maidenlady." Yvenza's face was unreadable. "I find myself in danger of coming to like you." She turned to her son. "Onartino, ring for someone to take her down below. And don't let me hear you offer to do it yourself."

"Magnifica, this won't do." The doctor spoke up with great courtesy and great firmness. "The maidenlady has been injured, soaked, and chilled. She must not suffer further abuse."

"Did you say 'must not' to me, Falaste?" Yvenza inquired gently.

"I speak as a physician. I trust you don't mean to kill her?"

"Correct."

"Then keep her out of that death trap of a subcellar or she'll take a fever within hours. Be certain of that."

"You seem much concerned for her welfare. Do you know who and what she is?"

"I do."

"Then you must also know that she won't escape punishment."

"Allow me to offer a suggestion. Punish her by setting her to work in the infirmary for the next week. I can use the assistance."

"Nonsense. That is a holiday."

"I don't speak of ladling soup and rolling bandages. She would do the real work—emptying bedpans, mopping up the vomit, changing soiled dressings, bathing infected wounds—all of it. For a gently reared young woman, that will be punishment indeed. And it would be of great help to me."

"If it's help you need or want, then you're welcome to borrow the servant of your choice. Any or all of them will prove more useful to you than this reluctant princess here. She'll take her lessons in the subcellar, and if she should happen to contract an ague, it will serve to drive the point home."

"Magnifica, indulge me," the doctor persisted. "I ask you in the name of my loyalty to grant me this personal favor."

"Do you, lad?" Yvenza hesitated. "Ah, you know me too well. When you ask so, I can't deny you. Very well, you may take charge of the girl, but mind you work her hard. She is not to enjoy it."

"I don't think it likely that she will."

"Then she's yours for the duration of your stay." Turning to Jianna, Yvenza observed, "Within the confines of the infirmary, you will obey Dr. Rione's commands without question or argument. You understand me?"

Jianna inclined her head, too relieved by her avoidance of the subcellar to resent this newest form of servitude. Out of the corner of her eye she glimpsed Onartino's face, which for once had lost its impassivity. He was eyeing the doctor with a look of sullen antipathy.

One of the cold drafts of Ironheart swept the hall, raising gooseflesh beneath her sodden garments. Jianna shivered. Her teeth started to chatter and she clamped her jaw, but saw that her reaction had not gone unnoticed by Dr. Rione.

"Magnifica, I've reconsidered," announced the doctor. "I'll have that meal after all. Is there soup in the kitchen?"

"There is always soup in the kitchen."

"Lentil onion?"

"See for yourself. After you've eaten and attended to your patients, come to me and we will talk."

"I'll look forward to that, Magnifica."

He looked and sounded as if he meant it, Jianna noted with wonder. And Yvenza's maternal smile had reappeared.

"Maidenlady, come with me." The doctor's courteous tone turned the command into a request.

She obeyed willingly, glad to remove herself from the dangerous vicinity of the matriarch. Onartino's gaze pressed her as she went. Through the galleries she followed Falaste to the kitchen, where a clutch of servants greeted him warmly. The doctor seemed a near-universal favorite. Jianna watched with interest as he returned the greetings in kind. As he spoke, he stripped off his hooded rain cloak, tossing it casually across the back of a chair. She saw then that his thick hair was a very dark brown, almost the same color as her own. His lean frame was plainly clad in serviceable garments.

"*Good to see you again, boy . . .*"

"*What's happening with the Ghosts?*"

"*Did you see 'em crunch any Taers?*"

"*Did you bring any ferret feet?*"

"*Welcome home, lad.*"

"Thanks. Here's your feet, Skreps." The doctor handed a small bundle to one of the potboys. "Try to make them last."

"You're the flashfire, Rione!"

"Tell that to Celisse and make her believe it." The doctor, evidently quite at ease, picked up a chair, placed it beside the fireplace, and turned to Jianna. "Sit here, maidenlady. Rest, warm yourself, and dry your clothing as well as you can. You'll have little leisure for it later on."

Again she obeyed willingly, removing her wet cloak and spreading it on the hearth, placing her wet shoes and stockings beside it, stretching her icy hands and feet toward the fire. The heat sent the blood coursing through her veins. Her fingers and toes tingled agreeably. An involuntary sigh escaped her and she let her eyes close. For a while she sat motionless, allowing the warmth to work its way clear through her. Her thoughts slowed and her mind emptied itself; she might even have fallen asleep for a moment or two.

The aroma of food recalled her to consciousness. She opened her eyes upon a bowl of thick soup and a heel of bread wordlessly proffered by the doctor.

"Thank you." She took the food. He started to turn away and Jianna, seized with some inexplicable urge to hold him a little longer, inquired inconsequentially, "Who is Celisse?" *Wife?* she wondered. *Sweetheart?*

"My sister."

"Older or younger?"

"Younger."

"She's not here at Ironheart?"

"Not these past three years."

"Everyone here welcomes you home. But you and your sister aren't—kin to the Belandors?" she probed. *Related to Yvenza? Or by-blows like Nissi?*

"No."

She paused, expecting an explanation, but none was offered. The doctor was civil enough but distinctly reserved, and if she pressed him further the conversation would assume the aspect of an interrogation. She nodded and began to spoon her soup. Falaste Rione took a seat at the kitchen table among the servants, with whom he ate and chatted on a basis of apparent equality.

She herself had never taken a meal at table with a menial, not even with Reeni, of whom she had been genuinely fond. The idea would simply not have occurred to her.

Was he a servant himself, then—some sort of privileged, upper-level servant? Surely not; not with that educated speech of his, the excellent quality of his manners, and the medical knowledge. Something in between?

The food was good and filling. As Jianna ate, her energy and optimism returned. The warmth of the fire was likewise comforting. Her skirts were starting to dry. She could gladly have stayed there eating soup and covertly studying the doctor for hours. All too soon, however, he rose from the table and approached her to announce, "Maidenlady, it is time to set to work. There is much to do."

· · ·

Aureste Belandor sat at his desk, blind eyes fixed on the oftblotted paper sheet before him. For the past half hour he had striven to pen a reply to the Magnifico Tribari's very courteous inquiry concerning the Maidenlady Jianna Belandor's delayed arrival, but the right words eluded him. The right words did not exist. For the moment he had given up trying, and his mind wandered the wooded slopes of the Alzira Hills.

The thump of a knock on the study door roused him from his reverie. Aureste blinked. "Come," he said.

The door opened and a Sishmindri head poked in.

"Woman," announced the amphibian.

"Woman? What woman?"

"No name."

"Throw her out. Don't trouble me again with such nonsense, or you will be whipped."

Incredibly, the Sishmindri ventured a reply. "You say, let this one in, else be whipped."

"Ah. That one. Why didn't you say so? Admit her."

The Sishmindri's head withdrew and then a familiar figure wrapped in a cloak of grey-brown frieze stepped over the threshold. Aureste eyed her without interest. "Well, Brivvia," he said. "Come forward. You may seat yourself."

"Thank you, Honored Magnifico." The Magnifica Corvestri's maid obeyed, perching gingerly on the edge of the same chair she had occupied upon the occasion of her previous interview. "Thank you, sir."

"What have you to tell me?" He made an effort to fix his attention on her.

"Well, firstly that I'm sorry, Honored Magnifico, truly I am, very sorry indeed, sir, and I hope you can forgive me."

"For what?" His interest remained minimal.

"For taking so long about it. You wanted quick action, you made that plain. But I must say it took some doing. There's usually guards or servants hanging about the corridor, and then there's a whopper of a padlock on the door. Getting past all of that was quite a trick, I can tell you."

Aureste's mind still sought the Alzira Hills. He controlled its wandering impulse with difficulty. What was the woman jabbering about? He had issued her orders, not long ago, although it now seemed vastly distant. She was to serve as his agent in Corvestri Mansion. It had all seemed important at the time.

"Well, I did it," Brivvia announced with a certain air of triumphant shame. "I got in."

"In?"

"The master's workroom. And truly, 'twasn't at all what I expected. I thought there'd be dead bodies all cut up and laid out on tables. And hearts and hands and heads and bowels scattered all over. And crystals sending out magic rays that would turn me into a sheep. But there wasn't none of that. It was just a room, an untidy room at that, stuffed with all kinds of trash, but nothing that scared me. Why, it was only—"

"Brevity, woman."

"Yessir. I searched, very thorough like you told me, and found nothing of no use to you. But I did the other things, Honored Magnifico," she added placatingly. "And they went off all right."

"Other things?" His mind slipped gears. For a moment he did not know what she was talking about.

"That little packet you gave me. I've tacked it to the bottom of the top drawer of the master's desk." She paused, evidently expecting congratulations.

"Oh. Yes." The exquisitely forged letters establishing Vinz Corvestri's connection with the Faerlonnish resistance movement were now in place, awaiting discovery by the first remotely competent investigator authorized to search Corvestri Mansion. Aureste found that he did not care in the slightest.

"That's what you wanted, isn't it, Honored Magnifico?" She was regarding him with a puzzled frown.

"It was."

"Went clear against my better nature, it did, but I followed your orders, sir. I'm not lying about this, either." No reply was forthcoming and she added, "I followed *all* your orders, if you get my drift."

"Then I am satisfied."

She seemed to expect additional commentary or inquiry.

Her frown deepened, and at last she prompted cautiously, "Well then, sir—would you like to see it, then?"

"It? What are you talking about?" His patience was beginning to fray, and he wanted to be rid of her.

"Why, you told me that I must bring something of my lady's, and I could see there was no help for it, so I've done what you said. Here it is. Take a look at that, sir." From some recess beneath her cloak, Brivvia produced a pair of gloves; very elegantly fashioned of the thinnest, palest grey kid, elaborately cut and pierced to display a lining of emerald silk.

Aureste's recollections stirred at the sight, for he recognized the gloves, although he had not seen them in nearly twenty-five years. The young Sonnetia Steffa strolled across his memory. She walked beside him along a path overlooking the sea. A stiff salt breeze had pulled some of her chestnut hair free of its confining pins. Now the shining strands whipped wildly about her head, and she was laughing, her eyes very bright and her cheeks very pink, her hands lifted to capture the fugitive locks—hands clad in those distinctive gloves. He reached out and caught one of her hands, felt the pressure of his grasp returned, and for a while they stood there blind to the world around them, while her hair streamed free in the wind.

And then, a different picture, a different place—this time, the bare and wintry garden behind Steffa House. Skeletal branches, withered stalks, dry fountains. Lifeless. Sonnetia sat on a small bench of white marble, gloved hands clasped in her lap. Her face was almost as white as the bench, but still the most beautiful face in his world. There was room for two on that bench, but he was not welcome to join her there. And now her voice echoed in his mind across the years, although he did not want to hear it.

"*. . . I did not let myself believe it, but all that they say is true. You have become the friend and the servant of the Taerleezis.*"

"*I've protected my House,*" he heard his own voice answer.

"*You have protected your own fortune.*"

"And yours as well. Do you think that your father would hold Steffa House, were it not for my influence?"

"Did my father ask any favors of you or your Taerleezi friends?"

"He didn't need to ask. I gladly do all in my power to assist your family. I had assumed—wrongly, it seems—that the preservation of your home would not displease you."

"The destruction of your honor displeases me."

Verbal attacks rarely troubled him, but Sonnetia Steffa possessed the power to penetrate his armor. Twenty-five years later, he relived the jolt of pained anger. And he recalled his own response. *"Come, this is absurd. You are only a young girl, without experience or knowledge. You prate foolishly of matters beyond your understanding."* In the years that followed, he had often wondered what course his life might have taken had he managed to hold his tongue.

"Certain matters are not beyond the understanding even of so foolish and ignorant a creature as myself." Her voice had been very quiet. *"I understand that you have cut yourself off from your nation, from your home, from your people. I understand that you are no longer one of us. I understand that I no longer know you, if indeed I ever did. And I understand that I cannot and will not join my life with yours."*

"You don't mean that; you speak in anger. You'll reconsider, when you are calm." He had taken a step toward her, and he still recalled the gesture—hand upraised in its grey kid glove—with which she had halted him.

"I am calm." Her white face and the tears in her eyes belied the claim. *"And I will not reconsider."*

"Sonnetia, there has always been strong feeling between us. It is there still, say what you will. You won't throw all that away on a sudden whim."

"It is neither a whim nor sudden. The division between us has been widening for months. You have not noticed."

He had not allowed himself to notice. *"We've had some few differences over small matters—"*

"Not small."

"But nothing to justify the ruin of our betrothal. Your father has consented, remember. Your parents and kin won't permit you to do this."

"Aureste, do you not understand? They will applaud me."

There could be no answer to that. For a while, he had stood searching her face for some sign of weakness or uncertainty, something that he could turn to his own advantage, but there was nothing there to use or control, which was one of the reasons that he so much admired her. Strength of will notwithstanding, her feelings for him ran deep; of this he had no doubt. Sooner or later her own emotions would erode her resolve, and then things would be right again. It was only a matter of time, or so he assured himself. Thus convinced, he had taken his leave, returning to Belandor House to await the retraction and contrition that never came. All that came, in fact, delivered by one of the few remaining Steffa servants, was the great sapphire ring that he had given to her upon her formal acceptance of his proposal. And from that chilly day until the present, he had never again set foot in that garden.

"Just what you asked for, Honored Magnifico." The voice of Brivvia intruded upon his recollections. "Clean and very nice, but not new. Could it be any better?"

As if from a distance Aureste heard his own voice return. "Is she not likely to miss these?"

"Not she. I found them tucked away at the very bottom of an old chest. She's never asked for them in all the time I've served her. She's forgotten they exist."

"Probably."

"You're content then, Honored Magnifico?"

"Content?" His lips turned down at the corners. "You've done well, Brivvia. Here." He flipped her a coin, which she caught neatly. "Now leave me."

"Yessir." She looked down at the coin and her jaw dropped, for it was gold. "Thank you, Honored Magnifico! Thank you, sir!"

She bowed her way out of the study, and he forgot her existence before the door closed behind her. For a long time he sat motionless, transfixed by the gloves and the memories they awoke. At last he roused himself from his trance, retrieved the casket from the bottom drawer of the desk, and added the newest keepsake to his collection. He locked the casket away again, and his mind was once more free to roam the Alzira Hills in search of his daughter. Sometimes he thought to glimpse her figure at a distance; she wandered among trees whose leaves were elegantly fashioned of grey kid lined with emerald silk. To the packet of incriminating documents hidden in Vinz Corvestri's desk, he gave no thought at all.

TEN

The maggots were exceptionally large, probably the largest she had ever seen; not that she had made a comparative study. They were mauve in color and startlingly visible within the dark cavity of the wound.

"Is it my imagination, or are those things glowing?" inquired Jianna.

"It isn't your imagination. They do possess a measure of luminosity. I bred them for that, among other things. It makes them much easier to see," Dr. Rione explained.

"*You* bred them? Yourself? Those slimy, repulsive little horrors?"

"Come, maidenlady. That's rather harsh. Perhaps they aren't the loveliest of creatures, but they are highly useful, and utility possesses its own beauty."

"None that I can appreciate. To me they're horrid, disgusting worms that eat corpses."

"You do them an injustice. True, they are the gluttons of the graveyard, but they're also the devoted drudges of the sickroom. You already know that a wound of the most trivial nature becomes deadly when a portion of the injured tissue dies, for the dead matter swiftly poisons the living, and the infection spreads throughout the body."

Jianna nodded sagely. In fact, she had known none of this, but did not wish to appear ignorant before the doctor.

"The only remedy lies in the removal of the necrotic flesh," Rione continued. "To this end the surgeon labors with his scalpel. But he is only human. His instrument is clumsy, his vision dull. He misses small quantities of dead matter, leaving them in place to renew the infection; else he excises too aggressively, needlessly deepening the wound. But these small creatures commit no such errors. They devour dead tissue down to the last particle but never touch living matter. Thus they cleanse the wound with a precision and thoroughness beyond the ability of any human physician. Now will you regard them with a kindlier eye?"

"Perhaps. From a safe distance."

"Oh, you'll be safe enough so long as the little fellows don't mistake you for a corpse, which they're unlikely to do—you are almost conspicuously vital. Now I want you to stand at my right with that bowl of maggots. The workers on site are sated; I'm sending in reinforcements."

"How can you tell that they're sated?"

"Their movements alter. And they exude a certain pensive melancholy."

"I'll wager that's not all they exude. Here." Jianna extended a moist earthenware bowl. A quick glance down at the squirming contents roused some distaste, but no terror or nausea. Her tolerance for such tasks was proving unexpectedly high. "Can you reach them?"

"He can't do anything if he doesn't stop chattering." The wounded Ghost on the cot spoke up in a slow voice slurred with kalkriole. He was extremely young, probably no more than fifteen or sixteen, small and thin, very pale beneath a multitude of freckles. The maggot-crawling hole in his lower leg promised inevitable amputation; but Dr. Rione continued to battle infection long beyond the point at which most physicians would have called for the bone saw.

"Awake are you, young Broso?" Rione observed with a smile.

"Wide awake," muttered Broso with patent untruth. His eyelids drooped. "Wide . . . wide . . . wide."

"Any pain?"

"Feeling fine. Bring on the worms."

"They're already at work. You go to sleep."

"Wide awake." Broso's eyes shut. He slept.

Using blunt-nosed tweezers, Rione transferred a number of maggots from bowl to wound. Jianna watched, admiring the deft economy of his movements. He was right about the change in the aspect of the sated worms. They were slow and placid, while the reinforcements were vigorously wriggly. It was easy to spot the difference.

"You needn't watch this," Rione told her. "I know it's hard for you."

"No, it isn't," she assured him.

"It isn't?"

"Well, of course it's revolting, but at the same time it's rather interesting."

"You surprise me." For a moment, his attention shifted from his patient to her face.

"I surprise myself." This was true. "I thought all this would be far worse."

"For most young women of your upbringing, it would be difficult to endure."

"What do you know of my upbringing?"

"Nothing definite, but I surmise that your life has been easy, pleasant, and all but devoid of ugliness."

"Until I came here. But that doesn't make me squeamish or spineless."

"Indeed. They keep reminding me that you are your father's daughter."

"I consider that a compliment."

"You might also consider setting that bowl aside and fetching me a fresh roll of bandages. Step lively."

The dressing that he had removed from Broso's wound was almost fresh, marked only with a few wet splotches. Most physicians would not have hesitated to reuse it, but Rione was unlike most physicians. She had already discovered that his habits and theories were distinctly unconventional. For one thing, he did not believe in bleeding his patients. His respect for maggots did not extend to leeches, and he simply dismissed the entire theory of sanguinary superfluities. This attitude in itself would have sufficed to establish his eccentricity, but there was more. He had no use for Troxius medals or protective appurtenances of any description. He did not believe in the application of friction or pressure to break a fever. He rarely if ever made use of emetics. He openly scoffed at the theory of malignant sendings. And strangest of all was his passion for cleanliness. She had never in her life encountered a doctor—or a sane man of any profession—so enamored of washing.

Rione demanded a mad perfection of purity. Everything in the infirmary had to be spotless, and a hard wipe with an ordinary cleaning rag wasn't good enough. All surfaces, even the floor, had to be scrubbed down with a harsh lye soap. The cleaning rags themselves had to be laundered, and that was nothing compared with the care expended upon bandages, towels, surgical instruments, anything that might actually come into contact with a patient's open wound. These items were boiled at length, then cooled and soaked in alcoholic solutions. Even the hands that touched the wounds, the instruments, or the bandages had to be doused in acidic solutions of stinging potency. The first time Jianna had been directed to plunge her hands into the faintly blue chemical bath, she had ventured to ask the reason, and he had replied very simply:

"Because it works."

"Works?"

"Helps to keep people alive. When bandages, instruments, and hands are kept clean, patient mortality declines."

"You really believe that?"

"I've observed the effect at first hand for years."

"The soap, the cleaning solutions—they're of arcane origin, then?"

He had smiled at that. "No, it's all ordinary. Even the soap."

"Then I don't understand. *Why* does it work? What's washing and scrubbing got to do with keeping people alive?"

"That is the question. I don't know the true answer—

nobody does. There are various theories, but nothing has been proved. The one thing I can state with assurance is that it does help. So give your hands a good soak, maidenlady. It's well worthwhile."

Yes, a curious character, Dr. Falaste Rione. His frank admission that he could not answer her question had won her instant approval, for it reminded her of Uncle Innesq, who—unlike his masterful older brother, Aureste, or his prissy younger brother, Nalio—was capable of confessing ignorance, upon occasion. Since then, the initial approval had only deepened. Nature had blessed Rione with exceptional talent. In Vitrisi and Orezzia, physicians possessing no more than a fraction of his skill tended appreciative Taerleezi patients and amassed considerable wealth. But Rione, evidently disdaining affluence, devoted his talents to the welfare of the Ghosts—a choice difficult to comprehend.

The Magnifico Aureste had always taught his daughter that Faerlonnish resistance was the hopeless cause of crazed fanatics unable or unwilling to accept reality. But Rione was neither unbalanced nor unintelligent; quite the contrary. He possessed one of the most lucid minds she had ever encountered, and his convictions were not to be lightly dismissed. Not that she understood how he had reached them, for the passing days had done little to erode his reserve. He was friendly enough, but hardly confiding. It was understandable under the circumstances, but the reticence had roused her curiosity, and of late she had developed a certain perverse ambition to win past his guard.

"Maidenlady, the bandages." His voice broke her reverie.

"One moment." She hopped into action.

"Mind the ankle," Rione advised.

"Oh—you know, I'd forgotten about that. I think it's all better now." The moment the words popped out of her mouth, Jianna regretted them. Better, far better to persuade her captors that she remained incapacitated and half crippled. If they believed that, then perhaps their vigilance would slacken, and perhaps her chance would come. But now a single unthinking response had alerted Rione to her full recovery. She slanted a quick glance at him. He was smiling, obviously pleased, and his expression was so reassuring and so engaging that her chagrin dissipated and she found herself smiling back at him.

"I'm glad to hear that, but comfort can be misleading. Recovery is probably not quite complete. I advise you to take care."

Should that be taken at face value, or was more intended? She was uncertain. Could he read her thoughts? Probably no better than she could read his, but then again he was uncommonly perceptive; he revealed that quality in every exchange with every patient. No telling what those penetrating grey-blue eyes of his took in.

Jianna turned away abruptly. Her own eyes, unsure where to turn, ranged the infirmary, moving from cot to cot. Ten patients present today, five of them in serious danger. Three infected wounds, one case of brain fever, and one shockingly mutilated survivor of Taerleezi interrogation. This last she could hardly bear to look at, despite her newly discovered fortitude. Her weakness would scarcely offend the patient, who—having lost both eyes, among other bodily parts—was unlikely to observe it. In any case, he was usually unconscious, so far as she could tell. From time to time, however, an issuance of moaning babble suggested wakefulness. He was moaning now, limbless form jerking, and she wavered, half inclined to run to his side, half inclined to run away. But no decision was required of her; the doctor was waiting for his bandages.

Jianna hurried to the cabinet beside the door, withdrew a fresh white roll, presented it to Rione, and watched as he wrapped Broso's wound. This done, he moved to the bedside of the moaning wreck and motioned her to join him. She obeyed with reluctance.

"Grezziu," Rione addressed the ruin firmly. "Can you understand me?"

No response, no evidence of comprehension.

"I am going to change your dressings," Rione announced, and his patient whimpered. "No, I won't hurt you. Calm yourself."

The whimpering intensified. The wreck writhed.

"Grezziu, you are among friends. You'll swallow a draught," Rione promised.

The noise subsided. The wreck lay still.

Rione poured a small quantity of a dark syrup into an earthenware cup. "Lift him up," he commanded.

Jianna stiffened. She did not want to touch the wreck—did not want to see him, hear him, or exist in the same universe with him—but there was no escape. Mastering vast repugnance, she bent, slipped an arm under the bandaged shoulders, and raised him. He was limp, deadweight, but surprisingly easy to move; perhaps his lack of arms accounted for it. His odor was both rank and wrong, suggestive of decay, despite all his physician's efforts. Jianna's gorge rose, and she turned a retch into a cough.

Grezziu began to scream, his cries deafening within the confines of the infirmary. Jianna started and almost dropped him. Her alarmed eyes sought the doctor's.

"Try to hold him still," Rione directed.

She did try, but the task was nearly impossible. What was left of Grezziu's body pitched and bucked wildly. His head thrashed from side to side.

"Hush. It's all right. Hush, please," she soothed vainly. The bucking and thrashing continued. Out of the corner of her eye, she noted several patients watching.

"Sit on him, sweetheart," one of the spectators advised helpfully.

"Choke 'im down," another added.

She did neither. Grabbing Grezziu's head with both hands, she held on tightly while Rione tipped the contents of his cup into the open, squalling mouth. Grezziu's struggles gradually subsided. He breathed a gurgling sigh and lay still.

Jianna drew back, and Rione set to work on the sleeping patient's bandages. She held herself rigidly still as the facial dressings came off. There was no particular reason for her to observe the holes that marked the site of Grezziu's missing nose. Nobody required her assistance at that moment, but somehow it would have seemed an act of cowardice to turn her eyes away. Likewise she willed herself to watch as the stumps of the amputated limbs were uncovered one by one, bathed, and bound with fresh linen strips. When the abbreviated remnants of Grezziu's genitalia were exposed to view, however, her equanimity broke.

Abruptly she rose and retreated to the far end of the room, where a partially open window admitted a current of fresh air. There she stood breathing deeply until her qualms subsided and her roiling stomach calmed itself. At length she grew aware that the infirmary window offered a grand view of the surrounding countryside. Probably the place had once served as a watchtower; from its summit she looked out over miles of forested hills. Jianna strained her eyes. Perhaps if she stared hard enough, tried hard enough, she might catch a glimpse of Vitrisi. Ridiculous, of course. The city was too far away; she couldn't possibly see it from this place. The road, then, or a path through the woods—anything that might point the way home.

"You are ill, maidenlady?"

She turned at the sound of his voice to find Rione standing behind her. He would be angry, of course. She should not have walked away without permission. He probably wanted her to collect bloody bandages or chase down fugitive maggots.

But he did not look angry, only concerned, and perhaps a little tired. He had been working steadily since the break of day, working far harder than she, never pausing until now. Moreover—it dawned upon her for the first time—he had kept her busy, but consistently spared her the worst of labors. He had not, for example, commanded her to bathe Grezziu's stumps; he had done it himself. All things considered, he had treated her with remarkable consideration.

"I'm well enough," she told him. "I just wanted air."

"Then step outside for a few minutes."

Kind. He was obviously kind, and the idea that she had dismissed days earlier jumped back into her mind: Perhaps he might be prevailed upon to help her. He assisted those in need, and she certainly qualified. She needed to enlist his sympathies, somehow.

"I'll stay," she returned firmly. "Just give me another moment."

"Take all the time you please. You deserve it."

"The Lady Yvenza wouldn't agree."

"Ah, the magnifica doesn't know how well you've been doing. Astonishingly well, in fact."

"Why astonishing?" she asked, absurdly pleased. Praise from a man of Rione's talents meant something.

"You've no experience, no training, and some of the sights you've witnessed in this place must be hard for you to bear."

"Some of them," she admitted. "I'm not squeamish, but that poor man Grezziu—"

"Man? He's no more than a boy. He's all of fourteen."

"That young? How horrible! Oh, if only they'd known that!"

"They? The Taerleezis, you mean?"

She nodded.

"Do you imagine it would have made any difference?"

"Why—why, yes, of course it would. They're not savages."

"Aren't they?"

"They're perfectly civil folk, most of them, with decent enough manners, if something coarse. Some of them like music, and play very well. I know, because I've met them. I've even sat at table with them. I . . ." Her voice trailed off. He was observing her thoughtfully, and all at once she found herself confused and oddly mortified.

"You've dined with Taerleezi guests in your father's house?" Rione prompted, quite gently.

She nodded again and her sense of inexplicable shame deepened, which was ridiculous. She had nothing to be ashamed of, nothing to apologize for, and neither did her father, no matter what the world had to say about him. Aureste Belandor was capable of accepting and adapting to life's realities. If the envious resented him for that, so much the worse for them.

Thus internally fortified, she was able to meet the doctor's eyes and answer with an appearance of assurance, "The Taerleezis aren't monsters, they're just people, not that much different from ourselves."

"I don't dispute that," Rione conceded drily. "Were our positions and opportunities reversed, we Faerlonnish would no doubt prove as cruel and tyrannical as our present overlords. But that has nothing to do with present reality. You've been sheltered, maidenlady, but you're no child, and you should understand that the Taerleezis you've dined with in Vitrisi are perfectly capable of chopping countless boys like Grezziu into hash. Oh, they wouldn't do it themselves, it's true. They are too civil and musical for that. But they issue the orders that cause it to be done."

"Well, a lot of these bad things wouldn't happen at all if only some people would settle down and stop making so much trouble. Stop burning buildings and attacking Taerleezi patrols and assassinating tax collectors and so forth. When they break the peace, they should expect consequences, shouldn't they?"

"Settle down and stop making so much trouble. There's something to that, I suppose. We Faerlonnish need only accept Taerleezi occupation and domination. Accept the confiscation of our lands and homes, the theft of our belongings. Accept the killing taxes and financial penalties that reduce us to beggary and starvation. Accept the punitive laws that rob us of all rights, safety, and freedom. Accept the insolence and contempt that strip us of dignity and self-respect. Accept all of this without a murmur of protest, and perhaps our appreciative conquerors will refrain from butchery. Have I correctly stated your position, maidenlady?"

He did not speak angrily or accusingly. His face was clear, voice low and soothing as ever, but Jianna felt like a pinned insect. It wasn't fair, he was surely exaggerating and twisting the facts, but she hardly knew how to refute him. For a moment or two she cast about for a reply and finally settled on a weak one. "I think it's only common sense to make the best of things that can't be helped."

"Oppression is a thing that can't be helped, then?"

"The Taerleezis won the war. It happened long ago, and there's nothing much to be done about it now."

"The Ghosts believe otherwise."

"The Ghosts stir up trouble, they get themselves killed or worse, and what good does it do? Nothing changes."

"Ah, this is sad. You're too young to give way to such despair."

"Despair?" she echoed, astonished. "What despair? I've always been happy. Until I was brought here, of course."

"Despair is an absence of hope, is it not?"

"I haven't given up; I hope for all sorts of things. I hope for good health, good fortune, and happiness for myself and the people I care about. But those hopes will never be realized unless I find my way back home and so, above all else, I hope to return to Vitrisi." She watched his face closely for a sign of sympathetic response.

"Your ambitions are lively but personal. They don't embrace the welfare of your country or countrymen. You've been raised to regard such larger hopes as unrealistic, but there are many among us not sharing your pessimism."

Jianna stirred uncomfortably. She wanted to argue, to insist that she was not at all pessimistic, that she had been blessed with a cheerful disposition. But she could hardly afford to contradict and possibly alienate him. Moreover, she found herself oddly prey to doubt. Like her father, she had always dismissed Faerlonnish resistance as a foolish lost cause. But what if she—and he—had underestimated the will and persistence of their countrymen? Aureste Belandor rarely miscalculated, but even he was capable of occasional error.

"Do you believe—I mean *really* believe—that the Ghosts can actually drive the Taerleezis out of Faerlonne?" Jianna inquired, half in challenge, half in genuine curiosity.

"Perhaps that's too much to expect at present. But I do believe—I mean *really* believe—that the resistance may chivvy the Taers into repealing the worst of the laws," he replied with a slight smile.

"Well, that would be something, I suppose." Frowning, she pondered and eventually grew conscious that he was studying her face. Her sense of not altogether unpleasant confusion expanded, and she felt the color warm her cheeks. Ridiculous. Holding fast to her dignity, she announced, "I'm ready to go back to work now. Is there anything more to be done for Grezziu?"

"Very little." Rione's smile disappeared. He lowered his voice. "I try to keep him as comfortable as possible, but there's no hope for him. He'll probably be gone within hours."

Jianna wondered whether her sense of profound relief was inappropriate.

. . .

Another day passed and Grezziu quietly died. His remains were interred without ceremony in the small cemetery at the foot of Ironheart's outer wall. The next day brought two new feverish patients—a brace of household servants, this time—whose care kept Jianna almost too busy for thought or worry for a while. Then one morning she awoke to a world dusted with frost. The air was cold, the last leaves were falling from the trees, and her sense of time's passage reawakened to jab like a spur.

Her sojourn in the infirmary had proved demanding but not intolerable; certainly not as miserable as Yvenza had expected. The infirmary, in fact, had served as a kind of sanctuary, for here Onartino never willingly ventured, and here she was free of him. But the respite was temporary, and each passing day surely brought the East Reach Traveler and catastrophe closer. Each day also advanced upon the hour of Dr. Rione's departure. Already he had extended his stay beyond his original intent, but he would not tarry much longer. And when he went, Ironheart would be lonely, loathsome, and unbearable as never before. There would be no more conversation, no more kindness, no more companionship—perhaps for the rest of her life.

Jianna contemplated her probable future, and the idea floating wraith-like at the edge of her mind finally coalesced. Since the wet afternoon of their first meeting, she had always hoped to enlist Rione's assistance, and now she had decided exactly what form that assistance should take: When he departed Ironheart, he would take her with him.

He didn't know it yet, perhaps he wasn't even thinking about it. He would hesitate, no doubt. But Aureste Belandor's daughter would overcome his reluctance. She would find a way.

She took to watching him, searching always for some sign of receptivity, some clue that the moment was ripe, but his face remained closed. He was kind, considerate, courteous— nothing more—and she needed something stronger to draw him to her and to conquer Yvenza's influence.

It was curious and galling. Falaste Rione was intelligent, strong-willed, and independent, yet he manifested an incomprehensible loyalty to Yvenza. More than loyalty—an esteem, a deep respect, even affection that seemed almost filial. But he was not her son, her foster son, or even her distant blood kin— Jianna had satisfied herself upon this point days earlier. He was not a servant, although the servants in this place seemed to regard him as one of their own. He was not a tenant or a retainer of any description. He seemed to defy ordinary classification.

Whatever he might be, she would reclassify him. Quite apart from necessity, something in her wanted to claim him.

She continued to watch, but the perfect moment never arrived, and at length she resolved to create one. Her ankle was perfectly healed, but now she began to favor it, moving about the infirmary with a subtle, barely perceptible limp.

Rione noticed at once. "Trouble?" he inquired. "Ankle bothering you?"

"Nothing to speak of." She smiled bravely.

"You're in pain?"

"Really, it's nothing."

"Better let me have a look."

"You've more important things to do."

"Let me be the judge. When did it start aching?"

"Yesterday evening."

"Any obvious reason? You didn't try running or jumping, did you?"

"No, nothing like that. I—I fell down, that's all."

"Fell down? How did that happen?"

"Please, I don't want to talk about it." Her voice broke. She turned her face away.

"Maidenlady, are you crying?"

"No." She produced a strangled sob.

"Come with me." He led her from the room, shutting the door behind them. They stood on the landing at the head of the cramped stairway, and for once they were alone. "Now tell me what happened."

Wasting no time upon further protest, she launched into her prepared tale. "Yesterday evening I met up with—with Onartino on the stairs. I think he might have been waiting for me. He blocked my way. I tried to get around him, but he put his hands on me. There was a sort of scuffle and I fell down. Only a couple of steps, it wasn't much, but my ankle has been sore since then." She darted a covert glance at the doctor, noting with pleasure the sudden grimness of his expression.

"He pushed you down the stairs?" demanded Rione, jaw hard.

"He pushed or I fell, it isn't clear. Does it matter? It won't be the last time, will it? I can look forward to a lifetime of the same."

"Not necessarily. You are a resourceful young woman. Once married, you'll learn how to live with your husband."

"I already know how to live with Onartino. I must surrender without reservation, accept without complaint all torments that he chooses to inflict, and then perhaps he'll refrain from maiming or killing me. Sound familiar? It should. Not long ago you reproached me for suggesting that Faerlonne should submit without resistance to the dominance of Taerleez. Don't the principles that you apply to nations hold true for individuals?" Inwardly she congratulated herself on the brilliance of this analogy.

"Maidenlady, you speak of personal matters, Belandor family matters. I am an outsider and must not venture an opinion."

"Oh, please don't take refuge behind propriety! You have eyes and ears, you haven't missed what's plain before you. You have an opinion. Why be afraid to express it?"

"It is a matter of obligation."

She studied his still face as if it were a puzzle to be solved. "Have you no concern at all for me, then? I'm not simply Aureste Belandor's daughter. I'm Jianna, a person whom you've come to know. Don't you care at all what happens to me?"

"I wish nothing but good for you. But come, your situation isn't that desperate. True, the circumstances are distressing, but you aren't much different from any other young maidenlady of high birth contemplating an arranged marriage not to her fancy. Once it's done, you'll come to terms with your new life."

"Oh, that's untrue, and you *know* it's untrue!" She took a step toward him and stared straight into his eyes. "You're not honest with me or with yourself when you say such things, and I thought you were better than that. This isn't an ordinary marriage. I'm being handed over like a Sishmindri into the power of a brute and a murderer who hates me for my father's sake. He'll enjoy breaking and destroying me; it will be his pleasure. He makes no secret of that, and you can't pretend that you haven't seen it!"

"I've seen that you're much in his thoughts. Anything for good or ill might come of that."

"Only ill. He'll hurt me, he'll defile me, he'll use me to fulfill his mother's ends, and finally, when I've served my purpose, he'll kill me. There's my future, Falaste. Does it mean nothing at all to you?"

He was silent for so long that she thought he would not answer, but at last he spoke as if the words emerged against his will. "Maidenlady, what do you want of me?"

"Your help," she returned, ablaze with sudden hope. "Please, please, you must help me, or my life is over. I'll die in this prison if you don't help me!"

"To get away, you mean."

"Yes. You'll be leaving soon. Take me with you. Save me, Falaste. You're the only one in the world who can." Instinct prompted her to place a timid hand upon his arm, to gaze up at him wide-eyed. Instinct told her, too, that he was scarcely impervious to her appeal. Excitement surged through her. He was going to yield, he *wanted* to yield; she could feel it.

"You must not ask me," Rione told her.

The reply took her by surprise. She stared at him, momentarily dumbfounded, but rallied quickly to reply, "But I do ask. I implore you. I'll beg if needs be. Help me!"

"Impossible." He spoke with visible regret. "I'm sorry."

"But no, it isn't impossible, not impossible at all!" Her excitement was rising and she made little effort to control it. Perhaps she might sway him with sheer intensity of emotion. "They mew me up every night, but they don't bother to post a guard; they know I can't get out. All you need do is wait until the dead of night, then come up and unbar my door. That will be easy, you're able to move around this place freely."

"Yes. The magnifica trusts me insofar as she trusts anyone. And then?"

"In the morning, when they find me gone, the hunt begins.

They'll scour the woods, but probably not before they've searched the house from top to bottom. You offer to join in the search. They'll welcome your assistance. Make certain that you are the only one to search the subcellar, though, because that's where I'll be hiding. Then, a few days later, when they're starting to believe that I've gotten clean away and their efforts to find me are falling off, you announce your departure. The night before you leave, come down to the subcellar, help me out into the courtyard and over the wall. I'll wait in the woods. In the morning, you make your farewells and depart. Then you'll double back, meet me secretly, and escort me on to Vitrisi, with no one at Ironheart ever to know or even suspect that you helped me—that you saved my life."

"Quite good." He nodded. "Remind me to call upon your talents should I ever need to plan an escape. Despite your undeniable cunning, however, you've neglected certain details. For example, the magnifica would know at once who unbarred your door."

"Bah, she could be persuaded that I bribed one of the servants."

"Not as easily accomplished as you seem to imagine, but that's not the only difficulty. You speak quite casually of concealing yourself in the subcellar for a period of several days. During that time, what would you do for food and water?"

"Store them beforehand."

"Provided you've time and opportunity. Blankets and candles?"

"Do without."

"Alone in the dark and cold of the subcellar, with the rats and insects to steal your food, and the stench of the cesspit always in your nostrils—you think you could endure it?"

"If I must. But it wouldn't have to be as bad as that—not if you'd place a blanket and candles down there sometime during the next couple of days. You could do it easily."

"And why in the world would I do all this and risk so much for you?"

"Perhaps because you don't want to see me tortured and destroyed. Am I wrong?" She was standing so near him that she could discern the striations of color in his eyes, true blue alternating with slate. His face was unrevealing, but for a moment she felt as if she could read his mind. He wanted to remain detached and impersonal, but his resolve was crumbling and about to crash in ruins. She had him. She knew it. Triumph shot across her mind and flared for a moment in her eyes.

And he caught it. His expression altered.

She knew at once that her face had betrayed her and instantly lowered her eyes.

"Look at me," Rione commanded.

Unwillingly she obeyed. He was studying her, his penetrating gaze seeming to plumb the depths of her mind, and it was all she could do to sustain the scrutiny without visibly squirming. She tried to think of something to say. Nothing occurred to her.

"Well, maidenlady." He broke the comfortless silence at last, his voice soothing and unruffled as always. "You've ambitious plans, but you can scarcely hope to carry them out if you're unable to walk properly."

The abrupt change of subject took her aback, setting off internal alarm bells.

"My ankle's not so bad," she assured him quickly. "By this time tomorrow it will probably be all better."

"I shouldn't wonder. Better let me have a look, though."

"Oh." She cast about for some means of putting him off, but found none. "Thank you."

He knelt and there was nothing for it but to draw her skirt back a few inches, exposing to view a slim ankle quite free of swelling. He did not trouble to draw the flimsy shoe from her foot, but took her ankle in both his hands and pressed experimentally. His hands were warm, his touch light and sure. Her nerves jumped, and she drew a sharp breath.

"That hurts?" Rione inquired.

"No." She remembered to grimace. "It's all right."

"And this?" He squeezed her instep.

She flinched emphatically.

"Maidenlady?"

"That hurt some," she lied. "But not badly."

"And this?" He pressed.

"Just a little." She decided to stiffen. "It's nothing."

"I agree," replied Rione.

"What?" This time her start was spontaneous.

"I said I agree. It's nothing. There's no swelling, no loss of flexibility, no apparent inflammation, no appropriate response. Your ankle isn't bothering you in the least, is it?"

"It's much better than it was." She swallowed. *Caught.* "I've been telling you that all along, haven't I?"

"You've been telling me much. The story about last night's meeting with Onartino, for example. That was a lie, wasn't it?"

"It's no lie that he's waylaid me in this house. It's certainly no lie that he's shoved me, hit me, and threatened me."

"But not last night."

No room to maneuver. "Not last night."

"And he's never pushed you down the stairs, has he? Last night or at any other time?"

"Not yet, but it's something he's certainly *capable* of doing."

"This weak equivocation only cheapens you. I begin to see why they keep reminding me that you are your father's daughter. You seem to share his famed penchant for deceit and manipulation."

His remote expression alarmed her. She had blundered badly in lying to him. Unless she could make it right, he would never assist her. Moreover, he would think ill of her ever after, a prospect she found remarkably disturbing. Perfectly genuine tears filled her eyes and she blurted, "I'm sorry, Falaste! I never *meant* to deceive or manipulate, I didn't *intend*—"

"The artificial limp, the well-crafted lies—they were purely accidental?"

"No, I mean I didn't *think* of it as deceiving you, I only thought about somehow persuading you to help me, that's all I wanted, and still do, because I need your help desperately. I'm doomed without it. There's no falsehood in that." Her voice broke and the tears streamed freely down her face.

For a while he stood looking at her, and she had no idea what was going on behind his eyes. When finally he spoke, his tone was kind and impersonal, as if he addressed a distraught serving maid. "Take such time as you need to compose yourself, maidenlady. You may come back to work when you are calm."

She gazed at him piteously. Ignoring the mute plea, he stepped back into the infirmary and the door shut firmly behind him.

ELEVEN

Early evening, and the lamps glowed warmly in the magnifico's study at Corvestri Mansion. Two men faced each other across the polished expanse of the desktop. One was nondescript to the verge of invisibility. The other was utterly miserable.

"Your wife's maidservant has been back to Belandor House," announced Lousewort. "Around noon today. Did you know that?"

Vinz Corvestri hesitated, uncertain. He had not known that, but a frank avowal of ignorance would underscore his lack of mastery in his own household, a weakness he preferred to conceal from his resistance contact. And it wouldn't even be true, because he *had* known, or suspected, in a way; or rather, he was not in the least surprised. Some part of him had been waiting for it.

"This time, did your agents manage to discover what she actually does there?" Vinz liked his own reply, which seemed pleasingly assertive.

"You're in a better position than anyone else to find out," Lousewort parried. "But our lads have managed to secure one other bit of information that may be of some interest to you."

Vinz could not bring himself to voice the expected query. He sensed deeply that he did not want to know.

Lousewort, however, required no encouragement. "It's about our friend Belandor. For days now, he's been gadding about town buying up muscle."

"Buying up what?"

"Muscle. Able-bodied men, wherever he can find them. In short, he's working hard to raise a force. I don't know another

Faerlonnishman in Vitrisi who'd get away with it. But seeing as it's the Viper's pet, the Taers just pocket their bribes and look the other way."

"A force. Aureste Belandor is raising a force?" Vinz longed to disbelieve, but knew from past experience that Lousewort's intelligence was reliable. "What for?"

"To maintain public safety, no doubt. What do you think?"

"That your levity is misplaced."

"I am justly rebuked. You're right, it's no laughing matter. Let's consider, then. Your wife's maidservant flits back and forth between Corvestri Mansion and Belandor House, while your greatest enemy musters a small army. What does all of this imply?"

"You suggest that Aureste Belandor plans an attack upon my home?"

"He probably means to raze it to the ground. Such a scheme is hardly beyond him. Weeks have passed since you spoke of launching your own preemptive strike. Our people are ready and willing to support this venture, but there's been no call from you. Have you devised a plan?"

"It is incomplete." In fact it was nonexistent. His initial enthusiasm had long since ebbed, and with it his resolve. He had let himself drift, buoyed on the hope that all difficulties might quietly resolve themselves without benefit of his direct intervention. Clearly the difficulties had failed to oblige.

"We can help you with that," Lousewort pushed. "We can supply men, weapons, and strategy. But we can't proceed without you, Magnifico."

"I know." He knew only too well.

"The middle Belandor brother, the crippled one, is known to possess arcane skills of a high order," Lousewort pressed on. "He'll have safeguarded the house. We'll need to call on your abilities to break supranormal barriers and disable arcane devices."

Vinz said nothing.

"This task lies within your power, does it not?"

Vinz nodded distantly.

"Are you quite certain, Magnifico? You understand, we'll be relying on—"

"I said *yes*," snapped Vinz, goaded. Beneath the apparent impatience lurked trepidation and profound reluctance. Lousewort and the others expected his active participation in an armed assault upon Belandor House. He had supported the Faerlonnish resistance movement for years, giving greatly if surreptitiously of his time, money, influence, and arcane skill. But never in all that time had he been called to violent action. And with good reason: He was not a man of action. He never had been, even in his youth.

"Good. Then let us set a date."

"Now?"

"What better time?"

Some other century? Vinz realized then that he did not remotely want to go through with it. The pictures flashed through his mind—fire, explosions, the clash of steel, the shouts and screams, the stink of smoke and blood—and he shuddered discreetly. He wanted no part of such ugliness and horror, but what choice was there? Threatened, he was obliged to defend himself. Moreover Lousewort's cronies of the resistance were depending on him, and how could he fail such insanely selfless patriots? No question about it, he was committed. *Trapped.*

"Let me know more of your plans, then," Vinz temporized. "Will you—that is, we—enter Belandor House by stealth? Or do you intend something more of a straightforward military strike?"

"In view of Belandor's resources, we—"

A tap at the study door cut Lousewort's reply short. Both men turned. The door opened, and the Magnifica Sonnetia stood on the threshold.

"Magnifico, a word if you please," she began and broke off at sight of the visitor. "Ah, forgive me, I did not know that you were occupied."

Startled, Vinz goggled at his wife. She stood tall and straight in a wine-colored gown whose fluid lines draped a figure still slender and graceful as a girl's. Her chestnut hair had yet to reveal so much as a thread of grey. And her face—in the forgiving lamplight at least—seemed miraculously untouched by time, as smooth and fine as it had been on the day that he married her, twenty-four years earlier. She was as beautiful as ever, and as remote. He had little idea what went on behind those clear eyes of hers; it might be anything, up to and including treachery.

A wave of wholly uncharacteristic rage swept through Vinz. His face suffused and he heard himself demand harshly, "What d'you mean by bursting in here without permission? This is my personal study and I expect you to respect my privacy, madam."

Her brows rose and for once her face was not at all difficult to read: It reflected simple astonishment. Following a moment's pause, she returned evenly, "Magnifico, I beg your pardon. I did not realize that you entertain a visitor."

"Didn't you? Have you gone deaf, then? Are you trying to tell me that you heard no voices?"

"Indistinctly. I assumed that you addressed a servant."

"Well, your assumption was wrong, wasn't it? Assumptions frequently are. Exactly what did you overhear?"

"Overhear?" Her look of astonishment deepened. "Nothing of importance."

"I'll be the judge of that. Tell me exactly what you heard, madam. And no evasions, if you please." It was curious. In all their years together, he had never addressed his wife in such tones or terms, never even dreamed of it. But now it seemed as if his mouth had taken on a reckless life of its own. He hardly knew what would come out of it next.

He could see Sonnetia's initial amazement giving way to affront. Ordinarily her anger would have reproached him. Today, for some reason, he welcomed it. Some part of him welcomed the opportunity to assert himself, to express himself, to *pay her back*. Some part of him had wanted it for decades.

"I heard you pronounce the words 'military strike.' " Sonnetia's spine was very straight, her voice chill. "And then I thought I caught the name 'Belandor,' not spoken by you."

"What more?"

"Nothing more."

"Your conclusions?" There was no immediate reply, and he commanded masterfully, *"Answer me."* It felt fine and he added for good measure, *"Now."*

"Magnifico, I have offended you and such was not my intent." Sonnetia spoke with mechanically perfect decorum. "Pray forgive my error and permit me to withdraw."

"I don't permit you. I command you." The word possessed such a delicious flavor that he could not resist repeating it. "I command you to retire. Seek your chamber, madam. Immure yourself and consider your duty. Do not presume to emerge without my leave."

She was staring at him, patently incredulous and offended. Her jaw tightened and he braced against an angry retort that did not emerge. Her eyes shifted briefly to Lousewort's attentive face and thence to the floor. Whatever her private sense of outrage, good breeding would scarcely permit her to defy or embarrass her husband under the eyes of a guest.

"According to your will, Magnifico," Sonnetia returned tonelessly, and withdrew, heels clicking a sharp tattoo on the marble floor.

Vinz shut the door after her. His heart was beating fast with a kind of exhilarated anger, beneath which doubt and guilt persisted. He had behaved abominably. She might not forgive him for days; she might never forgive him. But no, he reassured himself. He had merely asserted himself, as a man ought within his own house. He was master here, he was entitled to respect, and his wife should keep that in mind. As for her forgiveness—why, she was the one who should apologize to *him*. She, after all, was the one whose maidservant went bouncing off to Belandor House upon unspecified errands. She was lucky he didn't beat her for it.

Beat her? The idea was unsettling. He had never in his life lifted a hand against any woman, much less Sonnetia. But he could. She might stand an inch or so taller than he, but he was undoubtedly the stronger. He could chastise his wife anytime he chose to exert his rightful authority, and maybe he should, maybe that was what the situation called for. Maybe it was what Aureste Belandor would do.

Vinz slanted a covert glance at Lousewort, whose forgettable countenance revealed nothing beyond alertness.

"Well," he prodded, "what do you think, eh?"

"About the magnifica?"

"How much do you suppose she overheard?"

"Difficult to say." Lousewort shrugged.

"Think she might be something of a—well, a *liability,* then?"

"You'd be the best judge of that, or you should be."

Yes, he should be. And he *was,* Vinz encouraged himself. He was a magnifico of Vitrisi, as well as an arcanist of the first rank, and he was certainly capable of governing his own wife.

"I'll confine her to her own chambers for the next few days," Vinz decreed. Lousewort's face told him nothing, so he added, "She'll receive no visitors. She'll neither send nor accept messages. And I'll lock that maid of hers up as well. That should keep them both out of mischief." There, spoken like the magnifico that he was. He should have adopted an authoritative stance long ago.

"Quite likely." Lousewort appeared less than satisfied.

Vinz knew what was required. "The assault upon Belandor House," he proclaimed with stunning assurance, "will take place in three days' time. And there at last is an end to the Kneeser King."

• • •

"Is the sficchi ready yet?"

"How do I tell when the sficchi's ready?" Jianna inquired.

"Tell me how it looks," Rione instructed.

Jianna surveyed the contents of the beaker. "It resembles pond scum that's been carefully aged for a couple of decades, then reduced to a rotten jellied essence."

"Perfect. It's ready." He smiled.

Finally. Following her attempted cozenage, he had treated her with an impassive courtesy that she found surprisingly difficult to bear. It had only been a matter of some twenty-four hours, but the time had stretched into eons. Now at last he was starting to thaw. Her spirits lifted and her face brightened. Returning his smile, she handed him the beaker and watched as he applied the contents to the blistered flesh of a potboy recently splashed with boiling oil. After that came a session with the maggots, to which she had grown comfortably accustomed, even going so far as to assign some of the creatures pet names. Then there was the cleansing of assorted wounds, the changing of various bandages; dispensing of medication; the odorous draining and chemical cauterization of an abscess, accomplished all but painlessly, thanks to Rione's skill. Then the inevitable bathing of fevered limbs and bodies, and the emptying of bedpans—to which she would never accustom herself, no matter how often she was obliged to do it.

The busy hours hurried by. There was little to distinguish this day from its recent predecessors, save for her newly sharpened sense of time's gallop. Then came a change that drove all thought of time from her head, for a while.

It was late afternoon and the daylight was already starting to wane. The infirmary lamps had been lit, and Dr. Rione was toiling away in the yellow glow. But not for much longer, surely. His patients had all been tended; each lay as comfortably as circumstance and medical expertise allowed. A variety of lesser tasks had been performed. All was properly ordered and he might allow himself a rest, in Jianna's opinion.

"You might allow yourself a rest, in my opinion," she suggested.

"I might at that," he agreed and smiled at her expression. "What's the matter? You look as if I'd sprouted antennae."

"That would be interesting. But no, I'm only a little surprised. Usually you can't be pried from your labors."

"Ah, I know you must think me a dull, dour character."

"Not dull at all," she assured him. "Nor even dour, exactly. But serious, always serious. You think of nothing in the world but your work."

"Untrue, maidenlady. I am capable of levity, upon occasion. When I strain to the uttermost, I have been known to achieve frivolity."

"Never."

"Once or twice."

"Humor, perhaps. Frivolity, no."

"Get your cloak."

"Why?"

"We're going to step outside for a breath of fresh air, and while we walk about the courtyard, I'll prove my point. I will relate an amusing anecdote, certain to inspire mirth."

"Do you know any?"

"One or two."

"Oh, this should be splendid. Or at least instructive." Jianna found herself suddenly and unaccountably light-hearted. There was no sound reason, for the doctor's good humor signified little. Or perhaps it did, perhaps he would relent and help her after all. At the moment she hardly cared. He was still smiling, the expression wiping years from his face, and her sense of inappropriate happiness intensified. He was by no means the handsomest man she had ever encountered, with his middling slim stature and his pale scholarly face. Nonetheless, the intelligent grey-blue eyes, firm jaw, and mobile lips pleased her greatly. She never seemed to tire of looking. "I'll just go get—"

The infirmary door banged open with a vehemence that

startled her into silence. Those patients retaining consciousness turned to gape, and Jianna did likewise. One of the household guards stood on the threshold.

"You're wanted," he informed Rione. "Kitchen. Make it quick."

Jianna scowled, affronted by the fellow's manner, but Rione appeared impervious, merely inquiring, "Why?"

"Trecchio. Stung by a siccatrice."

"Where?"

"Hand."

"When?"

"Dunno."

"Right." The doctor's eyes shifted to Jianna's face, and he commanded briefly, "You come with me." Pausing only long enough to scoop up his leather bag, he was through the infirmary door and on his way down the stairs, the guard at his side.

Astonished, Jianna scurried in their wake, down the stairs and through the second-story warren. Down more stairs, and on the ground level she caught up with Rione, managing to claim his attention long enough to ask, "What's a ziktris?"

"Siccatrice."

"Some kind of a snake?"

"An arachnid. A kind of woodland scorpion."

"And he's been stung. That must smart. Pity." Her lip curled. "Maybe this will teach him a good lesson. Maybe he'll learn that the worm or the scorpion can turn."

"Maybe he will, if he survives."

"What, you don't mean that one sting from something that isn't a snake could actually kill him?"

"It might, if he doesn't receive prompt treatment. And even then, the outcome isn't certain."

Taken aback, Jianna said nothing. Throughout the term of her imprisonment, she had had few dealings with Trecchio. He had not participated in the murderous attack upon the Belandor carriage. He had manhandled her upon the evening of her arrival, earning her permanent enmity, but thereafter he had never again touched her; had never, in fact, taken much notice of her. Presumably regarding her as the rightful property of his older brother, he had kept his hands to himself and—saving the occasional unimaginative incivility at table—had troubled her not at all. Thus he had retreated to the periphery of her awareness, and she had all but dismissed him from her thoughts.

She thought about him now, however; concluding that she didn't actively wish him dead, but would hardly mourn his loss.

Moments later they reached the kitchen, with its warm atmosphere and its perennial population of household menials. Trecchio was not in evidence, but the arched door to the stillroom stood ajar and the guard's gesture ushered them through.

Jianna blinked and her nose wrinkled. The stillroom was dimly firelit, its air weighted with an indefinably alarming odor. Trecchio lay stretched out on the table. His eyes were open but unfocused. His doublet was off, one of his linen shirtsleeves rolled up, baring his right arm. Beside him stood his mother, plying a poultice.

Yvenza's eyes lifted to Rione's face. "My youngest has played the fool again," she observed. "Now he's paying the price."

An inarticulate mumble of protest escaped Trecchio.

"Shut up, boy," his mother admonished. "You're getting nothing more than your stupidity deserves."

"And what is he getting?" Rione inquired easily.

"See for yourself."

"Siccatrice, I'm told," Rione prompted.

"Stuck his idiot hand into the wrong bush. Now he loses it."

Trecchio's mumbling rose in pitch.

"Oh yes, sonny. Make up your mind to it." Turning back to Rione, she inquired, "Bone saw sharp, lad?"

"Perhaps unnecessary," he replied.

"Careful. I don't tolerate falsehood."

"I know. What point in misleading you, Magnifica? I believe that your son's hand may be saved, provided he's treated promptly."

"A fairy tale, I suspect, and he's like to lose more than his hand if you're wrong."

"I am not wrong, but he must choose for himself." Rione bent to address the sufferer directly and very distinctly. "Trecchio, I've a treatment that should spare you amputation, but it is my own invention and not generally known. Do you want it?"

"He's unfit to decide," Yvenza observed. "I give you permission, lad. Do what you like, without fear. If you fail, I'll not hold it against you."

Rione seemed not to hear her. "Trecchio, what's your answer?" he persisted.

Yvenza's brows rose. Jianna's did the same.

Trecchio's response was garbled but recognizably affirmative.

"There's the sweet salve for your conscience, ready and waiting should the need arise." Yvenza forged an iron smile. "What do you need?"

"Bathtub if possible, otherwise washtub, large quantities of hot water, clean towels," Rione requested. "Basin, dipper, rezhia moss packing if you have any. That should suffice."

"You'll have it. In the meantime, I suppose you'll want the place cleared out."

"But for the maidenlady."

"Ah?" Yvenza's gaze briefly skewered Jianna. "She's so useful to you, then?"

"She is a willing and able assistant."

"Willing. That is interesting. You will tell me more, but now is not the time. To work, then. When there's news, send word, even if I am sleeping."

Sleeping? Jianna wondered. *Her son may lose a hand or more, and she can sleep?*

Yvenza withdrew without visible reluctance. Rione seemed scarcely to note her departure. Already he was at Trecchio's side, stripping the poultice from the damaged hand. Jianna glimpsed a sunken crater of scaled grey flesh surrounding a dry white ulcer, a sight outside her experience. Her gaze sought Trecchio's face, which was grey and curiously . . . *shrunken* was the term that sprang to mind. He appeared marginally conscious.

Rione ran one fingertip lightly around the circumference of the crater, and a long shred of dry skin flaked off. Trecchio noticed nothing, but Jianna drew in her breath sharply. Repelled and fascinated, she stepped nearer for a closer look. The flesh surrounding the wound was shriveled and apparently dead. The ulcer marking the entry point of the siccatrice's sting was ruffled with translucent white scales. A brush of the doctor's finger dislodged a powdery shower of them.

"Help me get his clothes off," Rione commanded.

"Everything?"

"Everything."

Jianna was undismayed, for her work in the infirmary had inured her to the sight of naked bodies, but she could hardly fathom his purpose. Why strip a patient bare in order to treat a wounded hand? It was not the time to ask. She shrugged and set to work. Trecchio soon lay fully exposed to view, and the object of the doctor's scrutiny revealed itself at once. A scaly grey patch marked the patient's upper arm. Another—small enough to pass for a mole—blemished his right shoulder. Her eyes caught Rione's.

"Dried tissue," he answered the unspoken question. "Drained of nearly all its moisture."

He did not need to say more. He did not need to inform her that it was already too late to halt the malady's advance by means of amputation; that was self-evident. Trecchio was clearly doomed. It remained only to keep him as comfortable as possible throughout the final hours of a life unlikely to outlast the night. She wondered whether Yvenza's apparent indifference would sustain the news of her younger offspring's early demise.

At least the poor wretch didn't appear to suffer. It would not be necessary to pump him full of kalkriole. Probably it would be best to keep him warm, though.

"Can't we cover him up?" she asked. "I'll find a blanket or two, and—"

"Step out into the kitchen and see if they've assembled the items I requested," he ordered.

She looked at him, surprised no less by his curtness than by his expression, which was particularly intent. His face reflected none of the reluctant resignation reserved for those such as Grezziu, whose cases he deemed hopeless. It was clear at a glance that Rione still expected and intended to preserve his patient. She nodded and did as she was bid. Moments later she was able to report, "The things you asked for have been laid out on the kitchen table, except for the moss. Most of the servants are out of there, but there's still one of the boys pumping and heating water. The bathtub—I suppose it's a bathtub, it's shaped like a shoe and riddled with rust—is more than half full."

"Good." He did not glance in her direction. He was engrossed in some task that involved measuring, weighing, and mixing of powders, liquids, and unguents. A few minutes later, an airborne pungency tickled her nostrils, and she hacked a muffled cough. Rione settled back in his chair with an air of accomplishment. "There," he said.

"A draught?" she asked.

"A wash."

"You'll want some clean cloth."

"No need."

"Oh, it's going straight into the bathwater, then?" she guessed.

"Good girl. Here—" He handed her a calibrated glass

beaker containing a quantity of viscous dark fluid. "Pour that into the tub. And tell whichever of the lads is out there to get himself in here."

Once again she obeyed, watching as the dark liquid from the beaker infused itself through the bathwater in slow serpentine streaks. Moist warmth from the tub kissed her face, and her mind flashed on the bath at Belandor House, with its spectacular mosaics, its intricate bronze chandeliers, its perfumed atmosphere, its beauty and safety . . .

Tears intensified the wet heat on her face. She brushed them away and took a deep breath, drawing medicinal vapors deep into her lungs. A moment later Rione and the kitchen boy emerged from the stillroom bearing Trecchio, whom they dumped without ceremony into the tub. He sank without a murmur. Almost casually Rione pushed back his sleeve, plunged a bare arm into the aromatic water, grasped his patient's hair, and hauled the submerged head to the surface. Trecchio choked and gurgled.

"That's all for tonight. Off with you," Rione advised, and his nameless assistant exited smartly.

"Should I go, too?" Jianna inquired.

"Certainly not."

"What's left to do?"

"Much. Roll up your sleeves, maidenlady. You're going to be here for hours to come."

"Very well, but doing what, exactly?"

"More of the same. Repeatedly."

Despite his promise, there was nothing at all for her to do for some minutes thereafter, during which time she covertly studied the doctor. Her attention fastened easily and naturally upon Rione. Her eyes sought his face of their own accord, and his changing expressions held them. The vertical crease between his eyes, visible when he frowned, made him look older than his years but agreeably distinguished, she decided. Presently, however, a moaning outcry from Trecchio dragged her reluctant attention from doctor to patient, whose arms were flailing in the water and whose head was thrashing from side to side. His mouth was open, parched lips drawn back over dry gums, tongue slack and juiceless.

Disgusting, she thought.

He retched drily and her revulsion sharpened. Then a high-pitched woeful whimper broke from him and the sound of it touched something inside her. Despite her distaste and dislike, she pitied him.

"Softly, Trecchio. All's well. Dr. Rione is looking after you. Everything will be all right." To her own surprise she found herself trying to comfort him. Probably he could not understand her words, but the sound of her voice exerted a certain soothing effect and his feverish animation subsided. The swirling bathwater stilled itself, and she saw then that it had lightened, the bruised hue of Rione's infusion fading to tired violet.

"That's good," Rione murmured.

"What is?"

"The way you spoke to him, the use of your voice. Very good."

"Oh. Well. I just wanted to calm him," she returned, warmed to the core by his praise.

"Exactly right. Keep doing it."

"But what if—"

"Now hold him while I take a look at that hand."

Jianna nodded. He often required this service of her; it was one that she usually performed well, despite her lack of weight and stature. Her success lay less in her own expertise than in the magic of the doctor's hands, whose talent minimized the patient's pain and consequent struggling. Still, there could be no denying that she herself had developed a certain skill. Now she judged at a glance that Trecchio's recoil was likely to plunge his head beneath the water and accordingly positioned herself at his rear in readiness to prevent total submersion.

Rione took possession of his patient's hand, whose appearance was startling. The white ulcer and surrounding tissue had taken on a deep purple hue verging on black. Having absorbed quantities of medicated water, the dead flesh was now tautly distended. The entire arm was swollen and faintly violet in color.

Trecchio moaned and pulled back. Taking a firm grasp, Jianna exerted force and held him in place.

Employing the thinnest of steel blades, Rione proceeded to shave fine slivers of spongy purple skin from the edges of the wound. His touch was light and the tissue he removed was dead, but Trecchio responded with screams and contortions. The submerged body flopped wildly and violet bathwater splashed Jianna's face. Blinking, she tightened her grip, bearing down with all her weight to hold him as still as possible. Trecchio's wordless vociferation intensified. Reaching back with his free hand to grab a handful of her hair, he yanked hard, bringing her head down sharply on the lip of the iron tub. Jianna squawked and saw flashing color. Her grip failed and Trecchio tore free. Loosing her hair, he balled his left fist and drove a blow at Rione's face.

Jianna was not aware of the warning screech that escaped her, but Rione heard it and looked up from his work in time to dodge the flying fist. Trecchio grunted.

"Hold him down just a few seconds longer, if you can," Rione enjoined quietly. "Try."

She nodded and set her jaw. Locking both arms about Trecchio, she held fast, clinging grimly as he moaned and bucked. Waves of violet water overspilled the tub, drenching both Jianna and Rione. Seemingly oblivious, the doctor worked on. At length, he drew back and set his scalpel aside.

"You can let him go," Rione told her.

She obeyed. Trecchio slumped lax and motionless.

"Finished?" Jianna ran a hand across her forehead, pushing back the strands of wet hair.

"For the moment."

"Do we take him out and dry him off?"

"Not yet. We've scarcely begun."

"What next, then?"

"Next we replenish the water. Bring it back to its former level."

The big kettle hanging above the kitchen fire remained half full. Jianna poured the contents into the tub, halting when the bath temperature grew uncomfortably warm to the touch; added cold water from the full bucket that the kitchen boys had left by the hearth; and finished with another heated dollop that brought the bathwater to the right depth and temperature. Rione handed her another calibrated fluid measure. She dripped it in, and the water darkened.

This done, she refilled the kettle at the pump, returned it to its hook above the fire, then refilled the cold-water bucket. Thereafter she was free to resume her scrutiny of Rione, who in turn focused undivided attention on his patient. The doctor's eyes never wandered, and Jianna's mind began to fill with ridiculous schemes designed to draw the blue-grey gaze to herself. She might gasp, clutch her brow, and fall in a swoon. She might scream and claim that she had seen a ghost. She might walk across the few feet that separated them, take his face between her hands, and kiss him full on the lips.

This last thought held her by reason of its extreme absurdity. She was the good daughter of a great House and her kisses belonged to the future husband selected by her father, assuredly not to some glorified servant owing allegiance to her worst enemies.

A glorified *indifferent* servant, she reminded herself. He was civil enough and kind to her, as he might be to any stranger in need, but nothing more.

But she did not really believe that, she realized. Perhaps it was instinct, perhaps simple vanity, but something inside her insisted that he was less detached and impervious than he chose to appear. If she could bring him to acknowledge it, she might enlist his aid, or at least win a modicum of satisfaction.

But probably not this evening.

The quiet minutes marched. The bathwater lightened. Trecchio honked, flopped, and tried to drag himself from the tub. Jianna held him down while Rione shaved quantities of dead flesh from the injured hand. This time, the patient seemed a little easier to control. Perhaps Jianna was acquiring expertise, or else Trecchio's strength was waning. Either way, the procedure was completed swiftly, but not neatly. Jianna was drenched, purple-stained from head to hem, and Rione fared no better. Water streamed from their garments to enlarge the violet puddles surrounding the bath. Some of it found its way into Jianna's fragile shoes, which now squelched audibly with every step.

"Are we done?" she inquired optimistically.

"Not nearly," he returned.

She nodded, not surprised. "Going well, so far?"

"I believe so. Too soon to say."

She nodded again, then busied herself replenishing the bath and the kettles. When she was done, there was time to rest for a matter of minutes before the entire damp purple sequence recommenced.

Jianna presently lost count of repetitions and lost track of time. The strenuous activity, continual distraction, and discomfort filled her consciousness. The world reduced itself to flailing limbs, surging purple waves, moaning outcry, much pumping of water, filling of kettles, and feeding of fires; everything else faded to the edge of existence, but did not quite vanish. She was aware that late afternoon had darkened into evening and thence into deep night. She knew that the signs of household activity had ceased; presumably the servants were abed, for Ironheart was silent. She knew that her conscientious tending of the kitchen and stillroom fires throughout the hours had greatly depleted the woodpile; eventually she might be obliged to venture forth in search of fuel—an unwelcome prospect. And she knew that Trecchio's struggles were diminishing. His strength or else his pain was weakening; or perhaps both. He was responding to his doctor's treatment or else sinking toward death. Either way, he was unlikely to present much more of serious resistance.

But in this she soon found herself mistaken. Somewhere in the deep of the night between midnight and dawn, Trecchio rallied. A roar blasted from his lungs and he wrenched his right hand free of the doctor's grasp.

"Easy," Rione soothed. "We've nearly—"

Trecchio threw a left that connected solidly with the doctor's cheek. Rione pitched sideways to the stone floor and Jianna gasped as if she felt the impact along her own nerves. Even as she started toward him, Trecchio grabbed the edges of the tub and hauled himself to his feet, violet water pouring down his body. Once upright he seemed somewhat at a loss, weight shifting from submerged foot to foot, glazed gaze wandering.

Jianna approached with caution. "Best sit back down," she suggested gently. "That's the way to get well. Why don't you just—"

He swung at her and she ducked but stood her ground. "Stop that," she directed firmly. "We're trying to help you. Behave yourself."

He swung again and she dodged, but this time the blow caught her shoulder. The pain jolted and Jianna staggered. *A watered-down version of his brother.* It would have been easy to retreat beyond his reach, but instead she stepped toward him, jaw set and fist clenched to strike back. He stared at her without recognition or comprehension, muttered incoherently, and once again pity cooled her anger. He was off his head, after all.

"Easy, now," she essayed, as if quieting a restive horse. His face remained blank; impossible to know whether he heard her. "Easy. We're almost done, this will soon be over."

Something between a groan and a growl came out of him, and he hoisted one leg over the edge of the tub. His purple-dripping foot hit the floor and Jianna rushed forward without thinking to grab his arm and hold him still.

Not easily done. He tried to shake her off and she found herself caught in a hurricane, clinging stubbornly as he slung her to and fro. The bellow of a tempest filled her ears; Trecchio's wordless vociferation. He slammed her hard against the tub and she fell to her knees, maintaining a limpet grip on his arm as she went down. For a moment or two Trecchio strove to wrench himself free, then pivoted and grabbed her throat with his free hand. Her breath stopped, her eyes popped, and she released his arm at once, but he did not let go.

Amazing how much strength remained in that one hand. Her most vigorous struggles failed to break his hold, and it flashed across her mind that he might actually strangle her on the spot. She might die a premature and ridiculously pointless death here and now. Before there was time for terror to blot out thought, the pressure on her windpipe eased as Rione, back on his feet, adroitly toppled his patient backward into the bath.

Trecchio sat down hard, and a purple tidal wave overspilled the tub. Twice he attempted to rise, but his burst of strength was exhausted and now Rione restrained him with ease. Presently all resistance ceased. His eyes closed, and he subsided with a groan.

"Did he hurt you?" Rione turned to Jianna. "Better let me take a look at your neck."

"No need, I'm well enough. What about your face?" She saw that his cheek was already darkening. "You'll have a fierce bruise."

"It will give me character."

"You already have too much."

"Bane of my existence." He glanced briefly down into the tub. "He won't be any trouble for a while. Why don't you rest? Sit by the fire, dry yourself, have some tea and something to eat."

"Bathwater's low. I'll just bring the level up a bit, then rest."

He nodded, and for the first time since she had met him, she saw unequivocal admiration in his eyes. A disproportionate sense of satisfaction filled her, and her fatigue dropped away. She attacked her work with a will and spent the next twenty minutes pumping, heating kettles, toting, and pouring. At the end of that time the bath had been restored to its former depth and temperature. Rione added another measure of his purple infusion, and the water darkened. Trecchio responded with a restless stirring and a querulous murmuring, but his eyes never opened.

"Is it working?" Jianna asked.

"It is. Look at the marks on his arm and shoulder."

"Still there. In fact, they look bigger than they were. And deeper, raw, and generally . . . nastier."

"You're missing the most important change. Run your finger over the shoulder ulcer."

"I'd rather not."

"I understand. Only look, then. You used the term 'raw.' You might have said 'moist.' "

"Oh. Yes, I see. The dry tissue is gone. It's not spreading out; there are no new scaly patches. He'll live, then?"

"For decades, if his luck holds."

"Two-fistedly?"

"That is the question. Too early as yet for a definite answer, but I think his chances are good. Now, maidenlady, you will listen to me."

"I'm listening."

"You've been working like a slave and you must be exhausted. I want you to rest and eat."

"Gladly, if you'll do the same."

"When I can."

"You can right now. The purple potion in the bath will need several minutes to do its work, won't it? You've time."

"A quarter hour or so."

"At the very least. Come on, then. Sit down by the fire, dry off, and fill yourself. There's food all over the place—bread, fruit, sausage, cheese, cheese of several varieties, I know for a fact that there's plenty of cheese."

"I can't quite account for your preoccupation with cheese, and perhaps it's just as well. All right, I'll take that quarter hour. Did you say something about sausage?"

"I did. See for yourself."

To her surprise he obeyed, abandoning his post, probably not for more than fifteen minutes or so, but still actually turning his back on the bathtub and its occupant to focus, however briefly, upon food, warmth, and respite.

They found a couple of earthenware plates, filled them with edibles requiring no preparation, and seated themselves side by side on the hearthstone; whereupon Jianna discovered how famished and tired she really was. For the next several minutes, the rapid transference of food from plate to stomach occupied her full attention.

Eventually the edge of hunger dulled, the pace of chewing slackened, and she settled back with a sigh. Her back ached with fatigue, likewise her shoulders and arms, but the heat of the fire behind her was wonderfully comforting. Her sodden garments were starting to dry and the warmth was working its way through to her bones, but her feet, shod in soaked slippers, were still cold. She slipped the wet shoes off and looked at them. The ridiculously delicate kidskin trifles, once deep red in color and polished to a rich shine, were now stained, dull, and deteriorating. The right vamp was starting to split; the left sole had a worn spot on the verge of turning into a hole. They were the only shoes she had and, when they were gone, she would go barefoot, else wrap her feet in rags like the most miserable of Spidery beggars.

And once again the sense of time's flight broke upon her mind, reminding her that she should have been rescued long ago, for each passing day bore her on toward disaster. Her father should never have allowed her to remain in this hideous place long enough for her shoes to disintegrate. It was inexcusable.

But what if he's sick? What if he's dead?

Nonsense. Aureste Belandor was never ill, and he was too

strong to allow death to overtake him before the task of recovering his daughter had been completed.

Nobody's that strong.

"In soul?"

"What?"

"Insole," Rione suggested. "New leather insole with reinforcement where needed. And the split can be stitched up. There's still a deal of use left in those little shoes of yours."

"Perhaps, if only I had the leather. And something to pierce it with. An awl, maybe? I have neither of these things, and I don't think that Yvenza is about to give them to me."

"You'll find them if you try. I have every confidence in your ingenuity."

"You do?" Her fatigue began to recede.

"I do indeed, but you won't need to use it. A word in Deedro's ear should do the trick."

"Whose ear?"

"Deedro. Household steward. Lord of the Supply Closets. Don't you know Deedro?"

"Sparse grey hair, wattles, sour expression, always sucking on a foul clay pipe?"

"The very man. He's the one to ask."

"I don't think so. I've smiled at him a couple of times and he pretended he didn't see me."

"No pretense about it. He's extraordinarily nearsighted."

"And I did try asking him a question one morning and he sort of—barked at me. I thought he might be rabid, so I shaved off."

"You should never have approached him in the morning, when his aches are at their worst. He's no good until noon or thereabouts. Midafternoon would be best. Ask him about his left knee, then look interested while he tells you. That will put him in a good humor."

"You sound as if you speak from experience."

"Much experience. Some of my most vivid memories of childhood involve unsuccessful attempts to wheedle favors out of Deedro. It took me years to perfect the technique, but you should find it easy."

"It doesn't sound easy. So—you've known this Deedro charmer since childhood. You grew up near Ironheart?"

"I grew up within Ironheart. Didn't I ever mention that?"

Are you in earnest? When do you ever mention anything about yourself? "Not that I recall," she returned nonchalantly. "But how did you come to live here? You aren't kin to Yvenza and her people, are you? Nor a foster son, exactly. Nor are you a—a—"

"A servant?" he prompted.

She nodded.

"Many would regard me as such, but I choose to think otherwise."

"Explain the riddle."

"Maidenlady, I won't weary you with tedious reminiscence."

"Come, you've piqued my interest," she encouraged with an easy air designed to mask blazing curiosity. "Speak on."

"Very well. I should tell you then that I am the sole son of that Dr. Strazinz Rione who was personal physician to the Magnifico Onarto Belandor, years ago in Vitrisi. My father was much favored by the magnifico, who lodged our family— my father, my mother, myself—within his own palace. My very earliest recollections, so distant that I can scarcely distinguish them from dreams, are of that vast and glittering place."

"Belandor House? You once lived at Belandor House?" Jianna exclaimed, astonished and almost inclined to disbelieve.

"So I was told. I remember, just barely, a great vaulted ceiling, unimaginably lofty, with a vast round skylight of colored glass. This skylight bore the image of the sun, his face wreathed in flame, worked in a score or more varying shades of golden glass. Even the greyest daylight, filtering through that glass, took on the tint of the sun, and it seemed as if the lords of that palace possessed the power to rule the elements."

"You're describing the skylight above the central stairway. That *is* Belandor House! You really *were* there!"

"Or else someone told me. But I think I remember. In any event, I wasn't there for very long. The great change occurred, driving the Magnifico Onarto, his family, and a clutch of his retainers out of the city and into the wilderness. I don't remember much of that. It happened at night in the winter, I think. It was dark and quiet, swift and secret. My mother carried me. I remember cold air on my face. I remember shaking, because the arms that held me were shaking, with cold or fear or both. I remember being inside a carriage with strange sounds and an odd odor; scorching wool, I think. Someone must have heated the bricks for the footwarmers too hot. Then there's a long gap; I don't know how long. I next remember being here at Ironheart, much smaller and less grand a place than the magnifico's palace in the city, but still the same in some respects. My father continued on as personal physician to Onarto Belandor and all his family, and we Riones still resided within the magnifico's own household.

"Then the Magnifico Onarto died," Rione continued. "I've no picture of his face in my mind, but I still recall the sense of shock and outrage permeating all the household. Even at that age, I understood that some great tragedy had befallen us. Yet my own juvenile existence altered very little. The widowed Magnifica Yvenza assumed leadership of the household, a position to which she was well suited by nature. My father continued on as physician to the family of his dead patron, and we all lived comfortably enough beneath the roof of Ironheart.

"Some two or three years passed, and my father began to instruct me. I learned the function of his surgical instruments, the names and properties of the various medicinal plants that he used. He even permitted me to observe his exchanges with certain patients, and all of this I relished. It ended early, though. One fine day in spring, Strazinz set forth in search of some essential root or leaf, and committed the error of venturing too near the VitrOrezzi Bond, where he ran afoul of a band of Taerleezi horsemen. No witness has ever reported the details of that encounter, but it seems more than likely that the soldiers mistook my father for a Faerlonnish insurgent. They cut him down where he stood and left his corpse lying at the side of the road."

He paused, but Jianna said nothing, afraid of breaking the magical spell cast by camaraderie and firelight that had for once loosened his tongue.

"My father's murder occurred toward the end of my mother's pregnancy with her second child," Rione resumed. "The shock of the loss perhaps in part accounted for my sister's premature birth and the resulting complications. My mother lingered for a few days following delivery. Sometimes she knew me, but much of the time she was unconscious or delirious. Many of those hours and days I spent searching through my father's supplies in search of the right infusion or powder, the perfect remedy that would restore her. As a child I could not find it, and neither could anyone else. By the order of the magnifica, my mother received the best care that Ironheart could offer, but nothing could save her. She died and was buried not far from the Magnifico Onarto—yet another mark of Yvenza's esteem. It was generally supposed that the baby Celisse would soon follow her mother, but to the surprise of all, my sister thrived.

"What then was the magnifica to do with us? Two orphaned children, no kin to her, and arguably no responsibility of hers. Onartino—who is just of my age, and was at that time old enough to express an opinion—believed that I should be set to work in the kitchen and that my infant sister should be placed in a wicker basket and left at some cottager's door. No doubt there were many who agreed with him. Fortunately for us, the Magnifica Yvenza did not. Life at Ironheart is not luxurious, but the magnifica saw to it that Celisse and I received the same care, guidance, education, and privileges accorded her own sons. More than that, she took a personal interest in our progress, lavished time and attention upon us, and in short proved the most benevolent of guardians. Many's the time that Celisse or I fell prey to some childish malady and she brewed the restorative draughts with her own hands. Often she took pains to see that we received the toys or trifles that we most desired—a penknife or fishing hook for me, and much the same for Celisse, for even as an infant my sister never valued dolls, or sweets, or anything commonly regarded as girlish. And more than once, when Onartino and I quarreled, the magnifica ruled in my favor over her own natural son."

"Strange," Jianna mused. "Not what I'd expect."

"Ah, you don't know her, you've only seen the worst of her. She is capable of great generosity. Celisse and I aren't the only recipients."

"Nissi?"

"Sheltered here since infancy, although the magnifica has every reason to resent her existence."

"Why does Yvenza keep her, then?"

"Perhaps because her husband would have wished it, or perhaps she pities the girl. Or both. The magnifica is rarely disposed to justify her decisions."

"I've noticed that."

"She was more than good to my family throughout the course of my childhood," Rione continued. "And when I was on the verge of leaving childhood behind me, she bestowed the greatest of gifts. Had she handed me over to serve as an assistant to some cobbler or cartwright, most would have counted me fortunate. But she did much more. She'd noted my natural interest in my father's profession, she knew what I longed for, and she gave it to me. At her own expense she sent me off to the College of Medicine at the Zerinius in Vitrisi, where I studied for four years. My tuition, room and board, incidental expenses—she paid them all, while repeatedly dismissing or refusing my offers of eventual repayment. I did well enough at the Zerinius to win a position as under-practitioner at the

Hospital Avorno, where I continued studying for another two years. During this time I received a small stipend, enough to live on. Upon conclusion of my term at Avorno, I was deemed qualified under Vitrisian law to practice independently, and so I have done ever since.

"A home, a childhood free from want, an education, my profession—all these things are the magnifica's gifts. She has given me more than I can hope to repay in a dozen lifetimes while asking nothing in return beyond my loyalty. That loyalty is hers, along with my gratitude. Do you understand me, Jianna?"

Jianna's eyes widened a little. He had never before addressed her by name. His gaze was clear and very steady.

"I am telling you all of this because you deserve an explanation of some kind. My loyalty is owed to the Magnifica Yvenza," Rione said distinctly. "I may often disagree with her, but I will never betray her."

She heard him too well. His meaning was unmistakable and the finality of it unassailable. There could be no answer and no appeal. A sense of intolerable helplessness froze her mind. Her eyes tingled with incipient tears, and for a moment she came close to hating him. A groan from the tub spared her the necessity of reply. Trecchio was astir again, and the purple waves were sloshing.

"Ready?" Rione rose to his feet and extended a hand to assist her.

She nodded. Ignoring the hand, she stood up. In silence she resumed her post beside the tub. The water had faded again. Trecchio was writhing and muttering, but most of his strength was gone and his opposition to Rione's ministrations seemed all but perfunctory. The doctor toiled on, Jianna assisted, and the fresh energy born of the brief respite gradually faded, but her sense of impotent misery persisted.

There would be no help from him. He might pity her, even like her, but his first allegiance lay elsewhere and always would. There was no rescue in sight and virtually no hope.

I'll find a way out on my own, then. I'm not helpless. I don't choose to be helpless.

But choice had little to do with it.

The repetitive mechanical rhythm of work dulled the edge of desperation. Her back and arms were aching again, and the discomfort offered an almost welcome distraction. Her clothes were wet, her shoes were soaked again, and these small things helped to exclude wretched thoughts. Conversation with Rione was minimal; there was nothing left to say. She dimly noted the passing of the hours, and at length looked up from her labors to behold a patch of the courtyard greyly visible through the kitchen window. Dawn was breaking.

"It's done," said Rione.

Jianna glanced at him unwillingly. She had hardly allowed her eyes to rest on him throughout the preceding hours. He was pale, his eyes shadowed with fatigue, dark hair disheveled. His hands, always so scrupulously clean, were deeply stained with purple. A similarly deep purple, almost black bruise marked his cheek. She winced at the sight and sympathy undermined anger, which wouldn't do; she did not want to lose the anger.

"His convalescence will be long and painful, but he'll keep his hand," the doctor explained.

"It's a triumph of your skill, then. You are truly a brilliant physician." Jianna felt her face color. The tribute had slipped out of its own volition. She did not wish to flatter and please him; he had made it clear that he was no true friend of hers. She saw the response to her praise in his face and instantly lowered her eyes to the bath, where Trecchio wallowed in deep slumber. The ulcers on his hand, arm, and shoulder yawned wide, but the ashen craters and desiccated flakes of the afternoon had vanished. The wounds were angry, but now essentially ordinary in appearance and presumably treatable by ordinary means. Trecchio's face was profoundly still, smoothed empty of everything other than possibility.

Like a baby, Jianna thought, and the simile struck her as

strange, for she had never regarded him as anything beyond large, repellent, stupid, and dangerous.

He was scarcely dangerous now and, for this moment at least, she could wish him a complete recovery.

"Do we take him out, dry him off, and bandage him up now?" she asked.

"Not quite yet. I'll give the infusion a little longer to do its work. In the meantime, I want you to rest. You've more than earned it. You've been toiling valiantly throughout the night and you must be exhausted."

Valiantly. That and his look of concern kindled an internal glow that she deliberately extinguished. Concern? He had none for her, not in any way that really mattered. Favoring him with a curt nod, she turned with a switch of damp skirts, marched back to the hearth, and seated herself. For a little while longer she watched him tend his patient; disappointed and resentful though she was, it seemed that she could not refrain from watching him. But soon her eyelids drooped, her eyes closed, and her chin sank. The warmth of the fire softened her bones and her brain. There was no resistance left in her, and she sank without a struggle.

When she woke she knew at once that she had slept for hours, curled up on the hearth like a scullery maid. The sunlight angling in through the windows was strong and bright. A few kitchen servants drudged at their accustomed tasks. The morning was well advanced. The big rusty bathtub and its occupant had vanished. The puddles were gone, and the floor was dry. Dr. Rione was nowhere in evidence. All of this she absorbed almost unconsciously, for her attention fixed on the trio looming above her. The Magnifica Yvenza stood flanked by two of the larger household servants. Probably the pressure of their regard had awakened her. Serviceably clad in her customary plain gown, the magnifica appeared well rested and untroubled; indeed, her expression was positively benign. Jianna blinked and sat up, absently brushing fine ashes from her face. Nameless dread fluttered her belly. Every instinct screamed a warning.

"Awake at last, little maidenlady?" Yvenza inquired genially. "I trust you've slept well."

Jianna nodded and rose to her feet. The long rest had restored her vigor. She was ready and willing to run, but her path to the exit was blocked. Her mind whirred. Yvenza's air of guileless amiability somehow suggested impending doom, and only one possible cause suggested itself.

"Trecchio?" she forced herself to inquire. He must have died despite all their care, and now his grief-maddened mother desired vengeance.

"Idiot Boy is doing well," Yvenza replied. "Far better than his stupidity deserves. He'll recover and retain his hand, thanks to my Falaste."

Her Falaste.

"I am glad," Jianna murmured.

"Are you indeed? Now there's a pretty expression of sisterly affection."

Sisterly? Jianna could think of nothing to say.

"My dear child, I believe that I can divine your true feelings. During the term of your residence among us, you've come to regard my younger son as a brother, in much the same manner that you have come to view me as a foster mother. Tell me, is it not so?"

"Who could resist the charm of Ironheart and its inhabitants?" Jianna returned with a burlesque sweetness designed to mask mounting apprehension. Her tormentor was about to say or do something dreadful; she could sense imminent devastation.

"Ah, spirited as ever, I see. What an addition to our household you are. You know that I've regarded you as my daughter in all but name since the very evening of your arrival, do you not?" Without awaiting reply to a query clearly rhetorical, Yvenza continued, "Now at last, following so long and weary a delay, I'm delighted to inform you that the final difficulty has been resolved, and your full membership in our little family is about to become a legal reality."

Jianna felt the blood drain from her face. She said nothing.

"What, no questions? I will assume then that you understand me. Yes, I see by your face that you do. And not so much as a single witticism? Well, at times the heart is too full for speech. My own powers of communication remain unimpaired, and therefore I'll confirm what you've already realized. The East Reach Traveler has finally arrived, within the last half hour. He is ready, willing, and legitimately empowered to perform the marriage ceremony. Indeed, it would have been done already, were Onartino anywhere to be found. It seems that my lusty lad departed at dawn upon one of his hunting expeditions. No fear, however—he'll be back by sunset if not before, and then we'll proceed. Therefore rejoice, maidenlady—this is your wedding day."

TWELVE

What would Father do? The perennial question flashed across her mind, but this time there was no answer. No stratagem, no evasion, argument, threat, bribe, or plea would serve her. There was no room left for maneuvering, and Aureste Belandor himself would be powerless to escape the trap.

The thought was wholly unnerving, and for a moment Jianna gave way to uncharacteristic panic. Without thought or reason she made a dash for the nearest doorway, the exit out into the courtyard. One of the servants caught her before she had taken two steps. His hand closed on her upper arm, jerking her to a halt. Still driven entirely by instinct, she wheeled and raked his cheek with her fingernails. Her captor yelped but did not let go. Immediately the second servant caught her wrist. She brought her heel down hard on his instep, but the attack went unnoticed, neutralized by a pair of thick work boots.

"That was rude," Yvenza observed with a smile. "And silly. I believe it's the first time I've ever seen you display true stupidity. Probably it won't be the last."

"I'll never marry your filthy swine of a son!" Jianna yelled, too furious and terrified to govern her own tongue. "You can drag me to the magistrate, but I'll never speak the words, and without the words there's no marriage!"

"Quite right." Yvenza nodded without abandoning her air of tranquil amusement. "But we discussed this issue, as I recall, upon the evening of your arrival. Allow me to refresh your memory, in simple terms that you can't fail to understand. This night you lodge with Onartino. Whether you go to him as his lawful wife or as his whore—and thereafter, anybody's whore—is entirely up to you. But go to his bed you will."

"I'll kill myself before I let him touch me."

"I think not. Suicide is an expression of despair, and a creature of your temperament never loses hope."

"I'll kill him, then."

"Ah, there she is, the true daughter of Aureste Belandor. I thank you for the warning. I believe my son capable of self-defense, but in the interest of safety I'll relay your threat, which he may address as he sees fit. What a blazing night the two of you will enjoy, to be sure."

"We'll all of us enjoy a blazing night when I burn the roof above your head, you vile hag."

"Manners, daughter." Yvenza advanced a pace and slapped Jianna's face soundly. "I don't tolerate disrespect. In order to spare you further embarrassment, I am sending you to your chamber, where you may compose yourself and repair your appearance as best you can. Remove her," she directed the servants.

They obeyed at once, the two of them hustling Jianna out of the kitchen, along the corridors to the southwest turret, and up the stairs. She struggled and resisted every step of the way, mindless of the absurd futility. When they reached her room, they pushed her in, slammed the door, barred it from the outside, then hurried away, no doubt glad to be rid of her.

Still raging in the throes of desperation, Jianna snatched up the nearest breakable—the big earthenware water pitcher on the washstand—and hurled it against the closed door. The vessel shattered, its contents drenching the door and floor. Instantly she was down on her knees, sorting through the wreckage for a suitable shard. She found one quickly, a long triangular fragment with a sharp point. Earthenware was not strong, but how strong would it need to be to penetrate the soft skin of her throat? Just one resolute plunge, a momentary pain, and it would be done. And then she would be safe beyond the reach of Onartino and his rampant brutality; beyond the reach of Yvenza and her malevolence.

She raised the shard and pressed its point to her throat. Then she paused, terrified. The pain she knew she could endure. But the thought of nonexistence was insupportable, almost unimaginable. The world would go on and she would simply not be in it. She was eighteen years old, she had barely tasted life. It was too soon to go; *she hadn't yet had her fair share.*

And anyway—what if she cut her own throat and then her father, at the head of a rescue party, arrived at Ironheart an hour later? Or less than an hour later, but just in time for her to die pathetically and bloodily in his arms?

A creature of your temperament never loses hope. Yvenza had been right. She could not possibly kill herself, at least not yet. Jianna let fall the earthenware dagger and gave way to bitter tears, crying as she had cried her first night at Ironheart. Now, as then, her thoughts flew to her father. He had not come for her. He had failed her. *You shall not be trapped in a marriage that you do not desire,* he had assured her. Those had been his very words, he had *promised,* and what was that promise worth? The tears flowed faster. But even in the midst of her misery, she could not abandon all belief in Aureste Belandor's omnipotence. It was not too late for a miracle, and who was a master of miracles if not Aureste? He could still arrive in time to save her.

Hurry, she silently enjoined. *Pleasepleaseplease. I need you here today.*

. . .

"I'm leaving today," the Magnifico Aureste announced. "The Viper has finally delivered, in his own good time. As of noon I command a squadron of crack Taerleezi guards. That, in addition to the household sentries and the cannon fodder I've scraped off the floors of the local taverns, should suffice to settle affairs at the stronghouse."

"A single squadron, your household bodyguard, and tavern scrapings against a stronghouse?" Setting his nameless research aside, Innesq Belandor swiveled his wheeled chair to face his brother, who stood framed in the workroom doorway. "Is that enough to maintain a siege?"

"There will be no siege. The matter will be concluded quickly."

"You are counting upon arcane reinforcement, then. Aureste, I've tried to tell you—"

"I don't need arcane reinforcement. I've something less mystifying and more reliable—artillery."

"That is astonishing. Your favor with the governor extends so far, then?"

"No. His Excellency wouldn't dare place such weaponry in Faerlonnish hands, even mine, at any price. Another source supplied the two cannon."

"What other source?"

"Better for you that you do not know."

"I daresay. Hereafter you lose all right to reproach my supposedly dangerous arcane illegalities. Nothing I've ever done remotely rivals the magnitude of this offense. Aureste, you could be executed."

"In public, I trust. Joy will reign throughout Vitrisi."

"It is no laughing matter. If so flagrant a violation of the Faerlonnish heavy-arms restriction is directed to the governor's attention, he will have no choice but to—"

"Close his eyes, else lose the most generous of friends," Aureste concluded. "Don't concern yourself; Uffrigo doesn't wish to trouble me in that particular fashion. In any case, it's a risk I'm willing to undertake."

"Speaking of risk, have you considered the danger of launching a direct assault upon a stronghouse containing Jianna? If the cannon fire doesn't kill her, the defenders might. You would do well to proceed by way of negotiation."

"Excellent advice. When I reach the stronghouse, I'll send word to the inhabitants that their lives stand upon my daughter's health and safety. If they harm her—if she suffers the slightest injury, even so much as a bruise—then I will execute every man, woman, and child that I find within those walls. How do you like my diplomacy?"

"An empty threat, I assume. You would not commit such an atrocity." His brother smiled chillingly and Innesq suggested, "You hazard all, if you drive them to desperation."

"They've clearly striven to do as much to me. But come, enough of this. You must trust me to manage this affair competently, as I trust you to manage Belandor House in my absence. Keep the accounts up to date, no matter how they bore you. Maintain discipline among the Sishmindris and resist your own inclination to indulge them. Don't let Nalio do anything too overwhelmingly stupid. Keep your workroom door shut and try not to loose any forces apt to tear the place apart."

"I think it unlikely that you will return to find our home in ruins."

"Humor my vanity, brother. I choose to regard myself as indispensable."

"Am I mistaken, or are you not in a remarkably good humor, all things considered?"

"You're not mistaken. I am in a good humor. For longer than I care to recall I've waited here, knowing that Jianna needs my help but powerless to assist her. I've loitered, I've fretted, I've scoured taverns, I've waited upon that malignity of a Taerleezi governor's pleasure. Have you the slightest inkling how galling it's been?"

"An inkling. Probably not more."

"I've roasted like a pig on a spit. Now it's over, the paralysis has broken, and I'm free to move again."

"You will join this squadron you have bought somewhere beyond the city walls, I suppose."

"Yes, at Strevorri Field. The Viper demands discretion. My tavern scum is already on the move, shepherded along by the best among my bodyguards. The remainder of the household crew, their livery cloaked, ride for the city gates singly or in pairs. I myself travel in a plain little unmarked carriage, fit for a tradesman, accompanied only by the driver and a single armed retainer. I'll be more than anonymous, I'll be next to invisible."

"Any Sishmindris in your force?"

"I've no use for the frogs. Those amiable creatures I leave to you."

"And then?"

"And then we proceed along the VitrOrezzi Bond as far as Abona, where we leave the main road and take to the hillside trails. If we maintain a smart pace and our guide is worth his price, we reach the stronghouse late tomorrow night. The residents will wake to cannon fire."

"The residents. You've not been particularly communicative, but I gather that we are dealing with the former Magnifico Belandor's people."

"How did you discover that?"

"Better for you that you do not know. Have you the stomach to confront Onarto Belandor in person?"

"If he is still in this world," Aureste returned smoothly. "Why should I not?"

"There was a wife and a couple of children, I remember. You'll not wage war on the helpless?"

"If they survived, the sons grew to manhood long ago. As for the wife, I remember her well, and trust me, she was anything but helpless. As far as waging war on them goes, I've no such inclination. If my daughter is restored to me uninjured, I'll spare the lives of all, but there must be punishment."

"To what end? So long as Jianna is safe, what else matters?"

"Justice. Future safety and peace of mind. These outlaws have dared to strike at my family."

"These outlaws are your family."

"An attack upon myself signifies little, I'm inured to such things. But to aim at my nearest kin—my innocent daughter, my only child—"

"And your sister. Remember Flonoria."

"Always." The infinitesimal widening of Aureste's deep eyes suggested belated recollection of Flonoria's forgotten existence. "It must never happen again. These criminals will learn the consequences of such villainy. They will learn well."

"What will you do?"

"I'll know when I do it."

"Perhaps you should consider, when you are busy meting out punishment, that this attack has not been launched without cause."

"Indeed. Jealousy and bitterness are sharp spurs."

"What hand sharpened them?"

"My own, you'd say? No doubt these people hate me for accepting the title of magnifico, but what was the alternative? Should House Belandor, one of the Six of the Veiled Isles, have faded and failed for want of a master? Should every Belandor among us have followed the fugitive Onarto into the wilderness? Evidently Jianna's abductors believe so."

"Is that all of it, brother? Have they no other grievance or injury?"

"What do you suggest?" Aureste stood very still.

"Aureste, I am not quite the otherworldly dreamer that you take me for. I am crippled, but neither blind nor deaf, and even I, mewed up here within my workroom, have heard the rumors. It is widely suspected that you engineered the Magnifico Onarto's downfall. It is even said that you personally denounced him to the Taerleezis."

"And you choose to believe this slander?"

"I have carefully avoided choosing."

"There's a neat thrust. How long have you been nursing dire suspicions, my brother? And who are you to accuse me?" Aureste radiated righteous indignation. "You know nothing of these matters. You were little more than a boy when Onarto fell. You weren't even in Vitrisi at the time, but off drudging as apprentice to some foreign adept or other."

"Quess Orlazzu, of the Six, emigrated from Faerlonne after the war."

"Very well. The point is, you weren't here to see for yourself, yet you don't hesitate to believe the worst of me."

"I hesitate often. Listen, it is neither my place nor my desire to judge you, particularly now. I only ask that you keep the past in mind when you meet our kinsmen, and choose your course accordingly."

"The treatment that Jianna has received shapes their fate. There's nothing more to be said. If we continue, we'll quarrel, and that's the last thing I want."

"Or I. Go then, and bring her home safe."

"I will." All rancor forgotten, Aureste clasped his brother's hand, then turned and departed the workroom. His long, buoyant strides bore him through corridors unusually depleted of able-bodied guards and sentries. Presently he crossed the gleaming vestibule and passed through the front door. A humble little unmarked carriage waited at the foot of the marble stairs. He took his place within, signaled the driver, and the vehicle moved off. Seconds later the great gilded gates at the foot of the drive swung wide, permitting exit into Summit Street.

Through the Clouds the carriage clattered, as far as the White Incline whose steep grade descended from the exalted realms of wealth down into the heart of Vitrisi. There, as predicted, the commonplace conveyance attracted little attention, and its unpopular passenger went unnoticed. There were no flying rocks, no insults riding on the breeze, and it came to him that he had all but forgotten how pleasant it could be to travel as a normal citizen, object of nobody's detestation.

The passage to the northeast gate was exceptionally circuitous, as several of the thoroughfares offering the shortest route were blocked off with tall wooden stockades bearing the red X of the quarantine. A couple of the neighborhoods so confined were surprisingly prosperous, yet their smoky air, redolent of the mass funeral pyres, might have wafted straight from the Spidery slums.

The detours were navigated in time, and the sun was still at its highest, almost directly overhead, as Aureste's carriage departed Vitrisi along the VitrOrezzi Bond, en route to Strevorri Field and a rendezvous with a squadron of ruinously expensive Taerleezi guards.

. . .

Vinz Corvestri tried hard to concentrate on the words. The epic *Journey of the Zoviriae,* one of the classics of Faerlonnish literature, had always been one of his favorites. As a boy he had gloried in the huge tale of war, adventure, and heroism, identifying himself with the character of Soliastrus, powerful and benevolent arcanist. When fully caught up in the story, he had not infrequently forgotten to feed himself. Today he sought no such profound immersion, but only brief distraction; sought and failed to find it. The rhythm of the verses was as stirring as ever, the deeds of the characters as inspirational, but none of it had the power to tear his thoughts for a single instant from the prospect of the night's activities. The sneak attack upon Belandor House. *The preemptive strike,* he reminded himself. A project dear to the heart of the Faerlonnish resistance movement. A very necessary act of self-defense on the part of Vinz Corvestri. The plan was complete, he was inescapably committed, and there was no sense in agonizing over it.

Vinz fixed his eyes on the quarto page before him:

> Grey Soliastrus raised his staff aloft
> And called upon the power of his mind
> To catch the lightning bolt midway between
> The sky and mountaintop; to hold it fast
> Suspended motionless across the vault
> Of night. The lucent beacon overhead,
> Its flight arrested and its glory chained,
> Proclaimed the mage's triumph to the world.

Halt a lightning bolt in midair and hold it there? An impressive feat indeed, and certainly exceeding Vinz's own capabilities. Not that he would do it if he could. The poem never seemed to address the issue of the ultimate explosive liberation of all that pent energy. Sooner or later the lightning bolt would find release, complete its interrupted flight, and when it finally hit the ground, the gigantic discharge would probably incinerate all living creatures within a radius of miles. There would be fire everywhere . . . *There would be fire at Belandor House tonight.* There would be screams, glinting steel, blood, groans . . .

Vinz shuddered. He wanted no part of it. For two decades and more he had aided the resistance, giving freely of his time, his money, and his arcane skill. Had his involvement come to light, he would have suffered execution at Taerleezi hands, despite his rank and lineage. Throughout the years, however, he had always managed to hold himself aloof from violence. He was ill-suited by temperament, training, or physique to active physical endeavor; moreover, his talents were too valuable to risk in the field, or so he preferred to believe. Tonight, however, his cherished immunity lapsed. He would not only accompany the resistance attack force, he would actually walk at its forefront; unavoidably so, for he alone possessed the ability to overcome the assorted arcane safeguards doubtless reinforcing the mundane defenses of Belandor House. The commandos would never get in without him; there was no help for it.

The fury, the destruction, the wholesale slaughter . . . He could see it all, he could almost hear and taste it. Horrible. And all the more horrible, he could not help but consider, should the blood that would flow within hours happen to include any of his own. Not impossible. The guards of Belandor House were trained fighters and well armed. He, the Magnifico Vinz Corvestri, arcanist of the first rank—well, high up in the second rank, at the very least—could be hideously wounded or even killed. Mere hours from now, he might be lying dead in a puddle of precious Corvestri blood.

And that would be that. He would never see his son again. Or his wife. *Would she care? Would she even notice?*

Vinz discovered that his mouth was dry and his forehead wet. Drawing a deep breath, he sat up straight and squared his shoulders. His fears were puerile. The simplest of arcane air-shields would easily ward off the primitive blades and missiles of Belandor House's guardians. Not so much as a drop of his own blood would be lost. The destruction of the household members, the Sishmindris, the mansion itself with its many treasures—all regrettable necessities. And at the end of it all, the prize of all prizes—Aureste Belandor would be gone for-ever. Aureste would die at the hands of his own countrymen, as he had so richly deserved for so many years, and then at last there would be peace. No more fear, loathing, jealousy, suspi-cion. Only peace.

Worth one ugly night, wasn't it?

A light tapping impinged upon his cogitation. The door of his study creaked open, and his wife stepped into the room. Surprised, Vinz stared at her. Attired in a simple, exquisitely cut gown of ash-grey silk, her autumnal hair wound into a heavy knot at the nape of her neck, Sonnetia embodied re-mote elegance. Often her graceful self-possession discon-certed him, even after half a lifetime of marriage. Not today, however. Today, she was the one with cause for discomfort.

"Magnifico, a moment of your time," Sonnetia requested in her low, well-modulated voice.

"You have disobeyed me, madam." Whatever discussion ensued, Vinz meant to command it from the outset, to com-mand *her*. And high time. He had made a good beginning in the presence of Lousewort, three days earlier, and now he was determined to maintain his advantage. "I ordered you to your chamber, and that command has not been revoked. Yet here you are. I am displeased."

"I regret your dissatisfaction, sir. May our reconciliation re-store your good humor."

"What reconciliation do you propose?"

"I've spent the last three days confined to my apartment. Whatever the nature of my offense, I've been sufficiently punished. I've come to ask for my liberty."

I'm sorry. Can you ever forgive me? The craven words trembled on the verge of utterance, but he managed to hold them in. He had played the weakling long enough, and things were changing now. *She'll hate me forever.* Another feeble fear. She wouldn't hate or blame him for asserting his rightful authority within his own home. Once she got over her initial shock, she would come to respect him, perhaps even admire him. *For the first time.* But the respect he wanted did not yet exist, as her attitude—despite the punctilious propriety—too clearly demonstrated. Vinz studied his wife. Her beautiful, closed face displayed no trace of uncertainty or trepidation. There was not the smallest doubt in her mind that her husband would yield to her will, *as always.* He was so compliant, so fair and reasonable, so amiable and predictable. So eager to please, so *boring.*

But not always.

"In demanding your liberty, you take far too great a liberty, madam," he informed her. "You might have sent me a written petition. Instead you've chosen to flout my commands and quit your chambers without my leave. Your disobedience is unmannerly and unwomanly. When you've learned how to conduct yourself, we'll discuss the restoration of your privileges. In the meantime, you will return to your chambers and await my pleasure."

She was staring at him impassively, but he had the distinct sensation that he had gone too far and a qualm of doubt unsteadied him. He came within a breath then of retracting his words, apologizing, *crumbling,* but once again succeeded in controlling the impulse.

"My incarceration serves no purpose," Sonnetia observed quietly. "Various household matters demand my attention, and it is best that I resume my duties. Pray you, Magnifico, favor me."

Impossible that he yield the upper hand upon demand. Assuming an attitude of chill disapproval, he inquired, "Will you oblige me to repeat my commands?"

"What—is—the—matter—with—you?" Her enunciation was achingly precise.

Vinz shifted his weight uneasily. She had not raised her voice in the least and her face remained expressionless, but it came to him, as it did from time to time, that her habitual composure was achieved only by means of constant self-control. Not unlike a lightning bolt caught midway between the sky and mountaintop. And sooner or later, the lightning bolt would find release, and he did not want to be in her vicinity when it did.

Intimidated by his own wife? No wonder she didn't respect him.

"Leave me, madam," he commanded.

She did not obey, but remained where she was, motionless and staring at him. Her analytical scrutiny was well nigh unbearable. When he thought he could stand no more, she spoke. "You are not yourself."

"I am very much myself, perhaps for the first time." He could not suppress a certain audibly defensive note.

"You've been speaking and behaving strangely. It began the evening I walked in on you and that man here in this study."

"Forget about him. My visitors are no concern of yours."

"That wasn't the first time he's been here."

"I said, he's no concern of yours!" He heard the shrillness in his own voice and deliberately lowered the pitch to admonish, "I won't have you meddling."

"Your discourtesy and petty tyranny date from that evening."

"You will not speak to me in that fashion! I forbid it, madam."

"You were ill-tempered, unpleasant, and unaccountably

uneasy," Sonnetia recalled. "You very much wanted to know what I'd overheard, which amounted to no more than three words. Something about a military strike and the name Belandor. It meant nothing to me at the time, and indeed I'd never have given it a second thought, but for your peculiar behavior. I'm thinking about it now, however, and the implications are terrible. You are not—surely you can't mean to launch some sort of attack upon Belandor House?"

"How dare you interrogate me, madam? How dare you?" Vinz was doing his best to conceal his dismay. He had never confided in her, she had little if any significant information, and yet somehow she had guessed correctly. Was this the proverbial feminine intuition at work, or something more? Had she been spying on him? Relaying information to Belandor House by way of her maidservant, perhaps? Or was it simply a lucky hit, enabled by his own blunders? . . . *indeed I'd never have given it a second thought, but for your peculiar behavior.* Whatever the explanation, he could not let her know that she was right, and he most certainly could not allow her communication with anyone outside Corvestri Mansion. He marshaled his forces and returned fire. "I have ordered you back to your chambers. Obey me, madam. Now!"

"I desire an answer."

"Are you defying me?"

"I'll return to my chambers when you've assured me that you are not involved in some sort of resistance plot. Only give me your promise that you won't take part in anything dangerous and destructive, and I'll gladly go."

"I'm hardly obliged to *bargain* with my own wife in my own house. I am the master here—a point you seem inclined to overlook."

"Your choices and their consequences directly affect the welfare and future of our son—a point *you* seem inclined to overlook."

"You don't seriously imagine that I'd jeopardize Vinzille in any way?"

"If involvement in resistance activities results in your arrest and execution, then Vinzille stands to lose his noble rank and his entire Corvestri fortune. Have you considered that?"

Her husband's safety did not concern her in the slightest, Vinz noted without surprise. Her care was for her son. His sense of resentment deepened, along with his determination to assert himself. Swiveling in his chair, he grasped the tapestry bellpull that hung behind his writing desk and yanked it hard. A big liveried Sishmindri answered the summons at once.

"Escort the magnifica back to her apartment," Vinz directed. "Station yourself at the door and see to it that she does not emerge."

Sishmindri faces rarely communicated anything, but Vinz fancied that he caught a brief flash of astonishment in the great golden eyes. The amphibian's head dipped in mute acquiescence.

"I do not deserve this." Sonnetia was standing stiff-spined, eyes stormy with incredulous anger, but her voice remained low and even. "It is unbelievable. What is wrong with you?"

"Nothing. I've recalled at last that I am the Magnifico Corvestri."

"I don't understand you. And you don't understand me if you expect me to accept insult and humiliation. I've been a dutiful wife to you for all these years, but there are limits. I'll not tolerate abuse."

"You'll tolerate the rightful authority of your husband, madam. It is a lesson you should have learned years ago, but I trust it is not too late to teach you." Vinz snapped his fingers, engaging the regard of the Sishmindri, whose house-name he did not recall and whose real name he had never known. "Remove her."

The Sishmindri hesitated, visibly reluctant to lay web-fingered hands upon his mistress.

"It's all right, Teebo," Sonnetia resolved the amphibian's dilemma. "I'll go." Her voice was controlled as always, but the glance she cast at her husband communicated the deepest out-

rage. Head high, she marched out of the study, closely followed by her guard, and the door closed behind them.

Vinz expelled his breath in a sigh. It was over. He had engaged in a contest of wills with his wife and emerged the victor.
He had asserted his rightful authority, displayed appropriate
firmness and resolve, defended the secrecy of the night's venture. Save for her single disturbing flash of insight, things had
gone quite well, and he had every right to enjoy a few moments
of well-deserved self-satisfaction. But he was not enjoying anything. That look she'd given him! In all their years together, he
had never seen such anger in her eyes, and that wasn't the worst
of it. There had been something more, something akin to—
what? Reproach? Bewilderment? Something that stirred his
guilt and remorse.

Nonsense. He was tormenting himself over nothing. The
anger in her eyes—now, *that* had been real, the reaction of a
self-willed, overindulged woman unaccustomed to restraint.
He had granted her too much freedom, which she may or may
not have misused, but those days were over.

He did not care to speculate as to the manner in which she
may or may not have misused her freedom. Contemplation of
the impending mayhem at Belandor House was actually
preferable. Another few hours, and it would be over and done
with, one way or another.

Vinz stared out the window and willed the hours to pass.

. . .

Time trudged at its own pace and the afternoon yielded to
twilight that persisted for decades before giving way to night.
Vinz ordered a light meal brought to his study on a tray. When
the food arrived fifteen minutes later, he found that he could
scarcely touch it. His hands were cold despite the good fire
crackling on the grate, and his jaw muscles insisted on clenching.

Unacceptable. He needed that jaw in good working order
to achieve proper enunciation of the syllables designed to

focus mental force. And his hands: Much suppleness was required to perform the gestures that somehow—not even the most deeply learned arcanist really knew quite how or why—enhanced the ability of the human mind to draw upon the power of the Source.

Vinz rubbed his hands together, driving warmth into the fingertips. He forced himself to swallow a few mouthfuls of soup and felt himself warming from the inside. He cracked his knuckles and bent his digits backward as far as they would go. All seemed adequately flexible. He tried once again to lose himself in the *Journey of the Zoviriae,* but the face of his wife kept superimposing itself upon the page. Rising from his chair, he paced restlessly about the study, but the face did not go away. Then the thought of Belandor House sprang once more to the front, and again that was all there was.

The distant tolling of a bell touched his mind. His hands jerked, and his eyes jumped to the window. It was dark outside, but not yet late enough. The hours of waiting stretched out before him and they were infinite, they would never end.

But they did end at last. Eternity expired and distant chimes sounded the stroke of midnight. Ordinarily he would have been fast asleep at such an hour, but now he was extraordinarily wakeful, almost as if he would never sleep again.

It was time. Vinz stood up. A warm woolen cloak in an unobtrusive shade of charcoal lay draped across the chair in the corner. Now he put it on, but not before checking his pockets to verify for the hundredth time the presence of the tiny stoppered vials, the miniature leather pouch, the arcanist's necessities. For the hundredth time, he found all to be in order. Briefly he considered—for the hundredth time—the advisability of taking up a small lantern to light his path, and for the hundredth time rejected the idea. A light would only draw unwelcome attention, and he could find his way without it; he had only a very little way to travel, after all.

With the hapless sense of abandoning a safe refuge, he departed his study. Through the dim corridors of sleeping Corvestri Mansion he made his quiet way; down a secondary stairway ordinarily used by servants, along a humble back hallway to a side exit. Only once in the course of that journey did he encounter wakeful life: A Sishmindri sentry stationed at the head of the stairs dropped into a respectful crouch as the master passed, and once again Vinz thought to glimpse astonishment in the golden eyes.

Slipping the bolt, he pulled the door open and made himself step through into the night. The raw cold struck him at once, despite the protection of his cloak. Autumn had undeniably yielded to winter, and all his instincts urged him to shrink back into the shelter of his home.

Later.

Lifting his hood, he pulled the edge well forward to shade his face. He stood at the side of the house, with but a few feet of flagstone walkway separating him from one of the several small doors in the wall encircling his home. The doorway opened upon a small service alley that ran between Corvestri Mansion and its nearest stately neighbor. Never in an entire lifetime of residence had he passed through that particular portal. Even as a boy he had decorously come and gone by way of the grand front gateway. It had never entered his mind to explore a lesser path.

He strode to the door, unbarred it, and went through into the darkness beyond, where he paused, blinking. Seconds later his eyes adjusted and he discerned a faint glow at the mouth of the alley, toward which he groped his way. The glow brightened and presently he stumbled forth into Summit Street, where the big brass-and-glass streetlamps cast their strong light. Instinctively he ducked his head. The illumination here in this best of all neighborhoods was excessive; he might easily be seen and recognized.

Ridiculous. He was thinking like some sort of a criminal. But he *was* a criminal, Vinz realized; or very shortly to become one. He cast a quick guilty glance around him. The

street appeared deserted. No beggars huddled under archways, no drunks sprawled in the gutters; the Watch did not
tolerate such unpleasing presence here in the heart of the
Clouds. *The Watch!* His stomach tightened. Those vigilant
guardians of public order patrolled this neighborhood continually. He might meet up with them within seconds, and then
what? They would wonder what a respectable resident of the
Clouds—a titled magnifico, no less—was doing roaming the
street at midnight. They would offer to escort him safely back
to his own door, and if he demurred, what then might they
think? He quickened his pace, and the sound of his footsteps
seemed appallingly loud, likely to rouse his neighbors from
their slumbers. Along Summit Street he hurried, past the
proudest old palaces of Vitrisi, now largely inhabited by Taerleezi officials, and the insignificant distance that he actually
traveled seemed immense.

At length he reached the end of the street and beheld Belandor House, its arched windows dark, its superb filigree
rooflights aglow. The wrought-iron front gates were closed
and padlocked, but the armed sentries usually stationed before them were unaccountably absent tonight. Curious, but
good. He had dreaded braving the regard of those sentries. To
his right gaped the dark entrance of an alley, similar to that
serving Corvestri Mansion and all great Summit Street
dwellings, allowing tradesmen, mechanicals, and other nameless folk with their wagons and donkey-carts access to the rear
of the building. He had passed by such alleys thousands of
times, barely noting their grubby utilitarian existence. But
now the black gap in the world seemed to offer shelter, which
he accepted with gratitude.

Into the alleyway slunk the Magnifico Corvestri, following
its stygian course along the walled perimeter of the Belandor
property to the rear of the house, where a small lantern hanging above a low postern cast its light upon a silent gathering.
Six of them, he counted quickly, all heavily armed. Strange to

see so few. Somehow he had expected an army. They were not voluminously cloaked as he was, but attired in doublets, loose breeches, low boots—practical garments affording freedom of movement. All were masked, their black dominoes lending them an eerie uniformity. His own face should be covered, Vinz recalled, and he had not come unprepared. Now digging into one of his pockets to bring forth a grey fabric scrap, he pushed his hood back and tied the mask in place. They were all watching him as he advanced, and he felt a complete fool, fumbling with the strings beneath that collective faceless regard. Once the mask was in place, however, the resulting sense of anonymity offered distinct comfort.

As he drew near the quiet group, he caught a whiff of pungency on the damp air, something unknown and unsettling. He walked on and soon descried the source—a still figure stretched prone in a puddle beside the gate. It was a dead Sishmindri sentry lying in its own sharp-scented blood, the first victim of the evening's enterprise. And although he had expected to encounter something of the sort, a powerful revulsion swept through him. He faltered an instant and only with an effort of will compelled himself to continue his advance.

Then he was in their midst, the eyes in the invisible faces all fixed intently upon him, and he was a sedentary rotund amateur among these tigers of the resistance, yet it was up to him to lead them in.

"I will prepare myself," he informed his listeners, and his voice came out astonishingly calm and confident, even authoritative, as if he addressed a band of apprentice arcanists. And nobody ventured to ask him why he hadn't prepared himself well in advance, so there was no need to explain the very short-lived effects of his self-fortifications. Perhaps they already knew, or perhaps his air of assurance impressed them. In any event, nobody uttered a word and the silence stretched as Vinz swallowed the essential draughts, inhaled the requisite powders, and timed his mental exercises to the rhythm of his quietly spoken, practiced syllables.

The inner light dawned almost at once, accompanied by the familiar but ever-wondrous mental expansion. He touched the Source, and its power filled every emptiness within him.

I am truly a master, he thought, and the flowering of self-satisfaction might have choked his concentration, had it been given the chance. But a true master knew how to exclude even the most seductive of distractions. He focused his arcane vision as if through a spyglass of the mind, and the hidden reality of his surroundings surrendered itself without further resistance.

"No arcane safeguards have been placed upon this gate," he reported, hearing his own voice reverberate across great distance. "Only an ordinary lock and key. I can overcome the lock by specialized means, but the exercise will drain a measure of force."

"No need," one of his companions returned.

The voice was low, the face was masked, and a cap covered the hair, but Vinz's heightened perceptions easily identified the individual known to him as Lousewort. How could he ever have thought Lousewort nondescript, nearly invisible? The man's dedication, high courage, and determination all but blazed.

Lousewort gestured and one of his companions stepped to the locked door, pick in hand. The lock yielded with astonishing ease. The gate swung open.

Vinz stood motionless and sent his perceptions questing through into the Belandor property. No exceptional obstacles or pitfalls in the immediate vicinity of the gate, he noted, but some few yards farther on pulsed an atmospheric sensitivity, designed to detect strangers and no doubt alert the Belandor household to the unauthorized presence. The sensitivity was invisible, devoid of physical reality, but in his mind's eye he saw it as a sort of disembodied mouth, throbbing with red energy, alert to unfamiliar flavors and ready to loose huge, silent yowls.

A flex of the mind, supported by corresponding hand gestures, fused the lips together, effectively stifling utterance.

This done, Vinz advanced with caution, passing through the open postern into his enemy's domain. Without turning to look he knew that his masked companions were close behind him, and their sheer silence was remarkable. Not a twig or dry leaf crunched underfoot; they glided on like specters. *Ghosts of the Resistance.* In a back garden was a fishpond with a fanciful arbor, probably designed to please that pampered daughter of Aureste's.

Belandor House arose before him, pure and proud and seemingly inviolable. He had never before set foot upon the property, much less penetrated the house itself. *Unlike Sonnetia's maidservant. And Sonnetia herself?*

For a split second his concentration wavered, and in that moment he felt the lips of the muted atmospheric sensitivity begin to work themselves free. At once he pushed the potentially disastrous distractions out of his mind. No room for them now.

Once again master of his mind, Vinz sent his perceptions pushing toward the nearest doorway in the great house and found the way clear of impediment up to the immediate vicinity of the entrance, which was protected by a heavy atmospheric/receptive shield: a beautifully conceived piece of work capable of feeding and strengthening itself upon the energy employed to attack it. But the Magnifico Corvestri knew how to deal with such a device. The key lay not in direct assault but rather in a systematic undermining.

Vinz took a moment to gather his faculties, then performed the mental and vocal contortions that slightly altered the course of the energy flowing through him, directing the Source's power to another layer of his intellect and allowing him to bleed arcane strength from the shield. The process was not to be completed in an instant. At least four or five minutes passed, and Vinz was peripherally aware of his companions, their regard pressing hard. To these men of action, the minutes of waiting must have seemed endless, but not one of them complained, demanded an explanation, or urged him to hurry. It would seem that they trusted in his abilities. He would prove that their trust was not misplaced.

He intensified his efforts and felt the incorporeal substance of the shield begin to soften. Another minute's effort weakened the barrier to the point of ruin, and then he felt it collapse. The way was clear, and he could lead them in. He actually took a step or two forward before the training of a lifetime halted him. Perhaps his prudence was excessive, for the atmospheric/receptive shield had been thoroughly disabled, but proper procedure dictated a follow-up investigation, and accordingly he projected his arcane antennae.

A moment later his questing vision encountered a flash of hot dazzlement. Pain speared into his mind, sharp and deep enough to rock his concentration. He tottered, and one hand rose to shield his eyes; a useless instinctive reaction, for the radiance was not perceived by means of the physical senses. It took all the experience and technique at his command to retain mental control, and the effort left him gasping. Vinz opened his eyes. His companions, wholly ignorant of the arcane Retaliation seething in their path, were watching him closely—with some misgivings, he fancied, but the dominoes suppressed expression.

"Danger," he informed them, a little breathless, but voice still creditably clear and calm. "Wait."

Again they obeyed without question, unaware that he had very nearly led them all into a death trap. And how could that have happened, how could he have failed to note the existence of a sizable Retaliation hovering just behind the atmospheric/receptive shield? A corner of his mind was free to speculate, and an answer soon presented itself. His initial surveillance had missed the Retaliation because, at that time, the Retaliation had not yet come into being. The destruction of the atmospheric/receptive shield had triggered the generation of the second, far more lethal barrier. He had to admire the skill and ingenuity of such work, even while preparing to destroy it.

A few moments' effort served to project a ShadowSon—an insubstantial replica of a man, complete in every detail, but invisible to the untrained eye. The ShadowSon, gifted with a handsome transparent face and a look of boundless good nature, advanced cheerily upon the booby-trapped doorway. When he reached it, the Retaliation smote so violently that the white-hot play of force defining the outline of the ShadowSon was dimly visible even to the uneducated eyes of the resistance soldiers. There was an audible sharp intake of breath, but no words.

The ShadowSon, lacking corporeality, sustained the attack unmoved. The fiery atmosphere enfolded him, the small lightning bolts pierced him through, but none of it possessed the power to alter his look of amiable tranquillity. Presently the lethal luminosity bled from the air, the killing bolts faded, and the ShadowSon turned a guileless eye upon his audience.

Stay, Vinz enjoined in silence.

His creation obeyed and presently the assault resumed, its renewed fury dimly visible to untrained observers, blindingly brilliant to the eyes of Vinz. The glare crescendoed, the bolts of force arcing so plentifully and murderously that even the ShadowSon took note, gazing about him with an air of puzzled interest.

The bombardment diminished and slowed to a halt. The Retaliation's energy was entirely spent. The ShadowSon stood unharmed, eyes blinking in mild bemusement.

Well done. You are free, Vinz communicated.

Smiling happily, the ShadowSon dipped his handsome head in acknowledgment and ambled off into the night.

A final examination discovered no further danger. Vinz made for the entrance, the others close upon his heels. Through it without mishap and he stood inside Belandor House for the first time in his life.

It was a small mud-closet, plain and bare, clearly intended

for the use of menials. No hint of arcane presence. Vinz led the way through the closet into the workshop beyond, and his heightened senses permitted him to see clearly in the absence of illumination—a privilege denied the companions stumbling in his wake. Belandor House was large and its plan was unknown to him, but probably the place shared many features in common with other great Vitrisian dwellings of its age and kind. Thus he would surely find the chambers of state and significance—including the master suite, *Aureste's lair*—upon the first story above ground level. No need to use arcane power to guide him; better to conserve his resources.

Out of the workroom and into a narrow corridor Vinz led the way and now there was a very little light, just enough to define the boundaries of that space, its source not immediately apparent. Around a corner, and the light was far brighter, almost beating upon his dilated pupils. Several yards ahead rose a narrow wooden stairway. Upon the bottom tread sat the first human sentry so far encountered within Belandor House. It was an old man, white head bent over some sort of work in his lap. He seemed to be polishing a collection of metal buckles by the light of a tiny oil lamp. The sentry looked up, presenting an astonished wizened face, and it struck Vinz as odd that a gaffer of such obvious decrepitude should have been assigned guard duty in the dead of night. Were there no younger men better suited to the job?

Before there was time to ponder the question, a couple of his companions loped by him like masked wolves. The lamplight winked on plunging steel. A cry quavered and the old sentry tumbled full length at the foot of the stairs. At once one of the killers snatched up the lamp, then paused, evidently awaiting direction.

Vinz gasped, shocked and all but sickened. Despite all mental preparation, the speed and ruthlessness of the homicide had taken him by surprise, and now his focus blurred dangerously. His arcane perceptions wavered and for one hideous instant he looked upon his surroundings with the myopic eyes of an ordinary mortal, and saw *nothing*. A quick inhalation of a certain reddish powder restored equilibrium. Alarm and uncertainty receded. Vinz glanced about him, passing quickly over the dead gaffer. His surroundings seemed to glow with their own inner light, outer surfaces transparent, inner realities revealed. His companions were looking to him and now he could easily see the faces beneath the masks, not in terms of feature and complexion, but rather as aggregates of individual experience.

Without hesitation he led them up the stairs and out into a broad corridor whose marble floors, high ceilings, tall windows with brocade hangings, crystal, and gilding cosmeticized the magnificent public face of Belandor House. To the right, vast carven doorways opened upon a cavernous space whose far reaches were lost even to his enhanced vision—almost certainly a state ballroom or banqueting hall of some sort. To the left must lie the grandest personal suites, and in that direction he turned his steps. His followers trailed in his wake. Only one of them, the man carrying the oil lamp snatched from the murdered sentry, paused long enough to touch flame to a window hanging. The fabric ignited and fire ascended.

We won't be able to come back this way when we leave. The prospect failed to alarm Vinz. His last inhalation had fortified him beyond reach of distracting emotion, or so he believed. He did not relish the thought of the mansion's destruction, but at that moment it failed to prick his armored conscience. As for their ultimate departure, he did not doubt that his skills would discover or create a way out for them all.

Before them loomed an archway, its bland curve spattered with bright patches of arcane awareness. He darkened the patches in quick succession and led the men through. Fire bloomed in their wake. Smoke commenced a lazy drift along the corridor.

Thus far the invasion had proceeded in silence and secrecy. Now a side door opened and a rumpled individual, perhaps roused from slumber by the smell of smoke, stepped forth into the corridor. A servant, Vinz saw at a glance, young and stoutly built—the first remotely qualified human guard he had encountered within Belandor House. The young fellow took in the scene at a glance, and sleep fled his eyes. The intruders cut him down in an instant, but not before he managed to loose a resounding outcry.

That will bring them. The prospect that would ordinarily have unnerved Vinz Corvestri scarcely daunted him now. Should Belandor reinforcements appear, the strength of the resistance men, backed by the powers of a skilled arcanist, would easily defeat them.

And sure enough, another figure came stumbling into their midst, a manifestly terrified young woman, and she died before she could utter a scream. Compunction gnawed at the foundations of Vinz's confidence. Smoke scratched at the back of his throat. Firmly he excluded both distractions.

Find Aureste.

On along the corridor, around a corner, to another wakeful archway that had to be sent to sleep; then under it and on until his augmented instincts told that he stood within a few yards of significant prey, an individual of Belandor lineage. *The* individual?

The nearest door was unguarded and unlocked. He led them through it into a plainly furnished, almost ascetic receiving chamber, *not grand enough for a magnifico,* and thence into a simple chamber whose sole occupant, stirring from slumber, sat up in bed.

Vinz glimpsed a pale angular visage, heavy black brows, great dark eyes still smudged with sleep—*Aureste!*—then noted the haggard, almost fragile look of the face, the comparatively narrow shoulders and emaciated frame, the unusual length and delicacy of the fingers. His glance jumped to the wheeled chair waiting beside the bed. Not Aureste. This was Aureste's younger brother Innesq, a reclusive cripple.

He could not raise his hand against a helpless invalid.

Even as Vinz confronted his own reluctance, the detached and purposeful portion of his mind currently governing his thoughts told him that the apparently vulnerable cripple was in fact the most dangerous adversary of them all. Innesq Belandor was an adept of formidable power, capable of single-handedly defeating any assault upon his home and avenging himself upon the attackers, if given the opportunity.

That opportunity would not be given.

Almost before he was fully conscious of his own intentions, Vinz Corvestri narrowed the energy that filled him to a single, concentrated beam capable of altering the nature of the atmosphere immediate to the man in the bed. For one brief moment the air surrounding the target would open, drawing Innesq Belandor's life-force unto itself, a process that Innesq would probably experience as a paralyzing chill. Immediately thereafter the surfeited and nauseated atmosphere would regurgitate explosively, blasting the victim with his own stolen energy. It was to be hoped that Innesq would lose consciousness prior to immolation, but this could not be predicted with certainty.

Innesq was looking straight at him, sleepy confusion giving way to alarm, and Vinz could not let himself hesitate. Collecting his force, he held his breath and hurled his arcane bolt. What happened next defied a lifetime of experience.

In that split second of launching the attack, Vinz met his target's eyes and saw comprehension there. Innesq Belandor knew that he was doomed; knew, and displayed no terror.

Arcane energy impinged violently upon the substance of the air and, deep within the recesses of his mind, Vinz sensed the atmospheric transformation. But it seemed not as he expected or remembered; it was foreign. Beyond foreign, profoundly alien. Incomprehensible. Impossible. *Impossible.*

There was no time to ponder the implications before the atmosphere voiced its anguish in an arcane shriek so vast that even the uninitiated of the resistance caught the faint echo of it, and cast their masked glances about in search of the origin. To the two men present possessing highly trained arcane abilities, the sound was overwhelming. Innesq Belandor's face twisted and he pitched backward onto the pillows, struck unconscious or dead. Vinz was unaware that he himself uttered a cry. Pain clamored in his skull. For a moment he could neither hear nor see. He tottered and would have fallen but for the supporting arms of his companions. Seconds passed, and the atmospheric shrieking went on and on. His mind would give way, some part of him realized, if the assault continued. But even in the midst of torture and terror, some kernel of intellect remained free to marvel at this impossible failure of arcane principle that *could not fail.*

The air about him seemed to burn with furious, glorious light of a color not to be found in the physical world. It was the most beautiful thing he had ever seen, and it was killing him. But then he realized that the ineffable color and the shriek of the atmosphere were fading away and almost he imagined himself willing to endure the pain, if only he might continue to watch. Probably the resistance men were blind, but Innesq Belandor would see it clearly, if he retained life and consciousness. And if he did so, then he must be deprived of both forthwith.

It would have to be done with mundane weapons, for at that moment Vinz Corvestri could hardly stand upright unaided, much less wield the power of the Source. He would have to tell them to ply their blades quickly, while Innesq still lay dazed and defenseless, and he *would* tell them, just as soon as he regained his voice. In vain he strove to speak. Before the words could be forced out, a door in the opposite wall burst open and into the bedroom leaped a quartet of large Sishmindris garbed in the livery of House Belandor. All four were armed with stout truncheons—an amazing spectacle. Even more amazing was their ferocity. Their vocal sacs were gigantically distended, almost doubling the size of their heads. The small membranous frills edging their earholes were fully fanned. Their bulging eyes blazed, while their staccato croaks and hoots unmistakably translated to battle cries.

It was unbelievable, almost as much of an impossibility as the previous moment's lunatic lapse of arcane reality. Sishmindris were inherently submissive creatures, formed for servitude and never defying much less threatening their human owners. And if by chance there existed amphibians capable of resisting this law of nature, there remained the law of man, which meted out death to any Sishmindri caught bearing arms.

But law seemed the least of concerns to these creatures as they hopped to the attack. Or defense, Vinz realized. The four of them stood ranged between the invaders and the bed, positioned to protect the helpless Innesq Belandor. Another surprise, for it was common knowledge that the Sishmindris were defective in character, ungrateful and incapable of loyalty to their human benefactors. How did it happen that these particular amphibians were willing to risk their own lives in defense of Innesq?

There was no time to ponder the question as the Sishmindris charged, truncheons flailing. The amphibians displayed little skill but much enthusiasm, and their efforts were surprisingly effective. Only four of the invaders stood within the bedroom itself, and two of them were occupied in supporting a limp Vinz Corvestri. The other members of the party clustered behind them in the doorway.

Vinz heard a sickening thud as a truncheon slammed a human temple, and one of his companions went down. A wave of dizziness rocked him, and his eyes swam. He was dimly aware of his supporters drawing him backward out of the Sishmindris' reach and out of the bedroom. There was a chorus of triumphant croaks and then he was standing in the receiving chamber amid his companions. The door of Innesq Belandor's chamber banged shut in their faces, and he heard the snap of a lock.

They could break the bedroom door down, but it would take time and serve little purpose. Innesq Belandor was incapacitated or dead, his threat nullified, while the real quarry remained elusive.

Vinz passed a hand across his brow. His head hurt, and his ears were ringing. But no, there was nothing wrong with his ears, the sound was real. Somewhere nearby an alarm bell was clanging. The air coming in from the corridor was heavy with smoke. Distant cries signaled the awakening of the household. No time left to waste on Innesq.

"Leave him, he is not important," Vinz directed, managing to make it sound creditably authoritative despite the throbbing head. "This way."

He marched back out into the corridor, strides purposeful, and they followed his lead, which they might have been less willing to do had they any idea how sick and shaky he was, how unsure and confused. The wild inversion of arcane law moments earlier negated all that he had known throughout his life, and the shock still resonated along every nerve. Overwhelmed though he was, he never lost sight of the evening's true goal—*find Aureste.*

Not easily accomplished in an atmosphere so dark and stinging, so increasingly unbreathable. And worse yet when an eager hand touched flame to a set of brocade portieres. Fire jumped and fresh clouds of smoke choked the air. Vinz's eyes burned and watered behind his mask. He knuckled the tears away and reopened his eyes to behold a trio of household servants bearing down on him. One carried a crowbar, one wielded an ax, and one clumsily brandished a rusty sword. Where was Aureste Belandor's reputedly well-trained and well-armed bodyguard? Even as he wondered, his masked companions expertly dispatched all three household defenders. Evidently the murders did not go unnoticed. Not far away, some unseen woman began to scream.

To the left lay the entrance to another private suite, and he led them through just in time to glimpse nightgowned figures fleeing through a back exit. One of them, a mouse-faced female in a ruffled wrapper, was a little too slow, and someone cut her down while someone else hoisted a shovelful of embers from a fireplace and scattered them across the nearest bed, whose silken coverlet began to smolder. A thin tongue of flame licked the bedcurtains and climbed. Still no sign of Aureste. He was probably barricaded in his own bedchamber with his best defenders gathered about him. Surely he would be found there.

"Hurry," urged the individual whom Vinz had identified as Lousewort. "They'll have summoned the Watch by now."

He could not defeat the Watch, he realized. He had not nearly enough arcane force left in him to oppose a party of armed Taerleezis. That stunning reversal in Innesq Belandor's apartment had shaken him to the center, breaking his connection to the Source and robbing him of all but the weakest powers, hardly more than some apprentice might have summoned. But there was no need to let his followers know it.

"This way. Move," Vinz snapped, as if omnipotent. And still the assumed confidence of manner ruled them and they trailed him willingly back out into the corridor and on along its smoke-filled length to another entrance, another apartment, one whose formality expressed the self-conscious dignity of high rank.

The door was unguarded and unlocked. He led them through into a highly polished small foyer, and thence into what he took to be a private audience chamber of some sort. This was the place, beyond doubt: the master suite, Aureste Belandor's sanctum. And quite deserted, by all appearances. No servants about, no night-light burning, no sign of life. But that meant nothing. Aureste was probably lying in wait with his retainers, poised to counterattack. Or better yet, he was abed and asleep, probably in the very next room.

But the very next room was a study or office, and afterward there was an antechamber, and then at last there was the grand bedchamber that he sought, a lofty space graced with an enormous ebony bed, which was empty, its pillows undented, its dark damask spread undisturbed. The bed had not been occupied that night. One of the invaders promptly set fire to the bed hangings, then smashed a casement, admitting a current of fresh night air to feed the blaze.

Not here. Not here. *Aureste was not here.* And Vinz had no idea where in this great mansion or out of it his quarry might have sought refuge, and no arcane force left to launch an extrasensory search.

"Can you find him for us?"

The speaker was Lousewort, whose black mask had regained its opacity.

"Not by arcane means. The fires that your men lit have excited and confused the atmosphere beyond penetration, for the moment," Vinz lied, unwilling to confess the disastrous depletion of his powers. "We must conduct a mundane search."

"No time. We'll be taken if we don't get out now."

"We've time. Come, we've a mission to complete." Vinz strove hard to conceal his discomposure. "There will never be another such opportunity."

"Not worth our lives. We're done here."

"I'm not. I want to finish this once and for all. I *will* finish it."

"Then you are on your own. May your powers preserve you." Lousewort signaled his henchmen and in silence they made for the exit, evidently confident of their ability to win free of Belandor House without benefit of arcane guidance.

They were actually willing to abandon him. Vinz gazed after them, incredulous and appalled. After all he had done for them and all that he had risked, they were quite happy to leave him here to face his fate alone. Of course, they weren't aware of his present defenseless condition; they viewed him as an arcanist of ability. Which he was, but *not at the moment.* Just now he could hardly fend for himself. He did not know where to look for Aureste, wasn't capable of overpowering a vicious adversary by ordinary means, hardly knew how to find his way from the mansion without arcane vision to aid him, and certainly could not hope to resist or escape should he encounter the Watch. No, he could not afford to remain in this place on his own. Without further reflection, Vinz Corvestri hastened in the wake of his retreating comrades.

He caught up with them in the onyx foyer, just as they were exiting the master suite. Out into the corridor again and now it was uninhabitable, an inferno of hot, hammering, nearly unbreathable smoke-filled air, through which jumping flames and scurrying human figures were intermittently visible. Vinz gagged on the atmosphere. His eyes were streaming; he could see little. His headache pounded and his churning stomach threatened rebellion. Instinctively he reached out and grabbed the arm of the nearest masked figure. He had no idea who it was, but it hardly mattered; anyone able to keep him on his feet would do.

He never knew how they managed to find their way out. There was a blind eternity of heat, screaming lungs, and confusion, through all of which the support of his masked benefactor kept him upright and moving. A dozen times he would have sunk to the floor, there to rest and recuperate for just a little while, but his guide would not allow it, and he felt himself drawn smoothly most of the way, but propelled forcibly as required.

Then somehow he was outdoors, where the air was cold and clean, and his mind and vision began to clear. He blinked, dashed the cinders from his eyes, and saw that he and the others had miraculously made their way back to the same small garden gate by which they had entered the property—eons ago. His supporter, judging him recovered, released his arm and Vinz mumbled muted thanks, to which there was no reply. Belandor House stood tall and proud as ever, but orange light flickered from many a second-story window and, at the south end of the building, a shattered casement belched flame, the lawless brilliance startling as a scream.

The gate was still unlocked, the dead Sishmindri still sprawled beside it, his murder as yet undiscovered. The alley was empty and the way out was clear. In silence the band departed the Belandor property, each member pausing briefly at the mouth of the alley to doff his mask before drifting forth to vanish into the misty night.

Vinz found himself back on Summit Street, alone again, heading for home at a carefully moderate pace. The headache and nausea plagued him still, no doubt aggravated by revulsion, bewilderment, and crushing disappointment. Ugly images seemed to have branded themselves upon his brain. Again and again he relived the violence, bloodshed, and brutality of the past hour. Above all his mind anchored on that indescribable moment in Innesq Belandor's bedchamber when the arcane laws that he had known throughout a lifetime had shattered, and the universe had gone briefly mad. And yet, he recalled, not long ago his son Vinzille had described the accident in the Corvestri workroom in distinctly similar terms. *Wrong,* the boy had insisted. *Impossible. Natural law broken . . .* His very words, and an apt description of this night's occurrence. Impossible. *Impossible.* And trying to make sense of it caused his head to ache all the worse.

The night was quiet. He caught the faint echo of shouting voices carried on the breeze from the vicinity of Belandor House, but that soon vanished behind him. He made it uneventfully back to Corvestri Mansion, entered the house, and hurried to his own apartment without encountering anybody beyond the occasional Sishmindri sentry.

Back in his own bedchamber again, *home* again. A lamp had been left burning, and a fire danced on the grate. His surroundings were familiar, prosaic, and trustworthy. Here, comforting normality reigned. Here it was almost possible to imagine for seconds at a time that it had all been a dream; nothing had actually happened, and nothing had really changed.

He undressed himself without a servant's assistance, extinguished the lamp, and climbed into bed, where he lay exhausted but wakeful. The headache still throbbed. The recollections still burned. And above all, one thought claimed effortless supremacy: It had all been entirely in vain. All the care and planning, the difficulty and danger, the destruction and the bloodshed—all quite useless. For the object of the hunt, the Faerlonnish traitor and collaborator, the Kneeser King, the unspeakable Aureste Belandor had once again escaped retribution.

THIRTEEN

Jianna had been waiting for hours. This extended span was no trick of skewed perceptions. The changing angle of the pale sunlight slanting in through the window of her tower prison told her that the afternoon was well advanced. Evidently Onartino had not yet returned from his hunting expedition. *No fear . . . he'll be back by sunset if not before,* Yvenza had promised, and the shadows had grown long.

And then, it seemed mere moments later, the shadows were gone, for the sun had dipped behind the hills and brief winter twilight had fallen. She was standing at the window when she heard a slight scuffling at the door behind her, and she stiffened but did not shift her gaze from the darkening skies. The door creaked open and now she did turn to face a brace of servants—the same two who had dragged her from the kitchen to the tower hours earlier. Both men's faces were marked with red scratches. And both of them, she noted with miserable amusement, wore the stout canvas gloves that servants donned when dealing with angry cats or cornered rats.

"He's back," one of them announced. "Time to go down."

For an instant she considered resisting. But to what end? She could scarcely hope to postpone much less escape the inevitable. Best to preserve such dignity as she still owned. Squaring her shoulders and lifting her chin, she advanced with a firm step. Her guards, patently relieved at her complaisance, refrained from touching her. Down the stairs and along the corridor, the guards flanking her closely. Down another stairway, cold drafts of Ironheart chilling her face, and thence to the central hall wherein she had met Yvenza Belandor and the others upon the first evening of her arrival. She swallowed hard and walked in.

The air in the room was warm; a popping blaze advertised unusually lavish expenditure of fuel. The table was unusually laden and the room was unusually full; never before had she seen such a large group assembled beneath Ironheart's roof. Yvenza was there, attired in her customary plain, dark gown. Beside her stood Nissi, pallidly drooping. Behind them, Falaste Rione, neatly dressed and looking well rested, one cheek black with bruises. Many servants—guards and sentries, stable people, kitchen people, maids and scrubwomen— almost all of the household staff. Witnesses, no doubt; an entire population prepared to verify the ironclad legitimacy of the marriage. Her eyes flew without volition to the huge figure of Onartino sprawled in a chair at the table, a tankard of ale before him. He was still wearing the stained leathers, homespun, and muddy boots in which he had ranged the woods throughout the day. And one more figure standing beside the fireplace, the only stranger present—a short, wiry individual with a pleasantly weather-beaten face and a grizzled brush of beard. The East Reach Traveler.

"The little bride has arrived," Yvenza observed with pleasure.

"And a most lovely bride she is," the Traveler returned warmly, as if imagining that the decencies were to be observed. "Maidenlady, I greet you and offer my congratulations upon this happiest of days."

She looked into his eyes, crinkled smilingly at the corners, and saw only kindness there, at sight of which a pang of anguish pierced her heart. *Help me!* she wanted to shout at him. *You represent the law, help me!* Useless. He would take her for a lunatic if she tried it. Like everyone else in these parts, this man would defer to the will of Yvenza Belandor. And if by chance he did not, he would probably never walk out of Ironheart alive. Not trusting herself to speak, she inclined her head.

"Happiest of days indeed," Yvenza concurred tenderly. "Traveler, let us proceed."

"By all means. Let the bridal pair stand before me," the Traveler directed.

Jianna advanced as if walking underwater.

"Bridegroom, get up," Yvenza commanded. "Your shining moment has arrived, boy. Let's see a bit of youthful *bliss,* shall we?"

Onartino drained his tankard and set it aside. Rising unhurriedly, he took his place at Jianna's side. Too close. She resisted the urge to sidle away. Slanting a covert glance at him, she once again took in his intimidating height and bulk; her head barely reached his shoulder. His brown hair was lank with oil; it did not appear to have been washed in recent memory. Allowing her eyes to drop to his hands, she saw that the fingernails were rimmed with black crescents. She looked away quickly.

The East Reach Traveler was speaking, his voice pleasant and mellow, and she realized that he was performing the marriage ceremony. This seemingly kindly and genial person was in the process of tying her inextricably to a monster, and it was happening *now.* Her gaze shifted to the doorway and paused there, as if in expectation of her father's materialization. Even now it was not too late for him to save her, and surely he would come; nothing could stop him. But the seconds ticked by, the Traveler's voice burbled on agreeably, and Aureste did not appear.

There was a lull in the verbiage, followed by the sound of Onartino's flat monotone repeating the marriage vows and delivering the appropriate responses. And then it was her own turn, and still it was not too late. Her eyes flew instinctively to the face of Falaste Rione, but he was not looking at her. His expression was indifferent to the point of boredom, and his polite obligatory attention appeared to fix upon the East Reach Traveler. No help there. Why had she for one moment imagined otherwise?

Another lull and then, as if at a distance, she heard her own voice uttering responses. Her mind shielded itself; she hardly knew what she said. Meaningless, all of it.

No, not quite meaningless. When the Traveler voiced the traditional call for legitimate objections to the match, her breath caught and again she awaited miraculous intervention. And there was none. Nothing. No one.

By the power vested in me by the Independent City of Orezzia, as recognized and authorized by the sovereign state of Taerleez, I pronounce you man and wife.

The ceremony was completed. The Traveler regarded the newly married couple with a congratulatory air. An uncertain murmur of approbation tiptoed around the room.

It was done. She was a wife. She felt no different—in fact, she felt very little at all—but a few spoken words had changed everything. In witness whereof, a large hand closed on her upper arm and she felt herself effortlessly shifted about to face her new husband. Jianna forced herself to look up into his face, which, as usual, expressed nothing beyond a certain purposefulness. Her jaw tightened and her eyes narrowed, beaming naked defiance at him. His face did change then, the smallest of smiles ripening his full lips, and already the fear was starting to erode her protective numbness.

Extending one arm, he clamped his right hand on the back of her neck and pulled her to him. Divining his purpose, Jianna stiffened and tried to turn her face aside, but the vise of his grip held her immobile as his mouth descended like an avalanche on hers. He was kissing her so hard that the pressure was painful. Then it worsened as his left hand shifted to the hinge of her jaw, knowledgeable pressure forced her teeth to unclench, and he thrust his tongue into her mouth.

Disgust, helpless fury, and terror exploded inside her. Her eyes squeezed shut and she endured the unendurable.

It was her first kiss. Often in the past she had dreamed of the moment, her mind spinning roseate fancies wholly divorced from the present reality. Once upon a time she had actually looked forward to this. Along the edges of her mind ran the words of Reeni, murdered by the man who now ruled her: *. . . like a nightmare you can't get out of . . . a husband is like a rutting boar pig that owns you.* And it was all true.

He released her abruptly and she drew an unobstructed breath, then wiped her mouth with the back of her hand. *And this is only the beginning.* Her eyes scanned the assembled witnesses in search of outrage, consternation, or even simple disapproval, but found none. The faces about her reflected joviality, for the most part. There were even a few guffaws. Apparently these people perceived Onartino's demonstration of raw dominance as the appropriate enthusiasm of an eager groom. Perhaps they even told themselves that she enjoyed it, maidenly coyness notwithstanding. But no, that couldn't be true of everyone present. Her eyes flew once again to Rione's face and this time he was looking straight at her, clear grey-blue gaze taking in everything, seeing all that was being done to her, and unmoved by it. She told herself that he seemed troubled, for an instant persuading herself that it was true. But then he turned aside, addressed some remark to his nearest neighbor, who shrugged and chuckled, and she finally recognized his essential indifference. He liked her well enough, probably pitied her somewhat, but he wouldn't alter the course of his life on her account.

Well, let him enjoy his life as best he could. In view of his association with the Ghosts, it was a doomed little rivulet anyway. She would save herself without his assistance.

Too late. Trapped.

There were people milling about her; she heard a babble of voices and understood that they were expressing the conventionally joyous sentiments. And she wondered if they were deliberately mocking her, for surely all present, with the possible exception of the East Reach Traveler, recognized her for the sacrificial victim that she was. The servants and guards saw everything, knew everything. White Nissi, with her peculiar gifts, certainly knew. And above all, Falaste Rione understood her plight, but he was as heartless and hypocritical as all the rest, for here he came with a pasteboard smile and mouthful of platitudes to grasp the hand of Onartino, who endured the familiarity with unwonted affability.

"You're losing your little infirmary skivvy, boy," the groom announced. "There are better uses for her now."

"No doubt. My visit has concluded, in any case. I leave Ironheart tomorrow morning." Turning to Jianna, Rione recited unexceptionably, "Madam, accept my felicitations. Allow me to express my happiness on your behalf together with my warmest wishes for your future contentment and prosperity."

The words struck like daggers. The pain sliced through her and the tears rose to her eyes. She fought them down again. He probably did not mean to torture her. He thought that she would do well, at least no worse than countless other brides in less-than-ideal circumstances. He told himself that she would come to terms with her new life. But if she did not, her misfortune was no concern of his.

"I thank you, Doctor," she heard herself reply. She met his eyes, which somehow seemed not to see her. She had no idea what her own expressed. "I am grateful for your kindness, and your regard means much to me."

He inclined his head courteously and his expression, if any, was lost. Then he stepped aside and a grinning gaggle of servants pushed forward to offer their compliments. And then, inevitably, Yvenza was there, her smile radiating maternal benevolence.

"Dearest children," she intoned, "you have filled my heart with joy. Sweet Jianna, at long last I embrace you as a true daughter."

She did so, and Jianna stiffened but controlled her instinctive recoil. The symbolic assault ended and she felt herself released.

"Now and forever." Yvenza's eyes glittered. "Know that you are ours."

"And now that it's official—" Onartino snapped his fingers sharply, snagging the attention of the nearest servant. "Take her upstairs and put her in my room," he commanded. "Stand guard at the door until I get there."

"Come, come, son," Yvenza remonstrated, amused. "Contain your ardor. There's plenty of food laid out. Let your bride eat and refresh herself; she'll surely need all her strength. Gwetto has his fiddle in tune, we'll have some dancing. The occasion demands no less."

"I've already promised her a dance. She remembers." Onartino's lifeless eyes met Jianna's. "Let's give her some time to think about it. Take her," he directed. "I'll be up presently. Right now, I want a drink."

The designated jailer loomed at her side. She would not give him an excuse to touch her. Spine straight, she wheeled and marched from the room, not allowing herself to look anyone in the face, not letting herself see Onartino's brutality, Yvenza's triumph, Falaste Rione's indifference, the East Reach Traveler's blind good cheer, or the jocularity of servants. Out of the room, back along the corridor that she had so recently walked as an unmarried girl, back up the stairs, and this time she needed no guide through the darkening second-story warren. She had lived at Ironheart long enough to learn her way through the nested chambers, and she knew exactly where she was going. Too soon the big oaken door that she recalled from her previous visit rose before her. Her guard opened it with a ludicrous affectation of courtesy. She went in and the door slammed solidly shut.

She looked around her. The room was very moderate in size, even small. In keeping with all at Ironheart, its furnishings were spare, plain, and utilitarian. Oaken bed; washstand; wooden chest. No pictures, wall hangings, looking glass, or ornaments of any kind. No books, nothing to reveal the personal tastes or habits of the owner. No curtains at the one window, whose heavy iron grillwork precluded escape. The fireplace was dark, the atmosphere cold. A single lantern hanging from a hook sunk in the wall had been left burning; this unusual luxury was the sole apparent acknowledgment of the evening's significance.

He would be able to see her clearly in the lamplight. He would be able to see every inch of her. Jianna stood motionless, staring at the lantern. After a while the flame within blurred as if viewed through tears, but her eyes were dry and hot. Despite the chilly air her body was bathed in sweat, while a steel band seemed to compress her temples. In her mind's eye the flame grew and spread, consuming the bed linens, the wooden furniture, the oaken door, and then all of Ironheart, or at least all that would burn.

Not impossible. They really should have known better than to leave her that lantern.

But then, what good would it do, with all the household awake and aware? The smoke would be noticed, the fire would be extinguished promptly, and she herself—probably already half suffocated—would be punished severely. No, the only chance lay in waiting until the dead of night—by which time, her husband would have claimed her.

Better that she die. Better yet—better by far—that *he* die.

At her hand.

She would never escape the consequences, of course. Yvenza would destroy her slowly and horribly. Ridiculous even to consider. She had never committed a violent act. Surely she could never kill a human being.

She could kill this one.

Impossible, in any case. Onartino was huge and powerful. She could scarcely hope to overpower him.

Unless she took him by surprise.

Without a weapon?

Her hot eyes raked the simple chamber. And there beside the dark fireplace stood a poker and small shovel. She darted to them and snatched up the poker. It was iron, solid and heavy. It would do. But she had to get it right. The first blow had to kill or incapacitate. Then, wait beside her cooling husband for hours, far into the night. And finally, when the world slept—take the lantern and start the fire, the great and glorious consuming fire. And perhaps a miracle would occur. Perhaps, in the midst of chaos, she might escape Ironheart, run away into the woods, and finally make her way back home. Not probable, of course. Very unlikely, in fact.

But Aureste's daughter might make it happen.

Poker in hand, Jianna moved to the door and waited there, contemplating arson and murder.

• • •

Father and son faced one another across the table in the small dining room of the master suite, where the Corvestri family took its private meals. This particular evening, one family member was again conspicuous by her absence. The boy's attention appeared to be fixed on his dinner, but Vinz could sense the imminence of a question—and his instinct proved sound.

"How much longer will this go on?" Vinzille looked up from his plate to meet his father's eyes squarely.

Although he had been expecting something of the sort, Vinz was a little taken aback by the suddenness and directness of the query. Vinzille was only thirteen years old, but already a force to be reckoned with. And in another ten years? With his formidable arcane talent, his intelligence and strong will, not to mention his good looks, the youngest Corvestri was surely destined for greatness. The familiar sense of pride welled up inside Vinz.

"Won't you answer, Father?" Vinzille prompted.

"You're speaking of your mother's absence from the table?"

"Yes, it's been days now. Why are you treating her this way?"

You're too young to understand. Another few years and you'll be ready. The habitual response to difficult or embarrassing questions remained unspoken, for Vinz recognized with a pang that Vinzille was no longer too young to comprehend all too readily. He could scarcely explain the nature of his decision to discipline his wife, however. The boy should not be obliged to take sides.

"Son, it's my decision as head of the house, made for the good of the house. Also, it's a personal matter between your mother and myself."

"That doesn't explain much."

"I know it doesn't. But you must respect your parents' privacy, just as you've come to expect us to respect yours."

"I do. I will. Only she's unhappy."

"Has she said so?"

"No. I just know."

Vinz nodded. The bond between Vinzille and his mother was strong and close. Almost he might have envied it, but for his absolute confidence that his own link with the boy was equally powerful.

"Neither of you will tell me what the matter is," Vinzille persisted, "but can't it stop now? Can't she at least dine with us? I'm asking you to end the quarrel, Father. She doesn't know that I'm asking," he added hastily. "You mustn't think she put me up to it."

"I know she didn't." Vinz pondered. By this time, his wife had surely learned her lesson. She would have heard about the assault upon Belandor House, *the failure*, and she would doubtless suspect his complicity, but it was too late for her to do anything about it—that threat was defanged, if in fact it had ever been a threat. Her liberation would please Vinzille. And, not the least of benefits, life would resume its normality, of which there had been too little of late. Yes, it was time to forgive her. "Very well," he conceded. "At your request, the quarrel is ended. Your mother's privileges are fully restored as of this moment."

"That's more like it." Vinzille's eyes—green, speckled with brown, *Sonnetia's eyes*—lit up. He started to rise from his chair. "I'll go get her."

"No, not quite yet." Vinz motioned, and the boy resumed

his seat. "There's something I want to talk over with you. An arcane matter."

"What is it?" Vinzille demanded, instantly engaged, his fascination with all things arcane temporarily superseding every other consideration.

"I'm thinking of that episode in the workroom, not so long ago. The animate corpse, our attempted communication with it, and the results. You remember what you told me?"

"Of course, but I wasn't sure that you would. You didn't believe anything I said, you thought I was off my head, and I supposed you'd forgotten about it."

"I didn't disbelieve you, I just wanted more information. And now I have some, more than I really want. Because, you see, the same thing happened to me. Yes," Vinz answered his son's wordless query, "now I know exactly what you were talking about. I was attempting a straightforward Absorption/ Enhanced Emission—"

"Without calling me? I could've helped, or at least watched."

"It was quite spontaneous," Vinz hedged. "I don't think you were anywhere about. And as things turned out, I'm very glad that you were safely clear of the disaster."

"You don't have disasters. You're always so careful to follow the correct procedure at all times, to take no foolish chances, to get every detail exactly right."

Which is why, unlike you, I'll never be great. Aloud Vinz replied, "I did follow the correct procedure, I was careful as always, and the results were—impossible. The freakish contortion of the energy, the outlandish result—"

"What outlandish result?"

"The force that I dispatched to activate the Absorption was somehow dispersed in a violent, uncontrolled burst."

"You've told me that can't happen."

"It can't. The activity—the basic behavior of the energy that I touched upon—violated natural law that can't be broken in our world. Can't, but was."

"Yes, that's what I felt that day in your workroom. Just what you're saying. But you weren't hurt, Father?"

"Shocked, sickened, but not injured."

"And now you believe me?"

"Completely."

"Then may I tell you what I think it all means?"

"What, you've a theory?" Vinz's paternal pride swelled.

"Well, yes. I couldn't let something like that go by without trying to figure out what really happened, so I've been slogging through the dustiest old chronicles and journals in the workroom, and I believe I've found the answer. I think that the Source is about to flip."

"Flip. Interesting way of putting it. Enlarge upon your theory."

"I've read enough to tell me that the Source reverses its direction of spin sometimes. Not often—only once in eons—but when it happens, everything important in the world changes. All the laws, both natural and arcane, get turned upside down, everything we've always thought we could depend on gets smashed to pieces, and the world becomes a place that we don't know anymore. A place that's comfortable for our enemies, but not for humans. But it doesn't all happen in a flash. There are warnings first, things start going really strange. Sort of like a candle guttering for a while before it goes out. And I think that's what's happening right now."

"So do I," Vinz answered.

"You do? I thought you were going to tell me that my imagination is running wild."

"I might, if my own weren't running equally wild. Did you read the explanation? Do you know how the Source reverses rotation?"

"Not really. Some of the information was written in Pre-Quake Taerli, which I can't read well yet. And some of it is in Faerlonnish, but too advanced; I just didn't understand it all. As far as I could tell, the old writings claim that the Source slows down because it gets—well, dirty, or something like that—and when it's slowed down enough, it just naturally reverses."

"That's not at all a bad way of describing something that nobody—neither the greatest natural philosopher nor the wisest arcanist that ever lived—truly understands. Certainly I can't explain the workings of the Source to you, but I can tell you a little about the 'dirt' that slows its spin, and you'll find that it relates to your accident in the workroom. You know, don't you, that once the Source spun counter to its present direction?"

"Is that fact, or legend?"

"Fact, but almost lost in distant prehistory. It was a very long time ago, before mankind ever set foot upon the Veiled Isles. And by every indication, our islands at that time were literally another world—a place of alien, unrecognizable physical and arcane law. Men could not thrive in such an environment, but the Isles were not uninhabited. The land was ruled at that time by a race of sentient beings, neither flesh nor spirit, who scarcely existed as individuals. The intelligence and awareness of each was linked to all others of its kind, the collective awareness forming a single great Overmind of enormous power. This Overmind, it is believed, was capable of insinuating itself into unguarded intellects of all types and species, thereby ruling its hosts. In view of this ability, the Overmind's dominion over the ancient world was absolute.

"And perhaps that dominion would have endured forever," Vinz continued, "but for the great reversal. No one knows exactly when that occurred—millennia past, probably. At some point, however, the rotation of the Source altered, the character of its emanations changed, and thus all things changed. It must have been an almost unimaginably cataclysmic event, for the traces of it are present to this very day, scattered throughout our islands and clearly visible to those who know how to look. The laws of nature and magic rewrote themselves, and the power of the Overmind was broken. Men came to the Veiled Isles, farmed the land, and built their cities, while the previous overlords were all but forgotten. But the past is never wholly lost, and neither is energy. The Overmind was driven forth into the northern wilderness that we call the Wraithlands, and there it remained, its existence fueled by the archaic energy, the reverse energy, let us call it—the emanations of the ancient, alien world. There it slept and dreamed of the past, and the passion of its dreams permeated the world around it, the land and water and atmosphere, which began to vibrate to the old, forgotten rhythms.

"The Source, for all its power, is by no means immune to the influence of its surroundings. The force of reverse energy, continually applied, creates arcane encumbrances that accrete over the course of the centuries, impeding and eventually slowing rotation. Then, as you described, when it's slowed down enough, the Source just naturally reverses."

"Do we have to leave the Isles, then?" Vinzille asked, looking for one split second almost like a child again.

"It may come to that. It isn't clear yet. Now, you remember the account of the Overmind's ability to insinuate itself into unguarded intellects?"

Vinzille nodded, almost impatiently. His memory was remarkable. He forgot nothing, and his father knew it.

"Well, human beings are vulnerable, but our minds and bodies are such that we resist intrusion. When the Overmind invades a sentient being—a human, or even a Sishmindri—the natural defenses of the threatened organism are violent, the resulting conflict as devastating as any natural disease, and indeed outwardly indistinguishable from—"

Vinz broke off, astonished, as a trio of strangers marched uninvited into the dining room. Three Taerleezi soldiers, a lieutenant and a couple of subordinates. How dare these louts come barging into his private suite? *Unless they had come to arrest him.* He could feel his face cool as the blood drained from his cheeks. Not all of the arcane skill at his command permitted him to control that spontaneous reaction. He could, however, arrange his features into an expression of polite inquiry as the invaders advanced and halted before him.

"Magnifico." The lieutenant spoke brusquely. There was no salute. "We are calling at every dwelling along Summit Street to question the residents and to announce the issuance of Governor Uffrigo's General Order Fourteen in response to last night's rioting."

"Rioting?" Vinz echoed, genuinely perplexed.

"You claim ignorance of the attack upon Belandor House?"

"I know there was some sort of disturbance, but I've been much occupied throughout the day, and never heard the details. It was a—riot, you say?"

"It was an organized assault," the lieutenant informed him. "Something by way of an insurrection. A sizable squadron of trained commandos broke in, pillaged, raped, murdered, and ended by torching the mansion."

"Squadron?"

"Numbering some two dozen or more of heavily armed masked men."

"Rape?"

"One of the Belandor serving women declares that she was interfered with. Repeatedly."

"Murder?"

"A dozen people dead, some by fire, some by the sword."

"The Magnifico Aureste?"

"Not there. Out of the city, we're told."

"Who died, then? Any—of the Belandor family members?" Vinz forced himself to inquire.

"Yes, one. Unexia Belandor, the youngest Belandor brother's wife. The other casualties were servants."

Innesq lived yet, to wreak vengeance.

"The mansion was destroyed?"

"Much of it."

"And the—commandos, did you call them?—escaped unrecognized?"

"All but one, apparently killed by the household servants. He's been identified as one Guini Noli, cobbler, known subversive. Are you or any of your household members acquainted with this Noli?"

"Not that I'm aware of." And Guini Noli, cobbler, known subversive, was not about to contradict him.

"Can you account for your whereabouts last night, Magnifico?"

"Why, I was here at home." Vinz contrived to appear bemused. "My wife, my son, and a number of servants can vouch for my presence during the early evening. I stayed up late, though, working in my study far into the night while all the rest of the household slept, and I can't produce witnesses to verify my location in the dead of night. Am I under arrest, Lieutenant?"

"Any known resistance sympathizers among your servants?" The lieutenant disregarded the Faerlonnishman's attempted levity.

"I believe not, but I can't really answer for the household staff."

"Have you any personal knowledge of last night's events at Belandor House?"

"None."

"And you, boy?" The lieutenant rounded abruptly on Vinzille. "Do you know anything about this? Have you heard talk?"

If he thought to rattle or intimidate the younger Corvestri, he had underestimated his adversary. Slouched low in his seat, Vinzille waited several distinctly insolent seconds before replying with a mute shake of the head. His thirteen-year-old lips were faintly curved in a classic teenage sneer.

"If you receive any information, you're required to report it at the Clouds Watch Station. You'll have to go there within twenty-four hours in any case to sign in on the ledger acknowledging your receipt of General Order Fourteen."

"And what is this General Order Fourteen, Lieutenant?"

The lieutenant nodded to one of his followers, who handed Vinz a fresh broadside densely covered with small print and bearing a representation of the governor's seal. Vinz's brow creased.

"I'll save you the trouble of reading all that," the lieutenant offered. "It's a set of new regulations designed to ensure public safety. In the first place, it sets a curfew on every Faerlonnishman within the city limits. Any Faerlonnish national found walking the streets after ten o'clock at night will be subject to arrest and fine. Orderly good citizens are abed by that hour anyway, so there should be no complaint."

"Is there a curfew on Taerleezis, too, or is it just us?" Vinzille demanded, ignoring his father's quelling glance.

"The curfew applies to Faerlonnish-owned Sishmindris as well," the lieutenant continued serenely. "Sishmindris caught roaming after hours are subject to confiscation by the authorities. The head of every Faerlonnish household is required to produce a list naming every dweller beneath his roof, including family members, guests, tenants, servants, and Sishmindris. This list will be submitted to the nearest Watch station within the next twenty-four hours."

"Don't you want the names of our dogs, cats, and pet birds as well?" Vinzille inquired.

"Every human servant abroad upon the streets at any hour of the day or evening shall be clothed in the livery of his household, or else bear an armband marked with the family crest or the surname of his employer. Every Sishmindri will be tagged, branded, tattooed, or otherwise furnished with an identifying mark. Any Sishmindri lacking such a mark is subject to confiscation by the authorities."

"All of this is just an excuse to fatten your Taerleezi pockets," Vinzille accused.

"Hush, son," his father warned.

"Faerlonnish nationals shall carry their documents of identification with them at all times. Failure to comply with this regulation will result in arrest and fine.

"And finally," the lieutenant concluded, "Faerlonnish nationals are henceforth forbidden to bear arms of any description."

This was too much even for Vinz's practiced composure. "But you would leave us defenseless," he remonstrated. "What of our right to protect ourselves and our homes?"

"A stout staff or walking stick is not to be regarded as a weapon," the lieutenant observed.

"Inadequate. The cutthroats and footpads will rule Vitrisi."

"They already do." Vinzille cast a meaningful eye upon the Taerleezi intruders.

"If you are truly concerned for your safety," the lieutenant suggested, "you might always consider hiring a good set of Taerleezi guards, who are, of course, exempt from the arms-bearing restriction. Their rates are a little high, but under the circumstances you may find the investment worthwhile. Magnifico, you have now been properly informed of the new regulations. I trust you understand what is required of you and will comply." So saying, he turned on his heel and departed, trailed by his broadside-bearing minions.

Vinzille waited until they were alone before expressing himself. "Stinking Taerleezi vomit. They shouldn't be allowed to get away with it. Father, I've made a decision. I want to join the resistance."

Vinz stared at him, speechless.

. . .

Time was out of joint. She had waited there forever and would continue to wait there forever, somewhere outside of time. But at length a low murmur of masculine voices, just barely audible through the heavy oaken door, told Jianna that the waiting was over. Her husband had arrived.

She heard a bark of muffled laughter, and the voice was unfamiliar, probably the guard's. Would that guard remain on duty, salacious ear no doubt pressed to the door? If so, he would hear the thud of the blow, perhaps a groan, the sound of a heavy body hitting the floor. He would investigate, raise the alarm, ruin everything . . . But no. Even Onartino would not relish an audience on his wedding night. Moreover, he would not for one moment doubt his own ability to control his slender slip of a bride without assistance. Surely he would send the guard away. She listened intently, but caught no tap of retreating footsteps. There was a pause, the small scrape of the latch, and the door began to open. She lifted the poker, both hands locked on the shaft, and held her breath.

One chance, now, that's all you get, now, do it right, now, smashthatbastard'sheadinnownowNOW!

As he stepped into the room, she swung the poker with all her strength, recognized the pale profile and middling slim stature too late to arrest the blow, and did her belated best to divert it. He glanced up to behold the descending iron, jumped aside, and the stroke missed him by a hair.

"Falaste." She stared at him and wondered if she could be dreaming or mad. She was shaking uncontrollably, and her eyes were flooded with tears. "Falaste. Oh, Falaste."

"Ah, Jianna. I know you." He drew the poker gently from her grasp and set it aside. "I should have expected this."

"What are you doing here?"

"I've come to take you away."

"Away from him? Away from Ironheart?" He nodded and her heart lurched as if she had been reprieved from execution, even while she wondered yet if she were dreaming. "But you said—"

"Never mind what I said. Come, we haven't much time. Hurry."

"Wait, wait, what about the guard?"

"Gone."

"You didn't kill him?" she whispered.

"Hardly. I advised him to go downstairs to the party for some ale and food. I told him I'd stand guard in his place until he returned. I told him to take his time."

"He believed that?"

"Why shouldn't he? Ennzu's known me since we were both children, and I've never lied to him before."

She fancied that she caught a note of something like bitterness in his tone, but there was no time to think about it, for he was already exiting the bedroom, motioning her with a jerk of the head to follow, and she obeyed without hesitation.

A little lamplight spilled through the half-open door, faintly illuminating the room beyond. They crossed it and passed through another doorway into blackness. Night had fallen. No light filtered in from the outside; in any case, many of the rooms on this floor were windowless. Jianna clutched her companion's arm.

"Candle? Lantern?" she whispered.

"No need." His voice was similarly muted. "I know the way."

And he did. She'd thought that she had learned to navigate Ironheart's second-story warren of nested chambers, closets, cabinets, and cubicles, but in the dark she immediately lost her bearings. Not so Falaste Rione. He had grown up in this place and knew every cranny. Moving confidently as if gifted with arcane vision, he led her through the maze, pausing only occasionally to run his fingertips along a wall, a floorboard, a doorjamb whose shape and texture seemed to inform him. Jianna followed, placing herself in his care as fully and willingly as she had done upon the afternoon of their first meeting. Only once he paused at length, suddenly kneeling in the dark and obliging her to release her hold on his arm. She heard a scuffling, a scrape, and then his voice.

"Here, take this."

She extended her hands blindly and felt a soft bundle thrust into them. "What is this?"

"Woolen cloak. It's cold outside."

Outside. He was taking her out of Ironheart.

"Thank you." Her voice was unsteady. "You've left things waiting here for us? You've been planning this?"

"I haven't been planning anything, before the last hour. At least, I don't think I've been planning anything."

What happened? Why did you change your mind? What

about all that loyalty to Yvenza? The questions boiling in her brain remained unspoken.

In the dark she shook out the woolen folds and wrapped herself in the cloak. He took her hand and led her on until they passed through another doorway, and she felt a current of fresh air on her face, and then she could dimly see again. A deep, unglazed window admitted the night breeze and a suspicion of moonlight. By that faint glow she discerned an arched opening in the wall before her. She knew where she was, now. That window looked out over the courtyard. That archway opened upon a narrow flight of stairs leading down to the ground-floor gallery. She could see Rione well enough to make out the bulge of the pack slung over his back and to see that he now gripped something dark in his right hand—a piece of luggage? *His medical bag.* Of course. His most precious possession, by far.

She no longer needed guidance, but she did not let go of his hand, whose steady warm pressure was wonderfully reassuring. Her eyes and ears strained for the sight or sound of some wandering servant or sentry, but there was none; presumably they were gathered at that monstrous travesty of a wedding celebration. But not all of them; Yvenza would never have left Ironheart wholly unguarded. Rione could not possibly smuggle her out without encountering somebody, and then what?

Down the stairs they stole hand in hand, and at the bottom Rione halted.

"Stay here," he commanded, his voice so low that she barely caught the words.

She could see him fairly well—evidently a lantern or candle burned somewhere along the ground-floor gallery—and therefore knew that her own voiceless nod would be visible to him. He placed his bag on the floor with care, then stripped the pack from his back and set it down. Casually unencumbered, he stepped out into the gallery, and for a few moments Jianna listened to his leisurely confident footsteps heading straight for Ironheart's big front door. She did not need to look in order to know that a sentry would be standing watch there, and sure enough, the voices soon came echoing to her hiding place.

"Well, Neequo. Seems you drew the short straw this evening. Stuck here alone at the door, while every other man in the place is busy putting away all the ale he can drink." Rione's voice, impossibly easy, untroubled, normal.

"Falaste, lad." The guard's voice, genial and sociable, evidently addressing a friend. "You're right, I'm the saltcod tonight. What are you doing here?"

"I've come to do you a good turn. Seems that the magnifica has taken pity on you."

"That doesn't sound like our lady."

"Well, I asked her."

"Asked her what?"

"If you couldn't leave your post for some food, drink, and Gwetto's fiddling. I'll stand in for you here."

"She said yes to that?"

"She did. You're in luck." Rione's delivery was a masterpiece of amiable insouciance.

"Well, I thank you, lad. That was a friendly thought. I'm much obliged."

"Better go along while there's still some of that ale left. Take as much time as you want, it's all one to me. I'm in no hurry."

"Much obliged. You can trust me to return the favor one day."

I hope not, Jianna thought. Neequo was already hurrying toward that ale, the swift clump of his footsteps approaching her hiding place, and she held her breath as he drew level with the stairwell entrance, pressing her back hard to the wall, hardly daring to blink. She might have spared herself the worry. As Neequo passed the archway, she glimpsed a big, broad figure, muffled in homespun and thatched with shaggy hair—she had often seen him about Ironheart, but never knew his name until this night—and then he was past, invisible again, footsteps receding. *So easy!* Presently the sound faded away and seconds later she heard a low whistle, unmistakably a signal from Rione.

Pausing only long enough to scoop up his belongings, she stepped forth into the gallery and saw him waiting beside the door in a pool of light cast by a small oil lamp. *You were brilliant!* Only the need for silence and secrecy stifled her voice. *You hoodwinked him completely, and you made it seem so easy!* She said nothing, but admiring enthusiasm lighted her eyes and her smile as she sped toward him. Then her smile vanished as she drew near enough to read his facial expression, which reflected neither triumph nor satisfaction. Quite the contrary, his demeanor was distinctly—*grim,* she thought. *Down in the mouth. Or maybe troubled in conscience?* Troubled enough to turn his back on her? It was not too late for him to march her straight back to the marriage chamber . . .

She went cold at the thought and, as she reached him, a wintry draft sweeping in under the door heightened the sensation. She noticed then that Rione was not properly dressed for the outdoors and she asked without thought, "Where's your cloak?"

"On you."

"Oh. But couldn't you—" *have found someone else's to take?* were the words that popped into her mind, but she held them in, recalling that he eccentrically viewed the servant population of Ironheart as a collection of individuals, even friends, from whom he did not wish to steal. Yes, he would very probably regard it as stealing. "Couldn't you have found something?" she concluded feebly.

"No time."

She wasn't sure whether he meant that he'd had no time to secure an overgarment, or that there was no time now to discuss the matter. Pulling the door open, he stuck his head out, reconnoitered briefly, and slid through. Jianna followed, out the door, *out of Ironheart,* into the night that was cold but not unendurably so, partly thanks to Rione's woolen cloak, partly due to her own excitement. What next? He was already moving left along the front of the building, and she supposed that he was heading for one of the small side gates in the outer wall, unguarded, if such was to be found.

It was not. As they rounded the angle of the stronghouse, Jianna caught an orange glow of light—fire or lamplight. Rione, a pace ahead of her, turned and halted her with a gesture. Jianna shrank back into the shadows, whence she watched with fatalistic fascination as he continued on toward the source of the light. Before the exit sat a sentry, very comfortably ensconced there, with a brazier of glowing coals beside him and a three-legged stool beneath him. The sentry was engaged in roasting something over the coals, rounded blobs wafting the aroma of onions. He seemed absorbed in his task, and wouldn't it be feasible to sneak on past without drawing his notice?

The sentry looked up, spied Rione, and the opportunity was lost.

"Well, Prenzi. Seems you drew the short straw this evening. Stuck out here in the cold alone at the gate, while every other man in the place is busy putting away all the ale he can drink." Rione appeared disinclined to tamper with success.

"Oh, I'm well enough," Prenzi returned equably. "Not so cold, else you'd be dressed warmer yourself. What are you doing out here, anyway?"

"I've come to do you a good turn. Seems that the magnifica has taken pity on you."

"Oho, has she now?"

"She gives you leave to go inside for some hot food, drink, and Gwetto's fiddling. And a good fire, I might add. I'll stand in for you here."

"That's uncommonly decent of you, lad, and I appreciate the offer, but I'll just say no, with thanks."

"No?"

"With thanks."

"Prenzi, you're a good fellow, you deserve a reward now and again."

"But it wouldn't be no reward for me, see. You think I want to be indoors, shut up in some hot room, with all that noise and chatter? Then there's all that ale, and you're the one that told me to stay away from it. Bad for me liver, you said so yourself. Ruin me health, you said. Don't you remember saying so?"

"Now that you mention it."

"And that party food. Too rich. Gives me wind. You warned me against the greasy stuff yourself, more than once. Don't you remember?"

"I do."

"So you see, it's better by far out here, and here's where I stay."

"I see. I must confess, I'd no idea that you take my advice so much to heart."

"Like it was the law of the land. When it comes to leechcraft, you're the prince."

Jianna watched in mounting alarm. The health-conscious sentry clearly was not going away. She and Rione would have to circle back to some other exit, one presided over by a more pliable guardian, but to do so meant crossing the front of the building again, where the danger of detection was greatest. Why couldn't Prenzi just behave like a normal human being?

"Well, I'll treasure your esteem for—as long as it lasts." Rione's voice almost sounded melancholy for an instant, before the casual tone resumed. "I'll bid you good night, then. I'm going back in, I don't mean to waste that big fire the magnifica's got roaring away in there. Before I go, though—I almost forgot—would you mind taking a look at this? Nobody knows more about these things than you."

"What've you got, then?"

"Found it the other day. Can't identify it." Rione handed the other something small and dark. From a distance the object resembled a lump of mud.

"Well, let's see." Prenzi leaned toward the brazier to examine the lump by the light of the coals. Rione stepped behind to look on over the sentry's shoulder.

"Looks like the nest of an ordinary stonemudder."

"Isn't, though."

Jianna saw Rione withdraw something white from his pocket. Paper or parchment? Scrap of fabric? Handkerchief?

"No, you're right. Holes are too big. With straight sides, too. Curious, very curious. What could—oh, I've got it. This has got to be the nest of the blueback jonce. Now, that's rare."

"Are you sure?" Rione's right hand, clasping the white scrap, advanced smoothly.

"You can depend on it, lad. This little beauty must have been built last summer by a wandering tribe of blue—"

Rione's right hand pounced, pressing the white scrap hard over Prenzi's mouth and nose. His left arm clamped across the sentry's chest.

It was a potion or sleeping draught, Jianna realized. Perhaps kalkriole, or else something like it. Rione's medical bag contained an assortment of such soporifics. Prenzi struggled valiantly, but could not break the other's grip. Very soon he went limp and his attacker lowered him gently to the ground. Rione looked up and beckoned. Jianna hurried to his side. This time she never considered congratulating him. His face was set and pained. He looked as if he had received a blow. She did not dare speak.

Together they lifted the heavy bar from the gate and set it aside. As Rione took up his pack and bag, Jianna pulled the door open, wide enough to permit passage. They exited and, without a moment's hesitation, he headed for the woods at a run. Jianna easily kept pace. Her strained ankle had healed long ago. The night was clear and the half-moon overhead lighted the way. She cast one look back over her shoulder at Ironheart, then turned her eyes forward. Moments later they reached the shelter of the trees, where the night darkened, obliging them to slow their pace. The stray beams struggling down through the bare branches overhead offered minimal illumination, but it was enough for Rione, who followed the course of a nearly invisible path with apparent ease. She would have been lost without him—lost beyond hope.

"Thank you," said Jianna, inadequately.

"Don't thank me yet," he advised, neither pausing nor turning to look at her. Almost he seemed angry at her. "You're clear of the stronghouse, but well within their reach. They'll come after us, be certain of that."

"How soon?"

"As soon as Onartino goes to his room and discovers it empty. Or when Ennzu or Neequo returns to his post and finds that I'm not there. Or when Prenzi wakes up. Whichever comes first. An hour or so at the most. Probably less."

"That little! How long will it take us to make our way down the hills to the highway?"

"We're not going to the highway."

"How else shall we reach Vitrisi?"

"We are not going to Vitrisi."

"Not!" She halted and he did likewise. "I don't understand. What do you mean?"

"I mean that the magnifica's men will head straight for the VitrOrezzi Bond as soon as your flight is discovered. They'll expect you to run for Vitrisi, and they'll be haunting that highway before the break of dawn. Take that route and you'll find yourself back at Ironheart within hours."

He was standing very near her, but his face was a pale blur in the darkness under the trees and she could not begin to read his expression. His voice, however, conveyed absolute conviction, and she believed him completely.

"Another route, then," she urged.

"Impractical. Listen to me. Onartino is a master hunter and tracker. He knows every path and trail through these woods, knows them better than I do. Not even Onartino can track in the dark, though. He'll pursue you, beyond doubt, but he won't be able to bring his real skills to bear until daybreak, and by that time we'll be far away."

"Far away where? Orezzia?"

"In time, perhaps. But I know of another refuge, closer at hand, hidden from view, and offering greater protection. If we reach it, the forces of Ironheart can't touch you."

"What refuge? Where?"

"The campsite changes according to need. I know where it is now."

"Campsite?" The word seemed to leave an unpleasant taste on her tongue. "Whose?"

"I think you've already guessed."

"You're not speaking of the Ghosts!"

"I am."

"They're criminals!"

"They're soldiers and Faerlonnish patriots. More to the point, they're armed and quite capable of defending you."

"Well, and why should they? Why would they risk offending the Ironheart people for a stranger's sake?"

"Because you're with me," he suggested gently. "They know me, you see. Also, my sister is there, and her opinion won't be ignored."

"Those resistance brigands hate my father. The moment they hear my name, they'll cut my throat."

"They'd better not hear it, then. We'll devise a new identity for you, but now is not the time. Come, we can't tarry. I'll not force you, but you must decide. Will you come with me to the Ghosts?"

"I will." The words came out of their own accord.

"Good. For now, it's your best chance. And mine," he added in an undertone.

"Yours, Falaste?" For the first time, she thought beyond her own fears and considered the consequences of his actions.

"I have betrayed the Magnifica Yvenza. I have broken every promise of loyalty. She will never forgive or forget. My benefactress is now my enemy."

"Then why have you done it?" But for the darkness, she could not have brought herself to ask.

"Because I looked at Onartino this evening, and couldn't pretend that I didn't know he would hurt you."

He turned from her and resumed walking. She stood for a moment straining her senses to catch the sound of pursuit, then followed him into the dark.

. . .

The candles were burning low and Gwetto's arm was beginning to slow by the time that Onartino Belandor, eager groom, set his tankard aside and rose from his chair.

"I'm going up," he announced, voice perceptibly slurred with drink. "The rest of you can do what you like."

A few listeners mumbled ale-soaked encouragement. The population of the room was greatly diminished. The East Reach Traveler had retired early. Nissi had vanished long ago. Many of the servants, required to rise at dawn, had likewise withdrawn. Several others had simply fallen asleep on the floor. But Yvenza Belandor—upright in her chair and wide awake—answered clearly. "Think you can find your way to your bride without assistance? You've drunk yourself silly."

"Always the sharp side of your tongue. I don't need to hear it tonight."

"You've an ear for sweeter music, no doubt. Go your way, boy. Claim your bride, if you're capable."

Favoring his dam with a glare, Onartino took up a candle and departed the hall. The drinking, music, and dancing went on without him, although the pace of all was slackening by the minute. Yvenza Belandor remained seated. A beaker of wine stood on the table before her. Moderate in her personal habits, she rarely touched alcohol in the late evening. But tonight she drank, without apparent pleasure, her brows knit in an abstracted frown. Lost in her thoughts, she seemed scarcely aware of the tired festivities.

Minutes later, her unpleasant reverie was broken by the reappearance of her eldest son, who burst in violently, suffused face ablaze with unidentifiable emotion. Music and dancing ceased abruptly.

Yvenza regarded him with arched brows. "Forget something?" she drawled.

"She's not there," he reported. "She's out."

"What, Aureste's daughter? Nonsense. She's hiding from you, of course. You'll find her cowering under the bed or jammed up inside the flue."

"Are you stupid? The door's open and the guard's gone."

So startling was this intelligence that his impertinence went unrebuked.

"Who relieved Ennzu?" Yvenza inquired calmly.

"Nobody. Ennzu was ordered to guard that little bitch and he's gone. She's turned his head and he's run away with her. When I find him, I'll kill him."

"You won't have to look far. He's asleep in the corner."

Onartino followed his mother's pointing finger to the sturdy figure lying curled on the floor, an empty tankard still clasped in one hand. A few ferocious strides carried him across the room and the remaining merrymakers fell back, hurriedly clearing his path. Reaching the unconscious man's side, he drew back his booted foot and delivered a solid kick. Ennzu grunted and woke. Onartino stooped, seized him by the throat, and pressed. Ennzu thrashed desperately.

"Where is she? Is there any reason not to wring your neck? Where is she?" With each query, Onartino struck his prey's head hard against the stone floor.

Ennzu's eyes bulged in a purpling face. He tore uselessly at the hands that were strangling him.

"Did she pay you? What did she pay you with, you filth?"

Ennzu's head rapped stone. His mouth gaped and his struggles weakened.

"Do you want to die?"

Ennzu could not answer, but another voice spoke in his stead.

"That will do, boy. Give over." Rising from her chair, Yvenza advanced unhurriedly. "Let go of him. Now."

Onartino obeyed with reluctance. Ennzu sat up slowly, rubbing his throat with one hand, the back of his head with the other.

"That's better. Now you can speak. I suggest that you do so," Yvenza advised the man on the floor. "Explain yourself, and tell the truth."

"Explain what, Magnifica?" Ennzu's voice was hoarse and scared. "What?"

Onartino's fist clenched and Ennzu flinched.

"What happened upstairs?" Yvenza prompted. "Why did you abandon your post?"

"As for that, I had Your Ladyship's leave." Ennzu appeared uncomprehending.

"My leave? What is this foolery?"

"Begging your pardon, Magnifica, but you gave me your own leave to come down for some food, drink, and fiddling. I wouldn't've done it otherwise."

"Are you mad, or do you imagine that I am?"

"Neither, Magnifica. Rione came on up and passed the word. Offered to stand in for me for as long as I liked. If it came from Rione, it had to be good, so I thought I was in luck."

"Rione passed the word? Rione's the one who took her?" Onartino demanded. "Miracle Boy himself? Genius Boy?"

"Shut your mouth," his mother directed. Turning back to Ennzu and pinning him with her eyes, she stated very quietly, "You are lying."

"No, Magnifica, no. I swear. I left Rione standing guard at the bedroom door. I thought it was all right."

"I don't believe you." Yvenza's low, deliberate tone expressed a death sentence. "Try again."

"Oh, I believe him, all right," Onartino interjected. "I believe every word. Haven't I been warning you for the past twenty years or so? But when would you ever hear a word against your precious Rione? Well, what do you think of your darling now, eh?"

"Shut up." Yvenza did not trouble to glance in her son's direction. Eyes pinning the luckless Ennzu, she commanded, "Now, give me the truth. Don't fear to speak. You'll be punished, but not killed or maimed. I promise you this mercy—provided that you tell the truth now. Lie to me again at your own risk."

Ennzu hesitated for several miserable and terrified seconds before crying out, "I'm not lying! Truly, Magnifica, I've told you the way it was!"

"You persist in accusing Dr. Falaste Rione?"

"I'm not accusing anybody of anything! I'm only telling you what happened."

"Rione is loyal to the core. Do you really think I'll believe he's betrayed me?"

"Oh, believe it." Onartino's lips twisted. "Think of the bait. The big eyes, that white skin, the dainty finicking ways. You go and throw the two of them together, give her all the time she needs to sink her hooks into him, and then you wonder that your pretty boy peasant betrays you? What else would you expect?"

"Speak to me again like that and you'll find yourself stripped, tied to a post, and whipped bloody," Yvenza advised her son. Her attention returned to the servant. "And you. Last chance. The truth, or I'll feed your carcass to the dogs."

"Magnifica—"

The unhappy man's reply was cut short by the appearance of a white-faced Prenzi, who entered on unsteady feet, tottered across the room to confront his mistress, and announced in a carrying voice, "Magnifica, beg leave to report that Falaste Rione has run mad."

"Explain." Yvenza's face was blank.

"I was on duty at the southeast gate, and along comes Rione, offering to stand in for me while I go get myself some ale. It's like he doesn't remember that he's warned me against it, but I remember, so I decline with thanks. And then he goes loony and jumps me from behind. Uses some sort of potion that sends me straight off. The next thing I know, I'm lying on the ground and the gate's open. I close it and come on in."

"The girl," Onartino demanded. "He had the girl with him?"

"I didn't see anyone with him." Prenzi shook his head. "My eyes went bad. He used something on me. I'm sick; I'm going to puke."

"Well? Enough to convince you?" Onartino inquired of his mother. "Or do you need more?"

"I need nothing more. It is true, he has betrayed me." Yvenza spoke almost to herself. For a moment she stood very still, head a little bowed, expression uncharacteristically sad, even grieving. Then it was gone and she was herself again, her face cast in iron. "Be ready to hunt at the first light."

"I'm ready to hunt now," Onartino informed her. "She'll run for Vitrisi and Daddy. They'll head straight for the highway."

"Falaste will know better than that."

"She's got that fool bewitched, he'll do what she wants."

"Not impossible. I'll dispatch riders to the VitrOrezzi Bond."

"I'll lead them."

"No you won't. Right now you're stupid with drink. In your present state, you'd only hinder the pursuit."

"Garbage. You're just afraid of what I'll do to your beloved little Rione when I catch up with him. You're right to fear. I'll break him with my bare hands and take her on his corpse."

"Are you defying me, my son?" She slapped him hard enough to brand a red palm print on his cheek. "Try to remember your manners." He glared at her and she smiled. "Come, don't pout, be merry on your wedding night. We'll get your bolting bride back soon enough, and then you may do anything you please with her. She deserves no less. She has poisoned my Falaste."

FOURTEEN

The march from Vitrisi had gone forward without mishap. The Taerleezi soldiers, seasoned veterans all, had maintained good discipline and made good time. The Belandor household servants had proved similarly orderly, while the tavern sweepings, perhaps influenced by the demeanor of their companions, had displayed willingness and obedience. All had proceeded smoothly until Abona, where the force had turned off the VitrOrezzi Bond and taken to the hillside trails, whose narrowness and steep grade obliged Aureste Belandor to abandon his carriage in favor of horseback. The contents of the supply wagons had required redistribution, with transfer of some articles to muleback. This done, the expedition had pushed forward at a fine pace, but the adjustment had cost some time and dawn was imminent by the time Aureste confronted Ironheart.

There it rose, a heavy, stark stone fortress in miniature, its graceless square turrets visible above a girdling wall, darkly silhouetted against a night sky commencing its matinal fade to charcoal. Despite the lateness or earliness of the hour, the place showed surprising signs of wakeful life. Light glowed yellow at several windows. Perhaps Jianna sat sleepless beside one of them; perhaps she somehow sensed her father's approach. Aureste sent his importunate thoughts winging to the stronghouse, but caught no echo of his daughter's presence. There was nothing to tell him that she was there or ever had been, not the slightest quiver of the psychic recognition once afforded by his brother's skill. He had thought to achieve the same result by sheer force of will, but there was nothing at all. Perhaps truly nothing, now or ever again, because they had already killed the kneeser's daughter?

The thought was insupportable—and untrue. He had touched Jianna's mind and spirit, not long ago. She lived, awaiting rescue. Inside that stronghouse, just on the other side of that wall.

He issued commands and his soldiers, keeping to the shelter of the woods, made haste to fan out about Ironheart. And once that was done, the need for stealth lapsed and he could permit the men to kindle bonfires lighting their way as they advanced the two highly illicit cannon on carriages into position, aiming both guns low and straight at the big double gate in the wall at the front of the building. The gate was constructed of multiple oaken layers heavily fortified with crisscrossing bands of iron. It was well engineered to withstand the assault of the arrows, pikes, axes, or battering rams employed by wandering gangs of brigands or by the forces of neighboring rustic chieftains. But it had never been designed to withstand artillery fire. Cannon had never thundered across the heights and valleys of the Alzira Hills, but all of that was about to change.

Aureste regarded the quiet scene—the old fortified dwelling, silent and at rest beneath a barely lightening sky; Jianna's prison—and a tide of rage welled inside him. In his breast pocket reposed a written missive, addressed to the head of the household and offering clemency to all inhabitants in exchange for the immediate return of his daughter, alive and uninjured. He had promised his brother that he would extend such an offer, and he meant to keep his word. At the moment, however, the defenders had no particular incentive to accept. Assuming ample stores of provisions laid in, they might well imagine themselves capable of resisting a lengthy siege. It would serve the best interests of all were he to disabuse them of this notion.

Aureste made his will known. The cannon were loaded, the gunners applied lengths of smoldering cord to the touchholes, and a double flash of fire accompanied by a double roar split the nascent dawn. Two substantial projectiles hit the oaken gate at nearly point-blank range. A drift of powder-reeking smoke briefly obscured the scene, then cleared to reveal the gate in ruins, fragments of oak and iron lying scattered far and wide, at sight of which the soldiers raised a cheer.

Not a bad announcement of his arrival. Aureste smiled. Calling one of his Faerlonnish bodyguard to him—a youthful giant, skilled as a fighter, but also well-spoken and possessed of pleasing manners—he handed over the prepared correspondence, ordering the youngster to approach the stronghouse under a blue banner of parley. His emissary departed.

All watched in fascination as their fresh-faced comrade crossed the courtyard under his blue flag, marched straight to the front door, and was promptly admitted. The door closed behind him. Silence ensued.

Some quarter of an hour later, the young fellow emerged unharmed, hurried back the way he had come, and presented himself to his master.

"The message was delivered to the head of the household?" inquired Aureste.

"Aye, Magnifico. She got it and read it," the guard replied.

"She?"

"Aye."

"Tall, strapping woman? Of some years by now. Square face, square jaw, very forceful and resolute?"

"Aye, Magnifico. That's it, sir."

"Ah." Unmistakable. So the dead Magnifico Onarto's widow Yvenza still lived and ruled her wilderness stronghold. He remembered her clearly from a quarter century past. She had been a young woman then, but strong and already formidable. He would never forget the determination and persistence with which she had raised her voice against him in the last weeks preceding her husband's downfall, nor would he forget her nearly phosphorescent hatred. Had she been a man, he might almost have feared to let her live. But the new Magnifico Belandor could scarcely war on widowed women; to do so would have made him a monster or a laughingstock. Or both.

"Her reply?" Aureste prompted.

"She says that an offer of clemency isn't good enough. She says she wants what she called 'specific assurances' of safety and freedom for herself and all her people. She says she doesn't much care to treat with underage underlings. She says she'll meet with Aureste Belandor face-to-face in order to name a fair ransom and set the exact terms of the hostage's release."

"Terms? I refrain from slaughtering every man, woman, and child presently occupying this backwoods dunghill. Those are the terms I offer."

"She says she'll meet up with you in the front court, halfway between the gate and the house. And if anything happens to her out there, then the Maidenlady Jianna gets her throat slit on the spot."

"After which, everybody in the house dies by slow torture. Did you see my daughter in there?"

"No, Magnifico."

"What did you see?"

"The lady—Magnifica, her people call her—and a gaggle of her folk standing around with weapons drawn on me."

"Very well." Aureste reflected. Yvenza was fully aware of her captive's immense value and would negotiate accordingly. Concessions would have to be granted in order to effect Jianna's release. Once his daughter was safe, he would avenge himself. "I will meet with Onarto's widow."

A blue banner of parley was invariably honored, yet ordinary prudence dictated at least minimal precaution. Aureste took time to buckle on a steel breastplate, invisible beneath his heavy winter cloak. He bore both sword and dagger, and with him brought two helmeted Taerleezi guards, each equipped with conventional weapons, but one also carrying a very newfangled hackbut, the other bearing the blue banner. Thus attended, he approached the stronghouse, passing through the gaping hole in the wall and over the blasted ruins of the gate. Ironheart's front portal opened briefly. A trio of figures emerged and advanced to meet him: a woman flanked by two armed guards or servants.

Aureste eyed her keenly. Tall, as he remembered, but a dark gown and voluminous cloak disguised her outline. Her hood was raised against the wintry chill; no telling whether her hair had gone to grey, as had his own. Her walk was vigorous and elastic as a girl's. Her face was shadowed and even as they neared one another, he could not discern her features.

He halted and spoke without salutation or ceremony. "Madam, before I will consent to extend the hand of mercy to you and your household, I require proof of my daughter's safety. I wish to see her and to speak with her. If this demand is not met—"

The threat remained unspoken. She had continued her progress and now, almost eye-to-eye with him, somehow summoned a short, heavy-bladed sword from the recesses of her generous apparel and lunged. He was not altogether unprepared and yet so sudden and swift was the attack that her blade scraped the steel of his breastplate before his own sword found its way to his hand and he struck her weapon aside. Simultaneously her two followers drew blades on the Taerleezi guards.

She was remarkably strong and quick for a middle-aged woman. Her recovery was immediate and her renewed assault so fierce that she actually succeeded in driving him back a few paces. For all of that energy, however, her technique was crude, almost as if she had been carefully schooled by some bumpkin. He himself had perhaps lost something of speed but nothing of cunning, and a fluid feint penetrated her guard, bringing his blade to her chest. Some almost forgotten principle or lesson of extreme youth momentarily checked him, preventing the slaughter of a woman at his hand, and she seized that opportunity to jump back out of reach. The sudden movement displaced her hood, revealing short cropped hair topping a smooth and youthful male countenance.

Not Yvenza Belandor at all, not even a woman. A deception, a treacherous attempt on his life, enacted beneath the flag of parley. Anger flamed and Aureste lunged for the counterfeit Yvenza, who turned tail and ran for the house. One of the Taerleezi guards felled his opponent without effort. The other leveled and fired his hackbut. The shot roared wide, but the target—appalled by the introduction of unfamiliar technology—fled for safety. Both men vanished back into the house, and the door slammed shut behind them.

A brief flight of arrows winged from a quartet of second-story recessed windows. A couple of them missed. One of them pierced a Taerleezi throat whose owner fell, still clutching the blue banner. Another struck glancingly off Aureste's cuirass; had the arrow hit squarely, it might well have penetrated the steel.

Aureste turned without visible haste and went back the way he had come, followed by his surviving guard. Once clear of the courtyard, he ordered the two cannon advanced to the gap in the wall and trained full on the doorway through which his attackers had vanished.

"Break them," he commanded, and as dawn rose the bombardment commenced.

. . .

The destruction of Ironheart's front portal was easily accomplished. A duo of cannon blasts reduced the door to splinters and scrap metal, but gaining entry was another matter. From the smoking ruin of the doorway issued swarms of arrows, shot by invisible archers. Likewise invisible were the marksmen shooting from the narrow windows slitting the first and second stories. Attempted incursion provoked deadly flights reinforced by flung canisters of powder trailing short lighted fuses.

Equipped with the best helmets, body armor, and advanced weaponry, the expensive Taerleezis suffered few casualties. Aureste's own household guards, almost as well protected, fared similarly. The self-accoutered tavern hirelings, however, were suffering, and Aureste was obliged to order them back out of range. Tactical revisions were indicated.

Double cannon fire blasting through the demolished doorway into the bowels of the stronghouse doubtless wrought internal havoc. This accomplished, Aureste moved artillery and some men to the rear of the building, where a brief thunder of big guns destroyed the kitchen door, effectively dividing the defenders' force. Arrows winged from the rear windows, while the attackers' return crossbow fire bounced harmlessly off the stone walls. Aureste accordingly repositioned his cannon, ordering the gunners to sight on specific windows. Massive projectiles commenced battering Ironheart's second story, front and rear.

The day wore on. The cannonade continued, and the walls of Ironheart, stout though they were, began to display the effects of the judiciously directed pounding. Half a dozen windows had been enlarged from slits to jagged rents. No less than five defenders, attempting to fire from those formerly protected positions, had been picked off by Taerleezi marksmen. In the midafternoon, a well-aimed cannonball smashed through the second-story masonry dividing a pair of expanded windows to tear a great hole in the wall above the front door, whose defense waxed problematic.

Disinclined to sacrifice his own men without need, Aureste made no attempt to hasten matters. Another three hours of crashing assault wrought gaping damage upon Ironheart's front façade while claiming the lives of assorted defenders. Arrow flights from within thinned, but the raising of the white-and-black banner, signaling the attacker's demand for surrender, went unacknowledged. He had expected that communication to draw a counteroffer, bartering his daughter's life and safety for advantageous terms, but there was nothing. Perhaps they feared to provoke him with an ultimatum, or perhaps they had nothing to bargain with; they had already killed her. *Or his own cannon fire had killed her.*

He would roast the Widow Yvenza alive.

The bombardment continued, and now the plumes of black smoke billowing from the ruined windows hinted of interior fires blazing out of control. The white banner of surrender never appeared, but the force of the defensive volleys was undeniably diminishing. When the shadows were starting to stretch and Ironheart's façade was cracked, pocked, and riddled with holes, Aureste judged it time to throw his strength simultaneously against front and rear doorways. At the front, the resistance held firm. At the back, defense was weaker and a band of the skilled Taerleezis succeeded in beating their way into the kitchen, where the opposition of the homespun household guards and servants was swiftly crushed. The Taerleezis ranged efficiently and unstoppably through the ground-floor rooms and galleries, killing as they went. When they reached the front door, they engaged its defenders, who—caught between attacking forces—died to a man. Whooping guardsmen poured in through the front door, and after that it was only a matter of searching through the stronghouse to eliminate all remaining pockets of resistance. Before the winter daylight began to fail, the Taerleezi troops' standard flew from the tallest turret.

Ironheart had fallen.

. . .

When the stronghouse had been properly searched and its surviving defenders thoroughly subdued, Aureste entered. His immediate demand for news of his daughter drew no satisfactory response from the Taerleezi squadron leader. No female remotely answering the missing maidenlady's description had been discovered within the confines of the stronghouse; no living girl, no corpse, nothing. And it flashed through Aureste's mind in the course of a horrible fraction of a second that it had all been a gigantic error. He had misinterpreted, he had placed his reliance upon huge assumptions, he had willfully deceived himself, and all this costly, destructive effort had been in vain. Jianna was not here and never had been.

Not possible. Unacceptable. They were hiding her somewhere and he would compel them to relinquish her. He would use any and all necessary means.

He wanted a room in which to conduct an interrogation, and they led him to a chamber of moderate size, almost undamaged, apparently used as a dining hall. A long table still bore the drying remnants of a surprisingly lavish meal. Ordering the remains removed and the lamps lit, he seated himself and was immediately approached by one of his own household guards, the same youngster who had carried his written message into Ironheart hours earlier.

"Magnifico, a word," the youngster requested, guarded demeanor and suppressed tone conveying confidential intent.

Aureste inclined his head.

"Sir, we've sorted through the dead, and there's one of them you should know about. Middle-aged fellow, looking like he was hit by flying rubble during the bombardment, carrying papers identifying him as an Orezzian East Reach Traveler. That's somebody. Didn't know if you'd want these Taerleezi cocks getting wind of it. Orders, sir?"

"Remove all identification and burn it. Discreetly," Aureste commanded. "You've done well—Drocco, isn't it?"

"Aye, sir."

"Expect a reward, Drocco."

"Thank you, sir." The enterprising youngster saluted and withdrew.

No sooner had he left than another of the Belandor personal guards presented himself, bearing some sort of a bundle.

"Magnifico, we've found something, if you please," the fellow announced. "Found it in a little sleeping chamber up top."

"Show me," Aureste ordered, barely containing his impatience.

The guard shook out his bundle, which unfolded into a woman's cloak of garnet wool trimmed with bands of black fox. The garment was soiled and tattered, its once rich fur matted, but perfectly recognizable. It was the traveling cloak that Jianna had worn the morning she departed Vitrisi. She had been wearing it the last time he had seen her.

Hope and fear ignited inside him. He concealed both. Frozen-faced, he emptied the room of all save a handful of the most professional of Taerleezis, then ordered the surviving members of the outlaw Belandor clan brought before him. Their number, he knew full well, would not include the proscribed Magnifico Onarto. He could only hope that Onarto's widow still lived, for she, beyond doubt, had stolen his daughter and attempted his life, and she merited his closest attention.

Slow minutes passed before his prisoners appeared, only three in number. One of them, a towering and powerfully built young man, square and broad of expressionless face, pale-eyed, and seemingly unhurt. A second, another young man resembling the first in feature and coloring, but evidently wounded, his right hand and arm bound in bandages. A couple of guards bore him in on a makeshift stretcher, which they deposited upon the floor. And the third, the object of real interest, the Widow Yvenza; hair streaked with grey and face bitterly lined, but otherwise much as he remembered her from a quarter century past. Still tall, upright, strong, and vital. Still square and grim of jaw, still hard and compelling of eye.

She was inspecting him with equal attention, taking in every detail. The set of her lips altered almost imperceptibly, the minute change conveying eloquent contempt. He had forgotten that mute disdain of hers, forgotten how it had always roused his anger together with the uneasy sense that she saw him too clearly and understood him too well. He had all but forgotten, too, how greatly he disliked the woman, as he had never disliked her husband, the harmless, simple Onarto.

"Cousin Aureste." Yvenza shook her head as if bemused. "You've grown so very old."

Disregarding the taunt, Aureste inquired levelly, "These are your sons?" His gesture encompassed her two fellow prisoners.

"You ought to know them, cousin. You lived with my boys Onartino and Trecchio at Belandor House years ago, when my late husband in his charity took you in and sheltered you after the war. They are your own kin, closer to you than perhaps you realize."

The woman's voice and manner somehow contrived to hint at secret and highly satisfying knowledge. Ridiculous, of course. Vanquished and wholly powerless, she still imagined herself capable of besting him upon some mental level. He had no interest in continuing a battle that he had already won.

"Cooperate fully and I will spare the lives of your sons," he informed her. "Resist, and I will slaughter them both before your eyes."

"Surely not, cousin. You were never one to dirty your own hands in the presence of witnesses."

Her insolence under the circumstances was remarkable. Perhaps it sprang from despair, but she scarcely appeared defeated, much less hopeless, and still she maintained her air of secret knowledge. A pose, an attitude, that he would not deign to acknowledge.

"I'll not duel with you, madam," he told her. "The contest is over and I have won it. Restore my daughter and I'll allow you to live. But act quickly, my patience is limited."

"The duel." Yvenza nodded. "But can you truly count yourself a victor, cousin, so long as the prize eludes your grasp? This missing daughter of yours—this wayward wonder— shall we speak of her? How long has she been lost to you? Have you received no word from her, no intelligence of her whereabouts, no ransom demand? If not, how cruel the uncertainty! Tell me, do you not dream of her at night? Do you not imagine her helpless in the hands of strangers, imprisoned, tortured, dishonored and degraded, crying aloud for the father who never comes to her rescue?"

Aureste felt his blood surge. Suppressing all outward sign of rage and terror, he replied mellifluously, "I have come now.

You paint ugly pictures of the imagination, madam. How much uglier to see them enacted in reality, before your eyes, upon the bodies of your sons?"

"You speak recklessly, cousin, without consideration of consequences. Perhaps advancing age has begun to erode your intellect. There is no telling, is there, what sort of situation your daughter presently endures—assuming that she still lives. Your Taerleezi hirelings have searched this house from top to bottom and they've discovered nothing. You know now that she is not here—if in fact she ever was."

"Her cloak has been found. She was here, and may still be, locked away in some secret closet or cabinet. I will tear the house apart stone by stone, or perhaps I'll simply tear the flesh piecemeal first from your sons' bones, and then from your own."

"And still you will find nothing, for I'll satisfy your paternal curiosity so far as to assure you that your girl isn't here in this house, and that you may believe. Where then could she be? The possibilities are almost limitless. Might she, for example, find herself imprisoned in some hut or cave deep in the woods, guarded by those under orders to strangle her at a certain hour should they fail to receive word from me or mine? Distressing, yes, but at least a hut or cave offers shelter. What if she has none? What if she has been stripped and chained to some tree or rock, left naked to the winter winds and the appetites of beasts, both four-legged and two-legged?

"On the other hand, what if she is sheltered more closely than she could possibly desire? Have you ever heard the tale of the abduction of Count Moverna's oldest son? No? It is an education. It seems that the kidnappers—masters that they were of cruelty and cunning—placed the stolen child in a sizable box, which they buried six feet deep in a wooded wasteland, with only a narrow tube ascending from the box to the surface allowing passage of air. The ransom was paid promptly, the location of the box was disclosed, and the count's son was recovered, still alive, but so damaged by his ordeal that he was never robust thereafter, but grew up sickly, melancholy, and timorous.

"The child's suffering lasted only a matter of hours. What might the result have been had it continued longer? Who can begin to imagine the agony of a youthful prisoner, trapped, buried alive, lying there alone in the cold and the darkness of her grave? Can words convey her sense of horror as the endless hours expire, as the small store of food and water left with her is exhausted, as the air grows foul and nauseous with the stench of her wastes, as her voice grows hoarse with the screaming that goes unheard? Assuming that the air tube isn't blocked with mud or leaves, she might live thus for many days—each one a torturous eternity. These are such matters as you may wish to consider, cousin, before you go crowing to the world of your great victory."

He wanted very much to kill her. He wanted to plunge his sword into her vitals and watch her blood flow. At the same time he was conscious of the most abject desire to plead with her, to offer anything and everything in exchange for Jianna's safe return. Aureste indulged neither impulse. When he answered, his rich voice was particularly musical. "It would seem that you imagine yourself capable of bargaining with me, of naming demands or even setting terms. You delude yourself. For your own sake, abandon this folly."

"Your concern for my welfare is heartwarming. But what demands have I made, cousin? What terms have I sought? What have you to give that I could want, beyond your sorrow and undoing?"

"Your sons' lives, perhaps?"

"Your threats are empty. Touch any one of us and you'll never see that girl you treasure again. The hills are wide and the forests deep. You might search for a lifetime and never find her. If she is still alive to be found."

Despite her wretched position, she still plainly believed that she held the winning card. She would play it to the limit and beyond, play it for days, weeks, years to come—if he permitted it.

He would not.

"Madam, you are in error," Aureste returned gently. He regarded the two young men, her sons. The big one, uninjured, returned the scrutiny impassively. His eyes, pale and cold as slush, were also inexpressive as slush, his countenance as a whole perfectly unrevealing. The other one, wounded and stretched out on the floor, appeared at best but semiconscious. His eyes were closed, and from time to time an incoherent muttering bubbled out of him. Clearly an unpromising source of information. Engaging the eye of the nearest Taerleezi soldier, Aureste flicked an indicative finger and directed, "Dispatch him."

At once the soldier drew his sword.

"Wait." Yvenza's tone was so commanding that her listener obeyed. "Have done with these charades. You will not harm us. You cannot, you dare not. We both know this."

"One of us is sadly misguided." Aureste repeated his signal.

The soldier shrugged and plunged the heavy blade into the throat of the recumbent prisoner. Blood gushed extravagantly. The victim thrashed and floundered a bit, then died in a red pool. Something like a grunt escaped the watching Onartino; the first sound he had hitherto uttered. His fists clenched briefly.

Aureste's avid gaze fastened upon Yvenza's face. She was a mother whose son had just been killed before her eyes; her pain and grief must be unimaginable. And he wanted to see them. Every tear, every shudder, every aspect of her agony— he meant to drink them in. He wanted her to suffer at length; he wanted reparation.

But the Widow Yvenza offered little satisfaction. Her set face was every bit as expressionless as Onartino's as she met Aureste's eyes and announced evenly, "Your daughter is a dead woman. Her death will be slow—over the course of years— and very ugly."

"Not nearly so ugly as that of your older son, should you continue to resist me," he replied with a smile designed to freeze her to the marrow. Her composure and fortitude were extraordinary, but he would surely break her. "Give me back my daughter, alive and well, and I will give you your son, your only remaining son. Refuse, and you lose everything."

"You have lost everything, Aureste," she told him. "You simply do not know it yet. Your daughter is no longer yours."

That odd look of secret knowledge was back in her face, and it disturbed him, but he thrust his misgivings aside. The woman was acting, or mad, or both. He had no time to waste on her theatrics.

"Perhaps grief has unhinged you," he suggested drily, and in one corner of his mind he realized that he half believed it. The marble immobility of her face suggested lunacy. "I will endeavor to recall you to reality." Turning to the nearest of his Taerleezis, he commanded, "Take this woman's son, strip him naked, and beat him with truncheons, brazen knuckles if you have them, belt buckles, fire irons—whatever comes most readily to hand. Strike to cause maximum pain and injury, but do not kill him as yet, and see to it that he does not lose consciousness. You two"—he addressed a pair of soldiers—"place the woman in a chair affording her a good view, and see that she stays there."

The soldiers made haste to obey. Before they could lay hands on him, Onartino spoke up for the first time since he had been brought in.

"Enough," he snapped. "Back off. I'll tell you all there is to tell about your daughter."

"Hold your tongue, boy," Yvenza warned.

"Your stubbornness and your venom have just gotten Trecchio killed," Onartino returned. "So happy with your accomplishment that you're trying to do as much for me, Mother? There's no great secret here to betray. In fact, I say the stew's tastier if he knows. I've said so all along."

"And when he knows, what then?" Yvenza inquired. "When

he's learned all and has no further need of us, exactly what do you think happens next, my wise and judicious son?"

"Tell me the truth and I will spare your lives," Aureste reminded her, pleased to witness familial discord. "I have given my word."

"Your word?" She curved her lips in imitation of a smile. "The worth of your word is famed far and wide."

"Will you save yourself?" Aureste inquired of the son.

"As you value our lives, boy, hold your peace," Yvenza warned.

"Trecchio held his. I don't mean to follow his path. You can go on with your games and plots; I've had enough of them." Turning to Aureste, Onartino declared, "You already know that your girl has been in this house. Well, she's not here now. Seems the cunning little harlot managed to seduce one of the servants, and he ran off with her last night. We might have tracked them down by now if it hadn't been for you and your cannon and your Taers, so you've got yourself to thank for their escape. One more detail that you might like to know, though—before our little Jianna scoured off, she married me. The ceremony was performed by the East Reach Traveler before a roomful of witnesses, so it's legal and binding as you please. The girl's my wife now, wherever she might hide and however she may whore herself, she's still mine, subject first to my authority. When she's found, she's mine. So there you have it. Finished and done."

"You unutterable fool," Yvenza remarked, very quietly. "You have ruined us."

Just as quietly, Aureste inquired, "Where is she?"

"I just told you." Incredibly, Onartino appeared impatient. "She's run off. We don't know where."

"You expect me to believe that ludicrous concoction?" Aureste kept his voice low, but the rage and hatred, briefly lulled by the prospect of success, were reawakening. These backwoods brigand enemies of his had not only abducted Jianna, held her prisoner, and no doubt tormented her so far as they dared, but now they slandered her name, hindered his search, and insulted his intelligence. "You weave an absurd fantasy. Give me the truth, or I will rip it out of you."

"You have the truth. If you don't like it, that's your affair."

His captive's affectation of surly indifference was a creative touch. Had the tale possessed even minimal plausibility, Aureste would have found himself in danger of believing. As it was—

"You expect me to accept the idea that the Maidenlady Jianna Belandor consented to grant you her hand?"

"A woman will consent to anything when it's put to her in the right way."

"And you also claim that my daughter—a sheltered virgin— was capable of seducing some species of household menial?"

"She knew how on instinct. With some of them, it's just there in the blood."

"You are a liar." Aureste struck the other's face and his ring opened a bloody gash.

Onartino snarled and returned the blow. Before his fist hit flesh, a quartet of Taerleezis flung themselves on him.

For a moment Aureste contemplated the immobilized prisoner, then commanded his soldiers, "Follow your instructions. Strip him and beat the truth out of him."

They obeyed. At first Onartino fought back, struggling mightily to break free, cursing and even kicking. Despite his size and strength, he was no match for the Taerleezis, who swiftly cut the clothes from his body, then commenced beating him with their truncheons, belts, and fists. His cursing increased in volume and his struggles waxed in violence, for a little while. As the blows rained down on his unprotected flesh, however, his vociferation dwindled to grunts and gasps. The thud of a brass-knuckled fist on his nose coincided with a crackle of breaking bone and a spray of blood. A second such blow dislodged both his front teeth. Welts and cuts striped his torso and his resistance was visibly weakening when Aureste raised a negligent forefinger, suspending the assault.

Meeting the prisoner's pale eyes, gleaming balefully behind swollen and purpling lids, he asked, "Where is my daughter?"

"You stupid kneeser shit, what does it take to get it through your head that we don't know?" Onartino inquired in turn.

"Perhaps the mother is more reasonable than the son." Aureste turned to Yvenza, who sat flint-eyed and upright in her chair. "Are you ready to relinquish my daughter?"

She stared at him. Her lips resumed their contemptuous curve.

"Do you understand that you'll see him beaten to death before your eyes? Be assured that the spectacle will last throughout the night."

"And your daughter's fate will exceed it by a hundredfold."

"You have her, then? You know where she is."

"I will tell you nothing, cousin. I leave you to the joys of speculation."

"That is scarcely my sole joy." Addressing the Taerleezis, Aureste commanded, "The bastinado."

At once Onartino was lifted, laid out flat on the table, and held down while a pair of soldiers took turns beating the soles of his feet with cudgels. This particular torment, while leaving few visible marks, was notoriously painful, but the sufferer never uttered a cry, much less a revealing word. Whatever his shortcomings, he was clearly no coward, and for the first time it occurred to Aureste to wonder whether he could possibly have been telling the truth, or even part of the truth.

But no. The story was wildly improbable to the verge of impossibility. Jianna, kidnapped and held captive in this guarded stronghouse, escaping in the company of some peasant lover scant hours prior to her father's arrival? And even more implausible—Jianna married to this hulking, loutish son of her father's enemy? *The ceremony was performed by the East Reach Traveler before a roomful of witnesses, so it's legal and binding as you please . . .* So the oaf had claimed, and one of his own personal bodyguard, the promising Drocco, had reported the discovery of an East Reach Traveler among the dead, a finding that seemed to corroborate the story. But did not prove it, and the thing was just too fantastic for belief . . . *a roomful of witnesses* . . . He could question the surviving Ironheart servants—who would undoubtedly reply according to their masters' will. No dependable testimony there.

Frustration heated his anger. He relieved both by setting his men to work on Onartino's fingernails with pliers; but the extraction of all ten produced no satisfactory information. Likewise futile was the application of radiant red coals to strategic points of naked anatomy, although one such application, resulting in the sizzling destruction of the victim's right eye, did at last succeed in breaching Onartino's provoking stoicism. Roars of pain resounded beneath Ironheart's grim old roof. Aureste drank the outcry, which seemed in part to quench his own inner fires. A measure of relief stole over him, and he signaled his men to desist. His eyes turned to Yvenza, who sat motionless, unblinking eyes fixed on the spectacle before her.

"Give me back my daughter and all this ends," he offered once again.

Her gaze flicked him and turned away, as if from an object unworthy of notice. In that instant he saw that her eyes were astonishingly devoid of tears; devoid of fear, hate, grief, or any other readily identifiable emotion and therefore alien as the eyes of some visitor from beyond the stars.

Thrusting his misgivings aside, he nodded and the torture resumed, the Taerleezis now hauling their prey upright to endure a merciless rain of cudgel blows to the torso. But Onartino's response was disappointingly sluggish; his sensations seemed to have dulled. At last a poorly aimed blow glanced off the back of his skull to leave him sagging unconscious in the grip of his captors.

Annoyed, Aureste was obliged to order another suspension of activity. During the lull he repaired to a chamber more tranquil of atmosphere, there to dine on the best fare the indifferent kitchen of Ironheart could provide. Following his meal, he demanded to be shown to the chamber in which his daughter's cloak had been discovered. It took but moments to investigate the place, a very plain, chilly little room whose door could be barred from the outside. No furnishings beyond a small bed with a threadbare blanket, pot under the bed, a rickety table, washbasin and pitcher. No ornaments, no clothing or personal items, nothing to recall his daughter's presence. And then he noticed the crude wooden comb lying in the shadow of the basin and all but invisible on the wooden table. He picked it up and found tangled in its teeth a single long, dark hair. The right length, the right color. *Hers.* His eyes scalded for a moment. He slipped the comb into his pocket then returned to the interrogation chamber, renewed in energy.

Onartino had recovered consciousness. He lay supine and motionless on the floor, his large body crisscrossed with welts and bleeding cuts, splotched with purple-black bruises and red burns, knobbed with discolored lumps suggestive of broken bones. His face presented a shocking spectacle, with its burned-out eye socket surrounded by hugely swollen, livid flesh. He turned to look with his one remaining eye as Aureste reentered, his gaze unblinking and expressionless as a wounded lizard's. Similarly impassive waited Yvenza, still in the chair where the soldiers had placed her. The soldiers themselves sat at the table, indifferent to the bloodstains marking its surface as they consumed the meal that some servant had evidently been ordered to bring them. They snapped to attention as Aureste came in.

Advancing to Onartino's side, Aureste halted, looked down, and observed, "There's still time to save yourself. Where is my daughter?"

"Probably servicing sailors, by this time," Onartino opined, voice hoarse, words slurred but still understandable.

Aureste came within a nervespan of driving his booted heel straight down on the profane mouth, but controlled the impulse. The loss of all his remaining teeth might render the prisoner incapable of intelligible speech. Therefore turning to Yvenza, he inquired simply, "Well?"

There was no reply. She did not trouble to glance in his direction.

The beating resumed, this time with the soldiers focusing their particular attention on the prisoner's joints—knees, ankles, wrists, elbows, shoulders. Onartino was no longer able to contain his outcry, but the roars had given way to shuddering moans. No information emerged, however; nothing from the victim or from his stone-faced mother. Presently Onartino fainted. A bucketful of cold water only partially revived him, and once again the proceedings had to be halted.

It was clear that the Taerleezis were losing enthusiasm. The early rush of savage enjoyment had waned, their weakening victim's initially entertaining responses had fallen off, and their strenuous employment was taking on the aspect of drudgery. Well-disciplined soldiers, however, they dutifully carried on. Aureste's own satisfaction was similarly ebbing, along with his hopes. The punishment the prisoner had received should have loosened his tongue long ago, if in fact he concealed information of any description. It had become difficult to avoid considering the possibility that he did not. There were no secrets to reveal. He had told the truth from the beginning: Jianna had fled—assisted by some servant, perhaps someone with an eye to a reward, or perhaps simply a person possessing conscience and a sense of decency—and neither Onartino nor his mother had any idea where she was. And if in fact he had told the truth or some toxic version of the truth about her escape—had the rest of his story been true as well? The marriage, performed by the East Reach Traveler, before a roomful of witnesses, legal and binding as you please?

Ridiculous, impossible. And yet, what in the world could have inspired Onartino Belandor to invent such a lie, guaranteed to rouse the fury of his captor? And what had brought the East Reach Traveler to Ironheart, to die with its defenders?

The night wore on, the dark hours passed, and the weary torturers were relieved by fresh Taerleezis who plied their clubs, their dagger points, and their heated poker with zest but no success. Onartino—increasingly distanced from recognizable human normality—furnished no information and little by way of diversion. His moans waxed periodic and monotonous. His spasms seemed reflexive, almost unconscious, and novel techniques—including the amputation of two fingers from his left hand—tapped no fresh wells of anguish. His mother was not much better. Her eyes remained fixed on the scene before her, but the eyes were vacant, the intelligence behind them seemingly elsewhere.

Time dragged on. The Taerleezis grew tired and bored. Onartino's moans had ceased, and when they kicked him in the groin, he did not react at all. His one eye was open, but it was not certain that he retained consciousness. It had been hours since he had uttered a word.

Aureste commanded another cessation. Like his minions, he was weary; and perhaps unlike them, he was filled with disgust. The night was drawing to a close, and an infinity of torture had extracted no information from Onartino Belandor, who once again lay naked on the stone floor. Aureste looked into the single unseeing eye wide open in the distorted ruin of a face, and finally acknowledged to himself that there was nothing to be had; the interrogation had proved futile.

An uncharacteristic sense of defeat swept through him. He had overcome all obstacles and found his way to this remote fortified place, he had battered his way in, he had made himself master, and yet he had failed. The prize eluded his grasp, just as Yvenza had observed hours earlier. His eyes shifted to her. She remained upright in her chair, motionless and unfathomable, as she had sat throughout the night. But now, as if she felt the pressure of his gaze, she turned to look at him. Her face was petrified, but he fancied that he caught a cold glint of triumph in the depths of her eyes, and the sight was insupportable. His failure did not establish her victory; he would not allow it.

"Hours ago, you taxed me with falsehood," he reminded her

in a conversational tone, and there was nothing in her face to assure him that she heard or understood. "You slighted the worth of my word. The moment has come for me to demonstrate that I can be relied upon to keep my promises. I made one to you, if you recall. I promised that you would see your son beaten to death before your eyes. The task is all but complete, but not quite. Let us make an end." Still no perceptible reaction from Yvenza, not even when he bade the soldiers, "Finish him."

Obediently they stooped to their victim, and the thud of their clubs striking his skull was clearly audible. Onartino's limbs twitched briefly and then he lay still.

"Magnifico, he's done," one of the soldiers reported.

"Your choices visited this fate upon him, madam," Aureste informed Yvenza, every demon within him clamoring for vengeance. "Take consolation if you can in the knowledge that the loss belongs to both of us if, as he claimed, he was my son-in-law."

No reaction, no response. She sat like a graven image, but he assumed that she could hear him plainly enough.

"During the course of this night, I've come to acknowledge the reality of your ignorance and your incompetence," he informed her. "You abducted my daughter, but you could not hold her. She was too clever for you. She managed to escape, and now you truly have no idea of her whereabouts. Nothing is to be gained in questioning you further. Thus there remains only the matter of your punishment."

Still no sign that she heard.

"It is within my rights and my power to order your immediate execution," he continued. "But I'm disinclined to war on broken old women, and even less inclined to grant you the mercy of death. Better by far that you live on—childless, destitute, bereaved, a solitary homeless wanderer in the world, with naught but your memories and your misery to carry you along a beggarly road. Yes, I say homeless. I am turning you out of doors, madam. You may take with you such belongings as you can carry in a sack, and so you'll go your way. I myself return to Vitrisi and the beauty of Belandor House, but do not imagine, once I am gone, that you will likewise return to this stronghouse. There will be no Ironheart for you, no refuge and fortress, no seat of outlaw power; it is finished. Do you understand me?"

Now she did turn to stare at him, and he read perfect comprehension in her eyes.

Without diverting his gaze from her face, he commanded, "Take her away. Let her gather what she will, with the exception of money and jewelry, then put her out."

The Taerleezis moved to obey, and Yvenza finally spoke, in tones barely audible. "My sons."

"What of them?"

"Burial."

"I've no time to waste on ceremony."

"Give them to me."

"Ah, you stole my daughter, but expect me to give you your sons? I will take pity on you and offer my charity. If you've any of your household servants about, still alive and willing to bear the burden, I give you leave to carry the corpses away." Addressing his soldiers, he commanded, "See to it."

Head high, Yvenza departed, closely flanked by her sons' killers. The door closed behind them. Alone, Aureste expelled his breath in a sigh and let his shoulders sag. Dawn was breaking, and he realized that he was overpoweringly tired. His eyes traveled the room, with its two corpses—Trecchio on the floor in the corner, where the soldiers had placed him, Onartino still lying where he had fallen—and its bloodstains, countless bloodstains. He filled his lungs with atmosphere reeking of blood and sweat, urine, smoke, cooked flesh, and vomit, and his sense of revulsion returned full force, along with his sense of defeat. All that he had wrought—all the destruction, all the bloodshed—all of it was worthless. He had not rescued Jianna. He could not absolutely assert that she still lived, although he refused to let himself believe otherwise. And he had no idea where to look for her.

The dark desolate fancies spun through his mind. He could neither grasp nor control them; and would not, he realized, until he had slept. Exiting the interrogation chamber, he made his will known and was conducted to Ironheart's best bedroom—plain and simple but decent enough, with solid, mildly battered furniture, a couple of fraying tapestries on the walls, and an old-fashioned cupboard bed made up with freshly laundered sheets. Removing only his boots, he stretched himself fully dressed atop the coverlet, shut his eyes, and let sleep claim him. Just before he drifted off, it came to him as his last coherent thought that the bed he occupied almost certainly belonged to Yvenza. Here she had slept, presumably alone, for years; and further back in time, a quarter of a century past, she had shared this bed with her husband, the late lamented Magnifico Onarto. The thought was distasteful, even a little disturbing, but he did not let it keep him from slumber.

When Aureste next opened his eyes, the angle of light told him that it was midmorning. He must have slept some three or four hours, and the rest had done him good. He had recovered much of his wonted energy, along with his mental clarity. Apparently his mind had nourished and fortified itself while he slept, for his first waking thought reflected renewed optimism. He had failed to recover his daughter, but her kidnappers insisted that she had escaped on her own. If true, then she would head straight for Vitrisi and home. It was not impossible that he would find her waiting there upon his return. She would run to his arms; he would see her smile again.

So heartening was this thought that he was able to breakfast with good appetite before summoning the Taerleezi squadron leader and issuing orders for an exhaustive search of the surrounding countryside, to be conducted over the course of the next several days. His newfound sanguinity was at once undermined by the Taerleezi's firm refusal. The terms of the agreement, he was reminded, included the taking of the stronghouse known as Ironheart; only so much, and nothing more. Mission accomplished, the squadron was under the

Governor Uffrigo's orders to return at once to Vitrisi, where its skill in the art of crowd control was much in demand. Nor could the offer of higher pay and a generous bonus alter matters. The squadron leader was adamant: His men would depart for the city this very day. The Faerlonnish magnifico could accompany them or not, as he chose.

Thwarted again. He could scarcely remain at Ironheart or even within its environs on his own. Unprotected, he would be murdered within hours if not minutes. There was no choice but to leave with the Taerleezis. And perhaps not the worst decision, although it ran counter to all paternal instinct. As Yvenza had noted, the hills were wide and the forests deep. He might search for a lifetime and never find her. But there was another whose detective abilities far exceeded his own. Innesq's arcane guidance had served him well in the past and would surely·do so again. He needed Innesq's special talents now; it was indeed time to go home.

But he could hardly afford to leave Ironheart deserted. The door would scarcely have closed behind him before Yvenza and her people would be back inside, safe, comfortable, no doubt busy regrouping their forces and plotting revenge.

No.

Aureste issued commands that fell well within the designated scope of Taerleezi activity, and the soldiers busied themselves with careful placement of powder barrels—most of them grouped in the cellar, but others positioned along supporting walls at various levels of the building. Preparation for departure was completed. Wagons were loaded, mules hitched, horses saddled. The squadron withdrew to a safe position beyond the wall. A final warning was issued to clear the building of humanity; a trio of fleet-footed Taerleezis lit the fuses and exited at a run. Two or three minutes elapsed before a rumble shook the ground. The rumble rose to a roar and a searing blast shook Ironheart from foundation to roof. For an instant the world changed color as fire leaped for the sky. Rubble flew; clouds of smoke and dust billowed, all but obscuring the scene. For an instant the topmost turrets appeared to quiver; and then, with the thunder of an avalanche, the stronghouse fell. So strategic was the placement of explosives that the final collapse occurred almost vertically. The dust thickened, excluding all daylight, and flying pebbles pelted down like hail. Minutes later, when the atmosphere had partially cleared and the air was almost breathable again, it could be seen that the building lay in tumbled ruin. All that remained upright were a couple of sections of ground-story wall.

The soldiers whistled and cheered. Aureste's own mood was far from triumphant. Long before the dust had fully settled, he turned his back on the wreckage of Ironheart and rode away.

FIFTEEN

The journey back to Vitrisi was uneventful. Traveling once more in his anonymous carriage, Aureste discreetly separated himself from the Taerleezi troops at Strevorri Field. Directing his own household guards to follow him home in unobtrusive pairs and trios, he proceeded at his best speed to the city gates, through which he passed unrecognized and unnoticed. And once again, the absence of public execration was so agreeable that he wondered if he should take to traveling incognito at all times.

The ordinary little conveyance clattered through the busy city streets, but he scarcely noted the changing scene outside his window, for all his attention focused upon a single incandescent possibility: Jianna might have come home. If she had in truth escaped her abductors, she might well have reached Vitrisi by this time. He might see her again in a matter of minutes.

It wouldn't do to let his hopes soar too high. He could hardly expect such good fortune; life was rarely that kind. But he could not control the acceleration of his heartbeat or the quickening of his breath as the carriage neared the top of the White Incline. Then he was hurrying along Summit Street, with its mansions and gardens, and soon he came upon a sight that momentarily eclipsed all other matters, even thoughts of his daughter. To his left arose the lofty marble walls and archways of the landmark dwelling known for generations as the Gaessilico Palace, but now called Nerosi House, in honor of its current Taerleezi masters. And the gilded front portal of Gaessilico Palace, now called Nerosi House, was marked with a great red X, symbol of the quarantine.

The plague had come to the Clouds. Nor had the wealth and power of the residents, nor the height and splendor of their gleaming walls, succeeded in keeping it out. The Nerosi household members, masters and servants alike, were now prohibited from crossing the boundaries of their own property, until such time as a city inspector proclaimed the house free of contagion. Probably in recognition of the Taerleezi councilman Nerosi's wealth and status, there was no armed guard stationed before the door to enforce compliance with the quarantine regulations. But the name *Nerosi* would now be marked and, for any household member discovered walking the streets, the consequences would be grave.

Here. Even here, in the security and beauty of the Clouds. No safe refuge existed; money couldn't buy one. And Aureste, wont to regard wealth as the ultimate panacea, experienced a chilly internal qualm. He suppressed the sensation expertly. The rare difficulty in life immune to the influence of money must surely submit to arcane power. The uncommon talents of Innesq Belandor could be depended upon to preserve the health of his family members. If money could not keep them safe, then Innesq's powers would.

Thus reassured, he let his daughter return to the forefront of his mind, and her smile lighted his thoughts as the carriage drew up to the gilded iron gates in the wall surrounding Belandor House. Aureste frowned. No sentry, human or even Sishmindri, stood watch at the open gateway. He had been away from home only a matter of days, and already in his absence discipline and care were sliding. He would have a word or two for each of his brothers. He would—

Then his gaze traveled past the gate as far as the house itself, and his breath stopped, for Belandor House lay burned and disfigured before him, broken and mutilated as any victim of torture. The south wing, he saw at once, had been completely destroyed by fire. The roof had caved in, the few walls left standing were charred black, and every window frame was empty. The brightest, warmest, and airiest rooms in the build-

ing were gone. Nearly as dire was the state of the central section, whose grandly proportioned entry now yawned wide in
black ruin, and whose tower, once graced with a skylight bearing the image of the sun wrought in two dozen tones of
golden glass, had toppled. Only the north wing had escaped
with moderate damage. The walls and roof were smoke-
darkened but apparently sound. A number of windows were
cracked or shattered, but many remained intact. Probably
some of the north wing chambers were habitable.

The resistance. There could be no other explanation. They
had struck at him from time to time throughout the years and
he had always dodged, but this time the thrust had gone home.

He would find a way of returning it with interest.

And if they had harmed Innesq, *or Jianna,* he would use all
the considerable resources at his command to hunt them to
the death.

In vain he shouted for greater speed. The carriage seemed
to creep on toward the wounded mansion. The journey took
centuries but ended at last, and Aureste sprang from the vehicle before it came to a full stop. Then he was running, as his
middle-aged dignity had not permitted him to run in years,
hastening for the entry to one of the north wing's ground-
floor galleries, where a sentry stood watch—providentially a
human being, capable of human speech, but just now slack-
jawed with wonder at the sight of his master's undisguised agitation.

"My daughter," Aureste demanded. "Has she returned, has
she been seen?"

"No, Magnifico," the sentry responded, astonished. "No
sign of the maidenlady."

"And my brother? Is he safe?"

"Master Innesq? Or Master Nalio?"

"Innesq, you fool, Innesq!"

"Well—well, that's not so easy to say, Magnifico. Master
Innesq is alive, mind you," the sentry forestalled the question
blazing in his master's eyes, "but, well, something happened

during the fire, and it's not clear what it is. They're not saying much, and 'twere best you speak to a doctor about it. Or Master Nalio would know more than me, sir."

"Nalio is unharmed?"

"Yes, Magnifico."

"Innesq has been injured, but *Nalio* is unharmed?"

"Well, it's not sure that *injured* is the right word for it, Magnifico."

"You dolt, you're not worth talking to. Is Nalio inside?"

"Yes, Magnifico."

"Out of my way." The sentry stepped aside and Aureste rushed on into the north wing, where he paused, uncertain. The gallery had escaped catastrophic damage—the ceiling and walls looked sound, and only two of the big windows were broken—but the effects of the fire were very apparent. Every exposed surface was filmed and blackened with soot. The formerly gleaming marble floors were dull and gritty, the rich tones of bronze and carnelian obscured, the mirrors cracked. And worst of all, the splendid paintings in their gilded frames—some of them priceless masterpieces—had been dirtied and dimmed.

Aureste scarcely noted the damage. His eyes ranged the gallery, whose far reaches vanished into a wilderness of studios and half-forgotten archives. Then his attention shifted to the graceful, smoke-stained stairway curving up to the higher stories, with their assorted workrooms and their guest rooms designed for visitors of less than the premier level, yet deserving of a certain respect. The chambers were numerous and he had no idea which, if any, contained either of his brothers. In the past—and the time predating his Ironheart excursion already seemed far past—the gallery would have been alive with servants, retainers, or even Sishmindris to question. Today there were none, and he—unwilling to search the north wing room by room—lifted his voice in a great echoing shout.

"NALIO!"

Ordinarily he might have suffered a sense of indignity to

find himself unattended in his own house, bawling at the top of his lungs for his insignificant youngest brother. Today he did not think of it.

"NALIO!"

The summons was heard. Within moments Nalio came jittering down the stairs, a familiar meager figure, unbecomingly clad from head to toe in black. In mourning? *For Innesq?*

"What happened?" Aureste demanded harshly.

"Aureste, you're back. Oh, it was dreadful—dreadful! You can scarcely begin to imagine—"

"Stop there. Before you go any further, tell me what has happened to Innesq. Is he alive?"

"Yes, yes, our brother lives. But he's—"

"Hurt? Burned?"

"There's not a mark on him, not so much as a bruise; no outward sign to tell us why he is as he is."

"As he is? What are you saying? Speak plainly."

"He's unconscious," Nalio announced. "He's slept for the better part of four days. No one can wake him."

Four days unconscious. It could only mean that Innesq was dying. A deep, cold terror took hold of Aureste. He was going to lose his brother—as well as his daughter. He was going to lose all that mattered, or perhaps he already had. *You have lost everything, Aureste.* The Magnifica Yvenza's voice rang in his mind. *You simply do not know it yet.*

"Take me to him," he commanded steadily. "And as we go, you will tell me everything that happened."

"Upstairs. This way." Nalio headed for the stairway and Aureste fell into step beside him. "It was the night of the day you left. All was quiet, orderly, and normal but for the reduced household staff. Still, between the remaining servants and Sishmindris, there were enough to mount what ought to have been an adequate guard. Also, of course, Innesq's arcane safeguards were properly in place and active. So we retired for the night, suspecting nothing, only to be roused from our slumbers by the attack of an army of masked soldiers."

"Soldiers? In uniform?"

"No—no—I don't think so—I'm not sure—I can hardly say what they wore. They displayed the discipline, expertise, and ferocity of seasoned soldiers, that is what I meant."

"An army, you say?"

"No—no—perhaps more of a troop. Probably not above two or three dozen men. They *seemed* like an army, though. We woke from sleep—Unexia and I—and they were *there,* in our own apartment, and there was fire and smoke everywhere, and—and—and screaming, and madness—and they—they—they were killing—killing humans and Sishmindris alike, killing everybody. It was hideous, a nightmare. In the midst of the panic and confusion, Unexia and I were separated. I escaped the house by way of a north wing exit, but Unexia did not. The—the—the butchers killed her." Nalio's narrow face contorted. "They killed my Unexia."

"I am sorry." Aware that some display of fraternal sympathy was mandatory, Aureste strove to conceal all visible signs of impatience. He grudged the waste of a moment's thought on Nalio's mouse-faced nonentity of a wife when matters of infinitely greater import clamored for attention, but there was no help for it. "Mark you, your dear lady will be avenged."

"Thank you, brother. You liked her, did you not?"

"Enormously. She will be greatly missed. But, as to your account of the attack—you say that Innesq's arcane safeguards were in order. You're certain of that?"

"Yes, Innesq had inspected them personally, that very evening."

"How were they breached? Did the invaders possess arcane resources?"

"Innesq said they did. He even said who."

"What do you mean? You told me he was unconscious. When could Innesq have said anything?"

"Right after. The killers retreated, I don't know just when they left, it was confused, with everybody running and screaming, and smoke over all. A couple of Sishmindris carried Innesq from the house and set him down in the garden, where I found him. At that time he seemed shocked and weakened—his face was so white, he seemed more spirit than flesh—but he was awake and perfectly clear in mind."

Aureste stopped dead and wheeled to face his youngest brother. "What did he say?"

"He said that an individual arcane force overcame the arcane safeguards and supported the entire attack, including a stroke aimed specifically at him, although he thought that you were the principal target. He said that every arcanist's work is unique, the product of a single mind, whose action and interpretation are identifiable as a signature. He said that he confronted the attacking arcanist, whose face was masked, felt the vibration of the other's mind, and knew him, despite the mask. He said he recognized—he—he—he recognized—" Nalio swallowed hard and forced the words out in a rush, "He recognized Vinz Corvestri."

Vinz Corvestri. The name set off ancient flares. Sonnetia's husband. Hereditary enemy of House Belandor. Lifelong friend of the Faerlonnish resistance. The awkward, studious ninny who had dared to marry Sonnetia Steffa. The undeserving second-rater to whom she had given a son—the son that might have been his. Vinz Corvestri, who had dared to strike directly at Belandor House and its treasures.

Vinz Corvestri, who would shortly cease to exist.

"I see. And you're quite certain that Innesq was awake and clearheaded when he said this?" Aureste probed.

"He certainly *seemed* to be. Sick and weak, as I told you, but otherwise quite his calm, thoughtful self. Oh, I—will—will—will miss him!"

"Stop that. You speak as if he were already dead. I won't have it!" Aureste snarled, and then, with a conscious effort, moderated his tone. "He survived the attack and the fire. What happened next?"

"The fire gradually died. All of Belandor House might have fallen had the wind not shifted, driving the flames south and bringing the rain. Before dawn the blaze was extinguished and we survivors took possession of the north wing, which remains livable, more or less. The Sishmindris took charge of Innesq at once. They are quite devoted to him, have you ever noticed? They took him upstairs to a decent room and put him to bed. He thanked them for their care, they reported later, and they left him. Around noon one of them brought him a tray, found him fast asleep, and withdrew. In the early evening they tried again, but found him still asleep, at which point they notified a human. It was discovered then that his sleep could not be broken. He lies peacefully, he is warm and his heartbeat is steady, but he will not wake. So he has remained, without change, for days. Oh, I will—will—will miss—" Encountering his brother's eyes, Nalio cut himself off.

"Come then, take me to him," Aureste ordered calmly enough, and progress resumed.

Another few paces along a corridor only faintly smoke-sullied, to a bedchamber perfectly clean and fresh—presumably the work of Sishmindri hands—wherein Innesq Belandor reposed. He lay motionless on his back in the middle of a big, carven bed, head propped on a spotless pillow, arms slack at his sides. His eyes were shut, his breathing deep and regular. His face was pale, peaceful, and unutterably empty.

"He's been like that for days, now—laid out exactly as the Sishmindris left him." For some reason Nalio was whispering. "He hasn't moved so much as a fingertip. It is my theory that he's suffered an injury to the brain—perhaps an apoplexy— and he is now completely paralyzed. I think—"

"Leave us," Aureste commanded absently.

"If I'm right, then the removal of a sizable portion of his skull, resulting in the relief of intracranial pressure, might—"

"You may go, Nalio."

"Very well. Very well." Nalio's face flushed. Spine very erect, he took a step toward the door, then stopped and turned back. "You make it clear that I am not wanted. Before you dismiss me, however, there is one thing you should know. In your

absence, and with Innesq asleep these past few days, I have
been in charge here. I've supervised the staff, reorganized the
living arrangements to shift us all over to the north wing, dealt
with tradespeople and mechanicals, begun work on the search
through the ruins, the discovery and interment of the bodies.
I've listed property lost, property damaged, property saved—
it's a very thorough list. I've accepted estimates from various
laborers for removal and cleaning services. I've compiled a
short list of worthy architects, one of whom might be selected
to repair and rebuild the house. In short, I've assumed the duties of head of the household. And I've performed those duties
well, Aureste. Very well indeed; ask anyone. I am not without
ability, you know. I think you should be aware of that."

"I am." Aureste frowned, feeling himself distracted as if by
the pertinacious buzzing of a fly. "Be assured that I value you
according to your merits, brother. Now pray leave us."

Only partially mollified, Nalio nodded and exited, shutting
the door behind him with pointed emphasis.

He was alone with Innesq. Approaching the bedside, Aureste stood looking down at his brother. The face—a sickly
and haggard version of his own—had never been so still, so
uninhabited. Innesq wasn't there.

But perhaps he could be summoned back. If determination
and singleness of mind were enough to serve the purpose, he
would be recalled to life.

"Innesq. Wake up. Hear me. Wake." He did not raise his
voice, but invested it with all the quiet force that he could
muster. Bending slightly, he clasped his brother's warm hand—
his own was icy—straightened, and spoke again. "Come back.
You are needed here. We cannot do without you. Do you hear?
You are needed. Wake."

Innesq slept on. For the next twenty minutes, Aureste stood
holding his brother's hand. Sometimes he repeated his exhor-
tations; much of the time he was silent. Gradually the warmth
of his brother's limp hand infused his own. But Innesq never
woke, never even stirred.

At length, Aureste laid Innesq's hand down, turned from the bed, and walked out of the room. Grief and an intolerable sense of helplessness would slice like internal daggers if he gave way to them and he therefore transmuted the unwelcome visitants to anger. And it helped greatly. The surging red energy reinvigorated him, renewed his courage and along with it his resolve to avenge himself upon the authors of this attack on his home. The skulking fanatics of the resistance maintained a craven anonymity, but one of the invaders—the vilest of them, the one who had brought them past the arcane safeguards, Innesq's attacker—had been identified. Vinz Corvestri.

Vinz Corvestri would pay dearly. And his connection to Sonnetia—his offense and his protection alike, for the past twenty-five years—would not preserve him now.

A nearby door stood ajar. Aureste looked in and saw a bedchamber, a lamp burning within, coals glowing on the grate, the bed made up, a smoke-dimmed portrait of Unexia Belandor hanging on the wall. Evidently Nalio had chosen this undamaged room to settle in following the destruction of his own apartment. He was welcome to it. Aureste's eyes flew to the one object of interest that the room contained: a small writing desk in the corner, its surface laden with perfectly arranged stacks of ledgers, account books, and documents. Here Nalio must sit to compose those lists, those very thorough lists, of which he was so proud. Here, too, would be found all manner of writing materials.

Aureste strode to the desk and seated himself. Seeing no blank paper, he selected an empty page from the nearest ledger and tore it from the book. There was no dearth of pens and ink. Dipping a quill, he began to write; very quickly and decisively, with never a hesitation or a blotted line. The denunciation of Vinz Corvestri as both a patron and an active member of the Faerlonnish resistance movement almost seemed to write itself. The exercise was pleasurable as well as productive. It was almost with a sense of regret that he concluded with the suggestion that an investigation of Corvestri Mansion—and most particularly of the desk in the master's study—would almost certainly uncover clear evidence of the Magnifico Corvestri's guilt. This letter he left unsigned. He sealed it with red wax that bore no identifying imprint, then left Nalio's bedchamber to search the halls for some servant to bear the message to the Clouds Watch Station, there to slide it through the slot in the door under cover of darkness.

Selecting a female Sishmindri, he sent her off about his business, and the knowledge that he had taken definite action at last greatly improved his spirits. The Taerleezi guards of the Watch would act swiftly upon such an accusation as he had sent them. Probably they would descend upon Corvestri Mansion within hours, and even the most cursory search would yield rich results, thanks to his own foresight and the corruptibility of Sonnetia Corvestri's maid.

· · ·

Evening in the Corvestri family's private dining room, and life was good; normality once more reigned. Vinz Corvestri surveyed the scene with satisfaction. Candlelight gleaming upon fine china, silver, and crystal. An excellent meal; and the circumstance that gave substance and meaning to it all—his family reunited. Sonnetia was back in her rightful place, facing him across the table. She was gowned in the deepest shade of moss-green velvet, with heirloom emeralds glinting at her throat and wrists.

During the days of her incarceration, he had almost forgotten how beautiful she still was, particularly in the warm glow of the candles. And if she had been treating him with some coldness since her liberation—yes, marked coldness, no doubt about it—yet her courtesy and propriety remained perfectly intact; she gave him no legitimate cause for complaint, and probably never had. Right now, at this moment, he would never have dreamed of complaining, for she was smiling at Vinzille, laughing at some funny story of his. It was an expression never directed at her husband, but when he glimpsed it his breath caught, even after all these years, and he remembered why he had wanted so desperately to marry her.

And Vinzille was smiling, too, uncomplicatedly happy to have his mother back where she belonged. Since she had rejoined them, the boy had spoken no more of enlisting in the resistance, to his father's deep relief. Vinz's sole experience of true resistance activity had been more than enough for a lifetime, and the mere thought of his son's involvement sent his innards into uproar.

No fear of that now, though. And no fear either, it seemed, that his own participation in the attack upon Belandor House would ever come to light. Had the authorities discovered any incriminating evidence, he would have been arrested and charged by this time. Clearly they had nothing. He had pulled it off.

Catching the eye of a hovering Sishmindri, Vinz shifted his glance to the empty glass on the table before him, and the amphibian refilled it at once. He sipped appreciatively. First-rate wine, full and complex. He felt as if he could drink an entire bottle of it without ever suffering a morning-after headache. Yes, things were right again.

Thus lulled, Vinz was unprepared for the entrance of the Taerleezi authorities. They marched into the dining room unannounced, no less than eight armed guards squared into a miniature phalanx, led by an officer of familiar aspect. It was a lieutenant—the same Taerleezi lieutenant from the Clouds Watch Station who had delivered the notification of the governor's General Order Fourteen, a few days earlier. There had been no cause for alarm on that occasion, and there was no cause now or so Vinz assured himself.

"Magnifico Vinz Corvestri, you are hereby informed that the Vitrisi City Guard, acting on behalf of the Taerleezi Provisional Council, has authorized a search of these premises," the lieutenant announced professionally. "We are to investigate the entire building and all of its contents, not excluding personal property. There is no area of the house, no chamber, closet, or container to which we do not demand access. If you, or the magnifica, or any member of your household possesses keys, you will hand them over to me at this time. Should we encounter locked doors, drawers, or boxes that we are unable to unlock, they will be broken open forcibly. Do you understand all this, Magnifico?"

"Clearly, Lieutenant."

"Have you anything to declare at this time?"

"What should I have to declare, when I've no idea what you are looking for?" Vinz inquired earnestly. In truth he knew exactly what they would be looking for in the home of a Faerlonnish noble rumored to possess arcane ability. They would be looking for evidence of illegal arcane practice. The law prohibiting arcanism among the Faerlonnish was loosely enforced; indeed, it could hardly be otherwise. Nevertheless, conviction upon such a charge would impose a heavy fine, together with the confiscation of all demonstrably arcane materials, writings, supplies, and devices, much of it valuable and difficult to replace, and all of it intended for Vinzille.

Vinz thought quickly. The entrance to the passageway leading to his workroom was well concealed; it was not impossible that the Taers would overlook it. If they found their way to the workroom, however, he could claim that the chamber and its contents had been the property of his late father, who had practiced legally in the ante-prohibition days before the war; all of which was true. He could also maintain that he himself had never made illicit use of the workroom. They would not believe him, of course, but it might be successfully argued that legitimate inheritance of arcane equipment did not in itself constitute proof of illegal use. With any luck, he might even evade the fine. The Taers would carry off the arcane paraphernalia if they found it, and that would be a considerable misfortune, but not a killing blow.

"I'll cooperate to the fullest, Lieutenant," Vinz declared virtuously. "As for the keys, you won't need them, for nothing here is locked, so far as I know. How should it be otherwise, when we have nothing to hide? Magnifica—" He caught his wife's eye. "Have you any keys that should be handed over to the officer?"

"None." Sonnetia's tone was neutral, her face perfectly mask-like. Vinz's regard shifted to his son, whose eyes were practically aflame with indignation.

Don't let him say anything, Vinz silently enjoined the forces of the universe. *Don't let him annoy them.*

As if she heard the mute plea, or vibrated in natural sympathy, Sonnetia laid a light hand on her son's arm. He turned to her, and she gave her head an almost imperceptible shake. Vinzille folded his arms and stared down into his lap.

"Proceed with your search, Lieutenant," Vinz urged graciously. "If there's anything we can do to assist, or if you've any questions, do not hesitate to ask."

"We won't hesitate," the lieutenant replied with a note of barely suppressed sarcasm. Turning to his followers, he commanded, "Split into pairs, take upper, middle, and lower stories. You know what to look for. Sanzi, you're with me, we're for the study. Magnifico, you'll have one of your people lead us to your study."

"Certainly," Vinz conceded, mystified and uneasy.

"Jio." The lieutenant addressed the tallest and broadest of his men. "Stay here, see that no one leaves."

Jio saluted. His comrades withdrew. The guard—a remarkably husky specimen, built like a warehouse—drew a chair up to the doorway and seated himself. From that vantage point he regarded the family unblinkingly.

Dinner resumed. The candlelight glowed as warmly as ever, the food and wine were excellent as ever, but Vinz's appetite had flagged. In this he was not alone. His son's adolescent voracity remained unimpaired, but Sonnetia sat still and very upright, eyes fixed on the plate before her. Conversation, so lively minutes earlier, had given way to comfortless silence. Vinz's mind flew to the workroom and its valuable contents. Lost for-

ever? His father's extraordinary collection of scrolls, the Balhoriovny Separator, the antique instruments—the heirloom
treasures meant for Vinzille—were these Taerleezi vultures
about to carry them off? The suspense was acutely unpleasant.
No matter, Vinz assured himself. It would end soon enough.

It did.

Only minutes later, far sooner than he expected, the lieutenant and Sanzi were back again. Jio rose at once from his
chair. The lieutenant's expression of satisfied expectation was
disquieting. In his right hand he bore a packet of papers that
Vinz did not recognize.

"Magnifico Vinz Corvestri, in the name of the Taerleezi
Provisional Council, I place you under arrest," the lieutenant
announced with undisguised gusto. "Magnifico, prepare to
accompany us."

"What?" For a moment Vinz doubted his own perceptions.
The thing made no sense. The invaders shouldn't have located
his workroom so quickly. And if somehow they had made a
lucky hit, they hardly needed to arrest him on such a comparatively minor charge. "What for?"

"You are charged with arson, sabotage, subversion, and
mass murder," the lieutenant incredibly informed him. "We
have uncovered evidence of your long-term involvement and
participation in the crimes of the Faerlonnish terrorist gangs."

Terrorist gangs. The Taerleezi term for the Faerlonnish resistance fighters. The lieutenant was perfectly correct, but
how could he be so certain? For so many years, Vinz had been
so careful. What evidence could possibly exist?

"This is madness. I know nothing of terrorist gangs." Vinz
sought refuge in incomprehension. "There's a misunderstanding here."

"The proof is clear. These documents were discovered tacked
to the underside of a desk drawer in your study." The lieutenant
flourished his mysterious packet. "I trust you recognize them."

"No, I don't recognize them. What's that you've got there?
Let me see it."

"No need. You already know what I'm holding. The names, the dates, the selection of targets, the plans, the records of payments and purchases—a complete portrait of your resistance activities."

"This is madness," Vinz declared in all sincerity. Indeed, a dream-like sense of unreality was taking hold of him, as it had upon the night of the Belandor House raid. "I know of no papers. They aren't mine."

"Two or three mention you by name, although the majority employ the code name 'Nullity.' Sound familiar, Magnifico?"

"No, it doesn't! This is fantastic and absurd. Lieutenant, you went straight to my study and came up with those documents, whatever they are, in a matter of minutes. That was no accident. They're cheats, they're fakes! And you know it. You or your men planted them there to incriminate me."

"And why should we want to do that, Magnifico? What have we to gain? No, accusing the men of the Watch won't help you. Don't worry, though. You'll have the chance, in fact you'll be encouraged to tell your story, complete in every detail, to the interrogators at the Witch."

The Witch. Not the Clouds Watch Station. They meant to drag him off to a real prison, for serious offenders, who not infrequently progressed from the Witch straight to the gibbet or the block. Vinz's sense of unreality intensified. But here was Sanzi coming toward him with a set of very real manacles. He felt the touch of the cold iron at his wrists, and the alarm boiled up inside him, impelling him to send the Taerleezi guard staggering with a sudden shove.

"We'll put a stop to this nonsense here and now," Vinz declared with a desperate air of authority. "Lieutenant, I'll see those documents that you claim to have discovered in my study. I'll expose them as the forgeries that they are. I demand to see them." He took a step toward the officer, but Sanzi was back with the manacles and now he was angry. When Vinz again attempted resistance, Sanzi hit him; a short, sharp blow to the midriff that doubled him over. Before he could straighten or even draw breath, the irons closed on his wrists.

"Leave him alone!"

He heard Vinzille's voice, clear and precociously commanding, and his terror expanded. The boy would get himself hurt or killed if he tried to interfere. Vinz managed with difficulty to stand upright. He wanted to warn Vinzille, to silence him for his own sake, but Sanzi's punch seemed to have shocked his system; he could barely catch his breath, much less speak. But there was nothing wrong with his eyes, and he raised them in time to see Sonnetia's white-knuckled grip tighten on her son's shoulder and to see her mouth the words, *That's enough!*

Vinzille's independence was increasing with each passing day, but his mother had not yet lost all control over him. He looked at her, drew a deeply wrathful breath, and fell silent. Sonnetia's glance shifted to her husband. Vinz met her eyes and—as always—found himself absolutely unable to guess what was going on behind them. Her thoughts, her sensations, and emotions—apart from her obvious love for her son—remained closed to him. He did not even know whether she truly supported him or not; whether she desired his safety and freedom, or whether she would enjoy ridding herself of him once and for all.

It seemed to him at that moment that she was no true wife at all and never had been. She was little more than a stranger inhabiting his house. And the frustration and hopeless longing, the disappointment and resentment of decades welled up in a great, hot surge, restoring his voice but not his judgment. The suspicions of recent weeks were burning in his mind, fueled by the terror of the moment, and that heat consumed all normal restraint, freeing the unspeakable to fly from his lips.

"Have you a hand in this, madam? Did you plant the papers in my study, or was it done by that maidservant of yours who carries the messages between you and Aureste Belandor?"

Sonnetia's eyes widened in astonished incredulity, convincingly portrayed. Vinzille's expression conveyed bewilderment, no doubt genuine, and the sight pricked Vinz's confused conscience. He shouldn't have attacked the boy's mother, it wasn't right or fair; unless, of course, his accusations were true and he could prove their truth beyond question, right here, right now. And probably he could prove it, if only he could examine those papers that the Taerleezis had so very quickly and easily discovered; those papers surely bearing some revealing mark of origin.

"Let me see them." Vinz turned back to the lieutenant. Stretching forth his manacled hands, he advanced. "If they're evidence against me, I have the right."

"You have the right to answer all questions that are put to you," the lieutenant advised him. "Halt."

The command did not register. The packet in the officer's hand filled Vinz's vision. Deaf to all warnings, he pushed on toward it until a moderate blow from Jio's truncheon clipped the side of his head. He did not entirely lose consciousness then, but the world went dim and distant. He thought he heard a faraway babble of voices, he thought he glimpsed tall figures gliding through grey fog, but he could not sort them out. There was something wrong with his sense of balance. He could not have remained upright but for the support of strong hands. They were moving him along at breathtaking speed, and he had no idea where they were taking him, but somehow he knew that he did not want to go. Resistance was out of the question, however.

Presently the world darkened, the air hardened, he felt the cold breath of winter upon his face, and after that his memory lapsed.

· · ·

For some moments after they had taken Vinz away, Sonnetia and Vinzille remained seated at the dining room table, motionless as if paralyzed, until Vinzille collected himself so far as to demand, "What are we going to do?"

Sonnetia looked at him. He was still so very young, yet distinctly no longer a child. Moreover, his intellect and his talents were uncommon. There was no point in trying to put him off with evasions or soothe him with implausibly optimistic lies. He was old enough and strong enough to bear the truth. She would answer his questions honestly, to the best of her knowledge.

"There's nothing we can do, right now," she told him. "The Taerleezis are still ransacking the house, and the search will probably continue for hours, perhaps all through the night. Until they're done, they'll not allow us or any of the servants or Sishmindris to leave the building. As soon as it's permitted, we'll contact the authorities, learn the exact nature of the charges against your father, find out if a trial date has been set, and then decide how we may best assist and defend him."

"Don't you think we could best assist him by calling in a doctor? Those Taerleezi scum hit him. He was bleeding."

"I know. We'll try."

"They didn't need to do that."

"Of course they didn't. But they probably wouldn't have if he hadn't fought them."

"That was brave of him."

"I'd call it a mistake," Sonnetia replied levelly. "He lost his head and so he got hurt."

Vinzille appeared taken aback by her coolness. He hesitated a moment and then asked, "Will they let us visit him?"

"I don't know yet. That may depend on the charges."

"Do you think it's true?" Vinzille cast a quick look at the open doorway and lowered his voice. "Is he really a member of the resistance?"

Sonnetia paused the merest fraction of a second before replying, "He hasn't confided in me, son."

"Because if he is—if he fights for Faerlonne—then I'm very proud of him."

"I know. Best keep that to yourself, though."

"I will. I saw that he means to deny everything. He's claiming that those papers they found are fakes. He even said something about you planting them in his study. That was all to throw the Taers off, wasn't it?"

"It could have been." It was the first less-than-truthful answer that she had given him. There was no doubt in her mind that her husband had accused her in earnest.

"And then when he said something about your maid carrying messages between you and that putrid kneeser Aureste Belandor"—Vinzille's eyes were fixed very intently on his mother's face—"that was more slop for the Taers, wasn't it?"

"Perhaps. I can't explain what was in your father's mind. But one thing I can tell you with absolute certainty." Sonnetia was back on the solid familiar ground of undiluted truth. "It was fantasy. There's been no exchange of messages between Aureste Belandor and me. I've not traded a word with him in many years. There's no communication at all."

Her son nodded, and she saw that he believed her.

"We're going to bring him back home, aren't we?" the boy asked.

Sonnetia was silent.

SIXTEEN

A drop of partially frozen moisture hit Jianna's cheek, and she brushed it away. Another followed, and another. "Sleet," she announced.

"I've noticed," Falaste Rione returned.

Her eyes roamed in search of shelter. She saw wet grey tree trunks rising on all sides, thin bare branches crisscrossing overhead, skeletal dead undergrowth, a moist dark trail slicked with soggy dead leaves—nothing that offered the smallest hope of refuge.

Her gaze came to rest on her companion. Falaste's hair was flecked with ice, his face paler than its wont, the fading bruise on his cheek standing out in yellow-green relief. His lips were all but colorless. Throughout the course of the past three days he had never once complained, but doubtless he felt the cold—because of her. The good oilcloth cloak that she wore, with its deep hood to keep the rain off and its lining of heavy wool—that cloak was his sole warm outer garment. Had he not handed it over to her, he would have been comfortable enough. Of course, he had only done what any gentleman would do, but compunction smote her nevertheless, and she found herself suggesting once again, "We could share the cloak. Why don't you take it for a while?"

He shook his head without troubling to repeat the usual refusal, and asked in turn, "You all right? Need a rest?"

He did not offer food, she noted. The bread and portable foodstuffs with which he had surreptitiously crammed his pockets before departing the wedding celebration had sustained them for days, but now the provisions must be giving out. She did not wish to burden him further, but could not forbear asking, "We've eaten everything?"

"Not quite. There's still some dried fruit and nuts. Enough to meet our needs."

The soothing power of his voice momentarily reassured her, but then he ceased speaking and her fears resurfaced at once. This elusive campsite that they sought—he had said that its location changed often. What if he couldn't find it? What if they wandered through the cold and the wet until their supplies and strength were exhausted, without ever finding the Ghosts or any other source of aid? She slanted a sidelong glance at Falaste, whose demeanor was characteristically composed and purposeful. He had rescued her from Ironheart at the cost of the human ties that he deemed precious, and probably at the risk of his own life. He had guided and protected her, provided for her, suffered privation on her account, without ever uttering a word of reproach. He had proved himself beyond all question worthy of absolute trust—perhaps almost as worthy as Aureste himself—and she would trust him now.

"Why are you smiling?" asked Falaste.

"Oh," she shrugged, "just happy to be away from Ironheart, thanks to you. And so relieved that nobody has managed to catch up with us."

"Indeed." He did not return her smile.

"What's wrong?"

"You said it yourself. Nobody has managed to catch up with us. It's too good to be true. Onartino is an accomplished tracker."

"We've crossed rocky ground, waded through streams, obliterated our own footprints, and you even had us double back twice."

"Yes. But Onartino is an *excellent* tracker."

"You sound as if you expect him to find us—as if you don't really believe we have a chance."

"Quite the contrary. I expect success, but not without a

struggle. Each day I've searched for signs of pursuit—a moving figure on the slopes below us, a wisp of rising smoke—anything to mark the presence of hunters on our trail. I've spied nothing, and I can hardly account for it."

"Well, maybe you've overestimated Onartino's talents, or underestimated your own skill in covering our tracks. Maybe he's hanging around the VitrOrezzi Bond, looking for us there."

"Perhaps." Falaste's frown deepened.

His strides lengthened, and she scurried to keep up. The sleet was pelting down, driving hard on the wind, whitening Falaste's hair and frosting his doublet. He had to be miserably uncomfortable. The thought was remarkably disturbing.

"Maybe it's time to forget about the Ghosts," she ventured. "They may have abandoned this vicinity altogether. We could head for Orezzia. At least we know where it is."

"The Ghosts are close at hand, you may be certain. If we don't find them, they will find us soon enough."

Not nearly soon enough. She said nothing.

Another sleet-filled hour passed before Rione permitted a pause for refreshment. Brushing the crust of ice from the surface of a fallen tree, they seated themselves side by side. He handed her a fistful of fruit and nuts, took as much for himself, and for a few minutes they ate in silence. Now at rest, Jianna began to feel the cold, despite the wool-lined cloak. Rione had to be in a far worse state. She looked at him—ice-dotted head down, shoulders hunched against the wet wind—and on impulse unfastened the cloak at the neck and draped a portion of it over his shoulders, enclosing them both within the woolen folds.

He glanced at her, startled, and she assured him, "Plenty of room. It's big as a tent."

She expected opposition. To her relief, he merely nodded. Within moments the warmth of their bodies began to permeate the enclosed space beneath the cloak. Warmer yet if they huddled together, pressed up close, and wrapped their arms around each other. So eminently practical an instinct almost prompted her to rest her weight against him, but something stopped her—an acute self-conscious qualm. She looked at him again, hoping for unspoken permission or agreement, but he was surveying the terrain, his attention seemingly elsewhere. Her sense of discomfort sharpened and she wondered if he experienced anything of the sort himself, but his pale profile told her nothing. It was a waste of useful body heat, but they never touched.

The sleet was dwindling, but the sky remained dark. It was too early for nightfall, but the day was advancing and the night *would* come, another night spent lying on the rocky ground under the leafless trees, wakeful ears straining for the sound of pursuit. And tonight Rione would never get a fire started, with nary a dry twig to be found.

"Best move on," he said, as if reading her mind.

He rose, stepped away from her, and the world was cold again. She followed and they made their way along a narrow little trail, where the sharp stones underfoot finally punched a hole through one of her ailing shoes. Moisture seeped in immediately, and she clamped her jaw to contain all lamentation. Up a steep grade, then the ground leveled out, the trees crowded in, black branches interlacing above, and the dark day darkened further. For the first time, she wondered whether Rione might be wandering wholly at random. But no, that would be unlike him. *Trust him,* she admonished herself, and discovered with a sense of wondering pleasure that it was easy; she really did trust him.

On through the sodden gloom, last of the sleet lightly pattering, wet foot in the broken shoe going numb with cold, then a tiny atmospheric shiver, and a sound. It was no more than an insignificant thunk, near at hand, and she did not recognize it, but took instant alarm. Then her eyes found the arrow, its head buried in a tree trunk a few feet to her left. The shaft must have passed within inches of her face. Even as she stared, the thunk repeated itself, and a second arrow quivered beside the first.

"*Run!*" She tugged Rione's arm.

"Stand still," he directed serenely, then raised his voice and called out, "Falaste Rione, here for your sick and wounded. Borli Quiotto, is that you lurking back there? Come on out." There was no reply, and he added, "And bring my sister, if she's with you."

"Quiotto's sick, along with plenty of others," came a voice from the damp shadows. "And your sister's stuck in camp helping to look after them."

A moment later the speaker stepped forth into view—a short, skinny figure, armed with a bow, shrouded in homespun and oilcloth, with carrot hair framing a snub-nosed face. A very boyish face, surely no more than sixteen or seventeen years of age. Once again Jianna was struck by the youth and ordinary appearance so characteristic of the notorious Ghosts.

"Well. Trox Venezzu. Hope those arrows flew wide by design, else I'll fear you've lost your touch."

"Fear not." The boy grinned. "Could've punctured you like a blister if I'd wanted."

"Well, that's a relief." Rione extended a hand, which the other gripped briefly.

"Good to see you again, it's been too long," Trox declared. "I mean really too long; things have gotten bad. A gang of us have come down with the hot heaves. Four of the lads and one girl have died of it, everyone still upright rotates nursing duty, and we've been nailed down in this sewer of a glen for weeks now. And where have you been all this time? You've never stayed away for so long. What kept you?"

"Business at Ironheart," Rione replied easily. "Several of your comrades are there, you know. Now, what were you saying about the hot heaves? That's uncommon. Are you sure you've got it right? Describe the symptoms."

"That might get messy. Maybe not quite fit for the ears of your—ah—your lady here."

"She is my assistant and, I assure you, faint neither of heart nor of stomach."

"Your assistant. Oh, right. Should've guessed." Trox smirked.

"My name is Noro Penzia." Jianna spoke with confidence, having memorized the details of her false history days earlier. "I've been working for Dr. Rione for some time now. I'm not afraid of blood, wounds, or sickness. I'm not squeamish; I won't faint, or vomit, or shriek. You may speak freely, and I urge you to do so."

"Oh. Do you, now?" Trox appeared taken aback. His eyes shifted to Rione, who nodded confirmation. "All right, then. You've asked for it, remember. If you lose your lunch, missy, don't blame *me*."

He led them off into the woods, where there was no trail and they had to thread a path through leafless patches of ice-rimed bramble. As they went, Trox talked, limning the afflictions of his comrades in terms that might once have revolted Jianna, but now merely struck her as informative. She noted Rione's creased brow, and knew at once that he perceived the outbreak as significant and dangerous.

Twenty minutes of walking brought them to the Ghosts' camp, which occupied a clearing so secluded that Rione might never have discovered it on his own. Here beneath the sullen skies clustered a drab assortment of tents ranging in size from moderately spacious down to miniature canvas hovel, barely fit to shelter a lone sleeper. Off to the side, a few rough wooden lean-tos rested against the trees; probably a testament to the campsite's exceptional longevity. One large, open-sided canvas structure appeared to function as a makeshift stable; several horses and mules stood tethered beneath the conical roof. Two or three smoky fires struggled to survive the on-slaught of the sleet. Somewhere someone was overcooking cabbage and the assertive odor permeated the atmosphere.

Disappointed, Jianna surveyed the scene. Her experiences in recent weeks should have prepared her, but still some child-ish part of her had expected glamour and color; ferocious fa-natics, dwelling in romantic rusticity, vowing allegiance to antique ideals even while plotting mayhem. Instead she found drab poverty, ordinary shabbiness, everything . . . *dreary*.

There were sentries stationed about the perimeter, but nobody challenged Trox Venezzu and his companions. Within seconds Falaste Rione was recognized, and the pale-faced, hungry-looking Ghosts came poking out of their canvas containers to greet him. The scene recalled the doctor's reception among the servants of Ironheart, weeks earlier. Rione seemed to awaken fellow feeling among the lower orders. Or perhaps there was simply something in him that found a warm welcome wherever he went.

She herself aroused great interest. Jianna felt the pressure of many a speculative eye. They would be more than speculative, she mused, had their owners the slightest inkling of her true identity. She would likely be hacked to pieces on the spot. Bowing her head, she fixed her gaze on the ground and listened to the voices. Animated chatter, greetings, demands for news, a bouquet of medical complaints—aches and pains and warts and boils—and ugly accounts of the hot heaves. Assorted accents—Vitrisian, Orezzian, Frenisi—but the majority rural, ordinary folk of the countryside.

And then Rione's educated Vitrisian tones again. "First allow me to greet my sister," he was saying, "then lead me to your sick-house, and I'll set to work."

Set to work? Without so much as a quarter hour's rest, a few minutes' warmth beside one of the smoky fires, a decent meal or even a cup of soup? How like Falaste Rione. Of course, he would willingly permit *her* these comforts, but she did not intend to ask.

The distinct tones of a new voice pierced the convivial babble. *"Is my brother finally here?"*

The voice was melodic, the accent cultivated. The words brought Jianna's head up. For a moment intervening bodies blocked her view, then the speaker pushed through into sight, and Jianna's breath caught, for she saw before her a feminine version of Falaste Rione. Medium height, slender form, clothed in a simple grey gown the color of the tree trunks; dark hair plaited into a single thick braid that hung down her back; Falaste's fine, pale features; Falaste's grey-blue eyes. His sister unmistakably, the mysterious Celisse. Their connection proclaimed itself to the world.

Jianna stared from one to the other, charmed. It was delightful, really—a young woman, only a few years older than herself, who was a second edition of Falaste. She smiled, fully prepared to love Celisse Rione.

Brother and sister embraced closely, then Celisse disengaged, stepped back, and stared straight into his eyes to demand, "Where have you been? Why have you stayed away for so long?"

"Detained at Ironheart."

"You were needed here." It was an accusation.

"The magnifica has taken in a number of the wounded, Celisse. You know that. There was also illness among her own people, including family. Trecchio was stung by a siccatrice."

"Trecchio is insignificant," she returned. "These men here in camp are not. They are the soldiers and warriors, they are the true heart of the resistance. Here is where your first duty lies."

Jianna's brows rose.

"Does my younger sister believe it her place to instruct me?"

"It would seem that someone should."

"This is an old discussion," Rione returned with an unusual touch of impatience. "If we must resume it, let's do so later, in private."

"Why in private? There's nothing in the world I need or wish to hide from my comrades. Can you say the same?"

"I can say that I'd rather be working than standing here squabbling with you."

"Well, that's the first sensible remark you've made." Celisse produced a grudging smile. "Pardon me, brother, but sometimes I think you permit yourself too many distractions, and it provokes me, for your talents are too valuable to waste." As if in pursuit of the thought, her attention shifted for the first time to Jianna.

The eyes were Falaste Rione's in shape, size, color, and intelligence; the eyes were Falaste Rione's, frozen solid. A curious play of light, a hard crystalline glint, distinguished sister from brother. Jianna's nascent liking was frostbitten at first glance.

Celisse was openly inspecting her, unhurried gaze taking her in from head to foot. At length she turned to her brother and inquired, "Who is this girl, and why is she wearing your cloak?"

Jianna felt her cheeks heat.

"She is my assistant, the Maidenlady Noro Penzia. Noro, allow me to present my sister, Celisse Rione."

"It is a pleasure to meet you at last, maidenlady." Jianna willed herself to speak cordially. "I've heard much of your devotion to the Faerlonnish cause."

Celisse's eyes did not stray from her brother's face. "Why is she wearing your cloak," she repeated, "while you feel the cold? Has she none of her own? Is it a beggar you've brought here for us to feed?"

"I've told you that I bring my assistant," Rione replied evenly. "And the discourtesy of her reception does you no credit, sister."

The rebuke summoned a flush of color to Celisse's face, but her eyes never wavered. "I speak my mind. I tell the truth." She folded her arms. "I'll not apologize for that."

"You know nothing of this maidenlady's circumstances. In speaking your mind, as you put it, you flaunt your ignorance and ill nature. Now let's call a cease-fire, before we quarrel in earnest. Show me to the sick-house, if you will."

For a moment Celisse hesitated, as if loath to abandon the discussion. She glanced once more at Jianna, who sustained the anatomizing scrutiny with outward composure, then nodded and walked off, long dark braid slapping her back with each emphatic step. Rione followed, and Jianna fell in beside him.

The Ghosts were openly staring at her. They had listened to Rione's sister, registered the objections, and now the eyes were boring in as if seeking her center. Jianna kept her own eyes down. Soon she would be in another infirmary, a familiar environment, helping Rione to heal the sick and the wounded—a task she was truly well qualified to perform. The weeks at Ironheart had not gone to waste. She had learned much, and now, when Falaste Rione introduced her as his assistant, it was no lie. Certainly he could do without her, but he would feel the loss. And the Ghosts would soon see for themselves that she could earn her keep. Her spine straightened and her chin came up.

Celisse led them to a pair of large tents set up at one end of the clearing, at some remove from the other dwellings.

"Wounded and aguish." She gestured left, then right. "Hot heaves. Lean-to behind the trees, for amputations. You can sleep there."

"I can, but Noro can't. She'll need some other place."

"Will she? Really. I don't know where."

"I'm sure you can find her something, Celisse. If you set your mind to it."

"I'll see what I can do, since it seems to mean so very much to you. And later on, when you've done with your day's work, perhaps you'll spare your sister a few minutes of your time and we can talk—of ourselves, and of the fortunes of the cause. In private, if that isn't too much to ask."

"I'll look forward to it," he assured her, calmly refusing the bait.

She nodded and stalked off without another word.

"I apologize for her," Rione remarked as soon as Celisse was out of earshot.

"She hates me," said Jianna.

"You mustn't think so. My sister is an odd creature, given to powerful loyalties and prejudices. She can be a tenacious enemy, but as a friend she is devoted, fearless, and utterly self-less."

That woman will never accept me as a friend, Jianna thought. She bobbed a falsely optimistic nod.

Then all thoughts of hostile sisters and suspicious Ghosts fled her mind as she followed Rione into the first infirmary tent to discover the half dozen wounded tenants wrapped in threadbare blankets laid out on the canvas floor. But no, not directly on the floor. Beneath the blankets, quantities of spongy moss had been packed and shaped into flat pallets.

"They don't even give their sick decent bedding!" she protested in a whisper.

"Nobody in this camp will enjoy what you would call decent bedding," he returned in a normal conversational tone. "Where are they to acquire such luxuries?"

Jianna quoted poetry in reply:

> "The forest nurtured all her human guests,
> As if they were the children of her soil;
> As if she were a queen dispensing gifts
> To princes born of her green-shadowed womb.
> She fed and housed and clothed them royally,
> Dispensing riches with a lavish hand."

"*Journey of the Zoviriae?*" Rione cocked a quizzical eyebrow.

"I had to memorize large blocks of it as a child. Judging by the look of things around here, it would seem that the poet didn't know much about forests."

Rione grinned, then set to work and she assisted as he bathed and bandaged a trio of wounds, addressed the horrific results of a botched amputation, soothed the seizures of deep nerve distemper, and strove to preserve the fluids of some unfortunate whose skin seemed to be peeling off in wide red and white rags. It was clear at once that the ailing Ghosts of the forest camp were similar in type to the sick men and boys confined to the turret infirmary at Ironheart. But for the canvas walls and mossy pallets, it might almost have seemed that nothing had changed.

He finished with them, and she prevailed upon him with infinite difficulty to allow himself a twenty-minute respite before proceeding to the second tent, abode of the hot heaves.

He had told her what to expect and she had believed herself well prepared, yet the sight, sounds, and odors of the heaves nonetheless took her by surprise. The audible churning of perpetually outraged intestines made infernal music, and the color of the vomit seemed to defy natural law. Once upon a time she might have retched and fled. Now she set her jaw and did her job. It seemed to go on for a very long time—the bathing and cleansing, the cooling of fevered bodies, the dressing of countless lesions, the mixing and administration of the varied draughts. Long before it was done, her forehead was moist with sweat, despite the wintry atmosphere.

At last he straightened with a sigh, and she knew that he could do no more at present. She surveyed the scene. The sufferers were at rest, for the most part. Three of the luckier were deeply asleep. He would save most of these people, perhaps all of them, and it would never occur to him that there was anything remarkable in it. The impulse was strong to tell him how greatly she admired him, but she hardly dared. She said nothing.

"We're done for now, and you deserve a rest," observed Rione. "Speaking of which, we'd best make sure that Celisse has found you someplace to sleep."

"I believe Celisse would like to see me sleeping six feet under."

"Bad attitude, Noro Penzia."

"My name lacks poetry. Would it be too late to choose another?"

"Come along."

They exited the tent, stepping forth into the clean air that Jianna drew down into the depths of her lungs. The breeze carried the scent of cabbage, onions, bacon; evidently preparation of the evening meal was in progress. She had not eaten in hours, yet the odor displeased her. The effects of the sick-house assault upon her senses had not dissipated, and she wondered if she would ever want to eat again.

"It will wear off much sooner than you expect," Rione told her.

"Do you read thoughts, then?"

"Only faces. Yours is uncommonly expressive."

Before she could reply, the young archer Trox Venezzu came hurrying to them.

"News, Falaste!" the youth announced with enthusiasm. "Galcone's just gotten back with news you'll want to hear about. He said that Ironheart's been destroyed. Blown sky-high, hardly two stones left standing together. Dust, rubble, and a walloping great crater, that's what's left. Now, that's *news!*"

Jianna wondered if the sick-house miasma had scrambled hearing as well as appetite.

"News, or rumor?" Rione asked quietly. "Has Galcone seen with his own eyes?"

"That he has. Been there, looked down into the hole with his own eyes, sifted the dust with his own fingers. It's true."

"When did this happen?"

"No more than two or three days ago."

"Who was responsible?"

"That's where it gets fuzzy. Galcone asked around, but people have different stories. Everyone agrees that a Taer force did it. They even brought in artillery, and that's pure Taerleezi. Must have discovered the Ironheart resistance connection and decided to clean the place out. That's clear enough. Strange thing is, folk claim to have spotted a Faerlonnish presence. A few even spout tales of a Faerlonnish *commander.* Now, that doesn't make much sense."

Father. Jianna's heart jumped. She knew with absolute certainty. He had been late—but he had come.

"And the people?" Rione's shock was evident, and he seemed to speak with some difficulty. "The family, little Nissi—"

"Little who?"

"The servants, the infirmary patients?"

"As far as Galcone could judge, most of the servants were killed by the Taers, but some survived and got away. Don't ask for names. As for the infirmary patients, I couldn't say. But here's the thing. We know what happened to the family. The Taers spared the magnifica, didn't want to kill a widow-woman, so they chased her off into the woods. But they slaughtered the sons. Tortured 'em all night, then killed 'em. Onartino and Trecchio Belandor are both dead."

Onartino is dead. The words found their way home—it seemed a minor eternity before their meaning reached her— and a light dawned in Jianna's mind. The invisible shackles fell away, and the weight that pressed down on her vanished in an instant. She took a great gulp of clean air, the first unobstructed breath she had drawn in days, and a sense of inexpressible gratitude filled her, bringing the tears to her eyes. Her father had produced one of his miracles. The rutting boar pig that owned her was gone, and she was free.

Free.

⋅ ⋅ ⋅

By the side of a stream in the depths of the woods, no great distance from Ironheart's remains, rose a stony ledge whose prominent overhang—its sharp thrust accentuated by centuries of erosion—offered natural shelter from rain and wind. At some point in past ages, unknown burrowing hands had improved upon the work of nature, enlarging the space beneath the overhang to create a cave, open at the front but protected on all sides, roughly circular in shape, modest in size, but large enough for human habitation. The cave had not been occupied within human memory. But it was occupied now.

A small fire burning before the entrance offered indifferent warmth. Beside it huddled a woman, arms clasped about her bent knees, greying head bowed. Behind her, nearly lost in the shadows, two motionless forms lay upon a man-made ledge or platform of stone—probably intended as a bed, now serving as a makeshift bier. One of them was fully clothed, the fatal rent in his throat visible; the other was completely covered with a yellowing linen sheet.

Some four days had passed since a small group of household servants had accompanied the Magnifica Yvenza to this place and left her alone with the bodies of her sons. They willingly would have done more for her. Although their mistress had always cultivated fear and respect above affection, still they hesitated to leave her alone and unprotected in such a forsaken spot. She had insisted, however. Declining their offers of transportation to civilization, declining the offers of two or three to remain and serve her, declining even the offers of assistance in burying the two corpses, she had firmly sent them on their way. They had pressed upon her stores of provisions, blankets, fuel, lanterns, tools, even a couple of weapons, and these things she had accepted. And having provided for the magnifica to the extent that she permitted, they had taken their final leave of her.

Throughout the ensuing hours, Yvenza had sat on the ground beside the fire, scarcely stirring save to feed the blaze and herself, keeping both alive. Her face was empty, her eyes open but blind, the contents of her mind unknowable. Almost she might have been distancing herself from the world and everything in it; from life itself.

The winter sun was setting again. Already it had dipped below the level of the surrounding trees, but Yvenza never noticed. The world was far away, it was almost gone—until a light footfall and a soft intake of breath brought everything back again.

Yvenza looked up. For a moment, the glare of the firelight confounded her vision, and then she discerned a slight, motionless figure, wrapped in a cloak the color of the twilight and all but invisible in the deepening gloom.

"You," she observed as if in accusation. "What are you doing here?"

Stepping into the circle of firelight, the newcomer let fall her hood, revealing a peaked little face, wreathed in mists of weightless pale hair.

"I followed you," Nissi replied in her tiny voice.

"Why?"

There was a long pause before Nissi answered, "I have . . . nowhere to go."

"You don't, do you? Aureste's ruffians didn't hinder you?"

"They did not see me."

"That hardly seems possible."

"I am . . . easily overlooked, at times."

"I see. If I allow you to stay, you won't be comfortable, you know."

"I know."

"I don't want fellowship. I'll have no companionable chatter, no reminiscences."

"I will not be companionable."

"Then you may stay, for now."

Nissi bobbed her head, then stood there waiting.

"Well? Are you hungry?" Yvenza demanded.

Nissi shook her head.

"Thirsty? Sleepy? There's a spare blanket you can use."

"Not yet."

"Find yourself some occupation, then. Don't look to me for entertainment. I'm not your companion."

"I will see Trecchio and Onartino now," Nissi announced with surprising clarity.

"They're at the back. Mind your head; the ceiling dips."

In silence Nissi made her way to the rear of the cave. The two bodies lay in shadow, but she seemed to see them clearly. She went first to Trecchio, and spent some minutes staring down into his dead face.

"Good-bye," she whispered at last, and turned away from him.

Drifting to Onartino's side, she hesitated a long moment, then very carefully turned the sheet down to his shoulders.

"Oh," breathed Nissi, taking in the ruined face. Her lambent eyes filled. Very gingerly she laid a small hand across his blood-caked forehead. "Oh." For a time she stood motionless and staring as if paralyzed or stupefied. At last she turned away and with dragging steps made her way back to the fireside. Yvenza, gazing deep into the blaze, took no notice of her until she observed hesitantly, "Onartino's face . . . his face . . . it should not be covered up."

Yvenza did look then. "Want to enjoy the spectacle, do you?" she inquired. "Never thought you had it in you, girl."

"The sheet over his face . . . will make it harder for him to breathe."

"Have you lost your wits? He isn't breathing, he's dead. They're both dead. Don't you understand that?"

"Not . . . both." Nissi shook her head.

"Is this some sort of a game you're playing, or have you truly run mad?"

"Not both. Trecchio has left. But Onartino still lingers. Deep, deep inside, there is still a flicker."

"You are dreaming." Skepticism notwithstanding, Yvenza was already climbing to her feet and hastening to the rear of the cave. Nissi floated like a bubble in her wake. When she reached her son, she applied her fingers to the pulse point in his neck; twitched back the sheet and pressed her fingers to his wrist, then laid her ear to his chest. Straightening, she met Nissi's eyes and reported deliberately, "Nothing. Nothing at all. He's cold, he's dead, and there's the reality of it."

"Not reality. He is almost gone, but there is still the last fiber of the final thread. He cannot find his way back without help, the path is too dark, but my call can guide him. Let me."

"Who or what do you imagine that you are?"

Silence.

Yvenza studied the other. Nissi's eyes were enormous and luminous. Almost against her own will, she found herself demanding, "Why would you do this thing? He was never kind to you."

"He lives," Nissi replied, as if in explanation.

"He is finished, but I see that nothing will convince you. Very well, you may call him by any means you choose—this one time only. And when you are done, and you have learned that you cannot recall my dead son to life, then you will give up all arcane practice once and for all, and you will never speak of it again. Do you hear me?"

Nissi nodded.

"Then look to it." Yvenza returned to her place by the fire, where she seated herself with her back to the cave. For a time she heard nothing beyond the crackle of the blaze, but presently a soft murmuring issued from the shadowy space behind her. The voice was small, light, girlish, and the rhythmic utterance verged on exotic melody, but there was something about the sound that seemed to deepen the chill of the winter night. Wrapping her arms firmly around her bent knees, Yvenza strove to exclude the voice, musical though it was. In this she was only partially successful. Her former state of deep abstraction eluded her, she was dimly aware of time's passage, and eventually aware that the voice within the cave had fallen silent.

Yvenza blinked and returned to the present. The fire was dying. The cave behind her was silent, appropriately enough, as a tomb. It would seem that Nissi had lost her contest with death.

Yvenza took time to replenish the fire before reentering the cave. At once she spied a slight form wrapped in a grey cloak, curled up on the floor. Heedless of the damp and cold, Nissi lay fast asleep, head pillowed on one arm. Her young brow was creased, and tired shadows smudged the hollows of her face. Behind and above her, Onartino still rested full length upon the ledge, just as the Ironheart servants had placed him.

Nothing had changed, but for the disarrangement of the linen sheet formerly covering his entire body. Even in the soft glow of the firelight, the dreadful condition of his exposed face was apparent. She did not want to see him or think of him in such a state; he should be covered.

Yvenza started toward him. Before she had taken more than two or three steps she froze, transfixed by the slow, steady rise and fall of Onartino's chest. The spell broke and she advanced to his side, where she stood staring down at her oldest son— broken and mutilated, but alive.

SEVENTEEN

Thick mists veiled the northern hills, and a cold breeze drove rain into the face of a lone traveler. Grix Orlazzu paused to wipe the moisture from his eyes with a damp handkerchief. He pulled the edge of his hood forward a bit, to little avail. His wiry beard was thoroughly soaked.

He had come to the top of a stony rise that might on a rare clear day have offered a view out over a considerable expanse of jagged countryside. Today—as on almost every day in these desolate lands—the world was invisible, lost in limitless mist. He could see no more than a few short feet in any direction before the soft grey walls closed down. He could hear nothing more than the patter of rain hitting the dead winter grasses underfoot, and he had not encountered another human being in days. He did not, however, feel himself to be alone, much though he would have preferred it.

The evidence of his physical senses suggested solitude. But another set of receptors—the trained portion of his mind attuned to uncanny phenomena—spoke of an incorporeal presence; something vast, ancient, and profoundly alien inhabiting the fog. He had felt it for the first time some days earlier, upon reaching the border of that dim region known throughout history as the Wraithlands. Initially it had been a mere whisper of foreign intelligence brushing his consciousness; a subtle, almost tentative exploratory touch that a mind less acute than his own might have overlooked altogether. He had noted it at once, however, and he had immediately attempted to initiate communication, which had sent the visitor flying from his mind for hours thereafter. Almost the presence had seemed timid, but this early impression had been misleading.

He had pushed on into the trackless hills, and the alien consciousness had soon returned. Nothing timid about it now; its inquisitive attention had pressed with increasing insistence, and he had soon come to recognize this bodiless entity's gigantic size and power. That it was aware he did not doubt, but its thoughts and intentions were closed to him, with one exception. It wanted to absorb him unto Itself; it wanted to own all that he was. This was unmistakable.

He might have turned back, he might have sought a safer path. But the Wraithlands almost vibrated with the energy of the Source, energy that he was determined to tap. And so he had traveled on into the charged mists in search of the ideal locale, and as he went the attempted mental incursions waxed in power and frequency. His arcane mastery enabled him to repel them all, but the task demanded constant vigilance.

And he was vigilant now, as he stood at the crest of the rise in the rain. He could see very little of his surroundings, but his mind quested, probing the fog in all directions. He caught no sense of the vast Other's proximity, but sensed something like a small echo of its existence. He also recognized that he was not alone, but strain his eyes, ears, and mind though he might, he discovered no recognizable sentience.

On he went, his path descending now, and as he went the mists began to darken about him, for the short winter day was drawing to a close. In all likelihood he would have to sleep out in the open again this night—a prospect that held no terror, for the intense energy of these lands willingly expressed itself in the form of big campfires capable of burning throughout the night untended.

But he did not need to stop just yet, there was still some daylight left. He could hike on for a while longer in search of the right spot, which he would know on sight, on instinct.

He was certainly not alone. The pressure of hidden regard was all but palpable. Orlazzu wheeled suddenly and the mystery was solved. Only a few feet distant, an animal sat watching him. It was small, not much larger than a house cat—long, lithe, and low, with a blunt little muzzle, round blue eyes, and heavy front claws designed for digging. Its grey coat faded almost invisibly into the grey fog. Orlazzu smiled. He confronted an ordinary meecher, a commonplace burrowing creature found throughout the Veiled Isles.

"You're a bold one," he observed aloud.

The meecher did not move. Its blue gaze, fixed on his face, did not waver. Orlazzu's smile vanished. This creature of the wild should have fled at sound of a human voice. He took a long step toward it, and then another. Two more, and he stood within touching distance, but the meecher never stirred. Its blue eyes were filmed, and it was terribly emaciated. A light froth whitened its muzzle. Rabid?

No. Worse. *Occupied.*

Some sudden reckless impulse impelled him to ask aloud, "Can you speak?" And perhaps he was a fool to stand there out in the middle of nowhere, addressing the dumb brute in absurd expectation of a spoken reply, but he did not feel like a fool. He felt afraid.

No reply was forthcoming, but he saw comprehension in the filmy eyes, he was sure of it. The meecher sat motionless as a dead thing. Orlazzu backed away step by step. The blue regard never wavered. There was no overt menace. Just as he started to turn away, the meecher rose and advanced several unhurried paces, reducing the separation between them to a distance of some ten feet, whereupon it halted, watching him steadily. He took another step backward and again the meecher advanced, maintaining that ten feet of separation.

"Useless. I am not easily disconcerted," he warned. There was no answer. Turning his back with apparent finality, he resumed his trek. But as he went, from time to time he cast quick glances back over his shoulder to behold the meecher following a constant ten feet behind. The minutes passed, the mists darkened, and the grey animal all but disappeared from view, but its silent presence was unmistakable, the weight of its stare heavy on his back, heavier than ever, in fact, almost as if the creature were somehow growing—

He looked back and his brows arched at sight of two meechers, walking side by side ten paces behind him. The animals were almost indistinguishable in appearance, both skeletal and film-eyed. Meechers, he recalled, were habitually solitary creatures, eschewing packs, tribes, or colonies. Even in the aftermath of mating, they did not live or walk in pairs. He quickened his footsteps. The meechers kept pace. They were silent, but impossible to ignore. Minutes later, when he could no longer forbear stealing another look, he spied three of them close on his trail. And now he felt a distinct sense of invasive mental pressure, a distant reverberation characteristic of the unseen Other.

On through the mists, and the pressure increased. There were four of them behind him now, and Orlazzu began to consider emergency measures. Not that he couldn't hold his own, but the prospect of a night spent out of doors, the sleepless hours given over to constant watchfulness and arcane exertion, lacked appeal. Certainly it lay within his power to kill the meechers—they looked half dead already—but the thought of destroying the ordinarily harmless small creatures was repugnant.

Darkness deepened around him, and now five meechers trooped quietly in his wake. He would have to kill them—a regrettable necessity. But even as he slipped a faintly iridescent pale pastille into his mouth, even as he readied his mind for lethal action, the mists parted and a small structure stood revealed.

It was narrow and low, with walls of sod, stone chimney, and a thatched roof. Too insignificant to be called a cottage, it was not much more than a glorified hut. There was no immediately apparent explanation for its existence in that isolated spot. The land had never been farmed, and did not seem to lend itself to any conventional human endeavor. In all probability the shelter housed some misanthropic hermit seeking refuge from the bustle of humanity—a desire entirely comprehensible to Grix Orlazzu. But the hermit, if such there was, did not appear to be in residence. No light glowed within, and no smoke rose from the chimney.

Orlazzu marched to the door, the meechers padding close behind him. A crow swooped down out of the mists to perch on the roof, scarcely an arm's length above him. The bird appeared to be molting. Its plumage was dull and its eyes were filmed. When he exclaimed sharply and waved his arm, the crow remained motionless, its eyes fixed on him. The hairs stirred at the back of his neck, and he knocked on the door with more than necessary force. There was no response from within. After a moment, he opened the door and stepped inside. There remained enough feeble daylight to tell him at once that the little dwelling was empty and probably had been for some time. A layer of dust and grime overspread all, and the few articles of unfinished wooden furniture sported luxuriant growths of mold. Still, the place was habitable. Its walls and roof could support intangible reinforcement sufficient to thwart invasion and repel arcane assault. More to the point, the ground below and around the building all but sang with power. Surely at some point along the course of its vast underground circuit, the Source must pass directly beneath this spot. And the place was even furnished. Its true owner might always return, at which point he would have to surrender the new domain, but in the meantime—

"Home?" Grix Orlazzu murmured, half in statement, half in inquiry.

He shut the door in the faces of the attendant meechers, and the room sank into near darkness. An almost effortless flex of his mind kindled fire on the hearth and lit an oil lamp on the table. It was easy, so easy in this place. The Source seemed almost urgent in its willingness to bestow its bounty. Upon this ground, a skilled arcanist might hope to transcend the limits of a lifetime.

Thus it was the matter of mere moments for Grix Orlazzu to imbue the surrounding walls, roof, and clay floor underfoot with sufficient protective force to ensure his safety for months or years to come. This accomplished, he felt none of the sick exhaustion so often blighting the conclusion of significant arcane endeavor. Quite the contrary, he was alert, optimistic, and—hungry. At other times, in other places, he would not have been able to hold food down, following such a feat as he had just performed, but here and now he was quite hungry indeed.

Orlazzu's sack yielded bread, cheese, wine, and dried fruit. Seating himself at the table, he ate and drank moderately, then brought forth his copy of *The Drowned Chronicle* and read for hours by the light of the oil lamp. During this time he never sensed the slightest invasive touch of the Other's presence, nor did the hapless beasts absorbed into a greater consciousness disturb his new sanctum. The barriers were holding.

When his lids began to droop, he set the chronicle aside, banked the fire, extinguished the lamp, and took himself to bed, wrapped in his own blanket, spread out atop the previous owner's begrimed coverlet. In the morning he would give the hut and its furnishings a good cleaning; for now, he wanted sleep.

He did sleep, soundly and dreamlessly, until the dawn sent baby fingers of weak light poking in through the chinks in the closed shutters, and a tremendous assault upon the door commenced. Orlazzu sat up, wide awake. Someone was pounding loudly and imperiously. Emotion drove those blows. There was nothing uncanny or Otherly about them. There could be but one explanation: The hut's rightful owner had returned to find himself locked out of his own property. No wonder he was incensed.

Bad luck. Orlazzu muttered a curse. This hut had almost seemed made for him, waiting for him. He should have known that it was too good to be true. Now he would have to leave. And apologize—though it slid along the edge of his mind then that he need do neither. His powers more than equipped him to keep the hut if he wanted it—but he pushed the thought away at once, as he had pushed such thoughts away throughout his lifetime. It was natural and inevitable that an accomplished arcanist would upon occasion be tempted to employ his powers destructively, for the sake of personal gain or personal malice. But Grix Orlazzu had made the decision, many years earlier, to resist all such impulses. He had kept that vow and would continue to keep it. Therefore, with a sad imprecation, he rose and opened the door.

He found himself confronting a familiar chunky figure wrapped in an oilcloth cloak and hood. He saw a wiry black beard, beaky nose, heavy black brows above eyes of amber glass, and a swarthy square face, identical in feature to his own, but neatly upholstered in the finest glove leather.

A whirring of internal gears heralded mechanical utterance.

"Leftover, once known as Grix Orlazzu, I have overtaken you at last. Admit me, if you please," the automaton directed.

"What are you doing here, Junior?" Orlazzu's sturdy frame blocked the doorway.

"I have decided to rejoin you. And do not call me Junior."

"What shall I call you then? Inescapable? Unavoidable? Unmentionable?"

"You already know, Leftover. Do not pretend that you have forgotten. My name is Grix Orlazzu. I am the improved and perfected version of the Grix Orlazzu design. You may address me as GrixPerfect, or, as we are intimate, you may simply call me Grix."

"Very well. Grix. Why have you followed me? I left you with the cabin and all that it contained, everything that you could need, nearly everything that I had. Wasn't that enough?"

"Ah, how like an organic to think solely in terms of material possessions! You gave me *things* and thought they would suffice. Did you for one moment consider my feelings, my inner self, my needs, or the destructive effect on my personal development when you went off and abandoned me? Did you think of anyone beside yourself, Leftover? And are you going to let me in?"

"What for? You don't need a meal or a place to sleep. What do you seek here?"

"What do *you* seek here?"

"Enlightenment. Fulfillment. A place to work, so long as I can; to practice, and to develop my abilities to their fullest potential."

"That is what I want also."

"Very good. Seek elsewhere."

"I will not. My inner yearnings drew me north to these hills in search of a perfect locale. I was drawn to this spot, so humble in aspect yet so rich in promise. It seems that you were similarly drawn, and how should it be otherwise, when your mind is a primitive, incompletely realized first draft of my own? Are you going to let me in?"

"No, I'm not. This place is taken. You must find another for yourself."

"Impossible. No other will suit me so well. I've searched through these foggy hills filled with impertinent wildlife, and this is the one that I want. What right have you to keep me out?"

"I was here first."

"Immaterial. Listen, Leftover. You built me—or so you claim, although it hardly seems possible—but if it's true, then you are responsible. You cannot simply turn your back on me and walk away—I will not be treated so. You will do your duty by me, you will minister to my needs. I demand it. Do you understand me, Leftover?"

"No, I don't. What exactly do you want from me?"

"Consideration. Respect. Concern. Companionship."

"Come again?"

"Also, you will teach me to read."

"You were to teach yourself, as I recall."

"In the absence of all moral support—cast adrift, as it

were—I lacked incentive. You will teach me; it is your obligation."

"Sorry, Grix. You must shift for yourself now." Orlazzu began to close the door.

Instantly the automaton advanced its foot over the threshold, at the same time shoving the door with steel-jointed strength. Orlazzu was thrust backward from the entrance, and his simulacrum stepped into the hut.

"You are inhospitable," it complained.

"You are not invited and you are not welcome," Orlazzu scowled. "I am asking you to leave."

"I refuse." The automaton folded its arms. "I will not be slighted. I will have all that's owed me."

"Owed you? Insufferable junkheap!"

"You will act as a proper creator," the automaton insisted. "You will give me the attention, education, and affection to which I am entitled. Make no mistake about it, Leftover once known as Grix Orlazzu. I am here to stay."

· · ·

Evening had come and the lamps were aglow when one of the servants came to Aureste Belandor, bearing news that his brother Innesq was awake and asking for him.

"If this intelligence proves false, I will have you flayed," Aureste promised dispassionately.

The terrified servant hastened to reassure him. There could be no mistake. Master Innesq was conscious and clearheaded.

He scarcely dared to let himself hope. The news was too good; it was either an error or a brilliantly cruel lie. It took only a moment to traverse the few feet of corridor separating the room he had chosen for himself from the chamber in which Innesq lay. A guard stood watch at the door, a huge and broad figure that Aureste recognized readily. It was the youngster Drocco whose courage, discretion, and general good sense had shone during the recent action against Ironheart. The lad had distinguished himself, and for that reason he had been assigned a post of importance—protecting the life of Innesq Belandor. Yet Drocco did not appear to appreciate his own good fortune. Unkempt, uncombed, unshaven, and bleary-eyed, he was actually leaning against the door. As his master drew near, he straightened and attempted a salute, but the wavering gesture was sketchy at best. His manner and slovenly look suggested dissipated nights. At any other time Aureste would have reprimanded the drunkard, or even dismissed him on the spot. Just now he could not be bothered.

Casting a cold eye in passing upon the young offender—a look promising future retribution—Aureste entered his brother's chamber. And it was true, he saw at a glance. Quite true. Innesq was sitting up in bed, still pale as a tombstone, but wide awake, eyes clear and focused, even spooning some soup proffered by a solicitous Sishmindri. He was himself again; he would recover. Aureste felt a tight constriction in his chest. *Reprieved.*

"Aureste." Innesq managed a ghostly smile. His voice was faint but audible. "It is very good to see you again. Welcome back."

"I might say the same to you. For a time we weren't certain that you'd wake."

"I am sorry for the concern I've caused, but it was necessary. I am sorry, too, for your disappointment regarding Jianna."

"I came so close, Innesq! She was there, they admitted it freely. Had I arrived but a single day earlier— But wait, how did you know—ah, I see, the Sishmindris have already been filling your ears."

"No, it was not the Sishmindris." Innesq turned briefly to the amphibian at the bedside. "That will do, Ini. Thank you. You may go now." Ini departed, bearing the tray and soup bowl, and Innesq resumed his interrupted train of thought. "It was the young girl who told me. She was confused and frightened, but she managed to communicate."

"Young girl? One of the servants, you mean?"

"I think not. Her position in the household is ambiguous, I believe, and she speaks very little of herself. In fact, it was not until our last Distant Exchange that I learned she resides at Ironheart. She sees a good deal, however, and she let me know that Jianna had escaped."

"Some girl has been in here chatting with you?" Aureste's fears were resurrecting themselves. His brother seemed rational, but he was surely confused or worse. "Innesq, you've been unconscious for a long time. Frankly, we thought you were dying. Now you're back with us and you are going to make a full recovery. But you must have dreamed while you slept, and right now I think you're mistaking those dreams for reality. It's understandable. They may have been very vivid, and—"

"Aureste, stop," Innesq interrupted. "You do not understand. I am neither delirious nor delusional. Now listen to me closely. I've vital information and I want you to hear it all without digression and without interruption. To begin with, understand that my recent slumber was not the result of injury or illness. It was induced by arcane means—performed deliberately and voluntarily by me upon myself—because an astounding experience that befell me during the attack upon our home had convinced me of the need.

"Thus I proceeded, and in this condition that resembled unconsciousness but was not, I was able to contact other arcanists in the Veiled Isles and beyond. I exchanged information and ideas with these colleagues, gathered knowledge, and compared theories. Beyond that, I succeeded in dispatching my awareness to the northern lands, there to study the recent phenomena at their point of origin. All of this has led to a single conclusion, confirming the suspicions that I expressed weeks ago.

"It can no longer be questioned or doubted that the Source stands poised upon the brink of reversal. When its spin alters, the Veiled Isles will become uninhabitable—to mankind, that is. Those humans able to escape across the sea may survive, but most of our kind will perish. Not so with the Inhabitants, however. Those former lords of the land will resume their ancient sway, and presently their huge collective Overmind will occupy and own every living entity to be found throughout the Isles. Already it has begun. I have long feared and now I am certain that the plague raging in Vitrisi expresses the human body's violent resistance to arcane invasion. So far, the majority of victims have died and fed the fires. But the great reversal is approaching and the Overmind's power waxes day by day. Very soon, if not already, the invader's control will extend beyond the point of death, and then the walking corpses of legend will once more roam the world.

"The danger is great, but our human resources are formidable." The lengthy speech did not appear to exhaust Innesq Belandor. In fact, his voice strengthened as he spoke, and an inner flame illumined his eyes. "We have faced and overcome this threat in the past, more than once. We can do so again. It is a matter of cleansing the Source of its impedimenta, restoring the velocity of its spin and thus preventing reversal. This is a task far beyond the power of any lone arcanist, even the greatest, but requires the combined abilities of several, working as one. For these adepts we must look to the Six Houses— Belandor, Corvestri, Steffa, and Orlazzu in Faerlonne; Pridisso and Zovaccio in Taerleez. Unhappily, the connections among the Six have decayed in the years following the wars, and the Taerleezi ban upon Faerlonnish arcanism has further marred matters. I think House Steffa is dormant right now, and Orlazzu has all but vanished. Nonetheless, there are skilled practitioners to be found. I am not without ability. Vinz Corvestri's performance is consistent and reliable. The young girl out in the hills—she is surely of Belandor blood, and her natural talent is prodigious. She must be included. We need to begin assembling a group of adepts, and we must set to work immediately. Aureste, I trust I may rely upon your support and assistance?"

"Always." Aureste studied his brother. Innesq's face was ashen save for two spots of color burning on his cheekbones.

His great dark eyes were too brilliant. Excitement seemed to have reinvigorated him, feverishly. "You know I'll do all in my power to help you. At the moment, however, you'd best eat, take a little exercise, and build up your strength. And when you're quite yourself again and ready to resume arcane activity, there are two most urgent matters that you must address. One—I'd like you to shield what's left of Belandor House against the invasion of the plague. I count upon your abilities to protect all of us. Two—you must locate Jianna, or help me to make my way to her, as you did the last time. She's out there, Innesq. Alive and in desperate need of your help. Find her! Do it as soon as you can."

For a long moment, Innesq stared at him, and finally asked, "Have you heard a single word I've uttered? Have you listened, has anything reached your understanding? We are facing catastrophe. Our lives, our home, city, and land—everything stands in danger. Do you not understand that, or do you refuse to believe?"

"I don't doubt your sincerity." Aureste stirred uncomfortably. "And certainly you may count on my loyalty. But it's clear that the most immediate and pressing of problems merit immediate attention. Right now, Jianna is our chief concern. Now, before it's too late, before she's hurt or killed, we must find her and bring her home. Jianna comes first."

"No, Aureste. I am afraid she does not. I love my niece and value her safety, but as of now the project comes first. I must begin work. I must send out the call."

"You don't know what you're saying. You're weak, faint, and probably confused. Rest awhile, and when your head has cleared we'll decide what you're to do about locating Jianna."

"It is extraordinary, this ability of yours to exclude all that you do not wish to hear, as if an arcane shield enclosed your head. I have rested quite long enough. Would you be so good as to help me to my chair?" The wheeled chair in question, untouched by smoke or fire, stood beside the bed.

"Where do you mean to go?"

"My workroom. There is much to do. I must begin."

"Innesq, wait. Your workroom was destroyed in the fire." His brother's face reflected shock, and Aureste added truthfully, "I am sorry."

"Destroyed? Everything?"

"I think the Sishmindris rescued a few items."

"Where are they?"

"I'm not sure. I think in one of the rooms at the end of the corridor. Everything here is in disarray. You don't yet realize the extent of the fire damage. We've suffered a tremendous loss."

"I will see for myself. Help me to my chair, if you please."

"Are you certain this is wise? Oh, very well, if you insist. But wait, I'll have your bodyguard assist. He's younger and larger than I."

"Bodyguard?"

"He'll stay out of your way. But I mean to keep you protected, brother. You'll not be attacked or injured again. And please don't trouble to protest, I'll hear no argument." Stepping to the door, Aureste opened it and commanded, "Drocco, get in here."

The youngster lurched in. His eyes were filmy, the whites faintly yellow. Sweat dewed his forehead, a heavy stubble covered his chin, and a disquieting, almost putrescent odor wafted from his uniform.

"You're falling-down drunk." Aureste's nostrils flared. "And you stink. Go downstairs and have them send up someone sober. Then collect whatever wages you are owed and clear out."

Drocco's face did not alter. Almost he seemed too muddled to understand. An incoherent muttering escaped him, and he tottered forward into the room.

"I told you to get out." Aureste fell back a couple of paces. "Do you wish to be beaten before you go?"

Drocco displayed no sign of comprehension. His dull gaze wandered, encountered Innesq Belandor, and anchored there. His muttering intensified, and he wobbled toward the bed.

"Stay back. You drunken donkey, have you gone deaf?"

Still nothing of understanding, nor yet of obedience. Drocco's laborious advance continued, and a dash of doubt, or even something like alarm shot through Aureste. Interposing himself between the guard and his brother's bed, he promised, "Another step and I will thrash you myself."

"Aureste, no, do not touch him." Innesq's voice from behind him, filled with something beyond characteristic pacifism. "Do you not see? He is ill. It is the plague."

Plague. The word detonated like an infernal machine in Aureste's mind. He knew at once that it was true; the signs were clear enough, had he allowed himself to recognize them. The pestilence, here in the heart of all that remained of his household; the plague, come to rob him of all that was still his, including his brother's life—and his own. Innesq would go first; the infectious guard was heading straight for him. At that moment it seemed to Aureste that the disease, in the guise of a shambling figure named Drocco, was an enemy that could be fought and conquered like all other enemies. Without hesitation and almost without thought, he sprang to the fireplace, snatched up the poker, raised it, and swung with all his strength. The iron struck Drocco's forehead with a startlingly loud crack. The youngster dropped without a cry. Letting fall the poker, Aureste drew the poniard from his belt, stooped, plunged the blade into Drocco's throat, and stepped back quickly to avoid the rush of blood. Spasms racked the dying body.

"What have you done?" Innesq's voice was hardly more than a whisper. "Oh, what have you done?"

"Saved us all, I hope." Aureste tossed the poniard from him, watching as the final tremors stirred Drocco's long limbs. A last gurgle of escaping breath, and the guard lay still. "There, it's done. And it had to be done, Innesq. You must see that. If it's discovered that the plague has come to our house, we'll be placed under quarantine and left to die at leisure. We'll be trapped in here, and there goes all hope of finding Jianna. Nor could all my credit with Uffrigo prevent it. I can't allow that." There was no reply, and he continued, "We must dispose of this body, and do it without contaminating ourselves. Can you use your abilities to disinfect him, brother? Render him safe to handle? Or better yet, could you vaporize him?"

"I am afraid it is not quite as easy as that." Innesq's voice was almost pitying.

"I never said or thought that it was easy."

"Still you do not understand. Watch."

Aureste obeyed, looking on with a sense of nameless dread that sharpened to horror as dead Drocco stirred, opened his filmy eyes, and sat up slowly. The empty gaze drifted over Aureste, who went cold inside, then traveled on to Innesq, where it halted. Clumsily, his movements stiff and abrupt, Drocco rose to his feet. A trickle of blood still descended from the great wound in his throat—doubtless drawn by the power of gravity, for his heart beat no longer. For a moment he stood rocking from foot to foot as if in experimentation, then resumed his interrupted advance upon the bed.

Breaking his own stunned paralysis with an effort, Aureste took up the poker again to bring it smashing down on the back of Drocco's head. Again he heard a sharp crack, but the dead guard barely faltered. He struck again and again, to no effect. There was a curious roaring in his ears, through which he caught or thought he caught the sound of his brother's voice, rhythmically upraised. Now he changed his mode of attack, clubbing the knees until he felt bone and cartilage give way, whereupon the dead man staggered, one leg buckling beneath him. And now for the other, but Drocco's attention was finally shifting from Innesq to Aureste, as if recognizing him for the first time as a significant threat, and the big hands were reaching out. Aureste swung the poker again, only to have the blow arrested in mid-arc and the weapon twisted from his grasp. The poker went flying, and he stood unarmed. The way to the door was clear; he could certainly escape, but that meant abandoning Innesq to the mercies of this . . . thing. His eyes ranged the chamber. The poker lay some distance from him. If he could reach it, he might target Drocco's remaining good leg. Break that one, and the corpse should be effectively disabled.

Retreating to the bedside, he seized Innesq's wheeled chair, and—rolling the chair before him as a perambulating shield—made for the poker. He had taken no more than three steps before Drocco's hands closed on the arms of the chair. His shield was wrenched away, the poker was out of reach; he stood once more defenseless. But the dead guard carried a short, heavy-bladed sword, presently sheathed. If he could duck in swiftly and pull that sword from its slow-moving owner's scabbard, then perhaps a tendon-slicing slash might fell the corpse.

Almost as if telepathic, Drocco slowly drew his sword, which he regarded without comprehension. As he stood staring, Innesq Belandor's voice rose to a controlled crescendo, and a blessed rigor mortis seized the dead guard's body, petrifying every muscle. Drocco crashed full length to the floor, where he lay motionless as a fallen granite image.

Aureste turned to the bed where his brother lay, sweat-soaked, eyes closed, breathing in rapid, shallow gasps. In his weakened state he had called upon his arcane powers, without benefit of the stimulants or chemical enhancements that he would have utilized as a matter of course at the best of times. There was no telling the effect of such killing overexertion.

He hurried to Innesq's side, and what he saw terrified him. The hectic spots of color had vanished from his brother's face. His lips and the shadows beneath his eyes displayed a bluish tinge. His quick breath was labored, and drops of blood spotted his lips.

"Innesq." Aureste's own heart was beating hard and fast. "Innesq, you've saved us both."

"Aureste." Innesq's eyes opened. His perishing whisper could barely be heard. "Not saved. Now you have glimpsed what we face. Understand? Adepts must gather. Work together as one. As one."

"Impossible. You speak of the enemies of our House."

"No longer. Make peace. Even with Corvestri. Or all lost."

For the first time a measure of true understanding came to Aureste, and with it a recognition of the ruin he had wrought. Remorse, guilt, and shame rose up to scorch him; demons that could be exorcised only by way of confession.

"I have caused more harm than you know," he admitted. "Vinz Corvestri sits in prison, where I placed him, probably facing execution. And you spoke of a young girl at Ironheart— I did not see her, but I destroyed the stronghouse, blasted it out of this world. If she survived, she and her people will never make peace with us. This is my doing."

"Forget the past. New start. Must be—" Innesq's voice died away.

"I can't hear you. Stay awake. Try to stay awake."

"No choice. As one."

"Don't talk anymore. Just stay awake."

"Aureste. Understand." For one moment the voice was clear and steady. *"We need them."*

Innesq Belandor sighed, and his eyes closed.

ABOUT THE AUTHOR

PAULA BRANDON lives in New Jersey. This is her first novel.